BLACKTALON

WARHAMMER
AGE OF SIGMAR

BLACKTALON

LIANE MERCIEL

BLACK LIBRARY

A BLACK LIBRARY PUBLICATION

First published in 2023.
This edition published in Great Britain in 2024 by
Black Library, Games Workshop Ltd., Willow Road,
Nottingham, NG7 2WS, UK.

Represented by: Games Workshop Limited – Irish branch,
Unit 3, Lower Liffey Street, Dublin 1,
D01 K199, Ireland.

10 9 8 7 6 5 4 3 2 1

Produced by Games Workshop in Nottingham.
Cover illustration by Anna Lakisova.

A CIP record for this book is available from the British Library.

ISBN 13: 978-1-80407-642-2

See Black Library on the internet at

blacklibrary.com

Find out more about Games Workshop
and the worlds of Warhammer at

games-workshop.com

Printed and bound in the UK.

To Peter, Alexander, and Catherine.

The Mortal Realms have been despoiled. Ravaged by the followers of the Chaos Gods, they stand on the brink of utter destruction.

The fortress-cities of Sigmar are islands of light in a sea of darkness. Constantly besieged, their walls are assailed by maniacal hordes and monstrous beasts. The bones of good men are littered thick outside the gates. These bulwarks of Order are embattled within as well as without, for the lure of Chaos beguiles the citizens with promises of power.

Still the champions of Order fight on. At the break of dawn, the Crusader's Bell rings and a new expedition departs. Storm-forged knights march shoulder to shoulder with resolute militia, stoic duardin and slender aelves. Bedecked in the splendour of war, the Dawnbringer Crusades venture out to found civilisations anew. These grim pioneers take with them the fires of hope. Yet they go forth into a hellish wasteland.

Out in the wilds, hardy trailblazers restore order to a crumbling world. Haunted eyes scan the horizon for tyrannical reavers as they build upon the bones of ancient empires, eking out a meagre existence from cursed soil and ice-cold seas. By their valour, the fate of the Mortal Realms will be decided.

The ravening terrors that prey upon these settlers take a thousand forms. Cannibal barbarians and deranged murderers crawl from hidden lairs. Martial hosts clad in black steel march from skull-strewn castles. The savage hordes of Destruction batter the frontier towns until no stone stands atop another. In the dead of night come howling throngs of the undead, hungry to feast upon the living.

Against such foes, courage is the truest defence and the most effective weapon. It is something that Sigmar's chosen do not lack. But they are not always strong enough to prevail, and even in victory, each new battle saps their souls a little more.

This is the time of turmoil. This is the era of war.

This is the Age of Sigmar.

PROLOGUE

'I have come to use the stormscryers,' Brother Myros said, dusting smoke-stained ice from the steel and leather of his slopewalker's cloak.

Brother Kyrivus raised an eyebrow. It was unusual for any of the brothers outside his own small group of assistant stormreaders to venture up to his mountaintop laboratory, and still more unusual for anyone to request access to his instruments.

And this *was* a request, however intemperately phrased. It could be nothing else. Everyone knew that the stormscryers were as delicate and temperamental as they were crucial to the brotherhood's work, and that none outside Brother Kyrivus' trained dedicants were to touch them. The survival of Astrapis' citizens, and the prestige of the Cults Unberogen across this mountainous reach of Aqshy, depended on their accuracy.

Brother Kyrivus set his quill aside. 'Why?'

'You will, surely, have read the signs that a cataclysm is coming.' Brother Myros unwound the protective wrappings that shielded his face. Frozen cinders showered from their folds, tinkling against the stone floor. A hungry joy lit his face, as if the prophesied storm stirred some long-suppressed excitement within him.

It disturbed Brother Kyrivus more than he cared to admit. Of course storms were holy, and he was always awed to see Sigmar's sacred power flash its fury across the realms. Deep in his bones, despite all the suffering he'd seen them bring, Brother Kyrivus loved storms. It was why he'd chosen to dedicate his life to the Stormreaders of Astrapis.

But the grandeur of a storm was laced with terror, and its power always – always, especially in Astrapis – brought destruction. One never forgot that. And one never *wished* for it, or greeted the portents of its coming with glee.

Glee. Yes. It was glee that he saw in Brother Myros' face, and it stirred a deep apprehension in Brother Kyrivus' soul.

There *had* been troubling portents lately. For the better part of a year, the stormreaders had received warnings of an impending catastrophe, far beyond anything any of them had seen even in these tempestuous mountains. The urgency had increased steadily, until the instruments were nearly screaming at them.

Yet none of the signs made any sense. Brother Kyrivus had pored over them for months, trying to fit the pieces together, but they refused to join.

'I know of the portents,' he told Brother Myros, grudgingly.

'Storms that rip apart storms, lightning that spears apart lightning...' Brother Myros' voice thickened with longing. 'Thunder that cracks open the foundation stones of the Mortal Realms themselves...'

'That is not what the stormscryers saw,' Brother Kyrivus snapped. He knew how the cults' more florid preachers had rephrased the plain readings he'd given them, and he did not approve. Stormscryer readings were solemn pronouncements, to be delivered accurately and without emotion. They told the people of Astrapis when and how to gird themselves against the avalanches and shardstrikes that hammered at their mountain refuges, and it was imperative that they be given truthfully, and calmly.

The warnings were Sigmar's holy gift. It was disrespectful, bordering on sacrilegious, to sensationalise them. Worse yet were the priests who chose to interpret the readings as allegorical, inventing their own meanings for the portents rather than conveying Sigmar's signs as they were given.

Brother Myros, he knew, took a different view.

'No?' Brother Myros shook the last of the melting soot-snow from his cloak and strode into the room, eyeing the burnished faces of the instruments that filled the laboratory.

A thousand distorted reflections looked back at him from within rings of brass and silver. Long glass cases, tapped into the mountain's living veins, dripped glowing magmafalls into beds of purified ice. Within stacked crystal hexagons, arcs of captured lightning leapt, obeying a rhythm that only they, and Brother Kyrivus' stormreaders, understood. A subdued whiff of volcanic smoke and ozone, imperfectly contained, filled the air.

Brother Myros trailed his gloved fingertips across one of the hexagons, smiling as its sparks leapt up towards his steel-threaded hand. Cold light flashed across his cheekbones. 'There is a storm coming, Brother Kyrivus, a storm such as the Mortal Realms have never seen. And I wish to watch it from your stormscryers, if I may. Perhaps you'll watch it with me. You might find it edifying.'

'There is no storm in the readings for today.' This was only half true. The readings had been more ambiguous than usual lately, as if the looming clouds of future threats occluded the instruments. For the past few days, Brother Kyrivus had felt apprehension trembling through the dials and levers, and a disquieting confusion as to place and time.

There *was* a storm coming, as terrible as Brother Myros said, but he didn't know when, or where.

Not today, though. Surely not today.

'Come,' Brother Myros said, beckoning with a creak of his steel-laced glove. 'Let us see what Sigmar's stormscryer tells us.'

Nothing. No storm comes today. But Brother Myros seemed so assured that it shook Brother Kyrivus' own sense of certainty. He came forwards reluctantly, noting the ease with which Myros adjusted the dials and scanned the dripping magmafalls above the primary sense-lens. *He's used this machinery before. But when?*

Swallowing a shiver, Brother Kyrivus stood beside his fellow priest.

Blue and gold swirled across the stormscryer's sense-lens. At its base, a glimmering shard – a priceless crystal of pure prophecy, mined from the Spear of Mallus and refined in the free city of Excelsis – began to pulse as the stormscryer sent out its tendrils of magic, seeking the tiny disturbances of flame, sea, and sky that might spiral into storms.

Translucent sigils sleeted across the stormscryer's lens as the magic found, and discarded, nascent storm-motes that were destined to dissipate harmlessly, never strengthening into more than minor squalls. A brief golden flare signalled a storm that would expend its fury on desolate lands, threatening no lives; another string of sigils pulsed a dim azure for a temporally distant threat, one that might not come for fifty years.

Brother Kyrivus held his breath. If the sigils found nothing urgent, there would be nothing to focus them, and–

But no.

The sigils joined together, locking arm in arm, and swirled dense as snowflakes in a blizzard. When each sigil had found its place in the mosaic's complex dance, they all paled to near transparency. Now it was possible, through the constant flow of information that poured across the stormscryer's lens, to see what the divination had found.

Brother Kyrivus' amulet chain rattled as he started in astonishment. The stormscryer showed High Sinsmiter Orvandus, in full regalia, addressing Sigmar's gathered faithful on the high slope of Mount Escharon.

It was a rare fine day, as near to cloudless as the skies of Astrapis ever came. Golden light winked off the High Sinsmiter's ceremonial headdress, his double-headed lightning staff, and the gilded spears and hammers of his honour guard. The faces of the faithful, turned up towards the High Sinsmiter's dais in anticipation, were – for once – unguarded against wind-whipped cinders and ice flakes.

Thousands had come for the prayer. It was one of Sigmar's great blessings, a high holy day for the Cults Unberogen in the region, at which his worshippers thanked the God-King for protecting them for another year, and sought his blessings for the year ahead.

Astrapis' wealthy, arrayed in smoke-tipped furs and embroidered shearling, stood at the front, while the common people, in shaggy bearskins and soot-cloaks, craned for a view from the lower slopes. Many wore elaborate, bestial masks of dyed fur and carved horns, for a key tradition of the Escharon Prayer was commemorating Sigmar's defeat of the daemonic warbeast Irskallon, whose heart was said to burn beneath the mountains. Astrapis' violent weather, some said, was worsened by the daemon-blood that still flowed through the volcanoes in this part of Aqshy. Although the Sinsmiters officially dismissed this folk tale as superstition, they did permit worshippers to wear masks at the Escharon Prayer, for Sigmar's victory over Irskallon was real enough, and worthy of remembrance.

Sworn acolytes stood in disciplined rows to either side, prepared to fan out their weathershields against soot-snow, or raise sky-anchors against lightning. Even they seemed almost relaxed, though. Today their presence was as much a formality as it could ever be in these mountains.

'The Escharon Prayer?' Brother Kyrivus murmured. 'There is no storm here.'

All was well. The sky showed no danger. But he heard only confusion, even worry, in his own words. *Why would the stormscryer alight on this?*

As if he'd somehow read those thoughts, Brother Myros shook his head, a short impatient gesture, and gripped the hilt of his hammer as he turned back to the lens. 'My brother. The skies boil with warnings. The fires beneath the earth heave with its rising fury. And humankind, weak and corrupt, is ill-prepared to withstand what comes. Our only hope is to purge the sins that exist, and control what remains by ritual and force.'

'Ritual and force,' Brother Kyrivus repeated, unable to disguise his disdain. Brother Myros' faction of the Sinsmiters were extreme even by the standards of that militant cult. While it wasn't uncommon for the Sinsmiters to consign forbidden texts to the magma-belching burn pits of Astrapis, Brother Myros' sect didn't stop with destroying papers, or those who made a deep study of them. They'd burn the dealers who sold them, even if those merchants and booksellers claimed to be ignorant of the nature of their untranslated texts; they'd burn close relatives and confidants of those who delved into proscribed knowledge, on the theory that such individuals might have heard whispers or glimpsed sigils that burrowed deep into their minds without their knowing. Weavers whose cloth was used for unholy vestments, and drovers whose animals were sacrificed to the Ruinous Powers, were as much at risk as the cultists who performed such despicable ceremonies. Any faint shadow of sin, and any tenuous connection to wrongdoing, could consign someone to the Sinsmiters' flames.

To Brother Kyrivus, such harsh measures threatened to become worse than the evils that they purported to protect the Sinsmiters' flock from, but he'd never actually bothered arguing the point. Let the rest of the sect debate how best to protect humankind from its own worst impulses. His duty was to safeguard the people of Astrapis from the fury of its elements, and that was work enough for him.

Around the periphery of the scrying lens, the sigils began flaring with bursts of blue and white, sometimes burning gold or even amber before they faded. *Danger!* they shouted, so vehemently it made Brother Kyrivus flinch. *Imminent. Major. Wind, soot-snow, lightning. Storm. Storm. Storm.*

Above the Escharon Prayer, the skies remained clear.

'You scorn our methods, but humanity can only be saved by the strictest hand,' Brother Myros said. 'The Mortal Realms, the world our grandfathers knew, are vanquished, my brother. You know this to be true. Secret cults fester in every city and settlement that fails to keep vigilance against their evils. Beasts out of nightmare hunt the wilds, and the trees and stones themselves are twisted into monstrosity by Chaos. We fight, of course, and by Sigmar's strength some fragile hope survives, but our civilisation is always under threat, and never more so than now.

'As Chaos' dominion grows stronger, humanity weakens. Despair, cowardice, and hedonism take root easily in mortal souls already weakened by hardship and defeat. Now, more than ever, we must purify such weaknesses from our flock, lest Chaos conquer all. The High Sinsmiter is blind to this truth, but you – *you*, Brother Kyrivus – need not be. *Must* not be. We need you.'

'Why?' Brother Kyrivus asked uneasily, stealing a glance back at the scrying lens. On the mountainside, lay choristers stood in ranks and sang hymns of praise and gratitude. The music didn't carry through the lens, but Brother Kyrivus didn't need to hear the song to recognise the words on the singers' lips, or to feel a swell of matching emotion in his chest.

The ceremony was, at once, awesomely ancient and intimately familiar. Each year's prayer was another link forged in a chain that traced back centuries. *How can the instruments see disaster at the prayer?*

But the stormscryer, guided by the glimmering crystal at its core, was never wrong.

'A newborn revolution is a vulnerable thing,' Brother Myros said. 'You see the alarms in the prophecies. The instruments warn us that, though we act by Sigmar's will, we may yet be stymied by the foolish and recalcitrant in our faith, who do not wish to admit that their coddling of sinners has brought us to the brink of disaster. But just as the stormscryers tell our people how to survive the storm, so they tell us how to safeguard the Cults Unberogen.'

Brother Myros left the stormscryer's flurries of silent panic, striding towards Brother Kyrivus. Melted soot-snow dripped between the folds of his cloak and gathered in the creases of his gloves. In the instruments' flaring red glow, it had the look of blood.

'The stormscryers have spoken of a key,' Brother Myros said, staring hungrily at Brother Kyrivus. 'A proof, written by Sigmar's own hand, that will convince even the greatest doubters that the God-King approves of our measures. It will be humanity's salvation, if we can obtain it. The signs are... difficult to read. We do not know where it is, only that it exists.

'We must have it. Many in your brotherhood support our revolution, but they lack the skills of their master. They have not been able to read the prophecies completely, and so they cannot tell us where this key can be found. But you can. You can provide the proof we need to bring the Cults Unberogen to heel, and finally ensure that humankind armours itself properly against Chaos.'

'I can't,' Brother Kyrivus blurted out. If he could make himself believe what Brother Myros was saying about girding humanity against Chaos, he might have been tempted to try, but it was impossible. The same desires and weaknesses that made people susceptible to Chaos were those that made them human: fear, anger, pleasure, pride. One could not excise those emotions from a living soul, not with any hope of keeping that soul intact. It was madness to think otherwise, and blind cruelty to imagine that those feelings could be purged by punishment.

Anyway, it didn't matter. He couldn't do what was being asked. 'I've been trying to make sense of the readings for months. There is no logic to them. The instruments spit gibberish about places that don't exist. They predict configurations that defy the laws of nature. They don't make *sense*, Brother Myros.'

'I have faith. I have reason to believe you can find the proof we need. It has been whispered to us, and shown to us in secret signs. When we have it, our brothers and sisters in the other orders will believe the truth of our message. Already they lean towards us, knowing that the flame of pure righteousness is needed to purge humanity's sins, but… they need more to light the sparks in their own cities. Only a little more. You will provide this.'

'How?' Brother Kyrivus asked, utterly lost. He looked to the stormscryer for solace, and found none. Many of its sigils had darkened from amber to brilliant red, a colour he'd seen only twice in the thirty-four years that he'd served in the laboratory. It was difficult to make out the scene at the Escharon Prayer through their crimson mask.

That much red, all at once…

Brother Myros didn't answer. He clapped a hand on Kyrivus' shoulder, squeezing hard enough to make the threat plain. 'Sigmar will show you the way, and you will convey it to us. That is your purpose, Brother Kyrivus. And what use is a man without a purpose?

'Watch what happens at the Escharon Prayer, if you have any doubts. But do not venture too close. It would be prudent for you and your assistants to remain in your laboratory. Things may be… unsettled… closer to Astrapis. We wouldn't want you to be caught up in the confusion.'

'I understand,' Brother Kyrivus lied. His shoulders ached with tension. He hid it as best he could, scarcely breathing, as Brother Myros held his gaze a moment longer, nodded, and left.

Alone, Brother Kyrivus let his shoulders sag. He went to the stormscryer, feeling the instrument's distress like an echo of his own. He played his fingers over the dials, trying to soothe the stormscryer as though it were a restive beast, but the magic had its own will. Sigils blurred across the scryer's curved glass face as its glimmering shard poured magic into the device, seeking the unspun threads of the future.

A twin-tailed comet appeared amid the sigils. It was Sigmar's holy mark, the symbol that had appeared in the skies to herald the god's birth, and all his faithful knew it well.

Yet this one was broken. A black wound tore across its face, bleeding darkness over the stormscryer's view. The comet's two tails trailed limp in its wake, buffeted by the shadowy currents that gushed from its stricken heart. Brother Kyrivus didn't recognise the symbol, but he understood its disastrous import clear enough. *Sigmar wounded. His cults dying.*

It was an unimaginably bleak vision, one he'd never seen or imagined the instrument could produce, and yet Brother Kyrivus beheld it with a certain grim relief.

Sigmar has shown me this for a reason. I can stop it. I must *stop it.*

Brother Kyrivus swallowed. He had always imagined, if and when he found himself in the midst of history unfolding, that he would steer the course of events with wisdom and skill. Perhaps a little apprehension, as he often felt while deciphering the stormscryer's more obscure signs, but nothing like the queasy, disoriented terror that filled his belly now.

The reality was nothing like what Brother Kyrivus had imagined.

It was, instead, like being caught in a blizzard on the mountain-side: blinding, battering, and entirely overwhelming. Lost and frightened, he could only try to cling to something solid and hope to survive.

Faith would be his guide-rope. He would find High Sinsmiter Orvandus and warn him of... of something. Of the panic in the instruments, and the ominous things Brother Myros had said. Of the disaster that was about to strike the Escharon Prayer.

It was true that Brother Kyrivus didn't understand what was happening, but the High Sinsmiter would, or would at least know what to do in response. Orvandus had always been judicious in his counsel, and though he cautioned against hasty action and harsh judgement, he also understood the need for decisive leadership in moments of crisis.

High Sinsmiter Orvandus would have the answer, he was sure of it. Whatever the danger, the High Sinsmiter would know how to face it, if only Brother Kyrivus could reach him in time.

Relieved to have decided on a course of action, Brother Kyrivus threw on his slopewalker's cloak, pulled on his heavy gloves, and fixed a pair of goggles on his face. He hesitated, then swept the instruments' latest round of readings and sigil-scripts into his satchel. Perhaps seeing the tangible evidence of the stormscryer's alarm would help convince High Sinsmiter Orvandus and the rest of the Astrapene Council that the situation was, indeed, as dire as Brother Kyrivus claimed.

He shoved the satchel under his cloak and buttoned the padded leather securely over it, doing his best to hide the bulge. It felt like a theft, even though he was only taking the stormscryer's readings to the leader of his faith. If anyone was entitled to the information, it was High Sinsmiter Orvandus.

Still, Brother Kyrivus couldn't shake the sense that he was doing something illicit. Nodding tensely to the scattered assistants he passed in the halls, he hurried to the small emergency corridors that burrowed through the mountain's faces. He didn't want to use the main gates, not after Brother Myros had warned him against leaving the laboratory. Weather in Astrapis was unpredictable enough that the brotherhood deemed it prudent to maintain a honeycomb of seldom-used tunnels to the surface, in case the main gates were sealed by rockfalls, lava flows, or avalanches. He'd get out that way.

Alchemical lights sputtered along the upper walls. A chilly white glow filled the tunnels, tripling Brother Kyrivus' shadow into a host of thin grey figures.

The steel bars at the door were frozen in place, but this was not an uncommon hazard and Brother Kyrivus had come prepared. Pulling a duardin-made torch from his satchel, he pressed the bronze lever at its base and flicked the engraved runes behind the nozzle. Blue flames erupted from the torch's muzzle, melting the ice away in bubbling streaks.

Brother Kyrivus grabbed the handle in gloved hands and heaved. In a cough of steam and cracking ice, he was out.

As soon as he emerged, the wind was on him, ripping at his thick protective gear. The din of soot-snow beating against his cloak's armoured plating was deafening, but hardly any louder than the hammering of his heart.

Hunched against the blasting wind, eyes squinted behind his insulated goggles, Brother Kyrivus picked his way down. Several times the wind yanked his cloak hard enough to pull him off balance, or a foot slipped on the ice-slicked slope and he nearly fell.

The guide-rope hammered into the mountainside was barbed with cinder-fanged icicles. It tore his gloves to ragged clumps of padding over metal threads as he worked his way blindly down, hand over hand, feeling his way forwards in the blizzard.

Brother Kyrivus was sweating hard by the time he reached the smooth-sided lava tunnel that led to the plateau of the Escharon Prayer. His phair-skin underlayers clung to him, wet and heavy, though ice caked his beard and froze his eyebrows to the rims of his goggles.

He broke the goggles away with a sharp tug, pulling out clumps of his eyebrows, and hurried into the tunnel.

From here it was only another mile to the slope where the Escharon Prayer was being held. If the God-King smiled upon him, he could reach it before the ceremony ended.

He ran. The tunnel was slippery with alternating bands of ice and snowmelt as it passed over and under the mountain's fires, but Brother Kyrivus splashed and stumbled through. Sweating heavily, panting under the weight of his sodden garments, he emerged at the edge of the plateau just as the Escharon Prayer was nearing its climax.

No one noticed his arrival. The ceremony was nearing its end, and the worshippers were rapt in their celebration of Sigmar's faith. One small figure, standing at the mouth of a lava tunnel fifty yards away from the gathering, drew little attention.

High Sinsmiter Orvandus, standing with his face towards the assembled worshippers and his back to Brother Kyrivus, lifted his double-headed staff towards the heavens. His voice, rich and sonorous, rang through the syllables of the Escharon Prayer.

The invocation climaxed with the traditional call for Sigmar to grant his strength and resolve to his followers, steeling them for the trials of the year ahead. The High Sinsmiter brandished his staff with a flourish, and a crack of lightning split the air. It burst into dramatic cascades of sparks upon striking the staff, enveloping Orvandus in holy fury.

From that dazzling shroud came a scream.

It was high, terrible, inhuman. Brother Kyrivus sucked in a breath. He had never heard such agonised betrayal.

The High Sinsmiter's corpse slumped out of the light, sparks still dancing about his knuckles where his fingers had been welded to the staff's metal. His eyes had burst, weeping slimy tears into his beard. Smoke drifted from his open mouth like the shroud of his soul escaping.

Before Brother Kyrivus fully grasped what had happened, pandemonium seized the crowd.

As the lay worshippers screamed and fled, Sigmar's sworn servants attacked each other. Brothers pulled hidden daggers from their sleeves and drew the gold-chased hammers from their belts, stabbing and smashing their comrades in faith with sudden, terrible ferocity.

It was a coordinated attack. The targets, taken by surprise, had little chance to mount any defence against their murderers. An older woman turned towards her friends for help, only to be greeted by knives instead.

Brother Mendevus, a gentle and compassionate healer revered by the citizens of Astrapis, sank to the ground, slain by his own assistants' scalpels. Brother Adevos, a fierce old warrior, drove back his attackers with vicious curses and great sweeps of his hammer. He smashed one enemy's face, spun, and crushed another with a two-handed blow to the chest.

Adevos turned to run, trampling the arcs of blood his hammer had thrown on the snow, but a pair of arrows buried themselves in his back. He made it another few faltering steps, carried by momentum, before a third arrow found him. The hammer fell, red at head and grip, and Brother Adevos fell with it.

Other victims, younger, Brother Kyrivus didn't know. He had little interaction with the main sect, and was unfamiliar with many of its newer recruits. But he watched them die, and terror churned against disgust in his bowels.

He didn't know most of their killers, either, but in their faces he saw the hard lines of fanaticism, and on their chests he saw the insignia of the Sinsmiters – the same symbol, silver over blue, that their victims wore.

'Why?' he whispered, staring at the monstrosity.

No one answered. But, after a moment, one of the attackers noticed him. A greying woman pulled her knife out of a worshipper's back and, spotting Brother Kyrivus, ran towards him. Her eyes were blue and pitiless, and her gloves were seamed with blood. 'Are you with us?'

Brother Kyrivus stared at her dumbly. 'With whom?'

It was the wrong answer. The woman snarled and stabbed at him. Brother Kyrivus raised a forearm reflexively, and the blade snagged against the bands of metal hidden in his padded glove. His attacker ripped the knife free, tearing away leather and snapped links of chain, and struck at him again.

This time he evaded her. Though he practised less often than most of his fellows, owing to his laboratory duties, Brother Kyrivus was still a sworn servant of Sigmar, and like many Sigmarites, he had been trained in the elements of combat. He sidestepped the blow, ducking clumsily, and thrust his arm up to knock the knife away. 'I'm not your enemy!'

'You are. You just don't know it.' She swung again. 'The faith must be cleansed. Purged.'

Desperately, gracelessly, Brother Kyrivus hopped away. There was nothing else he could do. He was unarmed. Any large piece of metal could interfere with the accuracy of the instruments, and the stormreaders habitually left their weapons by the outer door. He hadn't gone out through the main gate, so he'd had no opportunity to collect his sword, and in his distraction, he hadn't thought to take another.

'Please–' he began, just as the knife came in again. It tore through the hole in his sleeve, and bit into his forearm. Pain lanced through him. Sudden tears started in his eyes, surprising him. It had been over thirty years since he'd been wounded in a fight, and the sheer madness of this one threatened to drive all other thoughts from his mind.

But, after a second, he caught his breath and his sense. 'Please,' he tried again. 'I spoke to Brother Myros. He needs me…'

Immediately the fanatic's demeanour changed. She lowered her knife, eyeing him with reproval, but without the hatred that had twisted her face a moment earlier. 'Why didn't you say so? Why aren't you wearing our sign?'

What sign? Brother Kyrivus almost asked, but fortunately he swallowed the question before it could betray him. 'I am the chief stormreader,' he said instead. 'I cannot wear anything that might interfere with our instruments.'

This seemed to satisfy her. The woman drew out her own iron amulet, which depicted a hammer over a twin-tailed comet, and held it up in a fist. 'Sigmar grant you strength, and purity in your strength,' she said, and turned away to hunt new prey.

'Sigmar grant you strength,' Brother Kyrivus mumbled, which seemed to be an acceptable response. She didn't turn back, at least, and he was left alone with his turmoil.

There'd been a crack in the woman's amulet. It split the holy comet's two tails and speared a crooked fissure into its heart. Perhaps it was nothing more than accidental damage, but it was the same sign he'd seen in the stormscryer, and it filled him with dread.

Heresy. The deadliest contagion in the faith.

Numbly, Brother Kyrivus started to wander through the carnage. He dared not return to the laboratory, and the only way down the mountain was through the bloody field. As he came to the bodies of murdered Brother Adevos and the two attackers he'd slain before falling, Brother Kyrivus stooped and lifted the amulet from one of those dead assailants.

It, too, had a cracked comet.

With trembling hands and quailing heart, he put it on over his own head. *It's only a disguise. Only until I can get to safety.*

By now the killing was nearly done. Corpses littered the prayer grounds. Sinsmiters walked among the wounded, snuffing out any signs of life. Whenever one of them glanced his way, Brother Kyrivus lifted the amulet with the broken comet, and they let him be.

Grey clouds had gathered over the ruins of the Escharon Prayer, and soot-snow had begun to fall. The light lacing of black softened the grisliness, making the corpses look less like people and more like sculptures carved from basalt.

It was a thin illusion, and easily punctured. Smoky-winged scavengers drifted down to take advantage of the stiffening feast. Their beaks punched up and down on the bodies like an inker's needles, spreading ugly designs in red.

Brother Kyrivus walked past as quickly as he could, trying not to see the dead, and trying not to be seen by the living.

He couldn't ignore the corpse of the High Sinsmiter, though.

Orvandus' golden mitre had melted in the lightning strike and was fused to the dead man's skull by fingers of cooled metal. His staff had rolled a few feet away. Its gems had fallen from the gilt halo that had circled Sigmar's sacred comet, leaving empty and malformed sockets gaping in the half-melted gold, and the comet itself was marred by the same twisting rupture that split the one Brother Kyrivus wore.

But how? The High Sinsmiter couldn't have failed to notice the mark of heresy on his staff of office, and he would never have borne such a thing to the Escharon Prayer.

After a moment, Brother Kyrivus spotted his answer. A thin splinter of rough dark metal had been driven into the comet's heart. It was a small thing, only visible now because the staff had been so badly damaged by the lightning strike. Most probably it had been buried when the staff was intact, and the High Sinsmiter had been unaware that the symbol of his office carried his doom.

Heresy and sabotage. Murder and betrayal. That was what Brother Myros had spoken of in the laboratory, and what he sought to enlist Brother Kyrivus to aid.

He had to flee. There was no safe refuge here, and no choice. For the sake of the Cults Unberogen, and his own conscience, Brother Kyrivus had to take what he knew to a true Sigmarite sanctuary. There he could warn the faith's defenders about the heresy that had sprung up in Astrapis, and the truth of the High Sinsmiter's assassination.

The soot-snow was falling harder and faster, clattering cinders against Brother Kyrivus' shoulders but casting a welcome cloak of concealment over his actions. He pulled his hood and goggles back on, stooped against the wind to hide his height, and pretended to look for survivors among the fallen. Occasionally he mimed stabbing down at a corpse, trusting in the soot-snow to lend plausibility to the attacks, while slowly but steadily retreating towards the lava tunnel.

He didn't dare use the main road, which led directly to the Astrapene Sanctuary and was most likely in the heretics' hands, or at best still being fought over. The wind-scoured mountain paths on the more exposed slopes carried their own considerable hazards, but Brother Kyrivus preferred to trust his fate to the elements.

For the moment, the soot-snow seemed to deter pursuit. Brother Kyrivus hastened back up the lava tunnel and then out again. Instead of returning to the laboratory, he followed a narrow, wind-battered trail that led to a small outpost where the stormreaders kept emergency supplies. A few lay worshippers lived there as well, hunting and trapping beasts they could sell to the Sinsmiters for food, or scavenging rare minerals from the mountainside.

Brother Kyrivus hoped to equip himself with food and travelling gear from the Sinsmiters' cache, and perhaps hire a guide who might help him find a hidden path out of Astrapis. As he reached the small cluster of ice-rimed shacks crowded in a mountain cleft, however, his spirits rose at an unexpected sight.

Shaggy, curly horned vedeskas crowded around the settlement's lone stable, their bearded snouts heavy with the icicles of their breath. The animals' insulated barding was marked with embroidered yellow circles. That meant they were owned by a merchant – an outlander, whose people might not understand all the prohibitions of their sect and had to be measured against a laxer standard than the Sinsmiters permitted each other.

Outsiders. People who had no part in the heresy that had consumed the Sinsmiters, and who might be persuaded to grant him passage. Truly, Sigmar had blessed his servant.

A heavily cloaked figure was harnessing the vedeskas to a stout wagon, its wheels ridged with ice-biting blades. The kerchief tied around the figure's goggled head bore a yellow circle, marking him – her? – as a merchant, and an outsider.

Praying that his luck would hold, Brother Kyrivus hurried forwards. 'Good sir! Good sir! Please, might I take passage with you?'

The muffled figure looked up. He couldn't discern gender, or even species, through its layers of armoured insulation, but somehow Brother Kyrivus had the impression that it wasn't surprised to see him. That it had, in fact, somehow been expecting him.

'You are a… holy priest of Sigmar? Why would you travel with us? We are but outlanders. Perhaps too impious a company for you.' The merchant's voice was as indistinct as its face. There was a foreign lilt to the words, but it was impossible to place.

Brother Kyrivus swallowed. He'd always been a poor liar. 'My sister is ill. I must go to her. But I can't… No one must know I'm neglecting my duties.'

The merchant's goggles stared at him, bug-like, through the blowing snow. 'They won't know you're gone? We don't want trouble.'

'No,' Brother Kyrivus lied. 'They won't know. There's been so much confusion today, I'm sure no one will notice one minor priest has gone missing.'

'Ah, the... confusion. We heard about that.' The merchant resumed cinching the vedeskas' harnesses, and for a moment Brother Kyrivus felt a sinking dread that he'd been dismissed as too much of a liability to take on. But then the merchant looked at him again, moving closer. 'Can you pay for your passage?'

'I do have a little money. If the price is not too high–'

'We can be reasonable. But we are going to Bemara. If you come with us, you will have to go there. Maybe that's not where your sister is.'

Brother Kyrivus could scarcely believe his good fortune. There was a realmgate in Bemara. It was said to be perilous to use, and it was in the hands of duardin who owed no allegiance to the God-King's faith, but it would take him far away, to Chamon.

Another realm. There, he'd be far beyond the heretics' reach. He could bring his warnings to other pious Sigmarites, and together they could puzzle out the warnings that his stormscryers had tried to give him.

'Bemara is quite acceptable,' he said.

'Then please, come with us,' the merchant replied, gesturing towards the rear of the wagon. 'Best if you ride in the back. Because of the... confusion. No one will see you there.'

'Of course.' Brother Kyrivus peered at the mechanisms that secured the wagon's backboard. He couldn't see how anyone could manipulate that frozen steel with snow gloves on, yet the merchant deftly unlatched them with a series of clicks, too fast for Kyrivus to follow.

The backboard swung down, and the merchant ushered him up. 'Keep your head low until we are off the mountain. We can discuss payment on the road.'

Hurriedly, Brother Kyrivus climbed inside. The wagon's interior was dark, cold, and mostly empty – presumably its cargo had been unloaded into the outpost. He fumbled forwards until his fingers closed around something soft and slightly warmer than the wind-rattled walls, and then sank down gratefully to sit.

A few snatches of conversation reached him from outside. Wind and distance stole their meaning, leaving only tone. One was harshly interrogating, while the other was full of oily placation.

The voices fell silent. The wagon began rumbling down the mountain road, jolting Brother Kyrivus with every bump and bite of the ridged wheels against rock and ice. The odour of unwashed vedeska filled the wagon bed, and the wind found every gap to claw at him between the boards.

It felt glorious. Tears streamed down the insides of his goggles, mingling with the meltwater that dripped from the outer casing to soak his beard.

Disaster was not inevitable. The stormscryers had warned him in time. The faith could yet be saved.

His fingers had thawed a bit, and the wagon seemed to have steadied, so Brother Kyrivus fumbled about in the chilly black for something he might use as a blanket. Whatever was under him was soft, and came up easily when he pulled. It felt too flimsy to be a pile of cloaks. Scarves, maybe, or interior lining meant to be sewn into sturdier gear.

Whatever it was, it held body heat, and was pliable enough to wrap around his shoulders. Hoping his benefactors wouldn't mind his use of their wares, Brother Kyrivus curled into the borrowed softness, and soon fell into an exhausted slumber.

* * *

A flash of silver light woke him. Groggy, Kyrivus thought at first that one of the merchants was shining an alchemical torch into the back of the wagon, but there were two small lights moving in parallel, not a single large one.

Eyes. He was looking at glowing silver eyes – no, goggles. One of the merchants had lowered the board that separated the driver's box from the cargo area and had twisted back to look at him through snow lenses.

Goggles didn't ordinarily glow, though. Perhaps these had some magic, or duardin-craft, that enabled them to see in the dark.

'Do you wish to discuss payment?' Brother Kyrivus asked, fumbling for the purse wedged under his cloak.

'Your presence is payment enough,' the merchant replied. There was an odd, vibrating resonance to his voice, almost a buzz, that Kyrivus hadn't noticed earlier. Something silver gleamed in his mouth, as if his teeth or tongue somehow reflected the light from his goggles.

'Is it?' Brother Kyrivus said, baffled but grateful. 'I'm in your debt, then. How long until we reach Bemara?'

'Not long. But long enough that I must have a new skin,' the merchant said. He smiled, and the silver gleam of his teeth grew brighter, bright enough to show that they were sharp, thin points against the lipless abyss of his mouth. 'You seem to have slept on them. Will you pass me one? It need not be yours. No, not yours, not yet.'

'I don't understand,' Brother Kyrivus said.

The eyes staring back at him began glowing more intensely, lighting the merchant's face from within like twin candles in a paper lantern, and with mounting horror Brother Kyrivus started to realise that there were no goggles after all. The merchant's skin was stretched oddly over bones that didn't look human, and his eyelashes were smouldering around the edges of that silver incandescence. A second later, the eyelids began to crisp and blacken.

Under those burning eyes, the merchant's smile widened. The corners of his lips cracked apart, and silver light dribbled from the rifts. 'I see that. Strange that a student of prophecy should be so blind. But no matter. You don't need to understand, Brother Kyrivus of Sigmar Thunderfool. You don't need to understand anything, ever again.'

Brother Kyrivus reached for a sword that wasn't there, and then cursed himself for an idiot as he realised that, for the second time today, he had blundered into danger unarmed. He drew in a breath to shout for help, not knowing who might hear him, and then let out a pained burst of air from his nostrils as his cry froze mute and solid in his mouth.

Crystal spikes speared through Kyrivus' tongue and erupted from his cheeks. A sharp, antiseptic tingling filled his mouth, followed by numbness shot through with pricks of pain when he wriggled against the crystal piercings.

'Good,' the merchant crooned, as though soothing an infant. The silver light had grown still brighter, and between the expanding circles of burning black that ate away at his skin, the bones of his face seemed to shift in a revolving, fractal infinity. Kyrivus imagined he could glimpse the broken comet spiralling among them, just for an instant, before it spun away into kaleidoscopic oblivion. 'Good. Now we will have peace. And quiet. All the way to Bemara, where glorious fate awaits.'

CHAPTER ONE

'How long are they going to do this?' Neave asked, squinting into the distance. The early morning light was dazzling but cold. Rocks dug into her belly, grinding against her Stormcast plate. Across the Ghurish plain, faraway figures circled around a collection of tents and rings. It could almost pass for a carnival, if one ignored the screams.

'Until their Great Flayer comes,' Shakana answered. She passed Neave her spyglass, pulling back under the false grass canopy that hid their sniper's blind. 'The Hidruspex will keep working on their prophecies until they've found whatever signs the Great Flayer is looking for this year. Then he'll come out and read the Great Prophecy rendered by those signs, and reward whichever cultist found it.'

'And we can kill him,' Neave said, putting the glass to her eye.

Through the glass, the Hidruspex cultists' camp clicked into view. At its centre, raised up over the rest of the camp, was a circular platform measuring some fifty feet across. Pennons streamed around it, each painted with messy scrawls of Chaos sigils that melted together into an eye-watering tangle of obscenity.

Around the central platform, unfolding like the petals of a monstrous flower, were eight smaller rings surrounded by fences of dirty bone. Four were aligned with the compass points and held cauldrons heaped high with red-stained resins. The others, knocked slightly out of alignment to skew the overall pattern's symmetry, held an archers' range, a pyre of wood and bone, and two great beasts of Ghur, each collared with a band of heavy, enchanted iron.

The nearer of the two was a massive yellow-and-black chitinous thing that resembled a spider, but with six gargantuan legs and six smaller, sharp-tipped piercing appendages tucked close beneath its belly. Swollen knobs capped its joints, dripping a clear, straw-coloured fluid that soaked its bristly fur and tiny, many-eyed head.

The other beast was shaggy, ursine, armoured with pebbled calluses across its shoulders and back and corded blue-white fur everywhere else. Patches of its fur had been shorn off, and the cerulean skin underneath was scarred with Chaos runes that wept watery red liquid. The beast snorted and swung its tusked head from side to side in constant agitation, as if trying to shoo away invisible flies.

South of the main camp, the cultists had erected a series of crude pens from bone and sinew, so raw that carrion birds still picked at the bloody flesh caught between the joints. People filled some of the fly-specked pens, while other Ghurish beasts were hobbled in others.

Adjusting the glass, Neave focused on the captives. Soldiers could be useful, if armed and freed to sow confusion. Civilians would only be slaughtered, though, and that was a higher price than she was willing to pay for such a small advantage.

She couldn't tell which these were. There were humans, duardin, aelves. Some were old, some young. One cage of dripping bones held a willowy golden-haired Lumineth with a blocky, patterned bandage wrapped around her eyes. Another held a manacled Daughter of Khaine, her face hidden behind a snarling steel mask fused to her flesh. Those two, and a handful of others, seemed like they could fight.

But the rest? Neave had no idea.

As a rule, she paid little heed to the details of Chaos cults' worship. There was no logic to their practices. While some might offer the illusion of sense, it was only a lure to draw unwary minds deeper into their madness, and she'd seldom found any strategic advantage to be gained by trying to decipher them. On the rare occasions that a Chaos cult's beliefs might materially affect the Blacktalons' mission, one of her companions could be relied upon to tell her what she needed to know.

'Who are they?' she asked. 'Can we use them?'

'They're people that the Hidruspex believe are "touched by prophecy". Seventh sons of seventh sons, babies born in full cauls, that sort of thing. One man was shot through both eyes by a chance arrow but lived, only to be seized by the Hidruspex.' Shakana shook her head. 'There are some true seers and diviners among them. I saw a glimmerwitch of Excelsis earlier, and a Khainite heart-eater. Mostly they're prisoners, but there are a few who came by choice, believing this Great Flaying would assist their own prophecies. The captives might help us, if freed. I doubt the others would.'

'And the beasts?' Neave shifted the glass, focusing on the behemoths penned in the smaller, more ramshackle rings.

These didn't look quite as fearsome as the two in the central arenas, but nothing that walked, flew, or swam in Ghur was less than lethal. Neave recognised venomous tsati birds in one cage, with their spiked blue legs and poisoned beaks, and a shaggy, eight-legged rhyrac that had already torn the floor of its pen to a shallow bowl of dirt in its distress at being confined. She couldn't put names to the rest, but she could see their deadliness.

'They've been captured because they have some association with prophecy, either in myth or reality. The Hidruspex dose them with all sorts of things to "enhance their powers" or "grant the true sight". They're shot with tsati venom and forced to breathe in burning visionweed, poor creatures.' Shakana shook her head, her braids whisking quietly against her armour. 'They've gone mad. They'll destroy anything in their path if we set them loose.'

That sounded like the beginnings of a plan. 'Would threatening their prophecy bring the Great Flayer out? If we disrupt the ritual and start freeing the captives...'

'Maybe,' Shakana said. 'Some Khorne Bloodbound had a similar idea two or three months ago, according to the field reports I read in Hammerhal Aqsha. It didn't go well for them. They weren't expecting the Hidruspex to put up much of a fight, and their overconfidence cost them dear.'

Neave couldn't help but smile. She sometimes teased Shakana for spending her time between missions studying their targets, whereas Neave herself preferred to do her preparations in the sparring halls. But there were, undeniably, moments when the studious approach had its benefits. 'I'd like to think we're more of a threat than some Bloodbound.'

'One would hope,' Shakana said dryly. 'It's still not much of a plan.'

'It might be all we have time for.' Neave drew the glass down and wriggled back under the ambush cover. 'They're going to start murdering captives soon, aren't they?' The arrangement of those arenas was too plain to mistake.

Shakana's expression tightened. She never liked admitting to any exigency that might force them into a disadvantage. But, reluctantly, she nodded. 'They'll start with poisons, just as they do with the beasts. Tsati venom, visionweed smoke, whatever else they think will heighten their prisoners' gifts. Then they'll start the Running of the Fates – channelling their drugged captives through their monsters' pens, shooting at them with mistletoe arrows, and otherwise narrowing their number. They hope only to wound their victims, but they don't mind if some, even most, die. After all, a prophet who can't see an arrow coming isn't much of a prophet.'

'I suppose that's one way to test it.'

'That's what they think. Then the survivors run another gauntlet of those eight big rings, and whichever survive that ordeal are presented to the Great Flayer in the centre. Where they will be flayed, alive, by him. The Hidruspex consider that a great honour, naturally.'

'Flay them?' All she'd learnt about the Hidruspex had ignited a familiar ember of anger in Neave's soul, but this final revelation blew it into flame.

She let it burn. The outrages of their enemies spurred her wrath, and the righteousness of that wrath made her a fiercer fighter. Neave's faith was intertwined with her fury, and it was, she believed, part of why she'd been chosen as a Stormcast.

Almost all of her mortal life was lost to her, but that was one of the few memories Neave held: the absolute ferocity that filled her when she faced her enemies, and the quick sureness of her hurricane axes in her hands. She didn't remember her foes' faces, or the causes that had brought them into conflict, but she did remember the red joy of combat, and she was certain that Sigmar understood, and approved.

The God-King had once been a warrior himself. He'd recognised the purity of the battle-flame that burned in her, and he had blessed her for it.

Shakana glanced up, then took out her typhoon crossbow and began checking over its gears and sights as she frequently did. It was perfectly calibrated, as always, and in her hands had the sleek, patient lethality of a serpent at rest. 'That's what the Hidruspex do. They perform all these rituals to distil their victims' prophetic gifts down to their strongest essence, and then they read the future from the secret maps of their skins. It's the interior of the skin that holds their knowledge, you see. The secret side, the side facing the heart. Not the side that's shown to the world.'

'So we'll want to strike before they start that.'

'Our task is to slay the Great Flayer and stop his prophecy. So yes, we'll want to strike before they start that.'

'I meant–'

'I know what you meant.' Shakana gave her a sidelong glance, the beginnings of a wry smile teasing at her dark lips. 'Yes, if we're going to save the innocents, we'd better hurry. Don't worry. I'll be ready when the signal comes.'

'Right.' Neave touched Shakana's shoulder lightly in farewell and wriggled backwards out of the sniper's blind, moving as quietly as her heavier armour permitted.

It wasn't that quiet. She could hear Shakana's sharp inhalation behind her, and hid a little smile at the sniper's exasperation.

Her best was never good enough for Shakana. Sometimes that irritated her, but today there was too much excitement coursing through Neave's veins for her to mind.

A clean kill on a deserving target, one whose death unambiguously made the Mortal Realms better and safer for all its people, was all Neave could ask for. It was why she'd been reborn as a Stormcast: so that she could serve Sigmar, and his faithful, and all the Mortal Realms in this way.

There were times, rarely and privately, when she harboured misgivings about why she'd been chosen, and what the endless cycle of Reforging cost her. But when Neave was given an assignment like this – a good kill, a *worthy* kill – those doubts melted away.

This was why she served. This made everything else worthwhile.

But it also meant the Blacktalons could not afford to fail.

She slipped down the hill, using speed in place of silence. She wasn't quiet; she *was* fast. A seam of rocks ran down the slope, washed down by the plains' infrequent but torrential storms, and Neave stayed on the stones to keep the grass from swaying around her. The high Ghurish grass closed overhead, enveloping Neave in feathery green, and then she broke off to follow another spine of rocks towards the Blacktalon camp.

A tingle of magic passed over her skin as she crossed the unseen threshold of Lorai's spell, and for an instant her vision clouded with a blue-grey haze of salt fog. Then it was gone, and she stood in a small clearing dotted with bedrolls, a soot-scarred fire ring, and scattered packs of supplies.

Hendrick sat on a rock near the firepit, sharpening his axe. Rostus squatted in the dirt nearby, playing with a deck of cards. The cards were tiny in the bald Stormcast's massive hands, yet he flipped them with unexpected dexterity. He cut the deck, shuffled, and fanned the cards repeatedly, finding the same red fish card on every draw.

'Are you practising cheating?' Neave asked.

Simultaneously, Hendrick and Rostus both spoke – the former in affirmation, the latter in denial. Upon hearing Hendrick, Rostus gave Neave a wounded look.

'I think it works better if you don't practise right in front of your intended victims,' Neave said.

'Ordinarily I'd agree,' replied Rostus, shuffling the red fish back into the deck before cutting the cards and riffling the halves back together again. 'But with you lot, I just wait for you to die a couple times and you're wide-eyed infants all over again. So, either you survive the mission, or I get to fleece you.' He spread the cards out, offering them to Neave.

She shook her head. 'Don't let Shakana hear you joke about that. Anyway, there's no time for card games. She's finished scouting, I want everyone in position. We're going to flush the Great Flayer out.'

Hendrick looked up from his work, his expression nearly as sharp as the axe in his hands. 'You've laid eyes on the Flayer?'

'No,' Neave admitted. 'But we think disrupting the ceremony is likely to force a fight. The Great Flayer and his cultists have put a great deal of effort into preparing for this gathering. They won't stand by idly and see it destroyed.'

'A plan after my own heart.' Rostus put the cards away and lumbered to his feet. Sitting, he'd looked massive; standing, he was beyond that. Neave had never seen any other Stormcast who approached his size. It was like having a walking mountain at her back.

Once, she'd wondered why someone so huge had been assigned to an assassins' squad. Then she'd seen him in action, and those questions had vanished. That wasn't the sort of thing you forgot, even after Reforging.

'Glad you approve.' Neave looked around, though she already knew the Idoneth wasn't in their camp. 'Where's Lorai?'

'She didn't care to let us watch her preparations.' Rostus leant back, cracking his knuckles. 'But she did say she'd be ready when you called for the spilling of blood. Said her little fish would taste it on the water-winds, so there wasn't any need to go looking for her.'

'All right.' Neave checked over her own axes. She didn't need to, really. They were extraordinary weapons, forged of sigmarite and starlight in holy Azyr, and could not be dulled or broken by ordinary means.

But she still brushed her palms lightly over the handles, just once, in the moments before an assault. Superstition, maybe. Or perhaps she'd developed the habit when she was a mortal, and her axes had been ordinary ones, and had kept it with her as some reflexive part of her identity ever since.

For that reason alone, Neave touched her axes. It wasn't to make sure they were still intact. It was to make sure *she* was.

'Are you ready?' she asked.

'I'm always ready.' Rostus flexed his shoulders and cracked his neck: a double boulder-slide, followed by a thunderclap. Neave winced before remembering that Lorai's magic would keep the noise from their enemies. Hopefully.

Rostus didn't seem perturbed. 'So it's the usual? I go in and smash things, Hendrick pretends to be my sneaky second while actually being anything but – no offence, Hendrick, you're fine at being second, you're just not very sneaky – and then the rest of you sweep in and massacre our astonished foes?'

'That does seem to be the shape of it.' Hendrick stood, sheathing his axe on the opposite hip from his shortsword. When he was satisfied that the weapons were secure, he strapped an ornately scabbarded greatsword across his back. Not a trace of a smile broke the older Stormcast's craggy, bearded face, but Neave saw the glint of good humour lurking deep in his heavy-browed eyes. 'Is there anything else we should know?'

'Be wary of poisons.' Neave relayed what Shakana had told her about the Hidruspex's fondness for tsati venom and other hallucinogens. 'The prisoners may not be thinking sensibly. Spare whomever you can, but be aware that they may be erratic. Beyond that…' She raised her fist in a ritual salute. 'May the God-King be with you and lend his blessing to your blades.'

'And yours,' Hendrick replied, returning the gesture.

'And yours,' Rostus said. He saluted and lumbered off. Hendrick followed him, loping smoothly through the camp. Age might have stolen the colour from the Old Wolf's beard, but it hadn't slowed his step.

Neave waited until she felt the shiver that told her they'd crossed through the boundary of Lorai's spell, and then she too left, running back along the brittle bridge of stones towards the enemy camp.

At the base of Shakana's hill, Neave veered down another dry wash that snaked towards the Hidruspex encampment. Brambles tugged at the Stormcast's cloak and lashed against her greaves as she raced to get between Shakana and Rostus' anticipated line of attack.

She'd barely got into position when the first explosion sounded. A few seconds later, a second blast rattled the rocks underfoot and set the grass dancing over Neave's head. Even before the rocks had settled, screams filled the air.

Rostus had arrived.

Neave burst through the last of the screening grass just as the screams changed in pitch, shifting from shock to rage and then a renewed wave of panic. That would be Hendrick.

A quick glance ahead confirmed it. Rostus was bulling straight through a phalanx of ritually scarred Hidruspex guards, smashing them aside like so many rag dolls clad in cloaks of human leather. Behind him, about fifty yards to the side, Hendrick had leapt from the tall grass to tear a second bloody path through the mass.

More cultists poured from the tents, howling in outrage that their sacred gathering had been disrupted. Only their guards had swords and spears. The others, interrupted in the midst of skinning lesser offerings, wielded flaying knives and hooked retractors dripping with mortal blood.

Their lack of weaponry didn't seem to matter to them. Shrieking curses, the Hidruspex hurled themselves at the Stormcasts. Steel and bone blades screeched and shattered against sigmarite plate. Cultists clawed with bare fingers as their knives broke apart, heedless of their companions pulped beside them. The Hidruspex fell as fast as Rostus and Hendrick could cut them down, but their sheer numbers pressed the Blacktalons back.

She hadn't heard surprise in their screams, Neave realised. Shock, yes. But not *surprise*. Somehow, they'd known this attack was coming. And the way the cultists were throwing themselves against the Stormcasts, with blind determination beneath their fanatic rage...

They were buying time with their bodies. *Why?*

Further back in the camp, horns blared. Other cultists rushed to the pens, snapping locks and throwing open gates.

The beasts of Ghur rushed out, bringing death on hoof and wing. Neave took a split second to watch them, calculating their trajectories so quickly that it took no conscious thought, and just as swiftly mapped her own course between them. She dived through the bleating, roaring mass like an arrow cutting through clouds, twisting her body and turning her steps to avoid the beasts by wordless, unerring instinct.

Trumpeting through the fleshy pipes of its throat sac, the rhyrac reared up onto its four hind legs and crashed back down, crushing the cultists who had liberated it under eight tons of enraged muscle. Gore spurted between its toes. Over its head, the tsati birds circled and cried, filling the air with flecks of feather and the pungent oily scent of their wings.

Hendrick backed away, slipping through the outer tents, but Rostus was bigger and slower and bogged down by the screaming swarm of cultists. The rhyrac shook red mud from its forefeet and stormed towards him.

Neave saw more Hidruspex hurrying towards the central arenas, herding captives before them. Some of these wore headpieces with crystal lenses around their foreheads and beads that jangled beneath their chins, and carried glass staffs filled with pickled eyes that sloshed up and down as they ran.

These appeared to be of higher status than the others. Whatever they were doing, it was likely important. Neave swerved towards them.

Rostus was on his own.

The tsati birds swooped down at Neave as she rushed the camp. Their iridescent wings beat a reeking vapour of oil and venom into the air, making the Stormcast's throat tighten. If she'd been mortal, she would be suffocating. Their hooked blue claws, beaded with poison, stretched out as they dived.

Neave twisted away from their talons and brought her axes up in a steel-edged blur. Three birds evaporated in puffs of blood and feathers. She pulverised two more before the rest of the flock split around her, shrieking in dismay.

When she slowed enough to see the world again, the crystal-beaded Hidruspex leaders were almost out of sight. A knot of cultist guards were rushing to intercept her. Their faces were blistered and weeping where they'd been spattered by the poisoned pulp of tsati birds. One was breathing blood, his nostril half dissolved by the caustic toxin.

Neave leapt around them, dodging those she could, chopping down those she couldn't. She vaulted over their knives and twisted around their spears, propelling herself off one cultist's back to spring over the heads of two others.

Fast as she was, the guards complicated her pursuit. Amid the braying, bleeding mess, she'd lost sight of the cultists in crystal.

They couldn't have got far. Neave spurred herself forwards faster. Swiftly, without breaking her momentum, she blocked a guard's spear thrust with one axe, crossed the other beneath it to cut the woman's throat, then bludgeoned the dying cultist down to trip the others. As the Hidruspex stumbled over their companion, Neave leapt onto a wagon piled high with untanned hides.

There. A crystal-topped staff bobbed between the tents, peeled eyes drifting like gelatinous bubbles along its length. Neave launched herself after it, kicking the wagon over in her wake.

She almost tripped over a panicked man. The Hidruspex had thrown their captives into the fray. Unarmed and blind with terror, they stumbled from their prison pens into madness. A careworn woman clutched at Neave and turned cataract-blue eyes up at her in supplication, but the Stormcast had no time to grant her succour, nor to listen to her prayers. Not when her prey was escaping.

Neave wrenched away, leaving the woman to fall beneath the trampling crowd. She caught a glimpse of Hendrick, then lost him in the confusion. He'd been running a parallel course, though, converging on the central dais.

Behind and to her left, the rhyrac bellowed another chorused cry, its throat sac rippling down the row of fleshy pipes. Rostus roared back at it, swinging his hammer at the beast. Blood painted the bare-armed Stormcast's shoulders and streaked red across his bald head, making him look as savage as the monster he faced. The grass around him was littered with Hidruspex corpses, their limbs and heads crushed by the behemoth's feet.

Rostus smashed his hammer into the rhyrac's skull, silencing its trumpeting forever. As the massive beast slumped to its knees, then to the ground, the Stormcast strode past its ruined majesty towards the centre of the camp.

The remaining tsati birds came for him. They whirled at Rostus in a spiral of poisoned wings, shrieking in glee at having found a slower target. Neave saw the first birds begin to dive, and then she plunged into the midst of the cultists' tents and lost sight of Rostus behind them.

The smoke from the incense cauldrons choked the spaces between the tents. In its velvet blue fog, people melted into apparitions. Cultist and captive blended together, equally indistinct.

A huge crashing noise boomed through the smoke, followed by

another. Screams pierced it like pipes, high and shrill. The smoke swallowed it all, leaving dizzy silence behind.

Within the space of a few breaths, Neave felt her head grow light and her legs faraway. She couldn't hear or feel her own footfalls. The cultists' crystal beads chimed around her, too loud, from all sides. The ringing reverberated strangely, collecting hallucinatory echoes. Vast shapes lumbered through the blurring blue. Or maybe those were only Hidruspex tents, and they weren't moving at all.

Chaos tricks. Neave slowed – she couldn't trust her perceptions, and running blindly at full speed was a trap in itself – but didn't stop. This wasn't the first time her enemies had tried such tactics on her. She took a controlled breath, then another, extending her senses outwards once she'd steadied. *Sigmar, show me the way through the maze.*

She heard it in the rush of the sea. The deep, rhythmic throb of the tide reached her through the mist, steady as a heartbeat. That, too, was a phantom, but it was one Neave recognised. *Lorai.*

The Idoneth was sending her own spell through the Hidruspex's illusions, creating a thread for Neave to follow.

She focused on the sound, increasing her speed as the crashing waves grew stronger and surer in her ears. Anything that approached her through the fog of incense, she kicked aside or cut down.

Some of the figures that fell before her might have been prisoners, lost in the haze or too drugged to distinguish an armed warrior as friend or foe, but Neave couldn't spare the time for hesitation. The only mercy she could offer was a boot rather than a blade.

Ahead, a dais rose from the smoke. The crystal-beaded Hidruspex had gathered there in a double ring, passing their grotesque staffs from one to the next as they shifted ranks in an ever-twisting braid. They were chanting in a cadence that was hurried but not rushed: a song that had gone to a quicker tempo without altering its beat.

Neave leapt out of the incense like an avenging spirit, smoke curling off her armour. With two quick strikes, she beheaded one cultist and eviscerated another. She kicked the headless body into a third Hidruspex, sending the live man and the dead one pinwheeling together off the platform's edge, then shoved through the gap she'd made in their lines to the centre of the dais.

In the midst of the cultists' ring stood a tall, bony-knuckled figure clutching an eye-filled staff. Its face was hidden beneath a deep cowl of tattered human skins, damp and red-stained about the throat. The other Hidruspex hurried to put themselves between the tall one and Neave, but their leader didn't flinch.

'Are you the Great Flayer?' Neave asked, shearing an axe through a Hidruspex's upraised staff and into the man's throat. Glass shards, pickled eyes, and blood sprayed across the platform.

The cowled figure smiled, showing rotten teeth, and pushed down her hood. She was an old woman whose missing eyes had been replaced by mismatched, pickled ones floating in oversized balls of glass. The raw meat of her sockets wept blood around the too-large orbs, and the blood ran down her wrinkles to fissure her face with lines of red, unholy wisdom.

'No.' The woman smiled, and the blood ran faster down her face. The innards of her eye sockets were magnified by the glass; Neave could see every distorted detail of muscle and nerve behind the bobbing orbs. Behind her, something enormous approached through the smoke. 'I am here to deliver you to him.'

'Then let him come and take me,' Neave snarled, smashing the last of the woman's defenders out of her way. The looming, smoke-clad apparition rose alarmingly high on the other side of the dais, but she stayed focused on her target.

The cultist's ruined sockets widened in surprise around her

borrowed eyes just before Neave's axes took off her head. The glass orbs rattled across the wooden dais, leaving dotted trails of blood as they skittered into the fog. Then the half-seen creature lurched out of the incense smoke onto the dais, nearly tipping the platform over with its weight, and the remaining Hidruspex collapsed into panic.

It wasn't just one great beast that had arrived. Both of the collared behemoths from the central pens had come to wreak havoc on their captors.

Roaring, the armoured ursine beast smashed a scythe-tipped paw into the nearest cultist, breaking the man into messy pieces that flopped loose in his ragged robes. The Hidruspex scrabbled away from the creature, only to find the black-and-yellow spider clattering towards them from the other side.

Its piercing legs lashed out, impaling two cultists on dripping spears. Only one had time to scream before it crammed both of them into the drooling lamprey mouth on its underbelly. The surviving cultists fled, vanishing into the smoke.

Neave was trapped between the monsters, and she still hadn't set eyes on her quarry.

Suddenly the near-bear flinched, jerking its snout upwards in pain. Streaks of lightning seared through the smoke, and wet red blossoms spread across its side as Shakana's shots struck home. The Chaos runes etched into its skin flared, burning the stubbly hair around them and making the creature bellow again.

Hendrick clambered onto the platform beside the wounded beast, using his axe to hook into the wooden boards so he could pull himself up. He landed in a crouch, blade ready, as more lightning flashed overhead. 'Thought you could use a hand.'

'A sword would be better.' Neave turned her axes towards the spiderlike thing, which had drawn back to regard her with a glittering, monstrous intelligence in its multifaceted eyes.

46

'I brought one of those too.' Leaving his axe embedded in the platform, Hendrick rolled to the side as the bear-creature swiped at him. He slashed at its paw as he came back up, opening a gash down the pad and severing three toes. The beast roared and pulled its paw away. Hendrick stepped in swiftly, opening a second smile across its throat with a single smooth stroke.

As the hulking bear-thing's life flooded out, the sigils on its hide finally smouldered into stillness.

The chitinous abomination jabbed at Neave with its sharp legs. It was still chewing on the robes of the Hidruspex it had seized earlier. The knotted tangle of their garments, dripping with effluvia, shuddered beneath its gnashing maw.

Neave raised a forearm to knock one of the spider-thing's spears aside. Even with a glancing blow, it numbed her arm from wrist to elbow. Poison dribbled across her bracers, thick as pus.

She shook it off and darted between the legs, using her axes to chop a path between them so she could run straight to her enemy's face.

And there *was* a face. It was wizened, tiny, almost completely hidden behind thick yellow-and-black bristles and the mound of faceted eyes that swelled over that wrinkled nub of flesh. But it was there, with an atrophied nub of a nose and a thin toothless mouth, and Neave had the sudden intuition that perhaps once it had been human.

She raised an axe to cleave it in two.

Then it spoke to her, and she froze.

'Neave. Stormcast, Blacktalon. Sigmar's chosen killer. Do you know who sent you here? Not your god. You were sent by the changeling fates. To be *our* tool, not his. You were sent because the future is in your skin. Because Sigmar's doom is in your skin. Because–'

The creature's face exploded.

Lightning danced over the sizzling stump of its neck and arced from leg to leg as the spider-thing, spasming, fell off the platform and back into the smoke. A second later, the typhoon crossbow's boom reached her.

Neave looked down. A barbed length of black-and-yellow chitin jutted from her armour. The far end, still oozing ichor, had been snapped off by the beast's sudden death and fall, but the tip was buried deep in the padding beneath her plate. With just a slight shift in weight, she could feel it scrape against her skin.

If Shakana hadn't shot the thing...

She shook away the thought. Shakana *had* shot the thing. That was all that mattered. Near misses were a fact of life for the Blacktalons. And if it had killed her, then she would have been Reforged, as she had been countless times before, and she would have returned to her duties as she always did.

There was nothing more to it. Certainly there was nothing more to what the Great Flayer had said to her. That had been an attempted distraction, pure and simple, and it had failed.

But as Neave sheathed her axes, she touched them one last time, brushing her palms over the hafts to reassure herself that they, and she, were still there.

CHAPTER TWO

'So that was the Great Flayer,' Shakana mused, gazing down at the crumpled enormity of the black-and-yellow spider. 'Probably. Are we certain?'

It wasn't an idle question. Twice before, the Blacktalons had been deceived, and had let their target escape after killing a decoy. Terrible tragedies had followed, made all the more bitter because they might have been prevented.

Those failures had occurred centuries ago, long before Neave came to lead the Blacktalons, but they were scarred on the Stormcasts' collective memory. None would soon forget the stories, and none wanted to repeat those mistakes.

Neave nodded. If pressed, she wouldn't have been able to articulate *why* she was so sure, but she felt it in her bones. Her flashes of intuition were a gift from her God-King, and she accepted them without question. 'Hendrick will confirm it during his communion with Sigmar, of course, but yes, I'm sure.'

'If you're certain, then you're certain.' Shakana had more doubts about what she called the 'god-flashes' than Neave did, but even she had to admit that they were seldom wrong. The sniper moved away from the platform's edge, surveying the rest of the destruction they'd wrought. 'Is there anything else we need to do here?'

'I don't think so.' Neave paused, wrestling through the conflicting emotions that surged in her chest as she looked down at the remnants of the Great Flayer. Somewhat awkwardly, looking at a point just past Shakana's shoulder rather than at the woman's eyes, she mumbled: 'Thank you.'

'For what?' Shakana raised an eyebrow, then snorted. 'Saving you? If you really want to thank me for that, you'll stop running blindly into things that can kill you. That beast didn't have a single attack it could make at range. You didn't need to put yourself at risk. No one did. I could have shot it before Rostus even breached their camp. It was right there, out in the open, the whole time.'

'We didn't know it was the Great Flayer then.'

'We could have!' Shakana tossed her braids angrily. Sparks ignited in her crossbow's heart, responding to the Blacktalon's agitation. Smoothing her palms over her sides, the sniper took a moment to compose herself. 'If we'd let Lorai use more of her spells to scry the Hidruspex, or captured some of the cultists and interrogated them…'

Neave flushed. 'Look, it's done. Our duty is fulfilled. That's all that matters. I wanted to thank you for your part in it, that's all.'

'As I said – if you want to thank me, you'll be smarter next time.' Shouldering her typhoon crossbow, Shakana turned to walk away, then paused. She glanced back at Neave, puzzlement rising above her anger. 'Why did you leave the kill to me, anyway? You could have slain the beast yourself. I saw the whole thing through my sights. You had a clear opening, and you froze. What happened?'

'I… don't know.' The memories were vaguer than she'd expected. Neave studied the familiar emblems on her blue-and-gold gauntlets, struggling to remember. 'The Great Flayer called me by name. It spoke of my fate, and the God-King's doom.' She paused and looked up, holding Shakana's narrowed gaze. 'But none of that matters. The rantings of devils and madmen are unworthy of our time. You made the kill. I'm in your debt. That's the end of it.'

Shakana opened her mouth to speak, but Neave put up her hand. 'That's the end of it.'

'If you say so.' Shakana shook her head doubtfully and walked away, leaving Neave to survey the ruins of the Hidruspex camp on her own.

The Blacktalons had chosen not to hunt down the surviving human cultists – once the Great Flayer had been slain, their work was done, and the priority shifted to the next mission – but some of the freed prisoners had. Neave had spotted the Khainite heart-eater devouring fistfuls of bloody prizes cut from Hidruspex chests, and other captives had taken equally grisly vengeance on those who had tormented them. Others were trying to group together for safety. A few were busy looting whatever they could from the tents.

Neave ignored them. Neither the fate of the decapitated cult, nor that of their former captives, was her concern. The Blacktalons were assassins, no more and no less, and the mortals would have to find their own way across the Beastlands of Ghur.

Sometimes that rankled her, but not today. She had other problems on her mind. Shakana's irritability, for one. But also...

Lorai had pulled the mangled remains of the Hidruspex cultists from the spider-thing's underbelly and was spreading them out over sun-baked rocks at the periphery of the camp. Once the Idoneth had realised that the gargantuan creature was the Great Flayer, she'd focused on its last work, believing that doing so might shed some light on why Sigmar had sent them to destroy the monster.

Neave had thought that the Flayer had simply seized its victims to consume them, but as she approached Lorai, she saw that she'd been wrong. With a cautious glance at the Idoneth to ensure she wasn't interrupting some delicate magical operation, Neave moved closer. She was glad to have something to take her mind off the row with Shakana, and she was morbidly curious about what the thing had been doing.

The victims had been drained of their bodily fluids, and it looked as though their muscle and fat had also somehow been liquefied and slurped from their bones, but the Great Flayer hadn't stopped there. It had flensed the skins from both bodies, and had cut and stretched them into a macabre rawhide lace.

It had worked with astonishing speed. No more than a few seconds could have passed from the time the Great Flayer speared its prey until Shakana blew off its head, yet in that brief span it had shaped both skins into… tapestries, or maps.

Maps of the future, Neave supposed.

She stopped a foot away, looking over Lorai's thin shoulder. Both skins showed the same image, replicated with uncanny precision, though the marks were made by old scars, birthmarks and chance wounds. It was impossible that the Flayer could have known what the skins would show before cutting them open, or that it had deliberately crafted its design.

Yet both hides depicted the same swirling vortex, carved in a ragged-edged spiral by the Great Flayer's spearlike appendage stabbing through each struggling victim. Both showed five points arrayed like a constellation of stars around the vortex, and both showed blackened bolts erupting from the vortex towards the same point on its periphery, though in one case the 'bolts' were made of blood-crusted hair, and in the other they were the remnants of a tribal tattoo ripped apart by some long-ago laceration and healed into uneven streaks.

The largest of the bolts, the one that seemed to be aimed squarely at the storm's heart, resembled a twin-tailed comet with a terrible wound splitting its head. Gaps in the skin trailed the broken comet, creating the impression that it bled darkness as it flew.

'Odd,' Neave said.

'Prophecy,' Lorai corrected. The pale, hairless aelf didn't look up. She smoothed and straightened the skins with matter-of-fact efficiency, then walked a slow circle around them, tilting her head from side to side as if she were trying to bring them into better focus. 'They almost show the shape of certain mountains in Aqshy, but... not quite.'

'It is not an error,' she added, forestalling Neave's question. 'The prophecy is drawn to Aqshy, but it is not anchored there.'

'What does it mean?' Neave asked.

The aelf turned slightly. Her eyes were unrevealing, and the iridescent veil over her mouth fluttered faintly with what might have been an exhalation of soundless laughter, or of mild annoyance. Or neither. After all this time, Neave still didn't know how to read the Soulscryer. 'You wish for me to delve into a Chaos prophecy?'

'No, of course not.' Neave grimaced. Was she cursed to say the wrong thing to *everyone* today? 'I only wondered if you could tell by looking at it.'

The chimes on Lorai's staff tinkled as the aelf shifted her grip, considering the question. 'No,' she decided, after the silence had stretched long into discomfort.

'Oh. Well. Thank you for... thinking about it.'

'I am finished with these dead things,' Lorai said, as if Neave hadn't spoken. 'I will now collect what is mine.'

Neave nodded her assent, stepping aside so that the aelf could drift past her. Lorai moved with unearthly grace, seeming to float over the earth rather than step on it. Her blue-green cloak was crafted of driftwood and water-weeds and sea foam, all enchanted together, and the scent of salt fog surrounded her. Save for the light, atonal ringing of her wind chimes, her movements hardly made a sound.

Lorai flowed across the sun-bleached grassland, moving back into the Hidruspex encampment. The surviving prisoners eyed the aelf warily. Some called out to her, and some moved to avoid her, but Lorai ignored them either way. She wasn't interested in those well enough to walk. Instead she sought out the dying, kneeling beside them whenever she found such a stricken soul.

Neave looked away. She knew what Lorai was doing. The Idoneth Soulscryer wasn't healing the wounded. Perhaps she granted them a measure of peace, but if so, it was a grim one. The aelf was siphoning off their souls, stealing what life remained to them so that she could use their soul energies to bolster the vitality of her own people, deep undersea.

That was the pact between them. It was a mark of the Mortal Realms' peril, and the unsavoury alliances Sigmar had been forced to strike in order to preserve any hope of humanity's survival, that the God-King had approved such a bargain.

The Blacktalons relied on Lorai's magic to find their targets and augment their missions, and in exchange they permitted the Idoneth Soulscryer to claim a tithe of mortal souls. Though Neave and her companions did their best to minimise collateral damage, they hardly ever managed to avoid it altogether. Lorai's price was paid in that blood.

Usually it was their enemies'. But sometimes it wasn't, and then Neave had to console herself with the thought that, at least, the aelf abided by their rule that no innocents were to be killed for their souls. If they were already dying, Lorai was permitted to claim them, even to ease their suffering by hastening the end. But no more. She could not murder those who had done no wrong.

It was a small mercy, at best, but that was the nature of the

Blacktalons' work. Neave had reconciled herself to it long ago. This was Sigmar's will, and she was only his tool.

She started to turn away, and then stopped as she saw Rostus coming towards her. The big Stormcast was streaked with flaking blood. Scarlet stained his bald brow, spattered the brown fur of his cloak, and smeared his breastplate. His arms were red almost to the elbow, and Neave guessed much of that blood had been spilled after the Great Flayer was slain.

Rostus, she knew, would fight to the death protecting innocents and allies, if he felt he could do so without compromising their primary mission. He still grieved the family he'd lost as a mortal, and a terrible determination burned in him to see that no one else suffered the pain that he had. With the Flayer dead and no new target yet in their sights, he would have been free to hurl himself against that old wound, bruising himself into numbness. Any Hidruspex who hadn't fled the death of their leader, and who had thought to prey upon the surviving captives, would have found a hard enemy in Rostus Oxenhammer.

Despite the bald warrior's grisly warpaint and evident exhaustion, there was a relaxed satisfaction in his stance that Neave didn't often see. It was rare for Rostus to be simply, genuinely *happy*, but it seemed he was so today.

'Good hunting?' she guessed.

'It was.' Rostus studied her shrewdly. 'What about you? I saw Shakana a few minutes ago. She looked angry enough to bite the Blood God's horns off. Didn't even stop to throw an insult my way.'

'It's nothing.' Neave shrugged. 'She thought I was being careless.'

'Were you?'

'I don't think so.'

'Ah, well, if *you* don't think so.' Rostus nodded sagely. He wiped a bloody hand across his breastplate, achieving neither a cleaner hand nor a cleaner breastplate. 'Can't see what she'd be upset about, in that case.'

'I take your point,' Neave sighed. She ran her fingers through her short-cropped hair, shaking out dust and wishing she could shake away her tangled emotions as easily. 'All right. I'll do my best to be more careful next time.'

'Good.' Rostus clapped a hand on her shoulder, leaving a red print behind. He quirked his mouth ruefully at the smear, but his eyes were serious above the half-apologetic smile. 'When it comes to that sort of foolishness, I've found it's best to listen to those who care about you, rather than your own instincts. We have a better sense of what you're really risking than you do.

'Anyway,' he added, clearing his throat, 'now we've got that settled, we'd better be off. Hendrick's about to start his communion.'

'Right.' Neave shaded her eyes and looked up, seeking Shakana's star-eagle. Anda would tell them where Hendrick was. 'Sigmar guard you and grant you strength.'

'And you,' Rostus said, raising his fist in ceremonial farewell.

Neave matched his salute and was off. She'd spotted the star-eagle circling in the sky.

Fifteen miles from the camp, a bald promontory rose from the plains, slanting over the grass like a spear hurled into the earth. High on its peak, some nameless tribe had erected a tower of bleached bones, lashed together with woven grass and sinew, around a core of ore-veined rocks. An immense auroch skull, its horns wrapped in misshapen fragments of steel, crowned the edifice.

Lightning scars striped the tower and the stone at its base. Overhead, scavengers wheeled. As Neave ran closer, she saw why: a small company of Hidruspex had been sent to desecrate the site. Evidently they'd been working on that when Hendrick arrived.

Neave stepped over the bodies, slowing as she reached the stone's base. Hendrick was halfway up the tower, climbing carefully to avoid overbalancing the structure with his armoured bulk.

Though the sky was clear across the plains, storm clouds had begun to gather in a knot over the promontory. Hendrick's cloak flapped in the rising wind as he continued his ascent, slow and stubborn, hand over hand over creaking bone.

A prickling anticipation crackled through the air, and crisp blue sparks danced along Neave's gauntlets. High above, electric arcs jumped between the steel-studded auroch horns.

Hendrick reached the top. He thrust his sword up at the sky, crying: 'Sigmar!'

Lightning speared down. It struck him in a blinding blue explosion, surrounding the entire tower in its nimbus and dazzling Neave so that she had to avert tear-filled eyes from the intensity of her god's glory.

A pulse of divine awe filled her chest, expanding her heart with such a swelling flood of emotion – so much certainty and purpose and absolute, glowing *love* – that, for a long instant, Neave couldn't breathe and could only stand there, stunned, as she felt the after-echoes of Sigmar's presence from afar.

The light died down. The winds calmed. The plains grass stirred and sighed.

Slowly, Neave's sight returned. She took a shuddering breath, feeling as if the blood had just unfrozen in her veins.

Hendrick came down slowly, hand over hand, and took a moment to gather himself as he stepped back to the earth. Clods of flash-fried dirt and black-frizzed grass crunched under his boots. Soot marks streaked his plate, and he moved with the stiffness of an ancient, long-neglected automaton.

It wasn't the lightning that had stunned him, Neave knew. Hendrick had been touched by the hand of Sigmar, and had been granted a glimpse of divinity. The knowledge of the gods had, for an instant, filled his mind.

She envied him, even as she was grateful that this particular burden was not hers to bear.

'Well?' Rostus asked, breaking the spell. 'Do we have a new target?'

'We do.' Hendrick coughed. A wisp of smoke escaped his lips. 'Rather, we have four.'

'Four?' Rostus echoed. He glanced at Neave, who could only shrug in return. The Blacktalons had never been given so many targets at once before. Usually they were only assigned one. Two, on rare occasion. Four was unheard of.

But if Sigmar willed it, it would be so.

'Four,' Hendrick confirmed. He dipped his head in a nod, then grunted and cradled his temples between his hands, waiting for his vertigo to pass. 'Five, originally, but the Great Flayer was one, and it is dead already. I believe they are the same five that the Hidruspex saw in their prophecies.'

That was strange as well. Why should they be shown a target they'd already slain?

Shakana squinted at the older Stormcast. 'What do you mean?'

'The vision that Sigmar gave me is the same as that on the tapestries the Great Flayer made of its followers' skins. I saw a... raging whirlpool, or perhaps a storm, reaching for five points just outside its grasp. Those five points were our targets. Four remain.

'What the Great Flayer sought – the prophecy that its servants caught and killed so many to find – that was *our* prophecy. Those were *our* targets. The Hidruspex were looking at a future meant for us.'

CHAPTER THREE

'Why would they seek out our future?' Shakana wondered aloud. Her star-eagle had flown down and alighted on her shoulder, where it studied the Blacktalons with hard, unblinking eyes. 'Did the Great Flayer hope to protect itself by foreseeing our attack?'

'I cannot say, but it was the same vision,' Hendrick replied. He paused, for Lorai was coming into view through the tall grass. At times, the Idoneth preferred to keep her distance from the Stormcasts, pursuing her own inscrutable curiosities. Most recently, she'd been absorbed in study of the Great Flayer's final skins. As Lorai spread out the macabre tapestries for them all to view together, Neave couldn't help noticing how shaken Hendrick looked. He hid it well, but she wasn't fooled by his mask of grizzled imperturbability.

'These are the same as what Sigmar showed you?' Lorai asked.

Hendrick shook his head. He traced the spiralling vortex on the nearer skin with a callused finger. His hand trembled slightly as he touched the mark, though Neave thought she was the only one who saw it. 'Sigmar's vision granted more... emotion... to what I saw. In that vision, this was a screaming black storm. It pulled life and warmth inwards, consuming it completely, and spat out bolts of acid hatred that corroded whatever they struck. There was an immensity of evil in it, hidden by the storm, but stunning in its power. Pure Chaos. That was what I felt. A vortex of pure Chaos.

'The heart of it, the source of the storm's evil, poured out from a broken twin-tailed comet. Despair gushed from the comet's wound like water from a mountain spring, and it was that well-spring of pain and hatred that began the storm. But it grew beyond its origins, and became... fiercer, hungrier, *worse*.

'It wanted to rend apart whatever it could, but above all else, it reached for five sparks along its edge. The storm seemed to regard them with... agitation. Fear, perhaps. Or great excitement, of the sort that comes shadowed by the spectre of disappointment. I don't know. All I can say is that its whirling grew even more violent and chaotic as it reached for them, and I felt a hideous yearning from its depths. I wanted very badly for it to fail, and I was afraid of what might happen if it did not.'

'These were Sigmar's feelings?' Shakana frowned as she leant over the skins, looking from one to the other, as if studying the two versions together might enable her to see what Hendrick described. The eagle hopped forwards on her shoulder, cocking its head to match the movement of hers.

Neave knew how she felt. She strained to see it too. But only skin and hair and stiffened scars greeted her gaze, and from the irritable cross of Shakana's arms, she knew the sniper was equally stymied. Hendrick's description cast a prickling dread over her, but there was nothing Neave could actually see or sense to warrant that sensation.

It left her feeling foolish, and annoyed, and slightly apprehensive despite the thought that she really should know better.

'I cannot say,' Hendrick admitted. 'The emotion was there, but I do not know whether it was the God-King's or my own. Only that it was overwhelming, and roiled in response to what I saw. But the vision moved quickly, and I had little time to study its details.'

'Could you make anything out about the five specks? The targets?' Rostus asked.

'Not as much as I'd like,' Hendrick admitted, 'but more than what the skins alone show. One was the Great Flayer. Of that I am certain. I saw it crushed under our weapons. As to the rest...'

He touched the centremost of the five peripheral spots. On both skins, it was slightly larger than the other specks, and more vortex tendrils reached towards that one than any other. 'In Sigmar's vision, this was surrounded by high, spiked crystal walls. It was a fortress of mirrors, each showing horrors in its reflection. On the highest spire flew a many-coloured flag with a blindfolded woman's face on it. A shifting garden of shadows and illusions tried to disguise the true fortress behind their phantasms, but with Sigmar's wisdom I was not deceived.'

'Well, that's clear enough,' Neave said grimly. 'The Blind Queen's Maze. We're headed to the Glassrift of Ghyran.'

The Blind Queen's Maze was a nightmarish labyrinth held by powers sworn to Tzeentch. Although it was an ancient and concentrated locus of the Change God's forces, it stood far from any known realmgate or point of strategic importance, and for that reason had never been prioritised above more direct threats. Neave recalled vague, old tales of a seer named Gerispryx who was said to divine the future from a hall of crystals that reflected visions on their panes, but she knew little of the Blind Queen's Maze beyond that and its name.

She relayed this to the others, then gestured to the points arrayed beside the Blind Queen's Maze. 'What did you see of these?'

'Only flickers. Nothing consistent.' Hendrick drew a deep breath. Some of the distress seemed to leave him now that he was no longer focused on the vortex. 'One of them was a pavilion made of rotting meat. Its guards were gaunt and wasted, but had enormous mouths and vast gullets that sagged over their chests.

'Another was a tree with roots made of bone that plunged deep into the bleeding earth. Flowers ringed the tree, and their faces were human, but covered in threads of pink mould. Then there was a library with books covered in ice. The books were holy scripture, but the ice splintered and slashed at my fingers when I reached out to read them, and my blood covered the pages so I could make nothing out.'

'Curious that we should be sent from one prophet to another.' Lorai's gaze was cool above the shimmering opalescence of her veil. She held each of the Blacktalons' eyes in turn, lingering longest with Hendrick. 'Gerispryx is known to me. She is a formidable sorceress, yes, but her true power is in foretelling. Few see as far or as clearly, even among the Changer's servants.'

'I wonder what we're meant to stop them from seeing,' Neave mused, looking at the torn skins.

'What's the point of wondering? We're assassins. Weapons. The arrow doesn't wonder why it's shot,' Shakana muttered. Plainly her temper was still foul from their last kill.

Neave chose to ignore her. 'The only solid lead we have is the Blind Queen's Maze? No one recognises any of the others?'

None of the Blacktalons spoke up. Rostus shook his head; Hendrick, perhaps remembering his vision, looked quietly pained. Shakana just snorted and stared into the distance, refusing to meet Neave's eyes.

'All right. Then we go to Ghyran. The nearest realmgate in Ghur is Tracha's Spin, but that'll take us to the Stifleswamps. Not ideal. Is there somewhere closer?' Neave asked it of them all, but the question was meant primarily for Lorai.

The Idoneth closed her eyes. Her pale, blue-tinged lids fluttered as she searched her memory for an answer. 'There is the Gnashing Gate, which opens to the Bay of Lotuses. Of course, it is perilous, particularly on this side.'

'Aren't they all.' Rostus heaved a sigh. 'Well, what's the matter with this one?'

'It draws insects. Many, many insects. In Ghur, that is… not a small problem. They are attracted to its vibrations. From time to time, the verminous mass grows so large, and so excited, that they shift the location of the realmgate. Fortunately for our purposes, it is not difficult to find when it moves, due to the size of the swarms surrounding it.'

'Delightful.' Rostus grimaced, shaking his heavy fur cloak as if dislodging imaginary vermin. 'And on the other side?'

'It opens deep underwater, deep enough that few land-dwellers can withstand arrival. Upon emerging, they are crushed by the sea. Your Stormcast blessings, however, should keep you alive long enough for me to assist you. At least, that should be so if I am not delayed by the swarm, or any other interference.' Lorai's voice and expression were utterly emotionless. She opened her eyes, gazing steadily at Rostus. The plains wind stirred a high, brittle song from her chimes. 'It is also always possible that the seas of Ghyran may have further surprises in wait.'

Rostus stooped for the Idoneth to clamber onto his back. 'Always been a safe wager, in my experience.'

Together, the Blacktalons set off for the Gnashing Gate. Already the remnants of the Great Flayer's convocation were almost gone behind them. Great armoured burrowers, ploughing through the earth as easily as fish in water, leapt up from the plains to consume the larger corpses, while winged scavengers and clouds of swarming insects claimed smaller pieces. Even the bloodied earth churned with hungry worms drawn to feed on any available morsel. In Ghur, life rapidly reclaimed its primacy, and no meal went to waste.

Leaving the carrion eaters to their work, Neave fell in beside Shakana. 'I'm sorry you're unhappy with how I dealt with the Great Flayer. You're right that it would have worked just as well your way, and it would have been safer. But what's done is done, and we succeeded. Can we put this behind us?'

Shakana gave her a sidelong glance. Around them, the plains grass blurred as the Blacktalons began picking up speed. Even among Stormcast, they were blessed with extraordinary swiftness, the better to travel the Mortal Realms striking down Sigmar's foes. Unless difficult terrain demanded it, they seldom rode beasts or vehicles in their journeys, since they moved faster afoot than all but the fleetest steeds, and could run far longer before tiring.

Without breaking stride, Shakana reached into an ammunition bag and drew out a green glass flask. It was ornately banded in gold and iron, and there were duardin runes on its label, though Neave couldn't make out the archaic script.

'Do you know what this is?' Shakana asked.

Neave turned to face forwards again. They were climbing from the plains onto a rocky plateau, where the grass gave way to bald earth and loose stone, and the footing was rapidly becoming treacherous. 'No,' she admitted.

'Right.' Shakana's grip tightened on the flask. Neave thought her fingers might have trembled, briefly – a rare lapse to see from the sniper's preternaturally steady hands. For an instant she thought Shakana might throw it away, but instead she stuffed it roughly back into the ammunition bag. 'Maybe it'll come back to you later. Things sometimes do.'

Neave didn't know what to say, so she said nothing. The slope grew steeper underfoot. Night was falling, and with dusk, the twilight predators of Ghur emerged. Vulpine forms flitted soundlessly across the slopes, sliding back into hiding when the Stormcasts passed. Leathery-winged aerial hunters snatched enormous insects from the air, cracking their chitinous shells apart in a loud chorus of nocturnal snaps. Toothy fish leapt from the streams, flashing liquid moonlight across their steely scales before splashing back into the dark.

One fish vaulted too high and was seized by a passing hunter. Curving backwards, the fish locked its ferocious jaws onto its tormentor's thigh. Knotted in mortal combat, the two beasts plummeted back into the river. The current bubbled around them, first white and then dark, as other creatures were drawn to the blood in the water and made swift, unseen work of their wounded windfall.

A moment later, the river was gone, lost behind rising hills.

'At least it's over for them,' Shakana said, and Neave realised she'd been watching it too.

She knew the sentiment too well to need elaboration. Any Stormcast who still held a semblance of humanity had spent many quiet hours with that thought.

They fought, they died, they fought again. With each death, they lost something of themselves: memories, most often, but sometimes it was some other remnant of humanity. The ability to be stirred by music, or the pleasure of a favourite perfume. Red blood might vanish from their veins, to be replaced by liquid lightning. Human eyes might transform into the incandescent fury of Sigmar's holy storm.

Bit by bit, Stormcast Eternals were blasted away by the continual violence of their existence. Even when they did not die, the endless immersion in blood and toil, and the slow erasure of their comrades, created its own unending hell.

For them, the battle never stopped. Their purpose was war. They had no other life, and the one they did have never ended.

New-forged Stormcast were sometimes too dazzled by the honour of having been raised to immortality by Sigmar to realise those truths at once. And it *was* a great honour to be chosen as one of his champions. Only the purest and most courageous were so blessed. Neave felt the truth and the glory of Sigmar's power glowing constantly in her chest, warmer and more vital than her own heart. She was deeply grateful that her god had deemed her worthy, and she strove to uphold his name.

But that blessing came with a bitter shadow. For a Stormcast, peace lay forever out of reach. They could gift it to others, sometimes, but it was never theirs to enjoy.

None of the Blacktalons was new-forged, though, and all had come to terms with the cost of their immortality. They'd succeeded in their last mission, and a new target lay ahead. Why would Shakana think about this now?

Something of Neave's puzzlement must have showed on her face, because Shakana glanced at her and snorted into the wind as they ran along. Then she sighed, her shoulders dipped, and her annoyance seemed to fade, reluctantly, into something more ambivalent. Sadness, maybe, though Neave couldn't guess why she'd be sad.

'I can't even have a proper fight with you,' Shakana said bitterly. 'I can't even have a proper *fight*. Because you don't remember why I'm angry, do you?'

'It's not really about the Great Flayer, is it?' Neave asked.

'No. No, it is not really about the Great Flayer.' Shakana sighed again, and looked straight ahead, and though they continued to run side by side deep into the night, Neave felt very cold, and very alone, as all around them the beasts of Ghur sang and shrieked and hunted and mated, caring nothing for the giants who passed them in the dark.

Three days later, Lorai led them to the Gnashing Gate.

The Idoneth was right: the realmgate did attract swarms of euphoric vermin. When the Blacktalons arrived, a buzzing mass of winged ant-like creatures was attempting to wrest the gate away from a rival colony of long-whiskered roaches. The roaches had buried their prize beneath the earth, and the winged ants were trying to dig it up while fending off the frenzied defenders' razored mandibles and corrosive sprays.

Most of the insects were at least as long as a Stormcast's leg, and so many of them clung to their treasure, and each other, that Neave couldn't see what was at the centre of the writhing mass. All she could make out was a house-sized heap of fighting insects, from which dirt, acid-dissolved wing fragments and dismembered legs flew.

'The gate's in *there*?' Rostus recoiled, staring at the mass of bugs. 'But they'll get inside my armour.'

'Good news,' Shakana told him, fitting a bolt to her typhoon crossbow. 'Where we're headed, they should wash right out.'

The eldritch tides of Lorai's ethersea pushed the weaker portions of each swarm aside, parting the cloud and leaving only the wriggling core. Lit by the silver-blue explosions of Shakana's shots, the Blacktalons hacked their way through the living mass. Ichor spattered their skin; twitching legs scrabbled against their armour. Their feet sank into a mire of acid-slick viscera, broken antennae, and cracked exoskeletons that slid treacherously under their weight.

Rostus spat as caustic pulp sprayed into his mouth. Filmy wings caught and crumpled in the joints of his heavy plate. 'I hate bugs.'

'I don't think they love you either. Come on. I can see the gate.' Neave hacked through another roach. An amber glow had begun seeping through the crush, growing brighter with each insect they chopped away.

Soon she could see it: a braided ring of stone shaped to resemble dried grass, twenty feet across, filled with opaque ochre light. It emitted a constant skin-tingling hum, not precisely unpleasant, but certainly not pleasurable enough to explain the insects' frenzy.

'It's here,' Neave shouted to the others. 'Jump when you see an opening. I'm going through.'

Then, trusting the Blacktalons to follow her, she leapt.

CHAPTER FOUR

True to Lorai's prediction, the Gnashing Gate spat them out deep in the Bay of Lotuses.

Neave plunged into water so heavily silted that it was like being thrown into an ocean of mud. Drifts of deep-sea weeds entangled her, preventing her from swimming for the surface with any speed. Even at this suffocating depth, Ghyran teemed with life.

Though the Gnashing Gate cast its amber glow on this side as well, Neave could see almost nothing. The water swirled with veils of brown silt and bioluminescent green, made even more opaque by the slurry of frantic insects that poured continuously through the realmgate and were pulverised by the weight of the sea. She had no idea how far they'd been thrown into the deeps, but the pressure was excruciating. Without Sigmar's power enhancing her body's resilience, she would have died upon emerging from the realmgate. As it was, she felt her vision blackening fast.

Just as Neave's consciousness began to crack in the ocean's grip, Lorai came through the realmgate. Instantly the water released the

Stormcasts, softening to an ethereal mist in which Neave and her companions floated. Now, with the ocean's density diffused, Neave could see that both the drifting weeds and the green-finned fish that darted through their fronds fed greedily on the pulp left by the insects that flowed through the gate from Ghur.

The seaweeds stretched out long stems that feathered into waving tendrils, sweeping through the slurry, while the fish's cheeks bulged and blew around toothless, sucking mouths.

Larger creatures, sleek and silvery, hunted at the edges of the floating forest, and still larger ones hunted those. Alarmed by the disturbance in their waters, they retreated into the concealing darkness, flashing dappled fins, as Lorai lifted her ethersea bubble higher.

Neave had just enough time to wonder how long the Gnashing Gate had floated here, spewing its endless stream of doomed insects, for the fish and water-weeds of Ghyran to have adapted their entire way of life to the realmgate's bounty. How many generations had lived, fed, and raised their young on that harvest? What would become of them if the gate ever closed?

Then Lorai carried the Blacktalons up through the bay to the shore, and Neave left that mystery behind, as she had so many others across the Mortal Realms.

High white cliffs, garlanded with wildflowers, shone above the water. Darkened forests, exhaling the rich scents of greenery and resin into the night, crowned their heads and wreathed their bases. The Blacktalons shook away seawater and gathered their breath, and they began running again.

Three weeks later, they reached the Blind Queen's Maze.

The labyrinth filled an entire valley. The Glassrift sat within a stubbed mountain range, worn down by time and scouring winds, and scarred by an ancient cataclysm whose name and cause were long forgotten. Over the centuries, Gerispryx had petrified the lush river valley and its surrounding woodlands into a tangle of sparkling, razored edges. From wall to rocky mountain wall, the Blind Queen's Maze glittered before the Blacktalons like an enormous crystalline cancer, stretching glassy tendrils up the slopes and burrowing into their rocky skin.

Within the walls of that cruel labyrinth, nothing lived. One by one, Gerispryx had slain the majestic old trees, solidifying the sap in their veins so that it burst out of their dying limbs in serrated spikes, or crushing them beneath the layered weight of stone leaves so that they sank into tortured sculptures in ripples of crystal and fossilised wood. Any animals that hadn't fled had been similarly mutilated, some standing as rags of fur on crystal bones, others no more than scattered bloodstains left to emphasise the curves of perfect, petrified musculature.

Just as she'd twisted the Glassrift's living creatures into monuments of torment, so Gerispryx had coaxed the natural stone and soil into similar contortions. Hollowed, winding spires rose above rock formations that resembled precariously stacked blocks, or blades fanned out of skeletal hands. The valleys and passes were obstructed by radiating crystal formations, delicate as the veins of a flensed body yet sharp enough to cut a trespasser to ribbons. None of the Blacktalons, save perhaps Lorai, could tell which of Gerispryx's creations had once been alive, and which only seemed to hold the memory of death in their limbs.

It was uncannily beautiful, especially when the light gilded the high peaks and flowed like liquid gold through the transparent boughs and limbs of the Glassrift's dead trees, but it made for slow going. Often the Blacktalons wasted hours, even days, when a pass proved to be unexpectedly walled off by crystals. In those moments, the valley's beauty struck Neave like a goad.

But, finally, they came to the heart of Gerispryx's stronghold.

Immense rough-edged oblongs of crystal hung in the air above the valley, suspended by invisible forces. These, too, appeared to be sections of the labyrinth. They were dotted with shimmering lights and honeycombed with passageways that showed through the transparent walls like traceries of dark veins. It wasn't clear how they might connect to any other part of the maze, however, since Neave could see no bridges or ladders linking the aerial crystals to each other, or to the ground.

'How are we supposed to get in?' Rostus grumbled, as the Blacktalons studied the hovering stones. In the long light of the dying day, they shone with a crazed pattern of mirror flashes and broken rainbows, impossible to unravel.

'We'll figure that out in the morning.' Neave began unloading her pack. In the Glassrift, the Blacktalons didn't need much to camp. Gerispryx's transformations had destroyed the natural climate, stripping away the vegetation that had once moderated the valley's temperature and moisture. Now the barren land was dry and windy, hot by day and cold by night, and haunted at all hours by the forlorn call of the wind through the shredding webs of crystal.

Even so, the altered environment wasn't extreme enough to trouble them. Just as the Blacktalons could run through the mountains for weeks without tiring, so they scarcely needed food or shelter, even under conditions that would kill an ordinary human.

Yet they were not entirely immune to hunger or fatigue. Although Neave wasn't tired enough for weariness to compromise her fighting skills, her muscles ached and her mind was foggy. She might not *need* a rest, but she wanted one.

Like most of the Stormcasts she knew, Neave believed that Sigmar had deliberately chosen to leave them with this connection to their mortal selves. It wasn't a flaw of Reforging that made them need these things. It was a mercy. A Stormcast who'd lost the pleasure of a hot meal after a long march through snow, or the bone-deep relief of a comfortable bed when weary, would be someone completely different, and completely inhuman.

So the Blacktalons needed a semblance of a camp, even if it was little more than a semblance. 'We have some cover here. We'll rest and recuperate while Shakana and Lorai scout. As soon as they spot our target, we'll plan our attack and move in.'

'Excellent.' Rostus let Lorai down gently, dropped his pack with far less care, and staggered off to find a flat rock face to collapse on. As the biggest of the Blacktalons, he always had the worst of it on any endurance run. 'Wake me when you need me, and let me die until then.'

'Wait.' Shakana had moved up to a higher point, and had begun scanning the valley with her spyglass. 'I think someone's attacked the Blind Queen's Maze.'

'What?' Neave climbed the short rise to join her. 'Is there any indication it's related to *our* attack?'

'Look for yourself.' Shakana passed her the glass. 'I've no idea whether it's related. This could be entirely coincidental.'

'Could be,' Neave said, dubiously. She put her eye to the glass. The undifferentiated glittering mass of the Blind Queen's Maze sharpened into labyrinthine complexity. Its walls and forks were dazzling mirrors, each one reflecting infinite false paths and non-existent barricades. Even from afar, the effect was hypnotic.

Smoke plumed from several points in the labyrinth. Beneath each of the spiralling grey smudges, a floating crystal had fallen from the sky, cracking open like a wasp's nest to reveal its swarming interior and devastating everything beneath. The lower labyrinth's walls were broken in sections, and tiny figures crawled across the rubble. Other figures, inert, lay sprawled in splashes of red.

Neave focused on the moving ones. They scuttled across the glass like scouting ants, fanning away from one another to explore the labyrinth and then abruptly regrouping around one or another of their group as they chose a direction to pursue. Most wore tattered red hats or scarves, and as far as she could tell from this distance, they appeared to be human.

Clearly they weren't the maze's original occupants. Anyone who knew the place wouldn't have had to spend so much time on blind searching.

And if they were still looking for something…

She handed the glass back to Shakana. 'You were right. Someone else is attacking Gerispryx. We need to move in.'

Leaving their packs and half-made camp behind, the Blacktalons headed into the valley, Neave at their fore. She wasn't concerned with stealth any more. Where delicate crystal snares blocked her passage, she simply shattered them with the flats of her axes and stepped over the shards. If the Blind Queen's Maze was under attack, she calculated, its defenders had more urgent concerns than her.

Caustic smoke swept up from the valley as the Blacktalons raced down the slopes. Faraway shouts and screams, and the crash of shattering crystal, came from both above and below. Burning debris rained from the nearest floating crystal hulk, and with it came pinwheeling bodies, flailing until they hit the ground.

Seventy feet above the ground, an aperture opened in the hovering stone. Neave saw a goggled, black-clad figure appear in the opening, then pull back as it spotted the Blacktalons. Light burst from its copper-gauntleted hands in three quick flashes.

Neave sprang to the side as the rock beside her exploded. Another burst of light streaked past her head. It hit a crystalline bush, engulfing its glimmering leaves and branches in an indigo aura. Shimmering with arcane energy, the crystal contracted slightly, as if it were under immense pressure. Then it exploded.

Shrapnel hammered Neave's armour and tore stinging tracks

across her skin. Behind her, Shakana cursed. Shielding her eyes against the explosion, Neave hurled an axe up at the half-seen foe in the floating labyrinth. But the goggled figure pulled back with blurring swiftness, and Neave's axe rang harmlessly against the wall, then tumbled back down.

Her lip curled in frustration, but there was no time to waste on a chase. She picked up her axe where it had fallen and ran on. Chunks of crystal littered the ground. Some were small enough to kick aside, but others she had to bound over or skirt around. The other Blacktalons fell steadily further behind her, unable to match her pace, but Neave didn't slow.

A half-toppled crystal wall sloped against a heap of rubble ahead, offering a path to a balcony opening thirty feet above. Just as Neave leapt onto it, the rubble heaved up, throwing her into the air.

Like a whale breaching the water, an enormous, heavily armoured millipede thrust its blunt head up through the labyrinth, shattering crystal walls and launching their fragments into a razored fountain. The bodies of the maze's defenders came up with it, smearing against its flanks as the beast's segmented sides ground them into mush.

Shaking off its victims' corpses, the millipede turned its head towards Neave as she came up from her fall. Fistfuls of tiny eyes gleamed like black bubbles beneath the artificial horns strapped to its blunt brow. It reared up, churning the air with dozens of serrated legs.

Neave hurled her axes at its underbelly as she ran towards the thing. They thudded into its underside, cleaving oozing starbursts into its chitin. She chased after them, jerking them out and slamming the weapons back in again.

The millipede emitted a high, deafening ululation of pain. Crystal vibrated and exploded in the intensity of its cry. It reared again, twisting to smash Neave under its mass as it crashed down, but she'd already dodged away.

Whirling her axes overhead, she slammed them into the millipede like climbing spikes, hauling herself up another segment with each swing. She pulled herself higher and higher, until she reached its horn-harnessed head. It thrashed wildly, trying to throw her off, but Neave hung on, her shoulders screaming, until its momentum had built to the point she needed.

She braced herself against its hide, gathered her strength, and wrenched her axes savagely through the monster's throat. The millipede, mortally wounded, flung her away in a shower of ichor-slicked shards.

At the same instant, Neave jumped. Her strength, added to the millipede's, propelled her high into the air, high enough that she slammed into the wall of a floating edifice.

Her armour cracked against the stone. Black stars flashed across her vision. Neave grunted and blinked them away, scrabbling for a handhold as she slid down.

As her heels slipped into empty space, her fingers closed around the stub of a baluster. Gripping it desperately, Neave hauled herself up. Slivered crystal snapped against her breastplate and rained into her hair as she pulled herself onto the balcony.

She lay there, just for a second, heaving for breath. Then she got up, shook off the splinters, and wiped away the blood that trickled into her eyes from a slash across her forehead.

A doorway stood gaping before her. Its barricades had been blasted away, and the runes inscribed about its threshold smoked with exhaustion. Whatever safeguards Gerispryx had set to protect this entrance had been destroyed.

Neave had left the rest of the Blacktalons behind her. The Blind Queen's Maze lay open ahead.

CHAPTER FIVE

Alone, Neave stepped into white stillness.

Silence surrounded her, but she could feel a faint vibrating hum along her skin. A sourceless white glow stretched into an indefinable distance on all sides, with no apparent ceiling or floor. Behind her, the exit had shrunk into a window that looked at least a quarter of a mile away. She could still recognise it, vaguely, but she didn't know if she could reach it. Somehow it felt even further than it looked.

Walls of faceted crystal divided the space into uneven, mirrored corridors. These had been violently vandalised. Most of the nearer walls had been smashed to jagged stumps. Angry fractures webbed the few that were still intact. Deeper in the maze, Neave saw blood and smoke smeared across the crystals' faces.

Neave moved cautiously, trying to use the walls for cover without looking at them. Even so, she glimpsed strange shapes moving in their surfaces. Some were her own reflections, or might have been, though they seemed to be hurt, or sick, or gripped by a raging malevolence that Neave didn't recognise, and didn't want to.

Most likely the images of herself in torment were meant to trick her into looking longer, and harder, trying to unravel the stories that this place promised to tell her about herself, and who knew what traps she might fall into then?

She eased past them, scanning the corridors and listening for any clue about what might lie ahead, or which path she should pursue.

The maze gave her nothing. There was no scent or movement in the air. Only the sound of her own breathing reached her ears.

Neave was isolated in a prison of her reflections.

There was nowhere else to go. She raised her eyes, steeling herself, and looked full into the glass.

Her face stared back, slashed into a hundred fragments, each one suffused with its own distinct expression of terror or hate. Neave tried not to gaze too long on any single one, but she felt something in the glass shift in response to her attention.

The images changed. Each of her faces distorted into someone else's, their expressions matching whatever Neave's false face had shown. Where she'd seen herself in terror, now she saw a sun-seamed human man's face frozen in fear. A cap of red leaves covered his head, and his cheeks were tattooed with long braids of sigils she didn't recognise. He opened his mouth to cry out, but only a puff of mouldy white threads came from his lips. Inside, his mouth and throat were choked with white fluff.

In the next shard, where Neave had seen herself enraged, she now saw an emaciated woman with sagging, pouch-like cheeks screaming at something unseen. Blood and saliva dribbled between her sharpened teeth. Suddenly she flew backwards, her chest torn apart by a flurry of flying razors from whomever, or whatever, she'd been howling at.

Movement flickered at the shard's edge. Neave could almost make out the assailant, and perhaps something in the background – a formation of broken mirrors that distinguished itself from the blank infinity she herself was in – that hinted at the location.

She scanned the image quickly, trying to memorise the mirrors' configuration, but she wasn't quick enough. Again Neave felt a presence manifest within the crystal, a deep and hidden intelligence that sensed and responded to her gaze. The reflection seemed to pull at her, tugging her centre of gravity forwards so that she leant on her toes towards the wall...

And suddenly she was *through* it, standing elsewhere, with the disorienting sense that she hadn't moved a muscle, yet was somewhere far from where she'd begun.

It was the same mirror-like maze, but it was different, too. The same white glow surrounded her, but here it was weaker. Shadows pooled beneath the crystal walls, and more of them were broken, with corpses sprawled amid chunks of bloodied stone. Fear-sweat and the heavy, not-quite-meat tang of boiled blood fouled the air. The vibrating hum was stronger, but less steady, like some battered duardin engine straining not to succumb to its damage.

Neave moved to examine the corpses. They seemed real enough. The woman she'd seen in the reflection was here, riddled with steel razors, just as she'd been in the vision. Others like her, with the same filed teeth and pouchy skin over wasted musculature, lay dead around her. They wore a patchwork of soiled finery over filthy rags, and very little armour.

It wasn't clear who had killed them. The bodies' positions and the nature of their wounds indicated that the fanged humans had blundered into a clearly superior force, which had massacred them without suffering a single casualty of their own. Most of the dead had been cut down in disarray, before they'd regrouped into any organised response. The last four had gathered around one of the crystal faces, defending it at the cost of their lives.

Why that one? Neave stepped over the bodies to look.

In the cracked crystal she saw herself surrounded by corpses. At first they were the real ones that lay at her feet, and then they melted into new forms, just as her face had been altered by the first reflection she'd gazed into. Neave stayed herself, this time, but the bodies around her became flyblown Rotbringers, or frozen civilians encased in cocoons of red ice, or the scorch marks of her fellow Stormcasts, slain and transmuted to lightning.

Some she'd killed, some she'd fought beside, some she'd failed to protect. So many bodies, over so many years.

Most she didn't remember, though Neave felt intuitively that these images were drawn from the truth of her history, and were not mere falsehoods as her own distorted reflections had been.

But none of them shed any light on why the fanged, pouchy-skinned humans had chosen this particular crystal to make their stand.

She looked harder. Carefully, trying not to give in too far, she let the magic reach a little deeper into her thoughts. *What were they fighting over?*

The reflected corpses changed. The dead Rotbringers and frozen villagers vanished, as their facets went blank.

The Stormcasts changed to a single man, wrapped in a padded cloak and face-shielding hood, who bore Sigmar's twin-tailed comet on his amulet and shoulder patch. A priest of some kind, but not of a sect that Neave recognised. Behind him, steep, snow-whipped mountains smoked against a stormy red sky.

Blood seeped from the bottom of his hood, where crystal glinted from the man's chin like a petrified beard. He cradled a bundle like a baby in his arms, and then suddenly the bundle was gone, and the man was gone, and his empty clothing lay crumpled on the ground with a cracked ball of spiny crystal at its centre. His reflection was still caught in the crystal, just visible among the spiky facets. In it, the man was screaming.

Around the spiked crystal ball, the man's empty clothes shuddered, as if shaken by some unseen hand. The heads of the twin-tailed comets on his shoulder and medallion split open, and wet blackness spilled from their wounds. The inky liquid dripped through the man's abandoned clothes to the earth. As it touched the ground, the scene erupted into a violent struggle.

Tree roots burst up from the black-smeared earth, grabbing at the bloodstained crystal ball sitting in the man's empty clothes. Fat, horned worms swarmed around the roots, biting and goring them. Gaunt shadows swallowed the worms in turn, dissolving their flesh into oozing darkness, and then multicoloured flashes of magic froze the shadows into crystal, and the tree roots pulverised the glinting shards.

Neave felt a pulse of hatred vibrate through her at the scene. It was the labyrinth's emotion, not her own, but her jaw clenched and her fists knotted in response.

This was the answer. This was why they'd fought. The forces of Chaos were vying for that spiked crystal sphere, and the spirit trapped within it.

But why? The mirror's magic reached for her, and Neave let it pull her through.

She emerged in another section of the Blind Queen's Maze, this one even more battered than the last. The labyrinth's white glow faltered into feeble, rapid pulses, scattering shadows over the scene of a massacre.

This part of the maze wasn't as featureless as those Neave had seen before. It looked like a laboratory, or perhaps a prison. Glass-barred cages, all empty and all damaged, surrounded dented, overturned healers' tables.

One wall was comprised of warped, living flesh stitched around glass tubing and rune-marked dials. Needle-thin siphons buried themselves in pulsing veins, sapping their fluids, while dismembered arms reached out of the fleshy wall to manipulate the levers embedded in their ulcerated mass. Bones and joints of enchanted crystal glowed within the flesh, continually healing its wounds. Though a terrible battle had been fought here, the arcane wall seemed almost intact.

Nothing else in the room had fared as well. Red-capped tribal warriors and sharp-fanged gauntlings lay broken amid the wreckage of the maze's crystal walls. Feathered Tzaangors and eyeless Arcanites, shimmering ichor dribbling from their crushed masks, were crumpled among them. The stench of Chaos magic hazed the air.

Whatever they'd fought over, however, had vanished with the victors.

Neave gritted her teeth. Not one of the corpses had been dead long enough to stiffen. Some of their wounds were still bleeding. She'd barely missed it, whatever it was.

Frustrated, and aware that her frustration was making her unwise, she stalked to the crystal pane embedded in the living wall. It was the only one left intact in the room. The dismembered arms around it, clawed and scaled and web-fingered, beckoned gleefully to her as she approached. Neave ignored their gesticulations, focusing on the glass in their midst.

Unlike the other mirrors she'd seen, this one was faceted with a dozen different faces and etched with runes about the base. Neave couldn't read those unholy marks and didn't care to try, but she surmised that this pane must be more important than the rest. Again she opened herself to its magic, seeking some clue about what had drawn so many servants of Chaos here and driven them to attack each other.

What did they want? Why did they kill each other? Neave tried to will the questions into the glass, hoping her thoughts would guide whatever spirit chose the visions in this place.

But what the mirror showed her, again, was herself, and the Blacktalons she'd left behind to forge ahead on her own.

Neave stood in the foreground of each image. In each one, she was staring at something unseen, always with the same caricatured expression of fatuous determination and a blinding gleam reflecting off her armour's holy sigils directly into her eyes.

Behind her, in the first reflection, Lorai siphoned the souls from a handful of huddled, shivering refugees even as they beseeched an oblivious Neave for succour. In the next, Hendrick, his mouth locked into a hard line, readied his sword to backstab her. Another facet showed Rostus collapsing under a swarm of giggling, biting Nurglings while Neave walked away, abandoning her companion to his doom.

Again and again, Neave watched her companions betray her, or saw herself betraying them. Across the Mortal Realms and the nightmarish domains of Chaos, in the sacred halls of Azyr and the poisoned fog of the skaven's Blight City, the scenes of deception and disloyalty repeated, century after century.

It wasn't those that caught her gaze, though. It was something simpler, and far more puzzling.

One facet of the mirror showed Shakana standing before an open balcony, gossamer curtains blowing in the wind around her. Gilded domes shone like banks of seashells in the city below. It was night. Somehow, looking at the image, Neave had the distinct memory of warm salt breezes and the scent of orange blossoms, although she didn't recognise the city or the scene.

In the reflection, Shakana wasn't wearing her sniper's armour, and she wasn't armed. She wore a billowing gown of sheer white silk, striking in its contrast to her dark skin. The wind wrapped the dress around Shakana's figure in a way that made Neave swallow.

She was so *beautiful*. She was so elegant, and proud, and... beautiful. The bottled-up frustration that always surrounded the sniper was gone. Shakana looked relaxed, and happy, in a way that Neave had never seen before.

And she was alone. Neave wasn't in that reflection. It was only Shakana, and the city, and a night that Neave didn't remember.

Neave wasn't even conscious of leaning towards the image, but the crystal flowed towards her and pulled her through.

This time, the labyrinth's magic seized Neave with a surge of malevolent glee, pummelling her like waves beating a rocky shore. It threw her off balance and slammed her against the rough, shifting sand of her memories, then prised greedily at her defences to see how much of her mental armour had come loose.

Uselessly she struggled in its grip. The magic held her fast, oozing around her like a pool of treacly filth, looking for any weakness it could use to seep into her mind. Neave tried to shake it off, to push it away, to do whatever she could in this disembodied struggle so different from the familiar rhythms of axe and muscle.

She had no strength here, or at least none she recognised, and that filled her with a blinding panic. She was a *Blacktalon*, one of Sigmar's deadliest warriors.

But she was alone, having run ahead of her companions. She'd left them all behind: Hendrick with his wisdom and patience, Rostus with his strength and dauntless good cheer, Shakana with her keen insights and unsparing perception. Even Lorai, whose cold and alien presence had somehow become peculiarly comforting over the years.

They were all gone.

Because you didn't want them. Because you wouldn't wait for them. Because you don't deserve *them.*

Those weren't Neave's thoughts. That wasn't her voice. It was the labyrinth's magic, gibbering madness into her head.

But there was enough truth to it, just enough, that the accusations were hard to shake.

Sigmar, grant me strength, she prayed. *Sigmar, show me the way. I need my friends. I need the Blacktalons. You gave them to me because you know I can't do this alone. Bring me back to them, God-King, please.*

The spell snapped. Neave stumbled back into reality, or something close to it, with a gratitude as immense as she'd felt upon being hauled out of the sea outside the Gnashing Gate.

It was another room, white like the first, shadowless like the first, filled with mirrors that didn't reflect anything around them. But this one wasn't empty.

'I was beginning to wonder whether you planned to join us,' Hendrick said.

They were all there. Shakana, Rostus, Lorai. The eerie white light blanched their faces and faded the insignia on their armour to a meaningless blur. In that bleaching radiance, they looked unfamiliar, almost sinister. Neave felt a stab of prickling fear that her comrades had been replaced by daemons wearing their faces, and then a deeper, creeping paranoia that the first thought hadn't been her own.

Had the mirror planted that idea? Was this all a trick to sow mistrust among the Stormcasts? Or was she still in the crystal, being deceived by phantoms?

'Where did you go?' Shakana asked, with a waspishness that barely concealed her relief. 'You left us all behind, Neave. We had to cut our way through dozens of defenders without any idea whether we were headed back towards you, or towards our target, or… anything. We didn't even know whether you were still alive.'

'I'm sorry,' Neave said, guiltily aware of how inadequate the apology was, and how little time there was to attempt meaningful amends. 'I saw an opening, and I took it. I shouldn't have left you, though, and I am sorry for that.'

Shakana quirked her mouth in eloquent exasperation. 'Right.

Well, we can discuss it later. Do you know how to navigate the labyrinth? We've been trying, but without much luck.' She gestured at the crystal walls. 'But now they're different. They were blank before you walked through. Now they show... this.'

Looking around, Neave saw that all the mirrors in the room showed the reflections she'd seen in the arcane walls earlier. Lorai stealing souls, Rostus dragged down by giggling Nurglings, Hendrick with his sword raised to Neave's back. Treachery and infighting, on every pane.

But now all of the Blacktalons could see the images. Could see Neave, blind and foolish, leading them into ruin, again and again.

For once, Neave couldn't guess what any of them thought. Even Rostus' normally open face was a lifeless plaster mask in the labyrinth's pale glow.

'Do you remember any of these things?' Hendrick asked her quietly. His expression was as unrevealing as the others', but a gruff gentleness softened the rumble of his voice.

Neave shook her head. 'No.'

'That's the trick to it,' Hendrick said. The grizzled Stormcast gestured to the walls without looking at them, and Neave realised that he was focusing on her to keep his attention away from the reflections' lures. He raised his voice, subtly but unmistakably, so the others could hear him. 'Much is taken from us when we serve Sigmar. That's true enough, and Chaos' cleverest traps are always laced with the truth. We suffer, and then the memory of that suffering is taken from us when we die and are Reforged. Perhaps that's a blessing, in its way. Think of what a torment it would be if, for eternity, you remembered every loss, every wound, every death.

'But it also opens us to lies about what we've done, and what we've lost, and whether it was worth it, because *we can't remember*.

'What's the truth? We don't know. We *can't* know, because this is a test of faith. Every day of our service is a test of faith. Our recollections are faulty. The histories we write can't capture every nuance. That leaves us vulnerable to lies like these, which attack our faith by reminding us that we must trust Sigmar to guide us in battle. We have no other option. Our comrades are as compromised as we are.'

'That's not true,' Shakana said suddenly. She'd been quiet through Hendrick's speech, as they all had. They'd all gazed at the crystal walls until, one by one, the Old Wolf's voice had pulled them from the Blind Queen's dreams.

But now the sniper broke the silence, with an undercurrent of hurt that Neave couldn't understand. It was as if she'd been personally attacked by the mirrors' visions, in some crueller fashion than the rest of them.

'Lorai remembers,' she said. It sounded half accusation, half plea. 'She remembers everything.'

The bald aelf stared back, unblinking, as all the Blacktalons turned towards her. Around her, the ghostly red fish that swam in the currents of the ethersea waved their gossamer tails and clacked their teeth in agitation, but Lorai herself betrayed no emotion. 'I do not remember everything. My memory is better than yours, but not without flaw.'

'You've never died or been Reforged,' Shakana insisted. 'You remember the truth of these things.'

'Some. Not all.' Lorai's sharp, delicate features looked even more alien in the labyrinth's glow. Her eyes were pits of darkness, washed with crimson flashes from the fins and scales of her spectral fish. 'Do you wish to ask me?'

It wasn't the first time the Blacktalons had asked her to recall what one of them had lost to Reforging, but ordinarily they only did it to improve their tactical knowledge or take better aim at an elusive target. They had never relied on Lorai to answer questions outside the scope of their missions, or to resolve personal disputes.

Certainly they'd never asked her to shore up their faith. The very suggestion made Neave uncomfortable, and it seemed she wasn't the only one.

'Faith is faith,' Hendrick said quietly. 'Your doubts cannot be salved by others. Once you begin looking to others to bolster a truth that should be between you and the God-King alone, it never ends.'

Shakana's corded hair swayed as she tensed her jaw. 'It isn't about that. But you're right. There's no point. She wasn't there, anyway.'

'I was there.' Lorai's gaze, infinite and pitiless, rested on Shakana. 'In the city of golden domes? That is Barak-Dul. We went to kill the daemon prince Ashul'vath. But we arrived early, and had to wait two weeks for the prince to come. You were new to the Blacktalons then, and did not wish to wear your armour in the city, lest his spies report our presence. I remember.'

'You weren't in that room. You don't know.' Shakana said it in a whisper. Spots of colour burned in her cheeks, almost hidden by her brown skin and the pallid light. But Neave could see it, and wondered what had the sniper so agitated.

'Are you all right?' Hendrick asked, interrupting the tension despite having pitched his voice low. The question wasn't directed at Shakana or Neave, but at Rostus, who had drawn away from the others, uncharacteristically quiet and remote. 'What did you see?'

Rostus stirred from his reverie. He lifted his great shoulders in a small, unconvincing shrug as he turned back to the Blacktalons. 'Nothing. It's not what I did see that troubles me. It's what I might.' He swept a hand across the bank of crystal faces, and the memories shown on each. They all reflected pain and loss, magnified and distorted by Gerispryx's malign spells, but not untrue. Never entirely untrue. 'If the Blind Queen's Maze is going to do this to all of us… I don't know if I can face it.'

'You can,' Neave said, staring hard at the crystals. 'You must. It's the only way through.'

CHAPTER SIX

Deeper and deeper the Blacktalons ventured into the Blind Queen's Maze, and at each turn the labyrinth extracted its toll of pain from them.

Neave bore the worst of it. She'd walked these crystal halls before, and knew her faith could carry her through. The maze assailed her with images of a shattered axe and a rusted helm, of a holy forge gone cold and choked with ashes, of Neave running down an endless dream-hall in black and white, pursued by a mocking shadow that wore her friends' faces as masks.

Some of the images she recognised. Some she didn't. The unfamiliar ones filled Neave with a colder fear than the rest, because she *felt* a powerful emotional reaction to them, but she didn't know the cause, and she couldn't guard herself against it.

All Stormcasts struggled with the limits of their self-knowledge. Some could accept it more gracefully than others. For Neave, that lack of knowledge had never been easy. She could force herself to swallow it, for a while, but eventually the desire to know who she'd been, and how much she'd lost, rose up again.

Over time she'd come to an uneasy peace with the uncertainty of her identity. But it was always a fragile peace, easily broken, and the Blind Queen's Maze drove spear after spear into the weaknesses in Neave's emotional defences.

She could piece together... some things. A mortal hero had borne that axe and worn that rusted helm, and Neave had placed the relics in an alcove to honour the long-dead woman's bravery. But there was... more to it, something deeper, something that hadn't just inspired her with another's heroism, but had... frightened her. Shaken her. She remembered the taste of that fear, but not the *why* of it.

The forge, too, was a thing half remembered. The Blacktalons had found it at one of Sigmar's sacred sites, a temple where master smiths honed consecrated weapons and holy warriors sparred to prove their prowess to their god. But the temple had been abandoned, its fires long starved and its sparring rings empty, when the Blacktalons came.

Neave remembered that much. What she'd forgotten was why the sight of the forge filled her with such sadness, and why she looked upon its ashes with dread.

She rubbed her forehead as she came through the glass, unsure whether she was trying to shake off the memories or coax them into coming back.

More than anything, Neave wanted the truth, but of course she wouldn't find that here. Only taunts, and absences.

'I need a rest,' she told the others. 'Someone else will have to take the lead for a while.' For reasons none of them knew, the Blind Queen's Maze demanded its tithe of suffering only from the first in a party to pass through its mirrors. Hendrick had guessed that perhaps Gerispryx enjoyed following her captives and watching their torments without suffering her own. That seemed as likely an explanation as anything Neave could invent.

Whether or not that theory was true, the Blacktalons had soon learnt that others could follow through the mirrors unharmed, if they moved quickly and to the same destination.

But no one came forwards to take the lead. They exchanged a glance, showing an apprehension that surprised Neave. It wasn't like the Blacktalons to hesitate in the face of sacrifice, however unpleasant. They'd seen what she had endured, and knew there would be no physical harm.

'I'd rather not,' Rostus admitted in a low rumble, avoiding the others' eyes. 'I know what the mirrors will show me, and... I don't want to see it. Them.'

'Sigmar has asked me to do some hard things,' Hendrick said, clearing his throat roughly in the hush that followed Rostus' confession. 'Ugly things. I fear the labyrinth will use them to shake our loyalties to each other, and to our God-King.'

Neave blinked at Hendrick in surprise. She knew Rostus couldn't bear seeing the faces of his lost family again. He seldom spoke of that pain, but he also didn't deliberately hide it, and all the Blacktalons knew at least the broad contours of the tale.

But she hadn't thought Hendrick would flinch at the prospect. What could he have done that troubled him so?

Before Neave could ask, Shakana shouldered her way to the fore. 'Of course they will,' she snapped. 'That's what they *do*.'

Neave saw the anxiety thrumming beneath the sniper's impatience, but she was grateful to Shakana for coming forwards. She was too tired and vulnerable to lead them through the maze again so soon, and they had no time to waste.

Shakana crossed her arms as she squared off before the nearest crystal pane, staring an angry challenge at her own reflection. 'But we need to get to our target. If you won't do it, Old Wolf, I will.'

The glassy surface rippled, teasingly, as if it enjoyed making Shakana wait for its sadistic game. Behind her, the featureless white maze shifted into a balcony overseeing the gilded city that Neave had seen in her own vision. Diaphanous curtains blew on either side of Shakana, and in the background was a small table set with two wine glasses and a canopied bed, upon which a vaguely glimpsed figure reclined.

In the reflection, Shakana's armour softened and paled into a flowing white gown, the same one Neave had seen earlier. Its silk clung to the Stormcast's curves and muscles, outlining her toned form alluringly. The figure in the bed lifted its head as if calling to her, and the Shakana in the mirror turned to respond with a playful smile, her eyes alight.

The real Shakana clenched her teeth, spots of dark colour burning high on her cheeks. She adjusted the crossbow on her shoulder, drawing sparks of lightning from the weapon as it clanged against her plate mail. 'Come on, let's go.'

'If I looked as good as you do in silk, I'd never wear anything else,' Rostus said, letting out an exaggerated whistle of admiration. Shakana glared daggers at him, but his joke did loosen some of the tension that ran through her.

'Sigmar strike me blind if I ever have to see that,' she muttered, pushing her way into the glass. It rippled and swallowed her, and the others followed soon after.

Neave waited until Rostus and Lorai had gone through. She would have waited for Hendrick too, but he waved for her to go first. 'After you.'

'All right.' Shaking off her distraction, Neave followed the others. She caught the hint of a sympathetic nod from Hendrick as she passed him, but he didn't say anything, and Neave wasn't in the mood to talk either.

So *she* had been the person in that bed.

Between the two glasses on the bedside table, Neave had spotted the same flask that Shakana had shown her after they'd slain the Great Flayer in Ghur. And of course there was no reason for the mirror to show them both the same vision unless it was something they shared. Or, rather, *had* shared.

Because Neave had lost that memory, and Shakana hadn't, and that was its own kind of pain.

They'd have to talk about that. Eventually. Not now. In this place, Neave knew, the urge to mend exposed wounds was a trap. That was why the maze prodded them so viciously.

She let herself look at the mirror's vision of happiness one last time, and then she too pushed her way through.

Other crystals met them, and other reflections: the Blacktalons laughing at Rostus as he tripped and plunged through the ice on a frozen lake that couldn't bear his weight; Hendrick patiently teaching Shakana how to follow the tracks of an elusive nightcat in Ghur, and rewarding her success with a rare smile of approval; a tavern in Azyr, under an unusually still sky, where they had drunk ale and shared tales deep into the night.

Neave read the stories in the images. She had no independent memory of any of these moments, and the loss ached with an unexpected, barbed bitterness. Even the *size* of what she'd lost had been unknown to her.

Lorai didn't feature in any of the reflections that the Blind Queen's Maze used to spur Shakana's suffering, and Neave thought she knew why: because the aelf, having never endured Reforging, remembered everything. The moments of joy and solace and friendship she'd shared with the sniper still bound them together. But the memories Shakana had shared with the other Blacktalons were now hers alone, and perhaps that hurt worse than if she'd lost them altogether.

A relationship is a chain of memories. The words came into Neave's mind of their own accord. Had Shakana told her that? When? Where? Neave scrabbled to remember, but the truth slipped like water from her grasp.

She could remember the words, though. *Break enough of the links, and nothing holds us together any more. That's what I'm afraid of. You die too often, and when you wake on the forge, you don't even know what I'm grieving. For you, it never was. We never were.*

Tears. There had been tears. Whose? Neave couldn't recall. *I have surer relationships with some of our enemies, Neave. At least they remember what we've been through together over the years. At least they know the stories we've shared. But with you–*

The mirror let her go.

Neave emerged in a close, suffocating darkness that stank of blood. Something wet squelched under her feet. Limp fingers crunched beneath her heel. Though the other Blacktalons, except Hendrick, had preceded her through the mirror, she seemed to be alone in the blackness with the dead.

It didn't last long. Just as Neave was turning to find her way back into the crystal – if she could – a pale light pulsed in the darkness, briefly revealing the enchanted pane, and Rostus' hulking shape stepped out. A moment later, Lorai followed. Then Hendrick, then Shakana, who looked shaken, though she recovered swiftly.

That wasn't the order in which they'd entered, but it wasn't a surprise that the mirrors would shuffle them as they passed through. Neave was only puzzled that it didn't seem to have happened before. Was this one different? Or was it merely the Blind Queen's malevolent magic at play, making them hunt for meaning where none existed?

Lorai lifted her staff. Aquatic green light spread from its chimes to drive back the dark, and its watery radiance shone over the upturned faces of the dead.

The Blacktalons stood in a vast black nothingness. Under their feet, faint reflections pooled. Around them stretched an inky infinitude, as ill-defined as the maze's earlier chambers, but rendered in black rather than white.

Around them hung a panoply of papers and parchments, inscribed with dense blocks of writing in a tight squarish script, or cramped and intricate diagrams penned by the same hand. These hovered in the air, held up by nothing. More trailed off into the nebulous void.

At the Blacktalons' feet lay a dozen corpses.

These weren't the tribal warriors with their red-leaf crowns that Neave had seen before, nor were they the fang-toothed creatures shrivelled inside bags of skin. The corpses in this room were scarred, muscular humans in black armour and goggled helms. They all had squiggles of darkness stretching up from their skin, as if fat black worms had burrowed just beneath the surface and then, finding themselves trapped, had thrashed fruitlessly to break through to the air. The inky coils spelled out venomous obscenities, and Neave didn't look at them long.

Chaos. That was all she really needed to know. These warriors were from yet another Chaos faction that had come to kill and die in this place.

And die they had.

Neave was wary of letting their cursed sigils burrow into her mind, but she looked long enough to see that some of the warriors had been partly petrified, their heads and limbs turned to crystal that had dropped bloodlessly away from the stumped pink remains of their forms. Others had been lacerated by flying shards, each about the size and shape of Rostus' playing cards.

'These are Champions of Vercaspior. Mercenaries among the Slaves to Darkness, born human and baptised in daemon-blood, as disciplined as such creatures can be. They are formidable fighters, but they met someone even more formidable here,' Hendrick said, studying the bodies with the same abbreviated, sidelong glances. 'Perhaps Gerispryx herself. I've seen these crystal blades before.'

'The one who killed them is not gone,' Lorai whispered, stretching her thin fingers over the dead. Their eyes opened blankly as her palm passed over them, and the aquamarine light from her staff shone up from their vacant gazes. A collective sigh, like the susurration of distant waves, emanated from their mouths. 'The pain of her presence lingers in the cold tide of their blood. Their hearts have stilled, and their rushing waves are silenced, but the fear remains. She is not gone. She waits here, hidden, for new prey.'

Neave's hands slid to her axes. 'She's here?'

A petrified head suddenly exploded, sending shrapnel and chunks of pulverised flesh flying. Then an arm, then another head, erupting in a wild syncopation of destruction. The papers hanging in mid-air shuddered, but stayed up, as glittering debris tore through them. Globs of coagulated blood smacked across the writing, then slid down the marred pages.

Shakana threw a gauntleted forearm up to prevent the shards from blinding her. Rostus, slower, grunted as splinters flew over the sniper's head to quill his cheek and the side of his bald head. If Shakana hadn't been standing in front of him, or quick enough to catch the rest of the assault on her armour, the volley would have torn out his throat.

The hanging papers in the distance drifted closer like parchment ghosts. Their blood-gelled writing blurred into meaningless grey smudges, then resolved into images much like those that had tormented the Stormcasts in the maze's mirrors. Loss, betrayal, meaningless sacrifice.

One hovered at Rostus' side, baiting his peripheral vision with images of his long-dead family. It showed his wife in happier days, visibly expecting. A new-born child, red-faced and yowling, moments after birth. Then their deaths, terrible and inevitable.

Rostus didn't look. His jaw clenched, and his breath hitched as if he'd taken an unseen punch, but he didn't stop scanning for the real threat in the room. He grabbed a handful of the quills sticking out from his head and hurled them in the parchment's direction, never turning to see whether they hit.

Lorai, though, was distracted by another shimmering sheet. This one showed the Idoneth kneeling beside an eyeless aelven child – a Namarti, born soulless and destined to die without the infusion of some other creature's soul. Neave gave the image no more than a sidelong glance, and couldn't tell whether the child was male or female, baby or toddler. It was young, though, and it had some resemblance to Lorai, though perhaps that was only because all Idoneth were similarly bald and bluish pale.

The child in the image looked sick, and Lorai was stricken beside it, both in her reflected likeness and in reality. The Idoneth couldn't look away, and Neave knew they'd have to win this fight without her.

As if tugged by an invisible lodestone, slivers of crystal began sliding together. A chunk of a broken scalp fused to a handful of other shards, each slotting into the next in a perfectly fitted puzzle. A single shape rose from the assemblage: a headless humanoid torso supported by four sprawling tentacles. At the centre of the figure's chest, dangling like a leathery medallion from a crystal chain, was a skinned human face, its toothless smile sagging vacantly below empty eyes.

The crystal flakes embedded in the corpses shivered and pulled themselves free, shedding drops of black blood. They flew to the figure and gathered themselves into wings, spreading glassy, dark-stained feathers wide.

As the last feather clicked into place, the wizened face's mouth curled up in a smile. Silver light spilled through the leather, pouring out from its mouth and eyes, and where it touched, the skin began to char.

'Old Wolf,' the crystalline creature crooned. Its words came in a chorus of fractured voices layered over one another, falling and rising unevenly. Some tickled Neave's ears with uncomfortable familiarity; others were utterly alien, their syllables mangled by clacking mandibles and scarcely comprehensible. 'How long it's been. You've brought new friends this time. I suppose your god couldn't salvage the old ones. Shall I take these from you too?'

'You're hurt, Gerispryx,' Hendrick said, circling around the creature with sword and axe readied. He kicked one of the corpses as he sidestepped by, making its limbs flop. 'Hurt badly, I think. You only talk when you're trying to distract me.'

The leather mask's eyes flickered at the corpse's movement. In that instant, a blinding explosion slammed into its crystal body, followed by a thunderclap that rattled Neave's teeth. Wing fragments battered Lorai's chimes, ringing them wildly. Shards spun off into the infinite darkness, shining like falling stars.

Shakana fitted another bolt to her typhoon crossbow. 'It's a good trick, talking,' she said. 'Works on all sorts of people.'

The withered face's lip pulled back in a silver snarl. 'You fools. Blundering blindly into prophecy. You've no idea what you're doing, or why you're here.'

'Killing you,' Rostus rumbled. 'That's why I'm here, at least.' He lumbered towards Gerispryx, hammer raised, only to find the corpses around his feet rising up into a grisly fence. Their veins, petrified to crystal in place of blood, burst out of the bodies and sprouted thorns as they tangled into a barbed barrier and rose higher. The razored thorns grabbed at Rostus' legs, scrabbling against his greaves and forcing him away from Gerispryx.

Shakana fired a second shot, but this time Gerispryx was ready. The sorceress lifted a crystal hand, and the bolt dissolved into fizzing sparks in mid-air.

Neave charged. She hurled an axe at the sorceress, scattering the dust of Shakana's disintegrated bolt. It slammed into Geri-spryx's chest, slashing open the leathery face. Silver light spilled out, along with a spectral moan, but the sorceress didn't falter. She seized Neave's axe and tore it away, and threw it contemptuously into the brambles massed around Rostus.

The crystal brambles kept spreading. They grabbed at Hendrick, jerking the axe from his grasp and twining around his wrist to prise at the plates of his gauntlet. He hacked at them with the sword in his other hand, chipping sparks and thorns and spatters of his own blood from the relentless vines.

Rostus was still entangled. The vines had risen to his chest, strangling him in jewelled barbs. None had cut deeply yet, but his sigmarite plate was scarred and scored, and his hammer remained firmly bound. He couldn't free his own weapon to fight, and he couldn't reach Neave's to return it. The big Stormcast bellowed in rage, but despite the furious bulge of his muscles, the brambles didn't release an inch. Groaning in protest, his plate mail began to cave in under the grinding pressure.

The corpses beneath the vines twitched. As if plucked up by invisible fingers, scraps of flesh and clothing rose through the thorns, clumping together into wet handfuls of rags and pulp. A silvery spark flew into the core of each one, animating the lump into something like a headless bat with two barbed tentacles in place of legs. Misshapen mouths, lined with splinters of bone and crystal for teeth, opened along the little monsters' bodies wherever the seams of their makeshift matter came together.

Shrieking from all their mouths, the tentacled bats flew at Neave. She dodged through the flock as best she could, bashing their dripping wings away with her remaining axe. A vine grabbed at her ankle, and she kicked it away as she leapt towards Gerispryx.

Another bolt from Shakana's typhoon crossbow howled past. Distracted by Neave's charge, Gerispryx failed to react in time.

Her hand came up too late, and the bolt exploded into lightning against her chest. Crystal cracked apart, bleeding silver light.

The bats came screaming down, battering Neave and Shakana with their wings. Their suckered, tooth-rimmed tails stabbed at the Stormcasts, leaving streaks of bubbling silver slime on their armour. Neave snatched one away from her face and crushed it in her fist, ripping the tail's mouths from her wrist as she flung away the body.

'You don't know what you're doing,' Gerispryx hissed as Neave closed on her. Up close, the silver light that filled her leather face was full of fractal shapes, spinning out and dissolving endlessly in its sickening radiance. 'In killing me, you serve Chaos better than any of its servants.'

'Shouldn't you want that, then?' Rostus asked, straining for a jovial tone even as crystal thorns climbed up his chest and reached for his throat. 'Not that it matters. Our orders are to kill you. So you have to die.' He made it sound almost apologetic, as though he were delivering unfortunate news about the health of a beloved pet.

Gerispryx took the bait. She hissed again, narrowing her luminous eyes in Rostus' direction, and in that instant Neave sprang.

Putting all her weight behind the swing, Neave buried her axe in the crack that Shakana's bolt had opened in Gerispryx's chest. She wrenched the blade sideways, splitting the fissure wide, and hammered an armoured fist into the bleeding light.

Again and again she punched into the gap, trying to find a heart, or a windpipe, or anything else that might let her kill the sorceress. But there was only light, and emptiness, no matter how deep Neave plunged her fist.

Still it seemed to hurt Gerispryx. The sorceress' leather face, hanging from a single seam as it flapped beside the rent in her crystal chest, opened its toothless mouth to howl.

Neave grabbed the face, tore it loose, and crumpled the leather so that it couldn't scream. Disgusted by the vibrations of its muffled cries inside her fist, she shoved the balled-up mask into the glowing infinity of the sorceress' chest and let go, casting it into the void.

A non-sound shrilled across Neave's body, like a scream at a pitch too high for her to register. In the corner of her eye, she saw Hendrick double over and Shakana clasp her hands around her midsection, both of them incapacitated by the screech. Rostus swayed in the vines, but remained too tightly gripped to fall.

Gerispryx exploded. The force of the blast threw Neave backwards, crystal shards ricocheting off her Stormcast plate. Silver light blazed across her vision, and then everything seemed very faint, and faraway, and somehow unimportant.

The bats screamed and fell from the air, smoke coughing from their melting cores. Rostus shouted curses as the crystal vines entangling him burst apart, ripping furrows of raw metal across his polished plate. Shakana, caught by one of the fragments, clutched her neck and crumpled to her knees with crimson spray bursting through her fingers.

Silently, unobtrusively, the hanging parchments went blank and grey. They drifted down like feathers in still air, their writings gone.

Neave, dazed, lay where she fell. She couldn't move. She could only watch, through dimming eyes, as Shakana bled and Rostus swore and Hendrick staggered blindly in the echoes of Gerispryx's death cry. Lorai slowly – not too slowly, Neave prayed, not *too* slowly – shook off the fading parchment's enchantment and looked about the field of ruin. The aelf alone was unhurt.

There was nothing more Neave could do to help her friends. Their fate lay with Lorai now, or else on Sigmar's forge.

Which it would be, Neave couldn't know, and couldn't change. But whichever it was, the Blacktalons had slain their target.

Holding that thought like a talisman, Neave let herself slip into the dark.

CHAPTER SEVEN

Neave opened her eyes to find Lorai kneeling above her.

'I regret that I was not better disciplined.' The Idoneth folded her hands, stained with Neave's blood, and likely the others', and leant back wearily on her heels. She looked drained, her eyes sunken and her bluish skin shaded with greening grey in the hollows. Fine lines stretched from the corners of her eyes and tugged around her lips.

That wasn't from the strain of her spells. Lorai had pulled the Blacktalons back from death's edge many times by bracing their souls against the raw shock of mortal injury, and it didn't exhaust her like this. Neave gripped the aelf's wrist in silent thanks, and reassurance, as she pulled herself up to sit.

'Why?' Rostus prodded at the side of his face where the crystal quills had been plucked out. He'd smeared sacred unguents over the wounds, and the skin was pink with new healing. 'Because you fell into a Chaos snare? They catch us all, from time to time. No need to feel guilty about it.'

'I was unprepared.' Lorai's gaze was distant. She blinked, twice, and a pulse fluttered at the side of her neck, making Neave think of a fish trying to catch its breath by flaring its gills. 'That memory is… old. Very old. From long before I came to the Blacktalons.'

'When did you think mine was from?' Rostus snorted, then shook his head in apology. 'I didn't mean that. I forgot myself. Gerispryx stung me, too. I only meant they attack us all. You can't block every blow. Sometimes they score a hit. Fume for a minute if you must, learn what you can from it, and move on. No use dwelling on it any further. That's what they want. But the past is past. It's gone. There's no changing… anything.'

'Not for us,' Shakana said, quietly. Dried blood crusted her braids, though the sniper's wounds were gone. She broke pieces of it away idly, watching the flakes scatter on the nebulous black floor of the Blind Queen's Maze. 'But it's different for her. How many decades has it been since you lost your family, Rostus? How many *centuries?* Do you even know? For us, the past truly is gone. But for Lorai…'

'It is the same.' The aelf stood, spreading her fingers wide as she lifted her hands. In a flurry, her spectral red fish surrounded her, nibbling the Stormcasts' blood from her skin. 'That life is gone. Carried away by the seas, crushed and dissolved. There is no use chasing bubbles in the foam.'

'Right, then.' Neave was terribly curious about the aelven child in Lorai's vision. Who was that? Had Lorai borne a Namarti child herself, or was it some other child who'd captured the Soulscryer's unfeeling heart? Of all her companions, she knew the least about the Idoneth, and Gerispryx's taunts had offered a glimpse of a secret Neave had never known.

But this wasn't the time to discuss that. Maybe there never would be a time. Duty came first, and the nature of the Blacktalons' work left little opportunity for such introspections.

'How do we get out?' Neave asked.

Lorai exhaled, relieved to change the subject. Her fish, satisfied, drifted back into the salt fog that surrounded the aelf. 'The maze will fade with Gerispryx's death. Its sustaining magic is already weakening. I can tear a hole in its reality easily enough, now, and return us to the valley.'

'Do it. We've no reason to waste any more time here.'

The day was fading over the valley of crystal vines. Long shadows drooled from between the petrified teeth of the trees on its slopes. The wind whistling through their needled branches still carried its eerie song, but it was a simple thing now, shorn of the eldritch echoes that had given it such disturbing reverberations earlier.

Hendrick, seeking Sigmar's communion and confirmation of their kill, had climbed to the highest of the stone trees on the valley's east face. Over his head, storm clouds swirled in an otherwise clear sky. Flickers of lightning flashed through the twilight, reflecting off the tree's crystal limbs and Hendrick's burnished plate mail.

Neave braced herself in anticipation of their god's arrival. In the corner of her eye, she saw Shakana cover her ears. Nevertheless, when the lightning bolt came, accompanied by its earth-shaking thunderclap, it staggered both of them.

Blazing with lightning, Hendrick fell from the tree in a shower of sparks and burning crystals. He hit the ground hard and rolled down the slope towards them, crunching glassy fragments under his weight. A haze of metallic blue smoke and ozone rose from his armour.

Hendrick opened his eyes as the Blacktalons gathered around him, but he didn't react to their presence. There was nothing in his gaze but lightning, flaring gold against blue. His lips parted, and he gasped out smoke.

Gradually, the divine light faded. The whites and irises of Hendrick's eyes returned. He sat up groggily, rubbing his eyelids hard. Bits of crystal pinged and popped around him as they cooled in the purple dusk. He stared at them glassily, uncomprehending.

'It doesn't usually take this long,' Rostus said uneasily. 'Is he all right?'

Neave could only shrug. She'd never experienced Sigmar's communion herself. None of them had, and none of them could answer. They could only wait, and watch, as the last of the daylight dimmed out of the crystal trees' embrace. Night fell, dotted with smouldering embers from the ruins of the Blind Queen's Maze.

Finally, Hendrick lifted his head towards his companions. Muscles jerked spasmodically in his neck and along his hands, but he seemed mostly in control of his body. His voice was hoarse, but recognisably his own. 'Our target is slain. We succeeded. But the threat has only grown more dire.'

'What do you mean?' Neave frowned.

Hendrick coughed up a wisp of smoke. He waved it away irritably, but weakly. 'The vision has changed. I saw the palace of illusions shattered. Its mistress was slain, her crystal throne empty. Whispering, muttering phantasms – which I took to be secrets, represented as winged spirits – flew out from its walls.

'Predators dressed in the barding of different lords chased after them, shoving against one another as they competed to bite these spirits out of the air. The most successful hunters' barding started to change as they devoured their prey. The emblems of their masters shifted to a bleeding, broken twin-tailed comet. That image… troubled me,' Hendrick said, after a reluctant pause. 'More than before. I felt, through the communion, that I… remembered it, and did so unhappily. Apprehensively, almost.'

'You think *Sigmar* knows that sign?' Shakana asked. She leant forwards, pressing her hands tensely against her thighs, and Neave felt herself doing the same. If this was a symbol that the God-King himself recognised – and *feared?* – then its importance was greater than she could imagine.

'I cannot say,' Hendrick answered, but the doubt in his tone was answer enough. He shook his bearded head and went on. 'We've eliminated another of our targets, and the vortex that I saw in the vision following the Great Flayer's death seemed to have lost another of its moorings. But the snapping of that line threw off sparks. Each of the remaining hunters caught those sparks, and became stronger in response.

'The first time I saw the cursed storm, it looked like a black thundercloud riven by bolts of acid. This time... it was still that, sometimes, but it took other forms as well. I saw it as a volcano, spewing geysers of blood-red varanite that warped the Mortal Realms into monstrosity. I saw it as a realmgate shaped like a daemon's vomiting maw, allowing the domains of Chaos to flood into the worlds of the living. All of them. Even Azyr. Raging armies of nameless, hate-filled things poured out, and I saw how the mortals were rent apart. Not just their cities and landscapes, even their bodies, but something deep in their core. The bonds that make them human. Shattered.'

Hendrick's voice grew rough, his eyes transfixed upon some undetermined spot, as if the images writhed and snarled before him still. 'Children were torn from their mothers' breasts by men with red eyes and murder on their breath – the aged and infirm left behind for the enemy to feast upon, as able-bodied warriors threw down their arms and fled. There were dead-eyed soldiers – they were so young. The walls of Hammerhal and Excelsis lay in ruins, and all the foul servants of darkness had turned their cathedrals into charnel pits.'

'*Sigmar* showed you this?' Rostus interjected, appalled.

'Hammerhal... and Azyr? But no creature of Chaos has ever breached the heavenly realm,' Shakana protested. 'Are you certain?'

'More than certain.' Hendrick shuddered, closing his eyes for a moment. He reached for his waterskin, but his hands were trembling too badly to uncap it. Neave reached over to help him, and he drank deeply, gasping over his next words. 'I saw the banners of Chaos hosts flying over the rubble of Sigmaron, and a figure of shadow, seated on the Anvil of Apotheosis. The sky was blighted behind it, and the stars wept red. The creature… laughed. In its laughter I heard screams. They were ours, and no one answered. Our God-King did not answer us. He couldn't because… *he wasn't there.*'

'It was only a vision,' Neave murmured, trying to console Hendrick in his agitation.

He didn't want to be consoled. Hendrick's fists shook in rage that he was too thunder-shaken to hide. His voice was low and filled with an anger and loathing that Neave had never heard him show so openly before.

'It was a warning,' he snarled, and the snarl was all the more terrifying for how it quavered, still reverberating with the echoes of the divine. 'This is what's coming. You didn't see what Sigmar showed me. You didn't *feel* it. If you had, you would harbour no doubt, none whatsoever, that we face the total annihilation of free life in the Mortal Realms. The conquest of holy Azyr by Chaos incarnate.'

'Chaos… taking Azyr?' Shakana whispered, stunned. 'Sigmar gone?'

It can't be.

Can it?

Neave looked to her companions for reassurance, and found only her own terror and confusion reflected back on their faces. For an instant it was like being in the Blind Queen's Maze again, caught in a disorienting caricature that only imitated reality to mock it.

But Sigmar would not show us anything less than the truth. And

Sigmar himself feared the sign of the split comet, so Hendrick had all but told them.

Therefore the possibility was real. Therefore the question the Blacktalons *should* be asking was…

'How?' Neave turned the question to them all. '*How* could Azyr fall?'

She watched them struggle to accept the enormity of the idea, and then begin to wrestle with how it might come to pass. In the distance, something exploded in the ruins of the Blind Queen's Maze, sending a flare of poisoned light and an earthbound thunderclap through the night, but the Blacktalons were so enmeshed in their thoughts that they gave it little more than a quick glance to assess any threat, and then dismiss it when they saw none.

'It's impossible,' Rostus was the first to conclude. 'The armies of the Ruinous Powers don't have the discipline or the coordination to bring down *all* of the Cities of Sigmar and trespass into Azyr. They're too fractious. This has always been our advantage. Even if they did unite to attack by some dark will, Azyr is guarded by defences none of the other cities have. It's Sigmar's *own* realm.'

'Maybe that's it.' Shakana's brow knitted as she focused on the problem, pushing past her immediate reaction of shocked defensiveness. 'It's true for us, too, that there is power in unity. What if that were destroyed? Only by undermining that which binds us all to our cause can I see every city, even Azyr, succumbing wholly to Chaos.'

'In Hendrick's visions, Sigmar was gone.' Neave looked around her, meeting each of the Blacktalons' eyes in turn. '*Sigmar* is that which binds me to my cause. He is also humanity's beacon. If the slaves of Chaos seek to see our faith riven apart, that's nothing new. Every day they threaten trust and certainty in Sigmar. And every day, they both triumph and fail. But if Sigmar were gone… How or why this could be, I couldn't – don't want to – say. But if he were somehow absent from these realms... there would be no beacon. No lodestone for a faith. There would be no faith at all, save in...' She frowned, unwilling to lend that possibility a voice. 'But how would he ever be gone? What could cause the people, the cult, to change allegiance on such a scale? Sigmar has warned us that it can be done,' she pressed. '*How?*'

'What always draws mortal souls to Chaos?' Shakana replied, gazing back at the burning wreckage of the Blind Queen's Maze, and the unseen bodies of those who had chosen to die within it. Regret, and condemnation, tinged her voice. 'Despair. Anger. Wounded pride. Pain that demands to be salved by the pain of others. Pleasure that cares nothing for its cost. But Sigmar's faith is a bulwark against those emotions. His believers understand the value of self-discipline, patience, humility. Why would they abandon those virtues for hedonism and rage?'

Neave mulled it over. 'I don't know. I suppose the only reason we exchange one virtue for another is when we stop believing in it.' Then the answer came to her, as obvious as it was stupefying. It had been staring her in the face, but it was so monstrously inconceivable that she'd failed to see it. 'They're attacking the cult. Somehow, our enemy believes they can bring about the collapse of the Cults Unberogen. They have, or think they have, something that can sever the mortals from their god, and leave their souls adrift to be collected by scavengers.'

'That must be the secret they're seeking,' Hendrick concluded. He stared, emptily, at his hands. 'That's what the hunters are vying to catch. A weapon, or an artefact, capable of causing spiritual calamity on such a scale that it would destroy the foundations of Sigmar's faith, and leave Azyr itself vulnerable to incursion by Chaos.'

'Then that's what we have to stop,' Neave said. She made herself sound confident, perfectly assured in the Blacktalons' ability to meet this threat as they had so many others. In her own heart, however, she quailed at the magnitude of their task.

Grant us strength, God-King, Neave vowed silently. *I know you would not give us a task beyond our skills. But grant us your strength, that we might prevail.*

Warmth filled her as she prayed. Golden radiance blossomed in her soul, and with it came the calm peace of confidence. *We can do this. We will do this.*

It was no mere bravado. The Blacktalons had tested and learnt their competence through pain, but that was precisely why Neave could trust its measure. She knew what it had cost, and she knew the extent to which it had been tried.

Each of the Blacktalons had suffered considerably over their years in Sigmar's service. They had lost more than they knew, or could acknowledge. Even if they were willing to look without flinching at their most grievous scars and deepest-buried secrets – and Neave was not, in her heart of hearts, certain that she was – too much of that pain had simply been erased.

We don't even know the full measure of the price we've paid. We never will. And still we pay, again and again, forever.

But it was necessary. It was worthwhile. That was the promise Sigmar made when he dragged their souls across his forge. That was why the Stormcasts endured.

That was the answer Neave felt in her prayer: *You can do this, and you will do this, because it is why you were forged. I would not have put you through such hardships, except to give you the strength you need to achieve the extraordinary. I would not demand such service of you, except that you are the shield that protects mortal life.*

You have endured these tests. You have prevailed. In this too, will you prevail.

Neave realised she was squeezing her fists hard enough to strain the finger plates of her gauntlets. She forced herself to draw a slow breath, relaxing by an effort of will.

'We can do this,' she said aloud, and this time there was certainty in her words. 'We've slain two targets already. Only three remain. To find them, we should consider who attacked the Blind Queen's Maze, and why. Sigmar's vision told us that all our targets are fighting over the same secrets, and we saw that there were corpses from multiple factions in the labyrinth. Gerispryx herself spoke of it.

'What can we learn from that? Who were they?'

In answer, Lorai lifted a corner of her cloak, and her spectral fish came streaming out to the starlit night. She stroked one thin finger along a fish's spiny back. The ghostly creature hiccupped out a glowing bubble, within which floated a dead man's head, crowned by one of the feathery red caps Neave had noticed earlier. Another fish coughed up a second bubble, this one holding one of the sharp-toothed gauntlings' heads, along with a crumpled mass of sodden leather, cloth and paper.

With the prick of a fingertip, Lorai popped the second bubble. She caught the wet mass of textiles, letting the head fall to the crystal-strewn dirt. Ignoring the head and its yellow rictus grin, the aelf stretched the soggy documents across the ground. Her fish swam circles around her shoulders, casting a swirling crimson light over her finds.

It was a motley collection. Lorai laid out scraggly leather pennons, garish banners slapped with gold paint and crude heraldry, woodcut-printed feast rosters, and invitations calligraphed in a flowing, sophisticated hand on what looked like human skin. Most of the pieces appeared to have been chewed.

Lorai circled a fingertip around a motif that was repeated on several of the pages: a simple face, just a circle with two hollows for eyes, such as a child might draw. The face's mouth was stretched in a grin that slashed across it from side to side, and that hungry smile was filled with sharp teeth. While the rest of the face was blank, the smile was lovingly detailed, as though that were the only part that mattered. 'This is the emblem of Pelokoa the Glutton. The pennons and banners, and the menus, are all invitations to his Travelling Feast. So they proclaim, proudly.'

'I don't know who that is, or what that means, but it doesn't sound terribly pleasant,' Rostus said.

Shakana straightened, and her star-eagle lifted its wings, a predatory gleam in its eye. 'I've read of him. Pelokoa the Glutton is a Slaaneshi Hedonite. He was human once, I believe, though he has been alive for centuries, and the legends have long claimed he cannot die. They call him Pelokoa the Undying, and Pelokoa Ever-Eater. Like many of his kind, he harbours aspirations towards godhood, or did. It's possible that by now he already thinks of himself as a god. The accounts I read were centuries old.'

'Yes. You are correct in all of this.' Lorai hauled the fallen head up by its scraggly hair and set it between the papers. Its lips were already pulled back to show the notched yellow teeth, but she drew them back further anyway. The fishes' red glow washed the teeth in scarlet, but Neave thought they might have been stained with that colour even in daylight. 'Those he sent here were cannibals from his Travelling Feast, and they carried open invitations for anyone who slaughtered them to join in their stead. According to these invitations, their master would be most eager to fill the empty seats at his table with such delightfully worthy guests.'

'That's thoughtful,' Rostus said, chuckling. 'I like it when our targets don't try to hide. Saves a lot of running. Shall we take them up on it?'

'Who's the other head?' Shakana asked.

Lorai coaxed the other floating bubble nearer, then popped its shimmering membrane with a swift jab of her fingertip. The red-capped head inside fell free, and she set it on a crystal stump near the other things she'd salvaged.

Now that the bubble was no longer obscuring Neave's view, she saw that what she'd taken for a feathery red hat was actually a profusion of scarlet leaves that sprouted out of the dead man's scalp like hair. Underneath it, the corpse's features were strangely and subtly wrong, as though his skin had been stretched over some uniformly round object instead of the bones of a natural human skull. His skin looked oddly soft and sunken, and pale pink threads peeped out of his nostrils and the corners of his lips.

Lorai spread the corpse's eyelids between her fingers. It had no eyes. Instead, a curve of smooth, green-tinted wood looked back at the Blacktalons from the dead lids, as if the entire interior of the head had been replaced by some enormous acorn. Fine rosy threads, like root threads or fungal filaments, stretched across the wood and connected it to the interior of the man's skin.

That explained the face's uncanny structure, Neave thought. Before she could say anything, Lorai took out a small knife and cut open the corpse's skin in a vertical incision from eyebrow to chin.

At the slightest touch, the skin peeled away from the seed inside. There was no blood, only more pink filaments and sticky clear sap gumming the dead man's skin to the seed's exterior. As Lorai continued dissecting, Neave saw that the leaves crowning the head sprouted from the seed's top, and the squiggled bulges around the corpse's chin were made by budding roots straining to break free.

'In a few more days,' Lorai said, 'perhaps a week, the head would have fallen free, and the seed would have taken root in the fertiliser of its bearer's corpse. Already, it was the seed and not the host that commanded the body's actions. No blood ran through that corpse's veins. Sap and fungus channelled the waters of its body, and held its life in their course.'

'What would such a seed grow?' asked Shakana, peering at it in revolted fascination.

The Idoneth shrugged and sheathed her knife. 'I do not yet know. I will study the secrets in the seed's sap, and read the flow of the life that sleeps within its shell. Perhaps that will tell us more. For now, all I can say is that whatever master directed this puppet to attack Gerispryx ordered its older servants, those that were nearing collapse, to sacrifice themselves to protect its other agents, who could be expected to live longer. I would surmise that those were intended to bring back whatever they sought in the Blind Queen's Maze. Whether they were successful, I cannot say, but we did not find their bodies. Only these.'

'All right. So we've identified two of the factions in Hendrick's vision – the glutton in the tent of rotting meat, and the tree with roots of bloody bone. We still haven't any leads on the library of frozen books.' Neave surveyed her companions. 'Is that about the shape of it?'

'There's the... What did Hendrick call them? Champions of Vercaspior?' Rostus ran a massive palm over his scalp one last time, finally satisfied that there wasn't a scratch left from his last fight. 'The ones whose bodies Gerispryx was hiding in.'

Neave shook her head. 'I'm afraid their presence doesn't tell us much. They're mercenaries. They'll work for anyone their grim masters approve, even ordinary mortals who have no allegiance to Chaos. All their presence tells us is that someone paid them.'

'Then we accept the glutton's invitation,' Rostus said. 'Because that's the target we can find.'

'I agree.' Shakana stood and brushed her hands against her thighs, ready to be done with the conference. 'When Lorai's finished with her spells, we might have another target in our sights, but for now, let's shoot the one we've got.'

'Where can we find the Travelling Feast?' Even as she asked it,

Neave moved beside Lorai to study the dripping documents herself. If these were 'invitations', they were ones that didn't seem to want their guests to arrive.

The crudely drawn maps offered no clues about their scale, orientation, or key landmarks. The written invitations were long on boastful descriptions of pickled thurppig nipples and slivered vadunesh tentacles in lemon sauce, and very short on details about how to get there. What little information they provided was wilfully coy, boasting of how the pavilion's aelf-blown wine glasses would reflect the glorious cloud-shimmer praised in the poems of Hansith the Flower-Weaver, and of how the ice in the sherbets would be utterly pristine, having been rushed down the mountains by relays of slave runners wearing atapok-hide sandals for speed.

'The invitations are not meant to be easily accepted,' Lorai said, seeing Neave's frustration. 'They are tests, and they are lures. One cannot decipher their clues without delving deep into forbidden lore and tasting poisoned pleasures, risking life and soul alike. That is why this servant of Chaos strews them so freely.

'But for us,' she added, brushing spidery fingertips over the gauntling's head, 'there are easier ways.' Under the Idoneth's touch, the head shrivelled into papery rags of skin over discoloured bone. Its eyes withered into raisins, vanishing into suddenly cavernous sockets, and its tongue curled into a dry, stubbled worm behind its cracked teeth.

All the water Lorai had pulled from the corpse's flesh rose up over the head, forming a translucent facsimile that shimmered with an eldritch blue glow in the night. It opened its mouth, emitting a watery, pained burble, like the prayers of a drowning sailor gasped into the sea. Tiny images flashed across its eyes and escaped from its lips on salt-scented bubbles.

Lorai absorbed all of this silently. More bubbles rose from the watery phantasm's neck towards its crown, dissolving the apparition bit by bit as they passed through. Within a few moments, the liquid image had evaporated into mist. The aelf closed her eyes, meditating on whatever she'd learnt, then turned back to the other Blacktalons in a rustle of stiff robes.

'The Travelling Feast is moving towards the Perennais Garden,' she said. 'This one did not know how to get there. But there are others in Pelokoa's caravan of seekers who do, and who have been charged with bringing the prizes from the Blind Queen's Maze to their master there. To find him, we need only follow them.'

'Assuming any of them got out of the maze alive,' Rostus grunted.

'They did.' Shakana was disassembling the sights from her typhoon crossbow so that she could stow it for long-distance travel. She did it smoothly, fluidly, with the understated satisfaction of a professional reflecting on the quality of a trusted tool. 'Wouldn't have been in Hendrick's vision if they hadn't. The glutton's still on the target list. If he's still a threat, that tells us his servants must have got whatever they were after out here.'

'She's right,' Hendrick said. His voice was still rough, but he'd recovered his breath and spoke with his usual certainty. 'The vortex was a greater threat with only three anchors than it was with four. Removing Gerispryx only increased the danger to the Mortal Realms. I presume this is because the lore and artefacts she held have now been redistributed among the others, strengthening and concentrating their ability to unleash the storm. If we are to stop it, we have to kill the remaining anchors, and we must do so swiftly.'

CHAPTER EIGHT

Pelokoa's servants set a pace that was murderous to them but by the Blacktalons' standards, nothing more than an easy trot. The mortals used magic and heavy doses of poisons to numb their riding-stags against weariness, allowing them to run the animals near to death without complaint, but even so it was trivial for the Stormcast Eternals to keep pace with them. Shakana's star-eagle flew high over the caravan's heads, tracking their position, and the Blacktalons ran hidden, parallel to their quarry.

From the crystal valley of the Blind Queen's Maze, the caravan cut through the forests and grasslands of Ghyran, never stopping to marvel at the verdant wonders of Alarielle's realm. Pelokoa's riders avoided the deep cool woods of the Sylvaneth and the blighted swamps of Nurgle's territory alike, and they skirted around the few settlements of aelves and humans in their path. They kept to the wilderness, believing themselves hidden, and they rode hard.

The riders had taken three prizes from Gerispryx's stronghold. The first was a skin-shifter, a faceless, sorcerous creature of smouldering silver energy clad in the burning rags of a human skin, which they'd fettered in a long, multicoloured chain of braided cloth and silken skeins that wrapped it from head to toe. Glass beads tinkled throughout the braid, and these seemed to contain some magic that bound the creature and tormented it.

Their second captive was a meek-looking woman with the hunched shoulders, habitual squint and soft physique of a scribe or scholar. Her captors hadn't bothered binding her, and whenever they stopped to camp, some of Pelokoa's servants would show her some papers and take notes on whatever she said. She was so cooperative that at first the Blacktalons were uncertain whether she was a prisoner or a collaborator, until one night when the scholar told her captors something they didn't care to hear, and they beat her senseless.

A prisoner, they concluded. A very frightened prisoner.

The third prize had to be called that, rather than a captive, because he wasn't alive. He wasn't even intact. Pelokoa's servants had carried off a man's torso, one arm, and part of a thigh, packing the pieces in coarse salt and herbs like dry-brined pork. When they camped, they checked on the pieces and sometimes blotted away moisture or changed the salt, but they never treated it casually. They kept it separate and always under guard, as if the salt barrel held a live prisoner who might escape, not several pieces of slowly curing meat.

On the dead man's arm, Shakana's star-eagle spotted the brand of a hammer engulfed in a lightning bolt, or perhaps a shooting star, but none of the Blacktalons knew what it meant. Mortal cults and churches of Sigmar were legion, and though the hammer seared over his bicep left little doubt that the dead man had been a Sigmarite, that was all they could tell.

'What bothers me isn't that they're going to eat him,' Rostus said, grimacing in disgust, when Shakana's star-eagle reported its observations to its mistress. 'It's that they're treating him like meat.'

'He *is* meat,' Shakana said, dryly. 'Anyway it's not as if you haven't seen beastmen roasting their victims over fires before.'

'That's barbaric, though. This is civilised. Well, almost civilised. That makes it worse. Pickling a fellow into salt pork is far more horrible than just eating him raw, because if you've the under-standing and resources to brine meat, then you're no mere beast. You *know* better than to eat people. You're just doing it because you *want* to. Not only that, you want to do it deliberately, with care and planning. And garnishes.'

'Right.' Shakana snorted, thinly amused, before she lifted a morsel of raw meat to her bird and turned her attention to Neave. 'What I want to know is, what are they trying to get that scribe to tell them? They've been at her every time they camp. Even when they're just stopping to water their animals, one of them questions her while they're waiting. They treat her well, too. Better food, a cushioned pallet to sleep on, a cover when it rains. What do they want from her? Why are they trying to win her over?'

'What does it look like to you?' Neave asked. Shakana, who had the best stealth skills among the Blacktalons, was the only one of them who'd got close enough to make any first-hand observa-tions. The rest of them had to rely on what she told them, either through her own eyes or her bird's.

Shakana held up another dead rodent. As the eagle snatched the furry morsel and swallowed, she brushed a finger affectionately across its glossy head. 'If I knew, I wouldn't be asking, would I? I can't read the gibberish they show her. It's no language I know. I'm not sure it even *is* a language. Looks like some sort of instru-mentation readings to me. Strings of sigils in different colours. Anda's seen them showing her star charts, too, and maps. Can't tell what they're supposed to be maps of, though.'

'Is it worth trying to free her?' Neave wondered aloud.

Shakana shook her head, but it was Hendrick who answered. 'If we attack Pelokoa's riders, we'll lose our chance at our real target. We can't engineer an escape from afar, either. It would only delay them as they stopped to recapture her, as they inevitably would. There's no sanctuary for a scholar in these wilds, and we can't hide her. The servants of Chaos must not know we're here.'

Neave nodded, gloomy but unsurprised. She'd known the truth of it before she spoke. But she'd needed to hear her companions reach the same conclusion, so that she could be certain that there truly was no hope, and that she wasn't giving up when there was anything else to be done.

She gazed off into the distance, listening to the nocturnal symphonies of unseen creatures. Night-blooming shimmerbells opened on their climbing vines, dotting the tree trunks with fragrant, luminous bursts of blue and violet that swayed gently in the breeze, illumining the rough mossy bark and spreading leaves of the sleeping forest around them. Much of Ghyran was a poisoned wasteland, warped by the Plaguefather into a heaving horror of blight and rot, but here they'd found a rare oasis.

From here she couldn't see the young scholar. She couldn't even see the orange glow of the riders' campfires. Only the faintest wisp of woodsmoke, undetectable to human senses, drifted across the forested hills to her.

They were phantoms to her, and she to them, and so it had to remain until the riders led the Blacktalons to their master's lair.

There would be no rescue, not until the Blacktalons had their target firmly in their sights.

Sigmar forgive me.

This was, Neave knew, her duty. Her task was not to save one scholar. It was to protect all the lives around her, all the fragile beauty of Ghyran's green, by slaying her appointed target. Otherwise, these hard-won islands of peace would fall back into the corrupted mire. *That* was her holy charge, and if she had to surrender one innocent to do it, then that was the price of her duty. She'd paid worse before.

But it felt like a sin, every time.

'Let's try to get a better look at what they're asking her for, at least,' Neave said at last, still gazing into the night-dark forests. She didn't want to look at the rest of the Blacktalons. Not yet, not while there was still some chance that she might change her mind. 'Tomorrow should bring rain. That'll make it easier.' Lorai's magic could disguise the star-eagle as a drift in the downpour, enabling them to send the bird closer than they could get on a clear day.

Shakana nodded. 'And the skin-shifter?'

The smell of woodsmoke was fading. The riders had likely doused their fires, and were preparing to sleep. If the Blacktalons struck now, they might be able to spirit that young scholar away unseen. Might be able to save her without compromising their mission. Maybe.

It was a gamble Neave couldn't take.

'The skin-shifter is less important,' she told Shakana, turning away from the shadowed woods. 'If it's possible to obtain more information safely, do so, but I think Pelokoa's forces only took that sorcerer because they wanted a prize to prove Gerispryx's defeat. They haven't interrogated him, at least not that we've seen, and they guard that salt barrel more closely. The skin-shifter doesn't seem to be of high value to them, and therefore I don't think that should be a priority for us, either. Focus on the scholar.'

Morning crept in grey and clammy, dense with a fog that left fat, cold droplets on leaves and skin alike. Wrapped in Lorai's magic, Shakana's star-eagle launched into the air, seemingly no more than a breath of wind amid the rain.

The Blacktalons waited, tense and silent, as the day dripped on. It took hours longer than usual for Pelokoa's riders to break camp, and they moved slowly when they did. They stopped early, and again failed to move for hours.

'What are they doing?' Rostus wondered, but no one had an answer to give him. The star-eagle didn't return, and Neave caught herself worrying that it had been caught. She could tell from Shakana's mute tension that she wasn't alone in that concern, but there was little either of them could do about it, and neither said anything.

Rostus practised his card tricks. Hendrick sharpened his blades. Shakana, who had more experience waiting than any of them, half-closed her eyes and slowed her breaths in prayerful meditation, so that she seemed to be a warrior's statue in the rain.

Neave went to watch Lorai cast her spells.

In the rain, the Idoneth seemed subtly relaxed, more at ease. Her robes absorbed the water and softened into living membranes, pulsing with gentle iridescence like the drifting shimmer of jelly-fish in the sea. The rain-slicked chimes of her staff clicked in quiet counterpoint to the falling drops, echoing their music with the beat of a phantom tide.

Neave hadn't intended to disturb her, but the bald aelf looked up with a slight smile as the Stormcast strode through the trees. 'You wish to know what I have learnt about our next target. Even before this one is devoured, you hunt the next. The shark swims and swims, always thinking of the next meal, and does not rest.'

'I'm just trying to distract myself from waiting for Anda's return,' Neave said.

Lorai's smile deepened from a hint to a real one that showed the tips of her small, slightly pointed teeth through the opal sheen of her veil. 'That can be true too. Often many things are true at once. So you wish to distract yourself from the eagle's absence. Do you also wish to know what my spells reveal?'

'Of course.'

'Then I must disappoint you. The river will lead me to its head-waters, in time, but it is always more difficult to swim upstream than down. This time it is particularly so.' Lorai plucked a red leaf from the head she'd been studying and held it out to Neave. 'It is almost as if the creature's maker was familiar with my arts, and sought by its creations to defeat me.'

Neave turned the leaf over in her hands. Its texture was subtly creased and soft as kidskin, its veins pronounced. The crimson colour was closer to that of arterial blood than that of any natural leaf she'd ever seen. It carried a faint, foul whiff of a week-old battleground – of mud and blood churned together, of terror and pain commingled in death, and of monstrous machines and sorcerous vapours used to slaughter more soldiers than any sword or bow could slay.

All of that, left to rot for a week in the heat, was what Neave smelled rising from the leaf as she bent it between her fingers. 'What *is* it?'

'Flesh becomes soil, and soil becomes plant. Life, death, another life. This is the way of things. Through this cycle of lives, the water remains the same, flowing from shape to shape.' Lorai took the leaf back and laid it carefully in the centre of a puddle that had formed in the crevice of a fallen tree nearby. 'But it becomes harder to follow when it passes through living veins, especially as one life becomes another. So it is with this creature. Born human, planted with a seed, and reborn as a plant without fully dying in between.'

'It smells of death.'

The aelf bowed her head in assent. Crimson ripples spread out from the leaf in the puddle, staining the water red. 'It is a foul magic, devised by a foul master. That is part of why my unrav-elling goes slowly. One must swim with caution through such murky waters.'

She paused, and looked up to the sky. Rain pattered across her face, and Lorai closed her eyes and smiled again, as though receiving the benediction of a kindly god. 'The bird returns. Go. You need distract yourself no longer.'

Shakana was soothing her star-eagle with soft words and a gentle hand when Neave returned. Anda was more agitated than Neave had seen in a long time. Her feathers bristled with jittery sparks, and her claws dug into Shakana's leather gauntlet hard enough to scratch the metal studs. The bird greeted Neave with a hiss, and she had the feeling that if secrecy hadn't been a concern, it would have shrieked.

'What happened?' Neave asked. 'What have you learnt?'

Shakana shot her a sharp look for her lack of sympathy, and pointedly spent another few moments calming her bird before she answered. Her voice was tight with a cold anger, teetering on the brink of fury, that surprised and puzzled Neave. 'The woman they captured is a Sigmarite scholar. She was a lay worshipper who assisted the Sisters of the Stormsceptre, a cult in Ghyran. Her main duties were translation and copying of holy texts.

'Gerispryx's forces took her from her cloister. She was being held captive in the Blind Queen's Maze when Pelokoa's agents seized her in turn. They've been hammering at her, again and again, to get her to translate some other Sigmarite texts they took from the maze. Evidently these are the same ones Gerispryx was trying to get her to translate, or similar. The ones they wanted her to translate are from Aqshy. Some place called Astrapis.'

Rostus listened quietly, his manner subdued. He'd been nursing a small, sheltered fire under a broad-leaved tree so that he could heat a battered copper pan, and he scattered a handful of weathered tea leaves over the water as it steamed. 'Since when do the armies of Chaos take an interest in holy scripture?'

'Since it gave them an opening to cause pain,' Hendrick answered. 'They studied the sacred texts to undermine the Convocation of Unsith's Peak. They learnt the details of the Hammersworn Church's high prayers so they could taint the Church's seventh-day mead and drive the brothers to slay one another in a frenzy. This is an old tactic, and it has often succeeded.'

Rostus poured the tea into a flask and offered it to Shakana. 'Drink. You'll feel better.'

Shakana nodded thanks to Rostus. The tea's fragrance seemed to relax her, slightly, and she breathed the sweet steam in gratefully. 'Both Gerispryx and Pelokoa were chasing the same legend, and both thought this scholar might help them find it. "Varstrom is the key to the storm. The key is in the cathedral. The key is in the scrolls." That's what her captors kept saying. They showed her maps, poems, star charts, sketches of old mosaics in crumbling cathedrals, and fragments of hides taken from the Great Flayer's camp. Above all, they showed her these documents from Astrapis, hoping she could tell them what, or where, this "key" was to be found.'

'What's Varstrom?' Neave asked. 'A person? A place?' She'd never heard the name before. It seemed no one else had, either, for no answer was offered.

Hendrick adjusted his oilskin cape, tucking his weapons' hilts more securely under its cover. 'Did the scholar answer her captors' questions?'

Shakana shielded her teacup against the drizzle, cradling its warmth in her palms. 'Not today. But it will not be long.'

Bleakly she regarded the other Blacktalons, ignoring the rain that gathered in silver beads on her braids and ran down her cheeks like tears. She kept the cup protected, though. 'She has given in. She has surrendered to Chaos. That's why the riders were moving so slowly. They were sealing her allegiance to Pelokoa, and through him to Slaanesh.'

No one spoke. Rain fell through the leaves and soaked the

Blacktalons in their armour. No one moved. Rostus' fire hissed, sputtered, and died. The ground was silvered with little lakes, each one dimpled in the falling rain, and the sound of the droplets striking them echoed painfully in Neave's ears.

Once she'd seen the survivor of a Bloodbound attack standing in the ruins of a chapel, washing his hands mindlessly again and again in the holy font. The fountain was broken, and its water shuddered out in gasping arcs. Soaked and unfeeling, the man stood in its spray, trying to rinse away the blood of the victims he'd failed to save, or the soot from the chapel's burned tapestries, or any of a thousand other things.

Neave hadn't asked. There was no point. The Blacktalons weren't healers, and she'd still had her quarry to hunt. She'd just left the man standing there, in the rubble of his faith, holding his hands out to that jagged spray.

The rain, now, had the same sound. Cold water falling, and sins that couldn't be washed away.

And, again, there was nothing Neave could do. She had her target. She had her duty.

Now, at least, it was a little easier. Grimmer, but easier.

Now there truly was no choice.

CHAPTER NINE

Two weeks later, they came to the Pillared Gardens, a dramatic formation of massive stone columns that rose up from the earth like mountains pared to their cores, or trees grown beyond all reason and frozen into rocky eternity. Dewy white clouds swallowed their crowns, leaving only the pillars' forested shoulders visible against the sky. Waterfalls condensed from those clouds tumbled down the columns' sides, pouring in torrents that looked delicate as veils of silver lace from afar, but were thunderous cataracts, awesome in their might, when approached.

The water's impact quaked the ground, a giants' drumline that jarred every bone in the body with sheer percussive force. Silenced by amazement and by the water's roar, the Blacktalons stood at the pillars' edge and looked at the misty maze of rivers, stone, moss and noise that lay ahead.

Pelokoa's riders had led them to the Pillared Gardens, and then had vanished at the base of one of the gargantuan stone formations. Shakana's star-eagle had marked which one it was, but had not been able to see where they entered or how they'd ascended, if indeed they had.

'We can't climb up,' Shakana told the others, putting away her spyglass. 'The stone is nearly sheer, coated in slimy moss in every crevice that'll support it, and hammered by waterfalls. Even if Lorai could somehow use the mists or cloud-rivers to carry us up, those pillars are enormous, and we don't know exactly where our targets have gone. If the pillars are hollow, they may be within. Or they may be hidden in some cavern or clearing behind the waterfalls, or they may have gone to the top. All I can say is that Anda hasn't seen them emerge, and I don't think we have much prospect of finding an alternative way in and surprising them. My assessment is that our best bet is trying to track them. We'll have to follow in their footsteps and enter by the same means they did.'

'Well, they *did* invite us,' Rostus said, shouldering his hammer. 'It can't be entirely impossible to follow them in.'

'No,' Shakana agreed, though she didn't sound confident. 'But there's a wide chasm between impossible and easy.'

Rostus grinned. 'Naturally. Sigmar never calls upon the Blacktalons for easy.'

Under a canopy of mist woven by Lorai, the Blacktalons slipped through the rivers and pools that spiderwebbed out from the cloud-washed columns, picking their way across precarious bridges of moss-slicked stone until they reached the one that Pelokoa's riders had entered. The riders themselves were long gone, but their steeds' split hooves had left faint impressions in the moss, and occasional scuffs on the stone, that Shakana used to track them.

She led them to a raging waterfall. Through its white-frothed crash, Neave saw the dim outlines of a gap in the stone's face, large enough for a rider mounted on a war steed to pass through, but blocked by a tangle of black-tipped thorns.

Even through the obscuring torrent, Neave saw that there was something abnormal about those thorns. 'I'd like a closer look at those.'

With a gesture, Lorai looped a shimmering tendril of water around one of the brambles and coaxed it forwards. As she pulled it through the waterfall, the thorns on the vine resolved into sharpened human teeth, each one rising from a pink ring of drooling gum. It coiled itself up into a sort of mouth, gnawing hungrily at Lorai's semi-solid conjuration until she released the water, and the vine, back to its original place.

'That's charming.' Rostus grimaced, looking up at the vast wall of brambles that barricaded the entrance. Water splashed his broad brow, making him squint. 'I suppose there's a secret password, or a code of some sort, that opens the door?'

'Guests summoned to the Travelling Feast are requested to provide a taste of their offerings to the table,' Lorai murmured. 'So the invitations say. If their offerings please the master's palate, they may rise to join his celebration.'

'If they don't?' Hendrick asked, but the aelf only answered with a shrug.

'You couldn't have told us this earlier?' Shakana shook her head in exasperation, and her star-eagle fixed its glimmering eyes on Lorai in an echo of its mistress' disapproval. 'I might have been able to hunt something down while we were following those riders. Sigmar knows the glutton's servants gave us time enough to look.'

'I do not believe any ordinary prey would satisfy Pelokoa,' Lorai replied. Spray misted over the Idoneth's skin and robes, drawing out their oceanic sheen. 'No doubt there is some fruit or beast of Ghyran that would serve, if prepared to the glutton's standards, but I do not view it as likely that we would be able to achieve those standards on the road.

'But a rare *ingredient*… That would suit. It would not matter that such a thing was raw and unprepared. That would only increase its appeal to Pelokoa. And, fortunately, we travel with the rarest of ingredients at the ready.'

Neave groaned as the Idoneth's meaning dawned upon her. 'Oh, no. You can't mean to offer *us*.'

'Only a taste,' Lorai said. 'But yes. How rare is the flesh of a Stormcast? You incandesce into lightning upon death. The only way to consume the meat of such a creature is to capture it alive, and cut pieces from that living body – a formidable task, and one that I do not believe Pelokoa's riders have often achieved. I suspect such an offering would be difficult for the glutton to refuse.'

'What does that mean?' Shakana scowled. She rubbed her gauntleted forearms, drawing herself close. 'A finger? A toe?'

There was a good chance, Neave knew, that such a loss would be permanent. If a Stormcast was dismembered while being slain, or moments before, then generally that Stormcast was Reforged whole. But when a Stormcast was maimed or scarred long before death, long enough for that new and altered self to be engraved on the Stormcast's mind and soul as the shape of their identity, then Reforging often failed to restore those wounds.

It was unlikely – Neave hoped – that they'd die within moments of offering Pelokoa this taste of their bodies. That meant a significant risk that the loss would be permanent.

'Suppose I could give up a toe,' Rostus said, reluctantly. 'I'd hate to ruin these dainty little trotters, pretty as they are, but then you already yell at me whenever I try to take my boots off.'

'With good reason,' Shakana muttered.

'So you say.' Rostus sniffed, miming hurt. Still, Neave could see a glimmer of relief in him. Since they'd left the crystal labyrinth, the warrior had wanted to acquit himself of his reluctance to share the burdens of the Blind Queen's Maze, and now he finally had his chance. No one thought Rostus a coward except the big Stormcast himself, but Neave knew that hardly mattered; *he* felt the shame of it, and that shame would torment him until he felt he'd sufficiently purged the sin. 'Anyway, if we need a toe...'

'We do not need a toe,' Lorai said firmly, 'and you need not remove your boots. A few drops of blood should suffice. To test the theory, at least.'

Rostus shook his head, though he too seemed relieved to leave his boots on. 'Well, all right, but that hardly seems much to ask. Wouldn't be a mission without a little bloodshed.'

Lorai swept her chime-topped staff towards the waterfall, beckoning the Blacktalons forwards. The torrent parted above the aelf's head, letting only a light mist sift down, and she strode into a cavernous chamber of river-smoothed wet stone and creeping moss. Toothy vines snaked tendrils along the cavern walls, and gathered into an impenetrable wall on the far side.

In the centre of the vine wall was a single strange flower bud, which moved sinuously through the brambles until it met Lorai at eye height. Then its green outer casing opened, revealing that it held not a flower, but a pickled human tongue that had been split repeatedly down the centre so that it could open with six bleeding petals made of flesh.

Rostus moved to stand beside Lorai, eyeing the macabre blossom with undisguised revulsion. '*That's* Pelokoa's taste-tester?'

No one answered. Shrugging, Rostus unsheathed his belt knife and swiped his thumb across the point. He held it out to the tongue-flower and squeezed a slow red trickle into its split mouth.

As soon as the blood flow stopped, the tongue-flower snapped shut. Its pebbled petals pulsed obscenely as it retreated back into the brambles' protective maw and gulped its offering. The vines rippled rhythmically and their teeth gnashed together, as if chewing, while the grotesque flower withdrew into its green bud.

Then the flower emerged again. It unfolded from the green

leaves, unfurling its blood-smeared petals, and the pebbles of its cut tongue swelled like infected wounds. A tooth burst from each distended lump, and the scraps of its fleshy coating sank down to become bleeding gums. Saliva ran between the mismatched teeth, spattering Rostus as the flower clenched and opened its petals in clacking, wordless demand.

'Now what?' the big warrior asked, tensely.

'You've intrigued it,' Neave said. It was a guess, but she felt confident she was correct. 'Now it wants more than a taste of blood. Now it wants a bite of flesh.'

'I don't like the idea of letting it bite me,' Rostus muttered, but he didn't retreat, and flexed a bicep as he readied himself for the ordeal.

'I don't either,' Neave told him. She studied the web of thorns another moment, trying to decide how Pelokoa's true guests would meet this test. 'If you were our captive, it might be difficult for us to offer you directly to the vine. Perhaps we'd have to worry about its teeth biting through your bonds, or your struggling hard enough to break free as we tried to push you into position. It would likely be easier, and safer, for us to cut a piece of flesh from your body and offer it to the mouth. But from where?'

Even as she said it, the answer came: 'Muscle. A Hedonite would want to taste your strength and know that it was being offered, helplessly, for his delectation.' Grimacing, Rostus removed his left pauldron and the armour from his upper arm. Neave swept the water from her face, regarding him with a mixture of determination and apology as she drew her knife. 'I'll try not to cripple you.'

Rostus firmed his jaw. 'Don't spare me. They wouldn't, and we need this to be convincing if we're to win an invitation to the glutton's feast.'

'I didn't say I'd spare you. Only that I'd try to leave you in fighting shape, as best I can.' Neave stooped in with the knife, turning her back to the waterfall to shield her work from its spray. She cut with quick, sure strokes, slicing a chunk out of Rostus' bicep that she gauged would fill the vine's gnashing mouth halfway. Enough to tantalise, but hopefully not enough to take him out of the fight.

Rostus sucked in a sharp breath, but held still under the blade. Sweat beaded on his brow and washed away in the cascade's spitting mist. He didn't look at the wound, and he didn't look at the wall of teeth when Neave went back with her offering, crimson drops spilling between her fingers and washing across the stone floor.

She pushed the gobbet of bloody muscle into the flower. Its petals closed so swiftly that they brushed her fingertips with knobbly, whiskered flesh. Its teeth grazed Neave's armour as they bit down on the meat she'd cut from her friend, and its breath puffed wetly against the back of her hand as she pulled away.

Shuddering, Neave stepped back warily to watch. She felt, more than saw, Rostus take an unguent-soaked cloth from Shakana and press it against his wound, and sensed his slight relaxation as the numbing poultice took effect. But she didn't take her eyes from the wall, and she kept her stance balanced, ready for anything.

The flower swallowed. Around it, the toothy vines spiralled outwards, parting to reveal a macabre archway that had been hidden behind their tangled mass.

It was made of bones and teeth and knots of gristly meat, some so fresh they dripped red blood, others decayed and stinking. Strands of bald sinew, pebbled tongue skin, and pink gum-flesh, all strung with slimy loops of saliva, criss-crossed the space within the arch. The web looked fragile enough to walk through, but it obscured whatever lay beyond.

'Look.' Rostus held out his injured arm. On the inside of his wrist, the image of a simple, childishly drawn face had appeared.

The shape of it was smudged in white, with indistinct dark impressions for eyes. Only its wide, grinning mouth had been drawn with any detail, as if this were the only part of any importance. Sharp yellow teeth filled that mouth, and it sagged at the corners with smiling hunger.

'The glutton brands the meat for his table,' Neave surmised. She remembered the symbol from the papers and paraphernalia Lorai had taken from Pelokoa's followers in the Blind Queen's Maze. It seemed logical that Pelokoa would put some mark on the offerings he'd personally selected. That way, none of his guests would consume what he'd claimed, and none of his visitors would try to substitute some lesser gift after gaining entry to the feast. Unscrupulous fishmongers sometimes tried to cheat their customers by selling a cheap catch under the name of a costlier one; Neave couldn't imagine the Hedonites of Slaanesh were any more honest.

She glanced up at Rostus. 'Does it hurt? Or… exert any other sensation upon you?'

'No. At least not yet, not that I've noticed.' Rostus drew his arm back, studying the mark for a moment, before covering it once again with his armour.

'Do we go through?' Shakana asked from behind. She sounded as tense as Neave felt. 'Is this the invitation?'

'This is the way the riders went,' Lorai answered, gazing at the empty air to the side of the ghastly archway, as if she could read some unwritten secret there. 'The water of their breath, their sweat, their hunger and their fear. They passed through these vines and into the mouth of their master.'

'Then we go in after them,' Neave said. 'Be ready.' For what, she didn't say, because she couldn't guess.

'I'll go first. Follow if I don't get eaten.' Rostus bulled through the threads of flayed tongue, raising his unhurt arm to protect himself as the grisly strands unravelled to lick greedily at him.

Undeterred, they slithered across his pauldron and through his shaggy cloak, matting the fur with streaks of saliva.

Then he was through and gone. Neave went after him, drawing on her Sigmar-granted speed to hasten her passage through the archway. The tongue strands reached for her, but she evaded most of them, and the few that snagged her chest plate or pauldrons tore loose as she bolted through the gate. They didn't coil around her as they'd done to Rostus.

But speed couldn't protect her from the archway itself. As she passed between its cursed bones, Neave felt a surge of hunger seize her.

She doubled over, gasping with the sudden clenched pain of emptiness in her gut. Neave felt as if she hadn't eaten in weeks. Saliva filled her mouth, and an overpowering lust for food overcame her. Not just any food. She wanted meat, and only meat, and *all* meat.

Neave craved the fresh, hot salt of a predator's kill, still kicking and gasping its last. The phantom smell of roasting tavern sausages and fresh-baked lamb pies drifted past her nostrils, making her inhale deeply with desire. Even the stomach-turning stench of carrion caused her to quiver with desperate hunger, and she realised that she wasn't feeling her own yearnings, but those of every carnivore in the Mortal Realms: wyvern, troggoth, or carrion worm.

They all fed on flesh. They all hungered for death. The timing might change, but the appetites didn't, and as she passed through the archway of tongue and teeth, Neave felt each and every one of those appetites acutely, and all at once.

She shuddered as she emerged into an idyllic forest of grapevines, fruit trees, and slanting shafts of golden light. Workers in shapeless smocks and gaudy carnival masks plucked pomelos and spotted drayfruit from the branches, handing them down to other servants, who sliced them onto silver platters. The vines' lower leaves and the ground about the workers' feet were spattered with blood, and the remains of dead servants lay sprawled and ignored in the foliage. They looked like they'd been partially eaten.

Neave was moving almost before she'd fully registered the scene. Sweeping her hurricane axes out, she chopped into the nearest workers, decapitating one and disembowelling the next. She kicked the ladder down from a nearby fruit tree, throwing its fruit picker to the ground, and slaughtered that one along with the servant who'd been slicing the picker's fruit on a platter. Bodies tumbled and limbs flew, but their masks never shook loose.

So swift was Neave's attack that she'd almost finished the massacre before Rostus landed his first swing.

His first was the Blacktalons' last. The last fruit picker strained to force a breath into crushed lungs, failed, and died.

Shakana stepped through the gate of tongues to join them. She absorbed the carnage silently, then scanned the orchard around them, lifting her crossbow with cool efficiency. 'Did any escape?'

'No.' Neave wiped her axes clean, an unnecessary habit from her mortal days, and sheathed them.

She regretted the killings, but only briefly. This place was sworn to Chaos, and Pelokoa's servants, however harmless they might outwardly appear, were saturated with its influence. Neave couldn't risk them sounding the alarm, or escaping from this place to spread their taint through the realms. She had no choice but to kill them.

The true tragedy, as with the Sigmarite scholar who'd succumbed to Chaos in captivity, was not in the servants' deaths, but in their corruption.

Sigmar forgive them. Sigmar forgive me.

She had never thought to spare them. As always, Neave moved too swiftly for such considerations: the instant that she registered a threat, she was already moving to eliminate it. Only now, after the killing was done, did Neave have the luxury of time and space to second-guess herself.

Were they truly corrupt? Might they not have been redeemed? These were servants, not soldiers; they might have been held here against their will.

But it was done, and there was no use dwelling on it. Neave was an imperfect instrument, and though the God-King might have – *would* have – done better, she lacked Sigmar's power, and his wisdom.

He might have been able to save them. But what she had were axes, and those were the tools she had used.

Hendrick and Lorai came through the archway, surveying the slaughter in turn. The Old Wolf nudged one of the dead servants' masks, grunting at the confirmation of his suspicions when the mask only tilted to the side, showing the crude stitches that held it in place.

Cutting the stitches loose, Hendrick pulled off the garishly painted mask. Beneath it, the servant's face was withered and jaundiced from long malnutrition. Her mouth had been sutured shut around a narrow tube that might have permitted her to suck up liquid sustenance, though the wasted figure under her loose-fitting smock suggested that she wasn't given much of it.

'Fodder,' Hendrick said, letting the corpse down with a gentleness that belied his gruff tone. 'I assume they were put out here to sate the appetite for blood that ugly gate ignites. The glutton's a thoughtful host, putting fresh fruit and meat out for his guests. Lucky for us, too. It might not be that unusual for newly arrived guests to kill their greeters. Might not raise any alarms.'

'It might not,' Neave agreed, 'but we'd be foolish to take that for granted. Let's assume the hourglass is running. If nothing else, Pelokoa knows there's a live Stormcast headed for his feast. One way or another, he'll be preparing to meet us.'

CHAPTER TEN

Shakana's star-eagle launched up through the orchard and out of sight, vanishing into a speck against the gloriously blue sky.

The rest of the Blacktalons slipped away, taking cover among the trees and grapevines, so that any new guests who came through the archway wouldn't stumble into their backs. They moved at a guarded pace, paralleling the orchard path at a safe remove. Until the eagle returned from its scouting, they couldn't know what dangers lay ahead, nor whether every step took them closer to, or further from, their target.

Pelokoa's gardens were beautiful temptations. Flowers speckled the grass beneath the apple trees and climbed alongside the grape-vines, adding their fragrance to the perfume of ripening fruit and sun-warmed straw. Picturesque meadows opened between the trees and luxurious swathes of moss lay cradled among their spreading roots, inviting amorous dalliances at every turn.

Only one of the bowers was occupied. A pair of Hedonites lay entwined there, licking the blood of their decapitated third partner off each other's bodies. Hooks and chains bound them to each other, and to their apparent victim.

Neave killed them both with swift blows of her axes, striking them down before they noticed her, let alone had a chance to disentangle themselves or cry an alarm.

She let the bodies lie where they fell. In this place, three headless corpses were as ordinary as one.

Nevertheless, Neave was relieved when the star-eagle plummeted out of the sky to rejoin them. Anda landed on Shakana's shoulder, preening at her braids with its hooked silver beak. The sniper tilted her head towards the bird, listening, as it clicked and hissed and flared its neck feathers.

'The path ahead doesn't seem to be guarded,' she translated for the others. 'It leads through a… garden, I think… and then comes to a great feast. Three structures, one of them larger and grander than the others. Many people are there, with blades, though that could mean either revellers or warriors. No obvious leader in sight, but the people near the grand tent were more ostentatiously dressed than the others.'

Shakana paused, her brow furrowing in confusion as she tried to parse her bird's clacks and head thrusts. 'There's also a large golden… machine… within a great tent. It's a… chair with a mask. Death chair. Death engine? Something of that nature. There are many blades around it, and many servants tending it as if it were a living thing. It's… eating some of them. Consuming them? I'm not sure.'

'Pelokoa's throne?' Hendrick hazarded.

Shakana shook her head. 'It's not just a throne. It's something complicated. Mechanical, magical, or living, I can't tell you, but it's some type of large device.'

'We'll investigate as we get closer,' Neave said. She started off at a trot, quick enough to cover ground but not fast enough to tire herself or charge blindly into danger. 'If they're guarding it, then it's important, and I want to know why. It may lead us to our quarry.'

Ahead, the path branched in three directions as it left the orchard. To the left, it swept down to a lovely little creek and a lightly wooded lake. To the right, it rose towards a scenic overlook dotted by artful follies. The landscape was so peaceful, and so perfect, that it unnerved Neave more than many of the open horrors she'd seen. Behind its illusions of serenity, Pelokoa's domain was no less soaked in blood and pain than any skull-stacked altar to Khorne. But its terrors were cunningly concealed, and its lures promised peace and luxury, not pain.

A tempting lie for those tired of battle. And who, in any realm but Azyr, was not weary of war? Neave felt the allure of that promise herself, even knowing the trap for what it was.

Sigmar held her strong, and the Blacktalons with her, but there were many in Ghyran and beyond who had no such bulwark. Without faith in the God-King to bolster them, and with only a few brief decades of life to enjoy... yes, she could understand the temptation. For such vulnerable souls, the relaxed delights of Pelokoa's gardens would be nearly impossible to resist.

All the more reason to destroy them.

Neave continued down the centre path, which took them through formal gardens of manicured hedges, regimented ranks of flowers and elegant stone urns. Each boundary between one garden and the next was delineated by an archway: a curious pattern of marble and onyx inlaid on the path, a pair of sculptured figures balancing a silver sphere between them, or a trellis draped in gossamer lumin-flowers, their lilac glow almost invisible in daylight.

At first glance, the decorations were as lovely as their surroundings, but on closer examination, all disguised obscenity behind a beautiful veneer. The patterns laid out in onyx and marble were tiny contorted figures, their bodies bent into sigils that spelled out paeans to Slaanesh. The marble figures were bound in agonised postures, and the sphere between them was a bulbous daemon that chewed on the fingers stretched out to it in supplication. The trellis was strung with hanging, cuplike lamps made of polished craniums, and the flowers that twined around it had been trained into place with knots of braided human hair.

'Avoid them,' Lorai murmured when the Blacktalons reached the first of these boundary gates. 'Each is enchanted with an accelerant to the appetites. Their natures vary, but I do not believe you would enjoy experiencing any of them, and all will distract from the task at hand.'

'Noted.' Neave gave the archways a wide berth, and the others followed her lead.

Three vast pavilions in brilliant but badly stained silk rose atop a hill ahead. Their sheer size lent them grandeur, and the silk that swathed them held a fine sheen despite its befouling, but a visual cacophony of ragged flags, pennons, and faded invitations dangled from the tents' eaves, giving them a tatterdemalion air.

Smaller tables dotted the grassy slope leading up to the tents. Revellers, servants and sacrifices swarmed around the feast. Most of them were armed, even the sacrifices, and past the gardens, cover dwindled from minimal to nothing.

Neave exhaled a controlled breath. It was as much frustration as she'd let herself show, but it was more than enough for the Blacktalons to know how she felt.

They still didn't know where their target was. A loud frontal attack *might* flush Pelokoa out, if the glutton's feast was as important to him as the Great Flayer's ritual had been to that fiend, but Neave wasn't sure that was so. This was just a feast, not a massive ritual convocation, and though there were mortal sacrifices being made under those hilltop tents, they had the air of vampires' kills or Khainite bloodlettings. Routine, and hardly worth dying for.

'Neave,' Rostus whispered urgently. He thrust his injured arm towards her, twisting it to show her the mark that had appeared on his wrist. Beads of blood speckled his skin where the face's yellow teeth seemed to bite in. 'It's pulling me towards the hill.'

'Towards the tents?' Neave glanced up the slope, eager for any indication of her prey.

'No. Something beyond them.' Rostus forced the words through gritted teeth. His fingers curled into a fist, and veins stood out on his wrist as he strained against whatever magic worked through the glutton's sign. 'It wants me to go and... lift my chin. To stand patiently and have my throat cut, like a stunned auroch at slaughter.'

'By whom?'

'I don't know. But I'm afraid I'll do it. The compulsion is... strong.' Sweat ran down Rostus' temples in forked rivers, spilling down his neck and vanishing into his gorget. 'I don't think I can hold much longer.'

'Lorai?' Even before the Idoneth responded, however, Neave had her knife out. She sheared it along the inner surface of Rostus' wrist, pulling the skin up and away from veins and muscle as she sliced.

It was swiftly done, and as neat as she could manage without compromising speed. Soon a raw pink blank showed on Rostus' wrist, rapidly masked with blood as his body realised the injury it had suffered. Neave had cut him so quickly that he hadn't even had time to flinch.

'Suppose it's a mercy you didn't warn me you were going to do that,' the big warrior grunted, clamping his other hand over the wound. A moment later, Shakana handed him another unguent-soaked cloth, and he pressed it down with a curt nod to the sniper. 'I'm starting to feel like a patchwork doll.'

'Did it help?' Neave asked.

Rostus nodded, closing his eyes for a moment. His nostrils flared as he sucked in a deep breath. Then, with a small sigh of relief, he mopped the sweat from his bald head. 'Yes. The urge is still there, but it's fading. It seems you guessed right. The magic was bound to the mark.'

'You cut him on a guess?' Shakana shot Neave a sidelong glance.

'She was right to do it,' Rostus said, firmly. He wound the cloth around his wrist, knotting it clumsily with his good hand, and tucked the ends away. 'I don't know how much longer I'd have lasted. Now, what's on the other side of that hill? What was I meant to sacrifice myself to?'

'That's where Anda saw the golden engine,' Shakana said, after a long beat of reluctance at changing the subject and another pointed look at Neave. 'It's surrounded by bodies. Some are guarding it, some are… fuel, I think. Anda wasn't very clear. But the chair, or engine, did seem to be killing people, or consuming bodies. Something of that nature.'

'If that's where Pelokoa is sending his choicest tributes, then that's the first place we should look,' Neave decided. If the glutton cared enough to put a magical sigil of such power on his feast meats, he was likely to oversee their preparation personally, or at least be close by while his cooks began their work. She didn't think he'd care to see such precious ingredients wasted. 'Lorai and Shakana will investigate the golden engine.' Those two could move the most stealthily, and were most likely to be able to comprehend what they saw. 'The rest of us will get into position and wait for word. If we're flushed, or we spot our quarry, we attack. Otherwise, we stay hidden as long as we can.

'Move quick and quiet. We have to find Pelokoa.' She hooked a tiny water-phial over her right ear, and the others mirrored her preparation. The phial, ensorcelled by Lorai, would allow them to whisper messages to each other within a limited range.

Shakana and Lorai broke off to the sides, both soon vanishing from sight. The sniper slid between the manicured trees with long-practised skill, while Lorai simply melted into one of the garden's fountains. Neave loped straight ahead, accompanied by Hendrick, who fell in beside her, comfortable and familiar as her own shadow. Rostus dropped into the rear, as he usually did, although Neave took care not to go so far ahead of him that she went beyond eye or earshot. She wasn't sure Pelokoa's magic had entirely released its grip on the Stormcast, and she wanted to be close enough to help if it tried to seize him again.

The only adequate cover nearby was in a cluster of artful follies gathered around a burbling stream. Gilt-roofed pergolas and flower-draped arbours surrounded a small bridge that arched over the water. Graceful trees trailed their branches into the stream on either side. Their boughs had been woven with strands of silver bells, which echoed the creek's music playfully but made them treacherous to hide among.

Still, there wasn't anywhere better in view. Neave motioned for Hendrick and Rostus to find concealment somewhere among the stream's follies. She took one of the pergolas, crouching low against the fragrant, sun-warmed wood.

Moments passed in tense stillness. The stream laughed through the latticed floor, and when Neave glanced down, she realised with a curiously unsurprised shock that the jewel-bright stones in its bed weren't stones at all.

They were skulls, mostly but not universally human, and they'd been partially enamelled with some opalescent material in pale pinks, blues and golds. The enamel was harder than bone, so that over time the water wore away the organic material underneath, leaving only delicate rattling shells. These clicked and swished in the stream, staring up with blank, dead smiles at the luxury offered to Pelokoa's honoured guests.

There must have been hundreds of them, perhaps thousands. Neave couldn't conceive of the lives wasted to create this artificial chorus of happiness. The enamel faces could just as easily have been made without skulls under them. There was no need for the killings.

But that wouldn't have sufficed for a Hedonite of Slaanesh. The pleasure of their excesses, alone, was never enough. Someone else had to be denied those same pleasures to give them their full savour – for what was the joy in waste, unless someone else starved while the feasters cast their unwanted food aside to rot? What was the beauty of a stream, unless hundreds of lesser wretches had been slain so its water could sluice over their sightless eyes?

And yet, if the visions foreseen by the Great Flayer and Hendrick's communions came to pass, this mockery of serenity might be the only peace the Mortal Realms knew.

What would the worlds be without the Stormcast Eternals holding Azyr's pure light as a beacon for the realms? Without the Cults Unberogen? Without *Sigmar*?

What hope would there be?

Neave didn't realise how tense she'd become until Hendrick's voice came through the phial hanging by her ear. It was a watery, distorted echo, inaudible to anyone else. 'Neave?'

'I'm fine.' *Calm. Focus.* She'd been breathing too hard; that had been what Hendrick heard. Deliberately, working upwards from her toes to her jaw, Neave tensed and relaxed the muscles of her body with exquisite control, her movements almost imperceptible. Her armour didn't even rattle. Bit by bit, she forced the tension from her body.

Hendrick wasn't fooled. 'You were distracted.'

She didn't bother trying to deny it. He'd led the Blacktalons too long, and knew her too well. 'Is it possible? What you saw in your communion, what the Great Flayer prophesied. A world without Sigmar?'

Hendrick didn't answer for some time. When he did, his voice was reassuring but measured, filled with the determination of a parent who acknowledged hardship but refused to surrender to it. 'It may be possible. The history of the Mortal Realms tells us that much. New gods rise, and old gods die. But that is why we have this task, Neave. Our duty is to eliminate the danger, and the Blacktalons do not fail.'

'No.' Neave's gaze strayed down through the pergola's slats, and back to the clicking, smiling ornaments in the stream. *So many dead faces.* 'We won't fail.'

'Someone's coming,' Rostus rumbled through the ear-phials. 'It's a large party. Musicians, acrobats, trick riders. Too many for us to kill quickly, and I doubt we'll be able to stay hidden from so many eyes.'

Neave listened, and soon caught the approaching blare of horns and drums. Each instrument was played with exquisite skill, but a terrible, cacophonous disregard for what any other musician was doing. Rather than playing in harmony, the instruments seemed to be at war with one another.

It meant the approaching party was unlikely to hear the Blacktalons before stumbling into them, but Neave wasn't inclined to take that advantage. Her target wasn't in that group.

'Move straight in,' she murmured to Rostus and Hendrick through the ear-phials. 'Run as fast as we can through anyone we don't need to kill, find Pelokoa if we can, hope one of the others spots him if we don't.' To Shakana and Lorai, she added, briskly: 'Our cover's flushed. We're on the move.'

With that, Neave slipped out of the pergola and ran towards the pavilions. Hendrick and Rostus broke cover to follow, and she kept her pace measured to avoid leaving them behind.

Even so, the Blacktalons whipped past the first tables in a blur. Intoxicating smoke poured from censers burning at the centre of each table. Thinly clad, carnival-masked servants bore flagons of spirits and jars of blended smoke weeds among Pelokoa's guests, along with platters of bloody meat and rare fruits. The servants were there for the taking as well, and the revellers weren't shy about indulging.

Neave saw dignitaries from a dozen cities and fiefdoms of Ghyran seated under Pelokoa's gaudy pennons. Most wore masks, but the arrogance of wealth was too ingrained to hide. It was in their postures, and in the regional finery they'd chosen. These were people who feared exposure enough to hide their faces at Pelokoa's feast, but not enough to take off their signet rings, or house brocades, or the pelts of the great beasts they'd slain.

They didn't entirely believe anything terrible could happen to them, not *really*, and if there was any truer tell of a wealthy mortal, Neave had yet to see it.

But she hadn't come to slay any princeling or clan chief. She ran past, Rostus and Hendrick at her heels, and if the revellers at these outer tables noticed the Blacktalons at all through their drugged hazes, they reacted too slowly to matter. Most didn't stir, too absorbed in their hallucinations or desirous of their next glass of wine to intervene.

Neave ran faster. Flags and servants blurred beside her. The three great tents of stained silk unfurled on the hill ahead. Teams of cooks, servers and attendants scurried like ants from the kitchen tents and cookfires at the hill's base to the guests' pavilions and back.

The grandest and most garish of the tents stood on the top of the hill, flanked to the right and left by smaller pavilions. As Neave curved up the slope, cutting through the cookfires towards the revellers they served, the Hedonites of Slaanesh rose to stop her.

These weren't dabblers and pretenders. These were the true swallowers of sin, and they did not wear masks.

A pair of matched, muscular albinos sprang from their feasting bench and came at Neave. Each of the women was well over six feet tall, and both were clad in identical golden breastplates and wide gold cuffs at wrist and ankle. With smooth gestures they snapped their ornaments into lobstered, spiked weapons that covered their heels and knuckles, and then they circled around Neave, swinging at her with wide kicks and sweeping punches.

They were fast, too fast to be purely human. The albinos laughed as they struck at her, and their laughter came out as puffs of reedy music. Gilt pipes protruded from between their lips: they'd been modified so that they could not speak, only trill their horrid songs. Bird skulls were braided into their hair, the eye sockets sealed shut with wax and the beaks fitted with smaller pipes that echoed the women's mirth as they whistled through the air.

They'd laughed too soon, though. Fast they were, but they weren't Stormcasts, and they certainly weren't Neave. She pirouetted between the women, axes flying, and their heads tumbled to the ground, blood spilling instead of music from the pipes between their lips.

Other Hedonites and minor daemons began closing in. Neave charted a course between the leaping Daemonettes and howling mortals, and then she ran for all she was worth. Hollow-tipped arrows screeched against her armour as she sprang up onto a table, kicking aside an elaborate centrepiece of roasted snakes glazed in sticky venom.

Neave waited just long enough for the revellers to converge on her. As they were about to close, she leapt away again. A sleek Daemonette with metallic paint on her eyelids, cheekbones and pincers struck at Neave as the Stormcast passed overhead.

The Daemonette's pincer speared into the gap beneath her greaves and stabbed up along Neave's right shin. Fighting not to lose momentum, Neave swung an axe back and shattered the pincer into splinters and pulp.

The Daemonette shrieked and jerked away, but the attack cost Neave precious seconds, and she stumbled as venom began to burn in the wound. A stinging numbness spread across Neave's shin, and with the numbness came a perverse pleasure that filled her with revulsion. The glutton's guests surged towards the wounded Blacktalon, and she might have been overwhelmed, had Hendrick not come to her aid.

Axe and sword alight with holy lightning, Hendrick hewed a gap in the Slaaneshi mob. He broke the wounded Daemonette's neck and eviscerated a spittle-flecked gourmand stabbing at him with a razor-tined serving fork, then kicked a chair into the crowd to open up a bit of space. 'Go!'

There wasn't time for thanks. Neave just steadied herself on her good leg, jerked a nod in Hendrick's direction, and sprang away, racing up the hill.

In front of the great pavilion was another cookfire, this one raised up on a gilt altar inscribed with obscenities. Whatever Pelokoa's cooks were burning on that fire gave off an awful, eye-watering smoke. It stung Neave's bleeding wound almost as badly as her eyes and throat, and when she glanced down, the Blacktalon was astonished to see pus dripping down the side of her boot.

At least she couldn't feel it. The Daemonette's poison was good for something. Gritting her teeth, Neave ran through the injury.

She could see what was causing the smoke now. Pelokoa's cooks were grilling long skewers threaded with rotund, squirm-ing daemons who moaned and twitched as their skin charred in the heat and the fat and ichor from their bodies spattered into the coals. The foul little creatures had been coated with oil and crushed herbs, but there was no mistaking Nurglings.

He's eating Nurglings?

Neave had never considered the possibility. The maggot-like daemons weren't merely revolting. Nurglings were walking embodiments of disease. Simply passing through the smoke from their sizzling fat had infected her wound.

How could anyone, even a daemon, hope to eat that and survive?

No time to wonder about it. The cooks had noticed her, and were coming with skewers and butcher's blades. Praying for her injured leg to hold just a little longer, Neave accelerated past them and into the pavilion. *Sigmar, grant me strength. And a path to my target.*

Behind her the sounds of fighting had grown louder. Rostus was pushing his way through the throng. There was no mistaking his battle roars, nor the frenzied pitch of the crowd screaming in return. Neave didn't dare look back. *Sigmar, grant him strength, too.*

Under the great pavilion were the most honoured of Pelokoa's guests, monsters one and all. Many were beautiful, inhumanly so, with skin like porcelain or onyx or iridescent glass. They had razors for fingernails and wore filigreed bones for crowns, and in their eyes was an empty hunger that had consumed whatever else they might once have been.

Neave charged straight at the largest of them, a hulking giant of a man whose well-oiled muscles glistened in perfect symmetry. He wore a spotted green cape of scales, imitating barbaric fashion, though the hide was too beautifully tailored, and its clasp of gold and emeralds too fine, to have come from any crude hunting camp.

The false barbarian wasted a precious second flexing for his admirers before he swung at her. That was all the opening Neave needed. She slashed an axe across his throat and slammed the other into his chest, hooking a foot behind his ankle as she did. The giant went over in a spray of blood and oil, and the smaller Hedonites scattered lest they be crushed.

Planting her good foot on the giant's chest, Neave used him to launch herself upwards. She grabbed onto a tent rafter, surveying the pavilion from above the roiling fray.

'Well, well,' said a cultured and melodious baritone, projecting effortlessly above the din. 'Are you the Stormcast I tasted earlier? There seem to be more of you than I had anticipated, and in less subdued form. But that is well and good. I don't mind a little hunt before the feast. It entertains my guests, and whets the appetite.'

Neave's attention snapped towards the voice.

At the back of the grand pavilion stood an enormous golden statue, easily twenty feet tall, worked into the likeness of a half-robed figure wearing a beatific mask. A table draped in purple and gold silks stood by the statue's base, and at the head of this table was the speaker.

'Pelokoa! Pelokoa Undying! Pelokoa Ever-Eater!' cried a chorus of slaves tethered in a ring about the statue. Golden chains pierced through festering wounds in their ankles held them in place. Agony laced their voices, and the pain in their cries of praise earned smiles from the sybarites watching the confrontation. Some of the guests, anticipating a show, were already beckoning for more wine.

Pelokoa the Glutton stood. He was nearly eight feet tall, swathed in gold and purple to match his table. Like his statue, he wore a porcelain death mask over his real features, but there the resemblance ended.

He was not made of gold, but flesh, and that flesh bulged and sagged under the weight of long overindulgence. Pelokoa's chest and shoulders were firm and well muscled, but his stomach strained against the folds of his robe, and his swollen legs had split open completely. Raw flesh oozed between broken crusts of scabbed white skin, the rifts widening steadily from his knees down to his feet. His toes had burst like crushed red grapes, and yellow crystals of gout winked from the joints between diseased bones.

'Come,' Pelokoa said. He held out a hand, and a servant rushed to provide him with a staff of sculpted bone with gilded blades at either end. 'Let us play, Stormcast. Let us play, and let us feast.'

Neave pumped her arms in a deceptively easy swing and tumbled smoothly from the rafter, landing in a cautious crouch to keep the weight off her injured leg. A path cleared through the crowd as the revellers moved aside, forming a ring that contained the Blacktalon and their master. Even the sounds of fighting outside diminished, as those who'd been battling Hendrick and Rostus pulled away to attend this new spectacle.

So you want a show. Turning a slow circle, Neave raised her axes overhead and clashed them together, showering blue and gold sparks over the crowd.

When she spoke, however, it wasn't to Pelokoa or his guests, but to the other Blacktalons, in a hissed whisper through her ear-phial. 'I've found the glutton. I'm going to kill him now.'

CHAPTER ELEVEN

After taking their separate courses past the revellers' camp, Shakana and Lorai reunited to investigate where Pelokoa's sigil-marked sacrifices were going.

A steady stream of captive animals, barrels of spirits and spices, and unfortunate prisoners, all branded with the same indistinct face and razored mouth, circled around the base of the feasters' hill to the other side. One after another, they entered a tent made up of smoke-stained hides. None re-emerged. Their bearers, empty-handed, returned to the festivities, but the offerings simply vanished.

It had been easy enough to approach the tent. Scattered copses of trees grew nearby, likely intended to provide firewood and spits for Pelokoa's cooks. They also gave Shakana cover, and so she'd been able to sneak close to the tent.

Getting inside was a more difficult challenge. Unlike the tents atop the hill, which were open-sided around their gaudy gilt poles, this one was fully enclosed. It was immense, easily two hundred feet to a side. The roof was pebbled with overlapping domes, as if a dozen smaller tents had been stitched together to create this single large one. Shakana guessed that when she entered, she'd find the interior structure was exactly that.

Painted faces, stark white with smeared red eyes and empty charcoal mouths, covered the tent's outer walls. They matched the face that had appeared on Rostus' wrist and that marked Pelokoa's other sacrifices, except the ones on the walls had no teeth.

A plume of green-tinged steam rose from a gap in the tent roof, and Shakana guessed that it was through this aperture that Anda had glimpsed the golden engine.

That would be her first target.

'Do you see any easy way to get into the tent?' she asked Lorai through the ear-phials. The Idoneth had stayed further back in the trees, where she was shielded from view and, ordinarily, wouldn't have been able to see anything herself.

But the aelf had a number of ways of seeing that weren't reliant on eyes, and she might have spotted something useful.

'No,' Lorai replied, dashing Shakana's hopes.

'Right, then.' The sniper drew out a knife. Its metal had been painted a dull greenish grey, with only the barest gleam of silver visible along the edge. 'I'm going to cut my way in.'

'I will await word here.' The connection went silent.

Shakana dropped into a crouch and moved forwards. The trees thinned to brush and open grass, and she crept even lower, dropping to her belly, as her cover dwindled.

The sacrifices and their bearers weren't looking at her, though. They sought out the tent with single-minded focus, and the looks of rapturous eagerness on the faces of those who bore Pelokoa's sign turned Shakana's stomach.

Why are they so eager to die? These people weren't in pain, as many of those who sought Nurgle's false mercy were. They weren't lost in a Bloodletter's rage or seeking some perverse transcendence outside their own flesh. They just… *wanted* it, as a youth yearned for a lover's kiss and a miser lusted after gems.

The sight sickened her, and it frightened her.

Though she'd sooner have bitten her tongue off than admit it to her comrades, Shakana was afraid of death. Or, rather, she was afraid of what came after.

Reforging took things, and it replaced things, and one never knew what Sigmar's forge might change. Usually it was only memories, but memories were not trivial losses. Memories were friendships, loves, rivalries, *identities*. She was still, privately, a little shaken by how cruelly the Blind Queen's Maze had tormented her with that.

And Shakana, who preferred to kill her enemies from afar before they ever knew she was there, feared death more than most, precisely because she suffered it less than most.

She remembered what her friends didn't. She remembered that they *were* friends, or had been, until death made them strangers with painfully familiar faces. Shakana, alone, still held the jokes that had lost their laughter, the stories that were forgotten, the grudges that had faded into indifference. Their original owners had lost those pieces of their identities, but she kept them close, treasuring the warmth and the occasional stings of remembrance.

As long as Shakana lived, so too did everything that she hoped, someday, to restore to her friends.

Death risked that hope, and everything it carried.

But sometimes there was no choice but to accept that risk, and go in close and personal. This appeared to be one of those times.

Another group of Hedonites and curly-horned beasts went into the scrawl-painted tent. The flaps swished and burped smoke in their wake. No one else was nearby, for the moment, and the size of those beasts suggested they'd take some time to slaughter and butcher. Anda was still circling high in the sky, tracing lazy circles that told Shakana that the next sacrifices wouldn't round the hill for a moment or two.

It was as good an opening as she was going to get.

Sigmar, grant me strength, Shakana prayed, and hurried across the open space.

She reached the tent wall. Quickly, Shakana scurried along the side until she judged that she was far enough from the entrance. Then she cut a narrow slit between two of the painted faces, just enough to peer inside.

Just inside the hide walls was a second framework built of hinged golden rods, like a skeleton beneath skin, that supported the immense tent. Between the rods, innumerable parchments and papers, all covered with sloped writing in the same careless but dramatic hand, had been sealed together with layers of unguents to create papier-mâché walls.

The papier mâché prevented Shakana from seeing anything, but fortunately it wasn't as thick or hard as it looked. She cut a second slash through the painted parchments, listened carefully for any indication of alarm, and pulled it cautiously apart when she heard none.

To her left, near-naked workers in thick leather aprons were slaughtering Pelokoa's tributes and hanging the corpses upside down on hooks to drain. The blood drained into drums, which other workers dragged away to an area Shakana couldn't see. When the corpses were adequately bled, they were hauled off to be either scalded in a steaming metal vat and scraped clean of hair and feathers, or taken directly to butchering.

The silence of the work was eerie. None of the sacrifices struggled or protested, not even the animals. They just lifted their chins and waited patiently for the knives, and barely sighed when the blades sank in. The splash of blood into the collecting drums was the loudest sound in the room.

About forty feet away, the butchery opened to her right. It was partitioned by bloodstained leather curtains, all painted with the same shapeless face as the exterior walls, but the workers' movements allowed Shakana to glimpse what lay inside: bodies, dozens of them, humans and ruminants and great flightless birds all hanging by the ankles as they waited to be cut apart. Others were being spitted, or cut into quarters, before being taken out to the cookfires.

Shakana's lips tightened. She couldn't stay outside the tent much longer, and the slaughtering pens were too busy to be safe. But there were far fewer workers among the hanging corpses, and far more places to hide between the dead.

She widened the gashes she'd cut in the exterior wall and inner papier-mâché barrier, contorted herself to fit between the golden bars, and slipped in. The outer hide was loosely hung, and it fell back into place behind her, sealing her in shadow.

No new sacrifices had arrived, and all the workers were busy in the butchery. For the moment, she was alone. Shakana listened intently, pinpointing the workers' steps and breathing, and the thud and rip of blades hewing dead flesh and bone.

Nothing sounded close. She parted the curtains and slid between the painted faces, moving swiftly to the side. Rows upon rows of hanging bodies hemmed her in, but they were only inert corpses, and they didn't trouble her.

The central aperture, through which Anda had glimpsed the golden engine, was somewhere ahead. Shakana hadn't been able to assess the full layout of the butchery, but she guessed that she'd have to cross it diagonally to reach the centre of the tent, where the engine presumably awaited.

Navigating more by sound than sight, Shakana worked her way through the dangling corpses to the far side of the butchery. Twice, when workers threatened to come near, she leapt up and caught hold of the golden rods supporting the slain sacrifices, tucking her knees tight against her chest so that she was hidden among the bodies. She held herself motionless, breathing shallowly, until they passed.

Then she came to the end of the hanging bodies, and froze.

Not ten feet away, the tent she was in overlapped with another. A wall of painted hides demarcated the change, along with a dip and rise in the roofs, but the doorway between the two areas was open. Through that gap, Shakana watched four servants toil over a table laid with freshly decapitated human heads. Sheets of dried translucent material hung from wire racks by the servants' elbows, and jars of cloudy liquid were set out on the table beside them.

Some of the servants were poaching heads in a cauldron of bubbling broth on the other side of the table. Others took the half-cooked heads and put them in ceramic moulds, where they were layered with pieces cut from the translucent sheets and ladlefuls of opaque liquid. Then, after the heads had sat for some indeterminate period, the servants turned them out onto ornate gold and silver platters, where they quivered in shells of shining aspic.

Overseeing the project was a one-eyed man whose corpulent, unhealthily pale figure was cinched into a painful hourglass by a waist corset of shiny black leather. Other than the corset and a broth-stained butcher's apron, he wore nothing but a pair of greasy boots. He wandered from platter to platter, tasting the meat jelly as it cured, adjusting the expressions on the heads before they went into the moulds, and occasionally barking reprimands at his subordinates.

The cooks working under him had a curiously uniform look, unlike the eclectic bunch Shakana had seen outside. While the servers seeing to Pelokoa's guests had all been chosen for their striking looks, whether that meant natural beauty or extensive augmentation, their variation was meant to be part of the display.

Not here. The under-cooks were all of a type: masked in iron bars, gaunt through the arms and torso, bloated from the hips down. They were all riddled with the scars of human bites, too, though some had more than others.

Among the heads, Shakana spotted the young scholar who'd been captured in the Blind Queen's Maze and had given herself over to Chaos during the journey. Evidently her conversion hadn't sufficed to save her life.

The salt-barrelled corpse pieces from the Blind Queen's Maze were there too, though these weren't being encased in aspic like the heads. They were just being poached in the broth pots and then laid out for consumption, as far as Shakana could tell. She wasn't inclined to spend too much time pondering the matter.

There was no cover around the cooks' table, and she couldn't see anything to be gained by investigating further. The golden engine didn't appear to be in this direction. Retreating back into the forest of hanging bodies, Shakana shifted course and tried again.

This time, she emerged to find herself standing before a short hallway formed from panels of papier mâché mounted on golden rods.

It was like stepping into a section of an oversized wasps' nest. The ceiling and walls closed in from the tent's exterior, funnelling downward in tight papier-mâché spirals so that there was nowhere else to go. Small, circular entrances, more like burrow mouths than doorways, opened to the left and the right. Whorls of writing coiled across the papier mâché, creating a dizzying, claustrophobic effect as Shakana was enveloped in their maddening embrace.

She wasn't sure which way led to the centre of the tent. Either way, she was so close that it was difficult to guess which side of the hall held the golden engine.

She'd veered right to enter the butchery, which meant that taking a left now would probably put her closer to the centre. *Unless the angles aren't what I think they are.* It was hard to tell, between the hallway's strange proportions and the writing on its walls.

Have to pick something. She went left.

Past the threshold, the corridor twisted abruptly, and a heavy, stained curtain of velvet painted with more charcoal-mouthed white faces blocked her way. Shakana pushed past it, and found herself facing a large room dominated by an empty stage.

Around the stage, arranged in concentric rows like the audience at a theatre, were dozens of decapitated heads preserved in aspic.

Is this what happens to the cooks' creations?

No one was present, except the heads themselves, so Shakana crept closer for a more careful look.

The heads sat in shallow saucers, garlanded by wilted garnishes of parsley and carved root vegetables. Many appeared to have been partially eaten, and they'd all been oriented in the same direction. One and all, they stared with lifeless, jelly-coated eyes at the blank boards of the stage.

'Lorai? Are you there? I need to know what I've found.' Using just the tips of her fingers, Shakana picked up a nearby saucer by the cleanest edge she could find. It held a mostly eaten Sylvaneth's head. Little was left but a delicately pointed chin, a few nutlike teeth in the lower jaw, and part of one striated brown cheek. Clear aspic quivered over the tooth-marked remains. There weren't any eyes in the head, and what was left of it could almost pass for a wooden carving rather than the remnants of a sentient creature, so it was the least repulsive option in reach.

Shakana slid the Sylvaneth's head onto the floor and uncapped her waterskin over the saucer, pouring out a measured flow. As the water settled, Lorai's head rose up from it, as if she too had been decapitated and added to Pelokoa's collection of grisly prizes.

The Idoneth seemed not to notice the unintended effect. She

looked about her surroundings, taking in the quiet stage and its equally silent audience, and then she turned to Shakana. 'This is curious. Keep pouring. I will come.'

Shakana nodded and emptied her waterskin into the saucer. Rather than overflowing the dish, the water lifted itself into a translucent replica of Lorai's thin, robed figure. Water flowed from her doppelganger's hand into the shape of her chiming staff, stabilised, and became solid. So too did the aelf.

One instant there was a faceless, fluid shape; the next, it was Lorai herself, stepping out from a cascade of water that splashed to the floor around her.

Even before the water hit the ground, Shakana had slipped back to the hallway. She drew her crossbow and crouched in front of the butchery, waiting to see whether any of the cooks or workers reacted to Lorai's arrival. But the sound of the Idoneth's watery spell didn't seem to have escaped the theatre, and no one came.

Once she was satisfied that they hadn't been noticed, Shakana crept back to Lorai. 'Well? What is it?'

'It appears to be a stage.' Lorai lifted a hand towards her staff's chimes. A puff of mist coalesced around them, silencing their song.

'I'd gathered that much. What are the heads for?'

Lorai didn't answer. The Idoneth walked in widening circles through the jellied heads, following an arcane pattern that only she could see. Her staff gave off a soft blue-green glow, and it seemed to Shakana that the heads' dead eyes were drawn to it somehow.

It was unsettling. Could the jellied corpses see her? Could they communicate with the cooks? Or with Pelokoa?

Every fibre of Shakana's being screamed to be gone before Pelokoa's servants spotted them, but Lorai didn't seem to share her urgency. She paced in her looping designs, agonisingly slow, heeding a rhythm that cared nothing for the danger they were in.

Finally the Idoneth stopped, gazing out over the glistening sea of heads. 'They are audience and dinner, playwright and performer. They are Pelokoa's prizes, and his prisoners, and the victims of his scorn. But…'

The aelf frowned. Levelling her silenced staff across the collection, she pointed out the cyst-raddled, hideously grinning visage of a bile troggoth. Putrid maggots spilled from between the head's rotten yellow teeth. They, too, were trapped in aspic, preserved so vividly that Shakana found it hard to believe they weren't still wriggling through the jelly.

Lorai moved past it, and pointed out a snarling Khornate warrior, her cheeks branded with Chaos sigils and her eyes turned to wet balls of blood. This head, like the troggoth's, had several bites fastidiously sawed out of its flesh by fork and knife. Shakana could see the punctures left by the fork's tines in the warrior's skin.

'These meals should have killed Pelokoa, even in his present state,' Lorai said. 'At the least, they should have threatened him with Nurgle's plagues, or Khorne's blood rage. These victims, his prizes, were blessed by the Ruinous Powers so that they could spread their cursed "gifts". Pelokoa consumed their tainted flesh, and did so willingly, courting their corruptions. He is no true daemon. He is a creature of flesh, mortal in origin. Therefore he should have succumbed, if not the first time, then at some point over the many meals he has made of such creatures. One cannot taste such things repeatedly without, eventually, swallowing more than can be resisted. Yet he remains unchanged.'

'That's fascinating,' Shakana said tersely, 'but is it going to help us kill Pelokoa? Because if it's not, we need to move on.'

The aelf looked at her with the blank, maddening serenity that Shakana had learnt signified profound frustration with her companions' failure to grasp the obvious.

'He should be dead,' the Idoneth said, patiently. 'Not only once, but several times over. Yet he lives. How?'

'If I knew that–'

The aelf lifted a pale hand, conceding the point. 'I do not ask you to answer the question. Only to consider it. I suspect Pelokoa has some means of enhancing his will and safeguarding his soul, and I suspect that it must be close. It cannot be far, for even one as convinced of his own invincibility as Pelokoa would not be foolish enough to put his salvation out of reach. Nurgle's plagues act quickly, and Khorne's rages are quicker still. Whatever counter-measure he uses, it must be ready within seconds when he feasts.'

Shakana nodded. She'd initially wondered whether Pelokoa forced these grisly delicacies on others, and made them choke down their final meals on stage for his entertainment. But if the glutton was eating these things himself, then she agreed with Lorai: he had to be using *something* to bolster himself against the nastier effects of his diet. Even if the spiritual corruptions didn't seize him, no mortal could feast on a Plaguebringer's flesh and survive. 'You stay here, and try to stay out of sight. I'm going to scout the other exit from the hallway.'

Silently she returned to the golden-ribbed hall facing the butchery. This time she heard guttural voices and heavy steps approaching, but just as Shakana readied her typhoon crossbow to obliterate who-ever was coming, the footsteps turned away.

Guests returning to the feast after delivering their tributes for slaughter, Shakana surmised, not iron-masked cooks coming to add more heads to those around the stage. She eased her fingers from the trigger, and after another moment, put the weapon aside.

Alone again, she crossed the papier-mâché hallway with two long steps and entered the other doorway. It, too, narrowed and twisted immediately, preventing Shakana from getting a view of what lay at the corridor's end until she was there.

As she moved down the short, contorted passageway, a glimmer drew her eye to the ceiling. It was no more than a chance reflection of her crossbow's contained lightning, but Shakana froze immediately, one foot poised in mid-air.

Shifting her weight near motionlessly, she looked up. There was a golden thread woven into the papier mâché, almost invisible against the golden rod that backed it. If her crossbow's lightning hadn't caught it at just the right angle to distinguish the thread from the rod, she'd never have seen it.

But she had, and every instinct warned of danger. Shakana tracked the thread with her eyes, following its course down and through the papier-mâché walls until she traced it to a tiny metal aperture, nestled in the stiffened paper pulp like a snake in grass, that opened at ankle height and faced across the passageway.

Alarm, or trap? Either way it was best avoided. Shakana marked its placement carefully and stepped over, holding her breath until her foot touched down and nothing happened.

Past the golden thread, the hallway ended in another chamber, roughly circular and, at forty feet across, markedly smaller than the theatre of jellied heads. Two iron-masked warriors armed with barbed bone blades stood guard at the entrance.

Fearsome as the masks were, they blocked the warriors' hearing and limited their sight. Shakana dropped them with a pair of quick shots to the throat, hitting each one neatly under the chin where the masks left their necks exposed. They dropped without a cry, smoke rising from the black-edged wounds, and she strode in between the twitching bodies.

The centre of the room was dominated by a shallow oval pool, twelve feet long and six wide, rimmed in gold and floored with white marble. An elaborate configuration of gilded pumps, pipes and faucets surrounded a golden, ovoid engine mounted at one end of the pool. One chute fed a continuous stream of finely chopped human limbs and less identifiable parts into the engine's belly, while two smaller pipes poured in greenish-tinted water.

The engine's presses and pistons churned this slurry to a pink froth, then emptied it into the pool in regular, rhythmic pulses, as if pumping blood from an imitation heart.

A stylised diagram of a male human body was inscribed on the bottom of the pool, its arms outstretched to either side. The body was larger than life-size; had it been standing, Shakana guessed that it would have been about eight feet tall, with proportions to match.

As she crept around the side of the pool, she saw that the diagram at the bottom of the pool wasn't merely a drawing. Body parts had been laid atop it like puzzle pieces, forming a fully intact male body. Though the parts had clearly been taken from different individuals, they were all perfectly shaped, and had been rubbed with some sort of unguent or ointment that gave them a waxy sheen. Pale green lines of magic criss-crossed the body like seams, showing where the pieces had been joined together.

Concentric rings of unholy sigils surrounded the anatomical diagram, and more sigils crowded the papier-mâché walls that curved high overhead. Even the golden pipes and the support rods in the walls and ceiling were etched with runes, and the oppressive force of their magic pressed down on Shakana, giving her a vicious headache and wracking her muscles with spasms that worsened with each step she took past the threshold.

She pushed the pain aside, trying to focus. Something about that water…

Shakana moved closer. Steam from the pool rose up to greet her, drifting ghostly green-tinged fingers through her locks. She inhaled, and vigour suddenly rushed through her, banishing the vice-like pressure that the chamber's magic exerted.

Aqua Ghyranis. The pool was filled with the restorative life-water of Ghyran, and a prince's ransom of it.

Now she'd seen the Aqua Ghyranis in the pool, Shakana recognised it pouring through pipes into the engine. That was the fluid that the device mixed with pulped flesh to create its pink slurry. Once it flowed into the pool, the slurry gravitated towards the seams that stitched the body parts together, filling them in with a meat paste that gradually solidified into pale, healthy-looking new flesh.

Shakana's ear-phial vibrated. Neave's voice came through. 'I've found the glutton. I'm going to kill him.'

'I'm at the golden engine,' Shakana replied. 'It mixes Aqua Ghyranis with pulverised bits of Pelokoa's sacrifices, then pours them into a pool holding body parts. It seems to be... growing a new body. The whole room reeks of sorcery. I'm not sure what the point of it all is, though.'

No answer came, but she hadn't expected one. Shakana turned, preparing to leave, and then paused as a sudden flurry of bubbles erupted in the depths of the pool.

A vicious wound opened in the submerged body's chest, cracking ribs and exposing the motionless heart. Then, just as swiftly, it healed under a fresh surge of pumped pink slurry. A second later, an even uglier gash tore across the body's neck, knocking the head to the side as vertebrae splintered and bloodless arteries tore open.

That wound healed too. The pool churned with even greater agitation, filling the chamber with fragrant steam. Struck by a sudden apprehensive suspicion, Shakana focused on her ear-phial. 'Lorai? You should see this. Neave, what's happening?'

'He won't die,' Neave said, her voice sharp with frustration even through the ear-phial's watery distortion. 'Pelokoa should be dead twice over, but his wounds simply heal.'

'One to the chest and one to the neck?' Shakana asked.

Footsteps were coming towards her. Many of them, running, with a heavy tread. Though the steam was now thick enough to obscure anything more than a few feet away, there wasn't much solid cover in the room, so Shakana moved to the side of the entrance and dropped into a crouch behind the fallen guards. She propped her crossbow on a guard's slumped bare shoulder, readying a shot at whatever might emerge from the fog. A steady patter of Aqua Ghyranis, condensed on the engine's rods and feeder pipes, dripped from the ceiling like warm, sweet rain.

There was a grunt and a scuff through the ear-phial as Neave blocked or evaded some unseen blow, and then: 'Yes. How did you know?'

Under Shakana's elbow, the guard twitched. An eye blinked open inside the iron mask. Aqua Ghyranis beaded on the rough metal and ran down the man's neck, where the wound in his throat had already healed to a faint pink mark.

The guard began to push himself up from the ground. Shakana moved back, took aim, and shot him point-blank in the forehead. At this range, her typhoon crossbow melted a hole straight through the iron.

Again the guard fell. And, again, a moment later he blinked away the blood and opened his eyes. The hole in his helmet was still steaming.

'Well,' Shakana told Neave through the ear-phial, 'I think I've found out why Pelokoa is called the Undying.'

'Oh?' Neave prompted a moment later. Her voice was strained.

The other guard had risen to his knees, and the approaching footsteps Shakana had heard earlier were almost at the doorway. She fell back another step, wiping sweat and Aqua Ghyranis from her eyes. The wall curved in from the right behind her, and the bubbling pool, fed by its golden engine, blocked off her left. There was nowhere to retreat.

No exit, no help. She was on her own.

Shakana willed herself to breathe. Masked shapes appeared in the doorway, shouting. The iron-masked cooks, and their one-eyed, corseted leader.

Inhale, exhale. *Aim, fire.* One down. *Aim, fire.* Two down.

She moved towards the engine, which offered the only solid cover in the room, even though it was poorly positioned away from the entrance and surrounded by a treacherous tangle of pipes. She could make a stand there, but there was a good chance she'd be trapped in it until all her enemies were dead, or she was.

More cooks were crowding the doorway. Her worst terror was coming true: hand-to-hand combat, badly outnumbered, no escape.

Inhale, exhale. It wouldn't do Neave any good to worry about her. It wouldn't do any of them any good.

'Yes. The golden engine keeps him immortal.'

CHAPTER TWELVE

'You can't kill Pelokoa.'

'What?' Conscious of the crowd's eyes on her, Neave didn't blink. She spoke softly, barely moving her lips, but her disbelief was clear.

'You can't kill Pelokoa,' Shakana repeated. Her voice held an iron calm, underlaid with a tightly gripped tension that told Neave the sniper was under attack, and that the circumstances didn't favour her. Something whistled in the background, and there was a sharp metal ping. 'At least I don't think you can, not while the engine's working. It'll just keep healing him. It may even be creating a brand new body to replace that one, if you destroy it entirely.'

'That's a problem,' Neave muttered. 'Can you stop it?'

'Maybe. I'll need some time.'

'How much time?'

No answer came. Another volley of fire echoed through the ear-phial, followed by silence.

'Pelokoa!' Neave cried. She drew another cascade of lightning from her axes, playing to the audience. Most Slaaneshi appetites were alien to her, and she was content to keep them so, but she understood their hunger for spectacle. 'I will end your worthless life.'

The crowd of revellers roared. Pelokoa threw back his porcelain-masked head and laughed, as Neave had known he would. *We all have to play our roles in this farce.*

'I shall eat you alive, little Stormcast,' the glutton answered, and there was a salivating thickness to his words that made Neave's skin crawl.

She didn't try to hide it. Let Pelokoa's guests think he had unnerved her.

Neave gave it a moment, then made a show of gathering her strength as she turned back to face him. 'Do you normally deliver all your threats from behind a mask? It must be much easier to boast when you can bury your cowardice in clay.'

Pelokoa snarled. Behind the mask's beatific smile and sculpted curls, his small eyes were hard with hate. 'I take the mask off when I feast. You'll come to know my true face well. I will keep you alive, Stormcast, so you can watch me enjoy every bite. There will be no lightning escape back to Azyr for you.'

He charged at her. The hilltop shook with every thunderous step, and yet for all the glutton's fearsome size, his bladed staff spun with deadly speed.

Neave danced away, but she couldn't get far. The crowd jabbed at her with barbed forks and blades, jeering as they drove her back towards Pelokoa.

Fine. Advancing on Pelokoa, Neave slammed her axes together again. They spat lightning, eager to bite into the Slaaneshi.

She feinted low, swinging at the glutton's legs, but Pelokoa drove her back with his whirling staff. The blades clipped over Neave's head, emitting an eerie, whistling wail. Though she had only meant to bait the glutton, buying time for Shakana to finish whatever she and Lorai were doing, he'd come dangerously close to cleaving off the top of her skull.

Ungainly he might seem, with those suppurating feet and split calves, but Pelokoa was fast, accurate, and ungodly strong.

She'd have to be careful. One mistake and she'd wake up on Sigmar's forge.

A roar in the crowd drew her attention. Hendrick and Rostus had joined the spectators. Both were bleeding from a score of minor wounds, but neither looked seriously injured, as best Neave could tell from a glance.

'You sent three to fight me? You should have sent a dozen,' Pelokoa laughed. 'Then I'd have enough of you Stormcasts to share with my guests. Three is scarcely enough for my own plate.'

His staff lashed out again, too quick for the eye to follow. Neave, watching Pelokoa's stance instead of his weapon, threw herself backwards. The reveller behind her wasn't so fortunate, and ducked in the wrong direction.

Pelokoa's blade sheared through the wine jug the guest had been holding, scattering fingers across the grass in a shower of wine and blood. The jug fell in two neat halves, cut clean as a Khainite offering's throat. The crowd gasped, and then it laughed. Gales of hideous merriment rang down the hill, and those who were too far back to have seen the bloodshed pushed forwards and strained up on their toes for a view.

Neave gestured for Hendrick and Rostus to stay back. She didn't dare explain why through the ear-phials. All three of them were too close to the Hedonites, and the risk of their whispers being overheard was too great.

She could only hope they'd obey the gesture. Her wounded leg was sending up flares of pain as the Daemonette's venom burned through its temporary numbing.

In a few more moments, she'd start to fail. If that happened, the

Blacktalons would charge to her aid, and no mute gesture would be likely to stop them. And if they still couldn't kill Pelokoa...

Come on, Shakana.

Pelokoa saw her weaken. He shifted the staff to a one-handed grip and drew out a glass bottle from his gold-trimmed velvet robe. The lower third of his robe was sticky and wet, and clung to his broken flesh where it brushed against his legs. Whatever was in that bottle reflected the sodden, contaminated colours of the once-fine garment, swirling with murky red and bruised purple. 'Does it hurt, little Stormcast? Do you want to feel better?'

He threw the bottle. Neave dodged, but it wasn't meant to strike her. Smoke spilled from the shattered glass. The revellers shrieked in excitement, recognising the smoke, and crowded violently to the fore as they vied to suck in great gulps of the stuff.

Not a good sign. But she couldn't retreat. The crowd pushed her into the thick red smoke. It smelled of dirty perfume and old sweat, of the stale air in a debauched emperor's pleasure rooms. Neave held her breath, but she couldn't do that forever, and she wasn't even sure it mattered. Where the smoke touched her open wounds, it filled her body with a languorous, repellent pleasure. It wrapped around her like soiled velvet, soft and luxuriant and rotten in every fibre.

She wanted the pain. She *craved* the pain. It was the poison's doing, but Neave still felt it, and resisting the unwanted impulse was another drain on her waning strength.

Sigmar, grant me fortitude. Sigmar, be my will. She couldn't do it on her own. *I need you, my god.*

Resolve sparked deep in her soul. Neave felt the surge of divine power in her chest, and could almost see it coursing like lightning through her veins. The God-King's might flowed through her, bolstering her own faltering will. With renewed determination, Neave pushed away the poison's temptations.

But in her distraction, she'd let the crowd get too close. The feasters struck at her sides and back, scoring shallow hits as Neave was forced to pivot on her bad leg. She couldn't evade them all, and they gloried in it.

A barbed fork snagged at her cloak, ripping away tufts of fur. A laughing reveller raked his gilt gauntlet across her side, and the golden claws came away dark with blood. He held up his hand and licked it messily, then crowed in triumph.

Pelokoa let his guest enjoy the moment. It didn't please him that someone else had drawn first blood, though. Neave caught a glimpse of a snarl behind the glutton's cracked mask. 'Flagging already, little Stormcast? You're forged of weaker material than I thought.'

'How would you know? Mighty Pelokoa has yet to manage so much as a taste.' Neave twisted away from a blade thrust. Pelokoa's staff, grazing her hip, caught the rip in her cloak and withdrew with a clump of bloody fur. 'Perhaps you can suck the blood from the cut your lackey managed. Seems he's a fiercer fighter than you are.'

The glutton roared again and bulled forwards. Neave side-stepped to the right. A woman in a purple cloak and not much else was leaning out of the crowd, shouting nonsense. Neave grabbed a handful of her cloak and yanked, throwing the spectator into Pelokoa's path.

He trampled the reveller without hesitation. Bone snapped under his gout-riddled feet. Neck or back, Neave couldn't tell, but the reveller went limp as a pithed frog under Pelokoa's weight, and the crowd howled in delight.

'Do I even need to use this?' Pelokoa held out his staff as if suddenly mystified by its presence in his hands. 'Perhaps I'll just blow you over. You look like a light breeze would end it.'

He wasn't wrong. Sigmar had helped her resist the corruption, but her wounds were mounting, and the poison was still in her, gnawing at her flesh. Neave closed her eyes, just for the briefest of instants. Even that felt like a surrender. Her axes felt like numb, tingling weights held in hands a thousand miles away.

Shakana, I can't hold out much longer.

Lying on her belly beside the pool, claiming what scant cover she could from the golden engine and its feeder pipes, Shakana switched her crossbow's arms out to their widest reach. The weapon's aperture dilated into full fury. As its magic gathered strength, Shakana lifted the crossbow and took aim through a gap between the pipes.

She'd hurt enough of the cooks to give the others some pause. Most of them didn't stay down for long, not with the pool's steam and unholy magic as intense as it was, but a stormbolt through the eye still hurt enough to hold them back.

And if Shakana did enough damage, they stayed dead. She'd finally blasted the two original guards past repair. Ugly work, and it had taken far longer than she'd have liked, but at least now she knew it was possible.

Pelokoa's servants had retreated to get their own crossbows, and launched a flurry of barbed quarrels at the Stormcast. Bolts screeched off the golden pipes around her and exploded as they flew between her crossbow's glowing arms.

In answer, Shakana fired into the middle of the crowd.

Lightning exploded across the room, accompanied by a concussive blast of thunder. Ghostly flashes filled the mist as the pool reflected and diffused the brilliant devastation. Before the cooks had a chance to recover, Shakana popped her head up to take measure of the destruction.

The one-eyed head cook was on his knees, coughing amidst the smoking bodies of his iron-masked subordinates. Blackened scraps of paper fluttered down from the scorched and battered doorway. The golden rods that supported the papier mâché had wrenched apart from the force of the blast, tearing the entrance wider.

Shakana tightened the aperture on her crossbow and drilled a shot through the cook's throat. His coughing burbled red. Clutching uselessly at his ruined neck, he fell.

They'd be up again soon, but for now, she was alone.

Shakana drew upon her ear-phial's spell, reaching for Lorai. 'How do I destroy the furnace?'

Only stuttered noise came through from the aelf's side. 'New flesh… Chosen to be perfect… That is how he is reborn… Ghyranis… Destroy it, and–'

Frantic screams, distorted cursing, a sudden sucking rush like the sea roaring through tidal caves. Then silence.

'Thanks, that's helpful,' Shakana muttered to no one. The cooks were climbing back to their feet again. Their iron masks were bent out of shape, their pale flesh streaked with blood and brain matter, but they'd never surrender.

They wouldn't be stupid enough to try exchanging fire with her again, either. The next time, they'd swarm her.

This isn't working. Her crossbow had gathered its magic once more. Rather than discharging its blast into the cooks, Shakana aimed it at the ceiling and pulled the trigger.

Dripping papier mâché and golden rods exploded in a mingled blast of steam and smoke. Slamming her crossbow back into its harness, Shakana clambered desperately up the pipes that fed into the golden engine. Even through her gauntlets, her hands blistered, and pain screamed up her forearms, but she only pulled harder in response. *The fastest way out is through.*

Barbed bolts hissed past her head and bit at her ears. One splintered against her eagle-headed pauldron, stinging her cheek with shrapnel. Shakana grabbed the highest cross-pipe and swung hard, clenching her abdominal muscles and kicking up at the top of her arc. Her feet punched through the hole she'd shot in the parchment ceiling, and she vaulted through onto the gold-ribbed roof. Behind her, iron-masked cooks climbed the pipes and clawed at her ankles, snarling in rage and pain. She smelled their skin frying against the heated gold, just as hers had.

A bolt found a weak point in her armour and lodged in the elbow joint, nicking the arm beneath. Shakana grunted, but retreated no further.

She fumbled her crossbow out again. Ignoring the bolts that whistled past her and the cooks that had nearly reached her position, Shakana waited a patient, torturous three seconds for the typhoon crossbow to finish gathering Sigmar's blessed power.

Another bolt jolted against her collarbone, missing her throat by inches. She absorbed the hit, rocking back on the roof but doing all she could to hold her aim steady.

Destructive fury gathered in her crossbow's channel. It coalesced into a thunderbolt, blue and gold and blinding bright.

Shakana took aim, and fired down through the hole at the golden engine.

Lightning engulfed the churning machine and all the tubes that fed into its unholy maw. For an instant its sigils burned with daemonic rage, searing red and visceral purple against gold.

Then it exploded.

Shakana fell prone on the rooftop, knocked out of her sniper's crouch by the blast. She sprawled wide and clutched at the rafters to keep from tumbling through.

Pelokoa's under-cooks were obliterated by the engine's demise. Superheated metal fragments ripped through the room, tearing them apart. Droplets of molten gold rained over their dying bodies, pitting black craters in their flesh.

The Aqua Ghyranis that had brought them back from death's

edge so many times escaped through the hole in a plume of green steam. Nothing saved them now. They died, and did not rise again.

The glowing strands of magic binding the pieces of the corpse in the pool faded with the engine's destruction. No longer bound by Pelokoa's spell, and no longer renewed by the foul slurry, the submerged limbs slumped away from one another.

It was an infinitesimally small shift, but to Shakana's eye, it was everything. Even before the dead engine coughed a last clotted belch of pulverised meat into the pool, and the pink sludge still drifting through the water covered the corpse pieces in fleshy silt, she knew the truth.

'Kill him,' Shakana murmured into her ear-phial, as she pushed back up to her knees and tightened the crossbow's arms once more. 'The glutton's engine is destroyed. Pelokoa will die.'

No reply came. Again, Shakana hadn't expected one. It was just as well; she was too exhausted to talk.

She'd survived.

Alone on the rooftop, witnessed by no one, Shakana gave herself the luxury of relief. She closed her eyes and let her head drop to her chest, making a silent sign of gratitude with her free hand. By the God-King's mercy and protection, she had cheated death once more.

Then, slowly, and yet all too soon, she opened her eyes, lifted her head, and shifted her position. Shakana brought her crossbow around to face the other direction, crouching with her back to the hole she'd climbed through and her elbows braced against the uneven roof. Up here, she had a limited but clear view of Pelokoa's feast.

The fight wasn't over. The Blacktalons hadn't brought down their quarry.

Death would claim more souls today, and hers might yet be one.

* * *

Kill him.

The words registered dimly. Neave was struggling just to stay on her feet. Pelokoa had battered her armour and lacerated her flesh, and her strength was leaking into the grass with her blood. Secure in the knowledge that he had the upper hand, the glutton was toying with her, baiting her for the crowd's baying mirth.

Step by step, he pushed her down the hillside, away from the feast tents and towards the cookfires at the bottom of the slope. His intentions were clear: he meant to end this fight by roasting and devouring her alive, just as he'd promised his followers.

Neave tried to circle to the right. Pelokoa cut her off, his too-wide mouth spreading past the porcelain mask in a ghastly grin. The edges of his smile split almost to his ears, showing sharp yellowy-grey teeth, as he forced her back with sweeps of his bladed staff.

Neave's injured leg buckled, and the unpleasantly sensual warmth that spread through the poisoned flesh grew stronger, as if sensing and preying upon her weakness. Sigmar's burst of resolve was a fading memory, though she strove to cling to it.

'Give in,' he crooned, slowing the staff and lifting it in a beckoning gesture. 'Embrace the lovely pain.'

Neave hurled both axes straight at Pelokoa's face.

He hadn't been expecting that. Few did, unless they were familiar with Neave's fighting style. The risk of being disarmed against a lethal opponent was too great; no ordinary combatant would take the chance.

But Neave was fast enough to chase her axes through the air.

Pelokoa swung his head to the left with blurring speed, dodging one axe. The other struck his temple, cracking the porcelain mask. Blood and ichor spurted through the broken curls in a gout of crimson and clotted, bilious green.

He bellowed and ripped the ruined mask from his face. Behind it, his face was a mockery of the smiling porcelain youth's. Once he had been beautiful, but decadence had ravaged that beauty. His skin had the sickly cast of the wine-soaked and smoke-pickled; his flesh sagged heavily from too many rich meals. An unhealthy yellow tint stained the whites of his eyes.

Neave registered all of this in a split-second blur as she rushed towards him. Before Pelokoa's mask was past his chin, she'd leapt up to grab her axes out of the air. As she fell back, she smashed an elbow into his mouth.

His head snapped back, and he roared again, fear mingling with the fury in his voice. Her heavy plate had gouged his cheek down to the bone, and the disfigurement seemed to enrage him more than the pain. Pelokoa grabbed Neave by the upper arm, stopping the swing that would have cut his throat. Chest heaving with exertion, he hurled her back to the ground.

She hit the hillside hard. Sparks flashed across her sight and blood filled her mouth. She'd bitten her tongue, or maybe the inside of her cheek. Hard to tell, and not important.

What mattered was that his wound hadn't healed. Everything else Neave had done to him had healed within seconds. The gash on his cheekbone hadn't.

Shakana was right. The Hedonite could die.

If I can kill him.

Pelokoa thundered down after her, shaking the earth with each step. Neave rolled away from him, partly because it was faster than trying to get up, but mostly because she wasn't sure she had the strength left to stand. She'd thrown everything she had into that lunge, and it hadn't worked.

Still somewhat dazed from the impact, Neave pulled her arms in tight and twisted her torso to gain momentum, rattling down the hillside as swiftly as she could. Her axes, clanging against her armour, threw a trail of lightning and blackened earth in her wake.

Pelokoa followed, unhurried and inexorable. The glutton was so tall and massive that he had to slow as he descended the steep hill, lest he lose his balance and fall. He couldn't rush down the slope as Neave had, and it gave her the barest glimmer of an opening.

Exhaustion had claimed her speed. He'd stopped her before, when she was stronger, and she couldn't hope to rush him again. But if she couldn't rely on swiftness to get past his reach, what chance did she have?

Sigmar, grant me fortune.

She needed Pelokoa to make a mistake, or else she needed a divine stroke of luck. Otherwise…

Neave rolled into the midst of the cookfires, clanging to a stop at the bottom of the hill. Servants scattered at her approach, abandoning their spits and pots.

The spits…

Neave heaved herself upright. Her head swam and her knees buckled, but she staggered to the nearest fire and seized one of the skewers threaded with squirming Nurglings. The hot, grease-smeared metal was scalding through her gauntlets, but she only crushed her fingers tighter into the pain.

Pivoting at the hip, Neave swung the skewer full force at Pelokoa. Shrieking Nurglings, their little bodies crispy and blistered, flew off the end and spattered against the glutton's body.

Half a dozen burst into boiling, reeking slime on impact. Two or three survived, only partly crushed. They wailed and gibbered, digging their filthy little claws into Pelokoa as they tried to find purchase on his body.

He swatted them away, his face contorted with disgust. Boils and oozing pustules bloomed on his flesh where the Nurglings touched him. Swollen discolourations flushed through his veins and stretched into painful-looking abscesses.

Like the wound she'd smashed into his face, these didn't heal.

Pelokoa's small yellow eyes were filled with terror, but he bared his teeth in a grimace that strained to be a smile. 'Did you mean to kill me with dinner, little Stormcast?'

'Seemed fitting,' Neave answered through gritted teeth. 'Isn't that usually how gluttons go?'

'Not I,' Pelokoa said, forcing a laugh. It broke into a wheeze as buboes climbed up his neck and burst, spattering his velvet cloak with gobs of filth. His lip quivered in petulant denial as he reached up to wipe the pus away. 'I, favoured of the Great Prince and blessed by their own lips, need not fear–'

He stopped suddenly, looking stricken as he gazed at his hand. The graceful symmetry and flawless skin were crumbling rapidly as the Nurglings' contagion consumed him. Strange knots deformed the bone. Curdled yellow tumours swelled into the spaces between his fingers, gnarling them into a useless fist.

On the far side of the hill, half hidden by the curve of the grassy slope, smoke and green steam blew from a rupture in the roof of a vast hide tent. Neave didn't know what it was, but Pelokoa stared at it as if someone were eviscerating his only child in front of him.

She seized on his distraction. The glutton was rotting before her eyes as Nurgle's contagions spread through his body unchecked, but that seemed to only make him more dangerous. The Plaguefather didn't always kill with his diseases, especially when they took root in more powerful victims; his plagues were meant to be shared, and often turned their bearers into juggernauts of blight.

The Blacktalons couldn't allow that to happen. Praying to Sigmar for accuracy, Neave threw her axes one last time.

The blades hit Pelokoa's unguarded neck, one after the other, cleaving through artery and bone. His head tipped drunkenly sideways, severed but for a thin flap of skin at one side.

It bounced against his shoulder. Then he fell, and it bounced against the ground.

CHAPTER THIRTEEN

With Pelokoa dead, the remaining revellers at his Travelling Feast fell into a panic. The Blacktalons killed a few, but neither the servants nor the guests stayed to fight. They fled, and Neave let them go.

'Pelokoa the Undying, the Ever-Eater, the Prince of Untarnished Perfection,' Lorai read aloud from the scraps of burning parchment that fluttered from the ruins of the glutton's pavilion. She plucked one and watched it burn between her bluish fingers. 'No more. His engine of renewal is shattered. He will not be reborn again.'

'Good. Then we're done here.' Neave's wounds still pained her, none worse than the poisoned gash in her leg. Its false warmth had faded, leaving only the hot, throbbing agony of spreading sickness. She sat on the ground and unbuckled her plate mail, then reached for a bottle of blessed unguents she'd brought from Azyr. The fragrant, silvery ointment healed her wound, and soon the pain faded as the blessed enchantments drove the poisons from her flesh.

'Perhaps not yet.' Lorai let the last scrap flutter away into the air, burning to nothingness. The Idoneth's eerie eyes, rings of grey and blue with a crimson centre, seemed to glow over her shimmering veil. 'I wish to study his theatre.'

'The place with all the jellied heads?' Shakana's nose wrinkled in disgust. Residual lightning flickered around her crossbow, leaping from its harness to dance about her armour. 'What's worth studying there?'

'It is more than a macabre feast, and more than Pelokoa's final gloating victory over his victims, though it is those things as well.' Magic blossomed between Lorai's hands in a ghostly waterfall that stretched and smoothed into a pane of undulating water. Its surface reflected an illusory image of the Sigmarite scholar who had been captured in the Blind Queen's Maze and borne here by Pelokoa's servants. 'Why did he take this one? What did he hope to learn from her? The answer will be in that theatre, somewhere. I believe it would be to your benefit to find it.'

Neave stood and tested her strength, flexing her knee and lifting her other foot slightly off the ground so all her weight was on the newly healed leg. It felt as sure as ever, though she needed a few seconds to recover from the expectation of pain, even after the wound itself was gone. 'If you think it's important, we'll look.'

'I should hope it's important,' Shakana grumbled, as she led them towards the sprawling tent on the far side of the hill. 'I would not choose to go back to that place otherwise.'

A few fleeing stragglers were still running from its door, but already the tent had the air of a place abandoned. The chalk-white faces painted on its hide walls fluttered in the breeze, their red mouths and empty black-smudge eyes somehow all the more monstrous for their childish simplicity.

Inside the tent, the air was heavy with the metallic odour of freshly spilled blood. Without a word, Shakana guided the Blacktalons through Pelokoa's slaughtering grounds. She stalked between enormous drums of congealing liquid and the twitching bodies of the recently dead, distaste bristling across every line of her body.

Next came a butchery filled with hanging corpses, bloodless and partially eviscerated. Some had been prepared for the spits; others dangled from ankle hooks. Shakana barely glanced at them, but she shook her head in quiet disgust as she and Neave walked past the carcasses. 'This was his meat. All these people. And they *wanted* to die for him, Neave. I watched them give themselves happily to the knives. He made them do that. It wasn't enough to kill them, or even to eat them. He had to make them want it, too. Pelokoa was a true monster.'

'He was,' Neave agreed. 'But thanks to you, he's dead.'

'Thanks to us,' Shakana corrected her, but the compliment earned a slight smile from the sniper.

Past the butchery, Shakana led them to the theatre of which Lorai had spoken. Here, concentric rings of jellied heads greeted Neave with vacant, half-eaten smiles. A stage stood at the centre of the rings, with curtains of tanned and embossed human skin folded at either side. Beneath the curtains, wooden boxes held piles of puppets with blank leather faces. Hanging lanterns filled with half-melted candles dangled overhead, emitting a faint, sour smell of boiled meat gone bad.

Lorai stopped beside one of the heads. It looked fresher than the rest, its fluted aspic casing unbroken. The head inside the broth-coloured jelly was sagged and wrinkled, as though the skin hung loose over a skull several sizes too small. Its eyes and mouth were ringed with black stains that Neave initially took for kohl, until she moved closer and saw that they were charred from the inside out.

'I recognise that one. That's the sorcerer they captured from the Blind Queen's Maze,' Rostus said. 'The one they kept with the scholar, but never bothered questioning.'

'I wish to see why they took him,' Lorai said. 'Why add his head to this collection, when they scarcely spoke to him while he lived?' The aelf paused for a moment, and when none of the Blacktalons voiced any objection, she thrust a forefinger into the aspic covering the sorcerer's gaping mouth. Deft as a fishwife gutting a trout, she hooked a glob of jelly within the mouth and pulled it out.

The head coughed, gagged and spat out more aspic. Its eyes rolled towards them, focusing slowly, and blinked unevenly through the jelly. A coruscating silver spark ignited somewhere deep behind its gaze, whirling more quickly as the head awakened. 'You are... Stormcast Eternals,' it said, in a thick, distorted voice that couldn't disguise its surprise.

'I always knew Gerispryx picked her pets on the basis of intelligence,' Rostus rumbled.

'You retain the knowledge you had in life,' Lorai observed. It was almost a question.

The sorcerer seemed to take it as such. 'Yes. Pelokoa himself came to gloat at me when they took my head for his pots. He felt I should be honoured to take part in a greater magic than any my mistress had managed. He promised that I would be part of the next performance in the Theatre of Flesh, though not the star. No, that privilege was reserved for Brother Kyrivus, stormreader of Astrapis... or at least as much of him as the glutton managed to capture.' The dead face's lips peeled back in a laugh that came out as a choked splutter of jelly.

'What is the Theatre of Flesh?' Neave asked.

'Why, you're in it.' The head's smile widened. It had no teeth or tongue, only that same silver glow behind its burned lips. 'Pelokoa's little effort at divining the future. Less barbaric than the Great Flayer's, I suppose, and somewhat better at ascertaining information about things in its very limited purview, but oh how limited that purview is. He can't see anything that was unknown to his little puppets, you see. His knowledge is limited to theirs. Fittingly for a glutton, all he can do is scavenge from their bones. *Our* bones, I should say.'

'What did he hope to learn from yours?'

The dead sorcerer laughed again. It was weaker this time, as if whatever magic enabled the head to speak was beginning to fail. The silver glow in its throat sank back, suffocating under the jelly's weight. 'Am I Pelokoa? I can't tell you that. Feast on my flesh yourself, if you want to find the answers he sought. His cooks brought them out in their boiling. They seasoned me with sorceries, and one who eats me will know what I knew. Try a taste. Swallow all the secrets you can stomach.'

'I will not do that,' Neave said firmly, keeping a tight rein on her disgust.

'Then you don't want your answers badly enough,' the head said smugly. Its mouth had gone dark, and the silver light in its eyes was fading to a midnight glimmer. 'But you might, if you like, light the candles in the Theatre of Flesh and see what that shows you.'

The silver light died, and the head went silent. Lorai pushed the aspic back into place over its lips, sealing it up again. 'The magic that allows the spirit to speak will regenerate in time as the jelly restores the flesh, but likely not soon enough for us to question it again.'

'Fine.' Neave glanced at the stage, dark and still, beneath its gloomy soot-stained lanterns and red-stained leather curtains. 'Was the head only taunting us, or is there real magic in that stage?'

'There is magic,' Lorai said. The chimes on her staff jingled softly as she shifted her weight, the only outward sign of the Idoneth's doubts. Her face remained smooth and secretive as a windless sea. 'It was not only a taunt.'

'Then I'll light the candles,' Neave said. She didn't trust the sorcerer's head, but she did trust its malice. Any sorcerer sworn to Gerispryx would have been both proud and deeply malevolent. Neave had no doubt that such a creature would bitterly resent being defeated and kept as a humiliating trophy by Pelokoa, and would strike back at the glutton as best it could, even after death. If it could burnish its own self-importance by puffing up the value of the secrets it held, and tempt Sigmar's holy servants into activating a Chaos spell out of desire to learn those secrets, so much the better.

She also didn't doubt that the head harboured equal malice against the Blacktalons, but under the circumstances, that was a risk she was willing to take.

An ugly, smoky yellow light bloomed from the candles as Neave lit them, spreading across the stage like dirty oil over water. Under its gaze, beauty drained away. Faces took on a sickly tint. A brownish-yellow stain tainted the Blacktalons' teeth and the whites of their eyes. Their shining armour dulled to muddy yellows and greys, while every crease and scar in their skin was underscored by harsh shadow.

Under the stage lanterns, the jellied heads were monstrous, pathetic things, as helplessly hideous as misshapen calves pickled in embalmers' jars. At the light's edges, where the leather curtains caught and pooled darkness within their folds, the shadows rose into slender figures with bulbous heads. They reached for the stage with imploring hands and incoherent mutterings, like beggars tugging at a passing merchant's robe.

The jellied heads' eyes snapped open in unison. Their jaws, if they still had any, chattered against the aspic. Smaller shadows dribbled from their neck stumps, stretching out into twisted semblances of the statures they'd had in life.

'How do we determine what it shows us?' Neave asked.

'I do not believe we can,' Lorai replied, 'at least not by any art I know. What it shows will be what Pelokoa chose.'

Neave nodded, crouching amid the heads as she turned her eyes to the stage. If any enemy came, she'd be ready.

The lanterns' light changed, softening to a diffuse red in one place, brightening to sharp pricks of white and yellow elsewhere. The stage faded from view, and in its stead came the illusion of a laboratory overlooking a mountainside scoured with windblown cinders and ash-black snow.

Two puppets rose out of the wooden boxes. They staggered onto the stage with drunk, lolloping steps. As they moved into the lanterns' reach, the lights painted faces onto their blank leather heads, and their shapeless sack bodies took on artificial definition.

Now the puppets appeared to be two human men, both in their middle years. They wore medallions depicting Sigmar's hammer and twin-tailed comet around their necks, and their robes were made of chainmail, soaked with blood from the ankles down. Their faces were set in hard lines, as if the younger of the two had never smiled, and the older had forgotten how.

Ignoring the crimson that puddled about their feet, the puppet-men gazed at a large round lens mounted on an unfamiliar instrument in the laboratory. In its view whirled a maelstrom of darkness spiked with agitated flares of lightning. Blood-red sigils poured across the lens in vertical scrolls, backed against blackness except when lightning ruptured the boiling sky.

'Only the pure may be spared,' the younger one said. He laughed, and blood began to run from between his teeth. It flowed into his beard, staining his armoured chest, yet neither puppet seemed to notice. 'Only the pure may survive. The unworthy must be struck down, lest they contaminate us with their sins and open the way to Chaos. Such is the word of Sigmar. Such is the truth in his scrolls.'

'This is cruelty, not righteousness,' the other puppet-man said. 'Not justice. This is not the Lord of Lightning's way.' His eyes widened in sudden fear, and he backed away from his younger companion.

With each retreating step he took, his eyes sank deeper into his head, until only empty black sockets were left. These ignited with silver fire that began to burn away his face from the inside out.

'By Sigmar's own hand is it written. Bow your head to the truth, or lose it.' Small horns had begun to sprout from the bloody-mouthed puppet's head. His eyes were wet and red, and when he blinked, there were no whites or pupils. Only raw crimson meat, and blood that trickled down his cheeks like tears.

The other puppet howled, a terrible mournful sound, and then sprang at his former companion with teeth bared. Silver fangs stretched out of his jaw, closing around the bloody-faced man's throat, and the two of them fell to the ground, punching and kicking and biting in a clatter of wooden limbs and thudding leather. Their painted medallions crashed into each other and cracked as if they'd been made of glass, not solid steel. A fissure ran up the heart of each comet, splitting the holy sign into the same defaced form Neave had seen on the Great Flayer's skins and in the visions of the Blind Queen's Maze.

The sound of the puppets slamming against one another was overlaid with illusory sounds of ripping flesh and agonised cries. The lanterns swayed, and their lights made the puppets' bodies writhe and mutate as they rolled together. One turned into a nightmare of weeping muscle and sinew; the other was consumed from within by spirals of fractal silver light.

Brother against brother, the puppet-men tore each other apart, and where their blood fell, daemons sprang up from the stone.

In the window above them, the storm raged harder. Lightning stabbed down from the black sky into a different realm each time: the green hills of Ghyran, a herd of bewildered auroch in Ghur, Aqshy's blazing plains, its soot-capped peaks. Again and again, wild lightning fissured across the realms, unleashing terrible, random devastation on innocent souls.

And in the scars of that lightning, the terror of Chaos arose. Blood and skulls fountained from the ruptured earth. Wounded mortals wept and wailed over the bodies of their dead. Once pristine rivers, now choked with corpses, turned to stinking soups of putrefied flesh and bone, and plagues bloomed unchecked across their shores.

There was no one to stand against the tide. No one to fight the teeming horde.

Lightning speared down over the great fortresses of Azyr, and no one stood on their battlements. Sigmar's cathedrals stood empty, their pews abandoned and their windows dark. Cold wind whistled through their towers.

Their inhabitants had killed each other. Neave knew this without having seen it. It was in the gloating sway of the theatre's lanterns, and in the bleak malevolence of the shadows that filled the vacant halls. The Sigmarites who should have defended those temples, who should have defended the *faith*, had slaughtered each other as the puppet-men had, leaving their realms and their followers unguarded.

Chaos had consumed the Cults Unberogen and those who depended on it, and there was no one left to mourn. No one left to pray over the graves, or beseech Sigmar to hold their souls close.

Perhaps the God-King wasn't even there to listen. Perhaps he was gone too.

No. It was impossible. Yet the visions of those hollow prayer halls, and that cold grey loss of faith, hurt Neave as badly as the scenes of bloody devastation. Maybe worse.

This wasn't a fight. This was what came when the last gasp of fighting spirit was gone. This was the death of hope.

Sigmar is gone from these realms.

Neave had not said the words aloud, yet the jellied heads quivered and clacked their spinal stumps against their dishes in excitement.

'Sigmar is gone from these realms,' the other puppets whispered from their boxes in a faceless chorus. The curtains echoed their words in leathery rustles. *'Sigmar is gone from these realms.'*

'So it is written,' one of the puppet-men croaked from the stage. He still wore his chainmail, and his hammer amulet, but beyond that he was a bloody, blasted ruin. His lips dangled loose from his teeth. One eye was gone. The other bobbed from a red string. 'So it shall be. The secret is in the scrolls. The promise. Sigmar will be gone from these realms.'

The shadows murmured and hissed their agreement, echoing the vision's promise. As the lanterns burned low, their enchanted lights shrank away from one another, and the illusion they'd created in concert vanished.

The ragged puppets stood, blank and faceless once again. Side by side, they executed jerky bows, then staggered back to their boxes, where they collapsed in heaps of wood and leather.

Darkness swallowed the stage.

'It can't be true,' Shakana whispered hoarsely. Tears stood bright in the sniper's eyes. She wiped them away with quick, angry flicks of a dark finger, banishing them before they could fall.

Neave swallowed. She wondered if her own face looked as stricken as her companions'. Hendrick's was nearly as ashen as his beard, and Rostus showed no trace of his usual jovial cheer. Only Lorai, utterly inhuman, was unaffected.

The vision of the Mortal Realms in desolation, stripped of Sigmar's faith and strength, had shaken them all. Even knowing that Pelokoa's theatre was nothing but spite animated by magic and artifice, Neave found it difficult to let go of the dread that chilled her.

How could humanity survive without hope? How could *she*? It would be like trying to live without the warmth of a beating heart, without friendship or fellowship or purpose. Without anything that made life worthwhile.

'No,' Neave said, setting her jaw. 'Not while the Blacktalons stand.'

CHAPTER FOURTEEN

'They keep showing us the same vision,' Neave said quietly to Hendrick, when the others were out of earshot. 'Sigmar being… driven from the Mortal Realms.' *Not slain*. She wouldn't say that word aloud. 'Leaving us.'

They were sitting by a small fire in a lonely part of Pelokoa's garden, near a steep, spiralling path that climbed down the great stone pillar and led back to Ghyran's wilderness. Either the glutton's magic had faded with his death, or he'd never cared to make it as easy for his guests to leave as it was for them to arrive. The Blacktalons had been unable to find any magical gateway that led back down the pillar, and were resigned to climbing down the treacherous cascade path.

Not just yet, though. They had to wait for Lorai to finish collecting her complement of mortal souls first. With merciless efficiency, the Idoneth hunted down the stragglers from Pelokoa's feast, slaying mortal cultists as they cowered amid the gardens and streams. At the earliest opportunity, she would return to her people to bestow her bounty.

When she couldn't physically distance herself from Lorai's work, Neave often sought out Hendrick's company. He'd led the Blacktalons before her, and he knew her better than the rest.

He knew Sigmar better, too. As the one who communed directly with the God-King, he had experienced revelations that none of the rest of them could begin to imagine.

So when Neave needed reassurance that the Blacktalons were truly serving Sigmar's interests by permitting Lorai to take her souls, it was to the Old Wolf that she turned.

And when she was afraid, as she was now, it was to him that she looked for wisdom and calm. Neave couldn't confess her fears or doubts to the others. But with Hendrick, she never had to. He knew her well enough to understand what wasn't said.

'They show it to us to weaken us. Lies and fears are their weapons, deadlier than claw or sword,' Hendrick said. He was sharpening his weapons, as he often did, and the rhythmic scrape of steel on stone filled the silences of his thoughts.

It was a comforting sound, Neave thought. Each stroke of the whetstone repeated the promise that the Old Wolf would be there for her in the next fight, and the one after, and the one after. *Sharp blades make good friends.* He'd taught her that, as he'd taught her so many things.

He looked up at her, raising grizzled eyebrows. 'It's to be expected that our enemies would repeat that vision. What greater fear can there be, for a Stormcast Eternal, than the prospect of infinite loss? Without the God-King, we're dust. His wisdom sustains us. His purpose sustains us. We endure what we endure because we believe in his cause, and because we know the justness of his faith. If you take that away, we're nothing. They know that. So they attack the obvious weakness.'

'But they *believe* it,' Neave said. 'They think it's something they can find. "The secret is in the scrolls," that's what Pelokoa's puppet said on the stage. That's what his servants pressed the scholar for, as well. "The key is in the cathedral. The key is in the scrolls." They wanted her to find a thing, some concrete *thing*, on a map.

'Pelokoa didn't design that puppet play for us. It wasn't meant to be a threat, or a taunt. He intended to watch it himself. It was meant to be a divination.' She took a deep breath, pressing her hands against her thighs. The holy symbols on her sigmarite plate glinted in the firelight, and Neave ran her fingers over them, taking solace in their solidity. When everything else was gone from her, every memory and shred of identity, this would be all that was left.

Faith. Duty. The reason the Stormcasts drew breath. She couldn't lose that.

Neave didn't remember who she'd been in mortal life. For the others, that memory could be a mixed blessing. Rostus was forever tormented by his failures as a mortal, and the family he'd lost because of those failures. Nothing he'd suffered as a Stormcast could compare.

But for Neave, there wasn't even the bittersweet comfort of being able to remember what she'd once loved and lost. Her existence as a Stormcast was the only one she had.

And if she was going to justify that existence, and the trust that Sigmar had placed in her, she had to be honest about what the Blacktalons faced.

'I think it's real, Hendrick. These aren't just the taunts of the enemy. I think these scrolls are some actual physical artefact the agents of Chaos are after, and if they get them, they can make these visions come true. I think our task is to kill the ones who are capable of finding and using that artefact, and if we fail, it might… It might result in Sigmar's faith being shattered. Brother against brother, believer against believer, just as the theatre showed. And Chaos, conquering the Mortal Realms, once Sigmar's no longer there to stand against its onslaught.'

She felt better once she'd said it. The thought still filled her with dread, but at least that fear was no longer hers alone. It had been named, and it had been shared.

Hendrick's whetstone paused. He glanced over again, his weathered face made even more rugged by the firelight. There was a measuring glint in his eye, and a grim approval in his tone. For her conclusions, Neave guessed, but also for her courage.

'I can't say you're wrong,' he said.

It wasn't what she'd hoped to hear, but honesty mattered more than comfort.

Neave nodded, and stood. 'I'll tell Lorai. No more time for soul-taking. We need her to find our next target.'

The Blacktalons seldom interrogated prisoners, for it was difficult to extricate the truth from the maze of lies and twisted desires that Chaos warped into mortal minds. Ordinary questioning was of little use on such captives, and the Blacktalons rarely had suitable magic at their disposal. Lorai's spells, though both powerful and subtle, were ill-suited to that task.

Harvesting souls sometimes gleaned a few glimpses of what her victims were thinking as they died, and occasionally Lorai could sift through those fragments to find something useful. Among the revellers of the Travelling Feast, however, she found only frustrated desires. They died dreaming of meals they hadn't eaten and captives they hadn't despoiled, and nothing in their souls was worth knowing.

The Soulscryer, however, had other tools at her disposal.

From a velvet-lined protective case, Lorai drew out an oyster shell as large as a halved melon. The exterior was barnacled and rough, the interior a smooth, irregular bowl of pale mother-of-pearl.

After filling her cyfar compass with water, Lorai sat cross-legged beside it, gazing into the green-and-blue iridescence. Shapes and shadows drifted through the water like phantom minnows, but they meant nothing to Neave. She hadn't the arcane sensitivity to follow whatever Lorai read in the water.

'Who's she looking for?' Rostus asked as he took a seat on the grass beside Neave, eschewing the soiled cushions that had spilled from Pelokoa's trampled pavilions.

'The source of the head-seed she found in the Blind Queen's Maze,' Neave replied. 'Whoever, or whatever, created those tribal warriors with the red leaves sprouting from their scalps and seeds inside their skulls. Our next target.'

'Ah. I'd forgotten. At least, I'd hoped to forget. We encounter too many ugly things in our duties. I don't miss those when Sigmar's anvil takes them from me. I wish it took them every time.' Rostus picked up a fallen guard's hammer and tossed it idly up the hill. It shattered a wine jug painted with grotesque figures, and he grunted in satisfaction.

'Do you really?' Neave asked.

Rostus started to say something flippant, and then saw her seriousness. He shrugged, perhaps a bit sheepishly. 'No, but also yes. It's important to remember one's enemies, both so that we aren't endlessly learning the same hard lessons from our battles, and so that we can take confidence in knowing we've faced worse things and won before. I don't, really, want to forget all that. Bad enough that I forget what I already have, and burden the rest of you with remembering it for me. Besides, you always get the stories wrong. No one ever remembers to give me proper credit for all the heroic deeds I've done.

'But it's also true that I don't care to remember every detail of every horror we've seen, and I'm not sorry when Sigmar chooses those memories for me to lose upon Reforging. I can always find more horrors to fill my head. I can't always find more friends.'

Neave didn't know what to say to that. She clasped Rostus' forearm with a gauntleted hand, and though the touch was only metal to metal, it carried the warmth of friendship.

'Ah, go on.' The bald Stormcast patted her hand once, awkwardly, and then tipped his chin towards the Idoneth. 'Looks like Lorai's found what she was looking for.'

'I have.' Lorai lifted her head from the cyfar compass. Enchanted light radiated from the water, blanching the aelf's face into an aquamarine pallor, and casting her eyes into deep gloom. 'I have traced its servants to its soul. It is an extraordinary thing. Seldom have I sensed a soul of such age and power. Its followers call it the Red-Seed God, and that is nearly true. Its enemies call it the Red Tree, and that is barely false.

'It is an ancient creature. Once it was an arboreal being, a tree in form but not in nature, blessed with a fragment of life-magic that gave it a deep sentience. Its life was slow and patient, and though it was only dimly aware of the warm-blooded creatures that scuttled above its roots and beneath its boughs, it bore them no ill will. The local humans venerated it as a protective spirit, for its power kept Nurgle's plagues at bay, and created a precious sanctuary for their tribe during the dark years of Alarielle's absence from her realm.

'In gratitude, its people brought it gifts. They hung feathers and crystals from its limbs. During droughts, they brought it water. As it grew older, they buried compost around its roots to feed it, and treasures to honour it. Centuries passed, and the Red Tree's tribe flourished, even as their world grew crueller. Generation to generation, they taught their children to serve and protect their god, for only by its blessing did they survive.

'Their devotion proved their undoing. A hero of the tribe captured a golden casket set with rubies and strange dark stones that swirled with their own secret stars. With great pomp, the tribe buried this offering at the base of the Red Tree.

'In that casket was an artefact of Chaos. I do not know precisely what it was, but from it flowed a taint so powerful and malevolent that, over time, even the Red Tree succumbed. Its intelligence bent towards evil, and with the same patient strength that had once made it a bulwark against Nurgle, it began manipulating its human followers to monstrous ends.

'Now the Red Tree radiates naught but hate. It holds the scuttling warmbloods in contempt, and loathes them for their weakness and dependence, even as it twists them to serve its wishes. I do not know why it has chosen to involve itself in this matter, but I can feel nothing but malevolence in its soul. Perhaps that is reason enough.'

Silence followed this recitation. The light in the cyfar compass died. Carefully, Lorai unfolded her legs and emptied the bowl, pouring its water back into a babbling creek.

'Do you know where to find it?' Hendrick asked.

'Yes. It will be difficult not to know, when we are close. The children of the Red-Seed God form a forest and an army around it. Their presence is… considerable.'

A silence fell over the Blacktalons. Shakana's star-eagle stamped its talons and ruffled its wings, sensing the agitation that its mistress concealed. Hendrick tightened a strap of his gauntlets with a sharp jerk, unlike his usual calm deliberation. Neave gazed into the distance, looking at the tatters of Pelokoa's feasting pavilion and trying to comprehend the bizarre enormity of what Lorai had described. *A tree that wants to murder a god. A tree that thinks it* is *one.*

Rostus cleared his throat, deliberately breaking the tension. 'Don't believe we've ever killed a deity before.'

'No,' Neave agreed. 'But if that's Sigmar's charge, then that's what we'll do.'

* * *

Weary but determined, the Blacktalons climbed down the water-fall path from Pelokoa's secret sanctuary. Lorai and Shakana took the lead, with Neave close behind them.

She was tired, more tired than she'd been in a long time. Norm-ally the Blacktalons struck a single target and returned to Azyrheim to rest and replenish their energies before setting out on another mission. This time they'd been afforded no such respite. The Great Flayer, Gerispryx, Pelokoa, and now this Red Tree: one target after another, none of them easy, with no real recuperation between.

Neave was running close to the ragged edge of exhaustion, and so were her companions. It wasn't only physical fatigue she felt. It was the unrelenting tension of knowing what was at stake, and the pressure the Blacktalons were under. Each target they slew only increased the urgency of their task, as each death further cleared the way for the remaining Chaos agents to pursue the scrolls that they believed would bring down the Cults Unberogen.

As she had a thousand times before, Neave pushed her tiredness away. It didn't leave her. It wouldn't leave until she'd returned to Sigmar's sacred fastnesses and had a chance to truly rest.

But she could ignore it. The Blacktalons' duty was not finished.

We do not rest until we're done. We don't need rest until we're done.

Together, the Blacktalons raced across Ghyran.

Much of what they passed was nightmarish, and a nightmare that could easily swallow them if they ventured too close. Where Nurgle had claimed dominion over the Realm of Life, the land itself writhed in fevered pain.

The Blacktalons skirted around desolate swamps where slimy water, blistering with diseased bubbles, lapped at the trunks of dead trees gone white and spongy with fungus. The wind, caught by a hundred thousand tiny holes in the soft, swollen branches, sang a slow, clotted song through those swamps, and foul gases burbled up from the black water in answer.

Elsewhere, the Blacktalons ran beneath boughs contorted into agonised curls. Weeping scabs pocked the tortured trees' bark, and dripping chrysalises hung from their limbs like malformed fruit. The corpses of stricken caterpillars fermented in those hollow shells, ripening until they erupted in wet, deadly bursts. There must have been thousands hanging in that silent, lifeless wood, and Neave wondered whether they would explode into emptiness or wait for some living creature to approach. They didn't react to the Blacktalons in any case, and she lacked the luxury of time to ponder the mystery further.

Yet not everything in Ghyran was warped. In places, Alarielle's forces had pushed back against those of Nurgle, or had maintained precious sanctuaries amid the blight, and there the Blacktalons found wonder.

They saw hanging jungles where vines grew into natural nets and captured clouds to drink, sweeping grasslands where rainbow-coloured feathered lizards flew over wildflowers, and towering forests of trees so ancient and enormous that entire smaller wood-lands had sprung up from the dirt and water caught in their sprawling boughs. Some of these held forests in turn, creating living terraces that rose step by step into the sky.

Despite her exhaustion, Neave marvelled at these miracles, and the hope they renewed in her soul. Where Alarielle had reclaimed her domain from Nurgle's warping influence, the Realm of Life had a soothing loveliness that no other realm could approach. The air and water were rich with subtle floral notes; the earth underfoot was soft and welcoming, layered with untold centuries of loam. The winds sang in harmony across bladed leaves and whistling seedpods.

It spoke to the part of Neave that was still, in some sense, mortal. Whatever was left of her human heart felt an abiding peace in the pure green reaches of Ghyran. There was yet hope. There was a purpose to their fight.

She loved it, and yet it was a remote love, like a memory stirred by a faded portrait, or a wisp of perfume lingering on an old dress. Too much of her was different, now, for Ghyran to touch her as deeply as it might.

Still, Neave breathed more deeply as she ran through Ghyran's hills and vales, and its serenity lingered with her until the Blacktalons came to the Red Tree's territory.

On the hills ahead, the rich greens of Ghyran changed to a mottled red, as if some cursed autumn had come to the land and, rather than changing green leaves to copper and gold, had stained them all into shades of crimson. The forest looked like it had been soaked in a godbeast's arterial spray, and the breeze that passed through its trees was warm, damp, and scented with iron.

'There is no way to evade notice,' Lorai told them as they reached the crimson wood. 'The Red Tree and its children share one mind. What they perceive, it knows as well. We have no choice but to cut a path straight through.'

Neave nodded. With a few gestures she directed the Blacktalons into a tight formation: herself and Hendrick at the fore, Shakana and Lorai close behind them, Rostus at the back. Anda lifted into the air, rising until she was a tiny speck against the clouds. The leaves obscured the star-eagle's view and limited her utility, but even so, eyes in the sky were always an advantage. Victories had been built on less.

The Blacktalons plunged into the forest. The red trees closed around them. Beneath their papery-barked boughs the air was still and breathless, thick with a discomfiting humidity. The ground was spongy and oddly humped and covered with frothy pink moss that clung to it like parasitic fungus on a dying body.

No young shoots broke through that moss, and no decaying foliage lay beneath it. Not a single leaf seemed to have fallen from the crimson trees. Ghyran's natural cycles did not touch these woods, which pulsed with the slow subterranean beat of their own heart.

That was no mere metaphor. Neave paused and examined one of the trees. Bluish veins snaked along its knuckled twigs and spidered down its trunk. The wood was warm to her touch, like living flesh, and when she nicked it, the twig recoiled in pain. Red sap trickled from the cut.

She let it go, and the Blacktalons moved on, surrounded by an oppressive hush. There were no animals in this wood, and no plants except for the pale-barked red trees and pink moss. No birds sang from the branches; no velmice skittered through the moss. Neave never saw so much as an ant walk among the leaves.

As they ventured deeper, however, she began to see bones. Mostly human, a few animal. They lay scattered at the base of the trees, entangled in roots and half buried by moss. Almost all the skulls were broken, though occasionally Neave spotted one with a slender sapling rising from its eye socket. In time, she supposed, the tree would grow too large to be confined, and that skull would break like the others.

The trees were younger and smaller in this part of the wood. Perhaps the Red Tree had demarcated its borders early on and filled in the rest of the forest later. Or, perhaps, someone had attacked it and destroyed this swath, requiring the Red Tree to replant the area.

Whatever the cause, the Blacktalons began to see saplings rooted in fresher bodies. Human corpses slumped beside young trees that grew out of their decomposed heads.

Some reclined against the earth; others sat almost upright, resting against their trees as if the decapitated body wanted to enjoy a summer afternoon in the shade. The corpses were soft and shrivelled, more like bags of loose leather than human bodies. They gave off no smell of decay.

None bore any signs of violence, apart from their missing heads. They seemed to have walked into position, sat down, and waited docilely for death to take them.

Neave crouched beside one of the fresher bodies. It was that of a young woman, hands folded peacefully in her lap, dressed in what appeared to be a ceremonial robe of braided and layered leaves.

Like the others, her neck ended in a bloodless stump of skin puckered around the sunken stubs of her vertebrae. Her head rested on the ground about a foot away, slack-jawed and eyeless. A sapling grew out of it, rooted through the foramen magnum. The trunk sprouted through an eye socket. Red leaves stretched through the other eye socket, the nostrils, and the head's soft, wrinkled lips.

Intent on studying the head, and the sapling that twisted through it, Neave didn't pay much attention to the body.

The dead girl's clothing rippled. Something bulged in her abdomen, and then in the pale leather of her throat.

An iron-tough tree root lashed out of the neck stump like a striking snake, hurling itself against Neave's side. It screeched along her armour, digging a gouge in the sigmarite as it prised for any trace of weakness. When it found a gap between the plates, it plunged in, burying itself with a sudden, terrible strength that no humanoid opponent would have been able to muster for a blow at that angle.

Neave fell back, gasping out a cry that wouldn't come. She grabbed at the root, trying to pull it out, but she couldn't gain any purchase. Oily sap oozed from the root's pores, and her fingers slid away helplessly.

She couldn't budge it. She couldn't breathe. She could only bleed, and feel it dig deeper into her guts.

CHAPTER FIFTEEN

'Neave!'

Shakana. The sniper's voice was afire with fear, rage, and… something else, something raw and wounded. Jolted back to awareness by Shakana's cry, Neave clawed out of the shock that had begun to swallow her wits.

A barbed crossbow bolt plunged through the root that twisted into Neave's guts. It was solid wood and steel, not the holy lightning that Shakana usually fired.

Understanding immediately, Neave grabbed either side of the bolt and wrenched at the root. It fought her, lashing from side to side like a coil of solid muscle. Pain sent blurring shots of black and gold across her vision, and her hands slipped from the bloody quarrel.

Hendrick's axe swept down, severing the root at its base. Once cut, it convulsed a final time and went limp. Neave grabbed the bolt again and, gritting her teeth, pulled the root loose.

The pain was incredible. Even dead, the root's ridged bark sawed against bone and muscle as it came out. Every finger's breadth of blood-slimed plant Neave pulled out made the bile rise in her throat. The sight of it emerging from her body like an enormous, ghoulish worm was even more revolting than the pain.

When the last of its gnarled tip finally popped out, leaving her body with an awful sucking noise, Neave shuddered and hurled it away.

Then she grabbed her axes and forced herself to her feet, turning to face the new threats.

The Red Tree's children were upon them. Headless bodies rose to their feet, sprouting pale shoots and crimson leaves from their neck stumps as they staggered towards the Blacktalons. More tendrils erupted from their hands, filling their palms with fistfuls of hungry, wriggling roots.

A shining volley from Shakana's crossbow levelled the first wave of headless bodies. They went down smoking. More came behind them, and Neave met them with axes in hand. Her blood was up, and the surge of adrenaline almost drowned out her pain and disgust.

She whirled and spun among the tree-corpses, chopping off arms and splitting torsos with brutal efficiency. None of the wounds bled. Red leaves burst out of one chest wound like some grotesque street puppeteer's trick. Another corpse cracked open to reveal that its torso held nothing but a mould-speckled hollow between brittle wooden ribs.

None of them made any sound. They never cried out, never cursed or roared in battle rage. The only noise was the thud of the Blacktalons' weapons into plant-filled flesh, and the occasional muffled cry or snarl when one of them was hit.

Hendrick hacked into one of the Red Tree's pawns. His axe stuck on something inside, refusing to come free. He put his foot on the dead man's thigh and wrenched the weapon loose. It tore away in a clump of tough, fibrous root matter and sticky sap.

The man fell. An invisible wind seemed to sweep through the rest of the horde, rippling over the corpses' soft, loose skin and whatever hid inside. They stiffened and relaxed, and Neave had the sense that some unspoken understanding had passed between them.

She hewed into another, jerking it forwards with one axe so that she could use the other to cleave it open from shoulder to hip. Inside the hollow space of its torso she saw a knot of thick white fibres coated with viscous liquid. It was smaller than her fist, but expanded rapidly even in the time it took the body to fall.

'They're changing!' Neave shouted to the rest of the Blacktalons. 'Adapting! They're growing the root balls that trapped Hendrick's axe.'

'We can't cut through them all!' Rostus bellowed back. He swung again, bashing aside half a dozen headless bodies. Corpses fell before him, some broken, others trapped by the sticky residue that spilled from their crushed companions.

Neave moved faster, seeking to rip open a path through the Red Tree's pawns. It was like trying to cut a line through the sea, or swimming through a nightmare. Each stroke of her axes was slower than the last, as the headless bodies swelled with gummy fibres that bogged her down more heavily with each blow.

One of Neave's axes stuck in a woman's side, pulling the Stormcast off balance. The wizened corpse of a pot-bellied old man lunged at her unguarded flank. Roots erupted from his wrists, tearing open his tattooed arms. They slammed into Neave's armour, searching for an opening.

Again Shakana saved her. A blast of lightning from the sniper's crossbow threw the body, and its sharp-tipped roots, back in a scorched heap. Neave jerked her axe out of the corpse that had held it and continued her fight.

It was only a matter of time until they were overwhelmed. Early on, the Blacktalons had had the upper hand, but since the headless pawns had filled themselves with sap-sticky roots and turned into walking traps, the tide of battle had turned.

Though they were concealed by his sigmarite plate, Rostus could feel the raw spirals scored around both arms and a laceration across his scalp. Shakana was moving stiffly, with a pained hunch, and the right side of her armour dripped red. Neave could feel the mounting toll of her own wounds, hard as she tried to ignore them.

'We need to get out of this forest,' she grunted.

'We can't,' Shakana snapped back. 'Our target is here.'

'Ready your shot.' Lorai lifted her staff high, gathering the air's moisture into a visible stream of mist. It gathered around her in a thickening cloud, cool and briny in the humid wood.

At the edges of the misty current, the headless bodies shrank and stiffened as the water was drawn from their leathery skin-shells and the vegetal matter within. They dried to brown husks, their bones clacking with every movement like beads in a rattle. Lorai pulled the water from their bodies until she'd desiccated all the corpses in sight, and then gestured to Shakana. 'Fire.'

The sniper drew a bolt from the case behind her back. The tip was a fiery orange crystal alight with the magic of Aqshy; the shaft was tightly wrapped with a coil of parchment inked with holy prayers. It hissed steam as it cut through Lorai's mist cloud, and exploded in flame as it found its target deep within the mob.

Tinder-dry, the corpse went up in a pillar of fire. It burned without a sound, neither flailing nor struggling. The crinkled red leaves growing from its neck stump blew away like fiery kites, trailing their own sparkling streamers as the heat of the blaze lifted them into the air.

They struck other corpses, and those too burned. Soon the conflagration had swallowed the whole mute army.

Burning bodies lunged at the Blacktalons, trying to drag the

Stormcasts into the inferno, but their fists and steps faltered when they struck Lorai's mist. The Idoneth solidified fog into an extension of her ethersea, transforming ordinary air into a semi-solid barrier that held the corpses at bay long enough for each of them to be consumed. From the other side of a wall of hovering water, Neave watched the dried-out horrors burn.

Finally the last of them crumpled into ash and smouldering bone. With a twist of her staff, Lorai let her spell dissipate, suffocating the embers under a drift of salt mist that left the charred wreckage beaded with diamonds.

'We do not have much time,' Lorai told them. 'The Red Tree's strength has been diminished, but it will soon return. I doubt I will be able to drive its pawns back so easily again. Like an ordinary tree besieged by insects, it learns from our attacks and adapts its defences to defeat them.'

'Plenty of trees get killed by bugs before they find a trick that works,' Rostus said. He wiped blood from a gashed eyebrow, brushed sap-sticky leaves away from his cloak, and shouldered his massive hammer. He could feel that his arms were bruised beneath his armour and purpling with every movement, but he paid them no mind. 'Let's see that this is one of them.'

Neave loped deeper into the forest. Though they were nearing its centre, the canopy thinned overhead and the ambient light brightened, for there were few great old trees left to bury the Blacktalons in shade. Most of the forest was made up of saplings, sprouting from heads that still had their skin and hair. Bare spots in the moss marked where their headless bodies had lain before rising to attack the Stormcasts.

Other scars, too, marred the wood. Raw gashes in the earth remained where ancient trees had been uprooted. The trees themselves were nowhere to be seen, though new seedlings dotted the torn dirt.

Seeping black stains, wet and mushy, wended through the pale pink moss like poisoned creeks. Nothing grew in these, and Neave avoided them instinctively. She didn't know what had caused them or what they meant, but nothing good could come of such foulness.

The Blacktalons came to a gentle rise, its pink moss and red-leafed seedlings bracketed on either side by weeping streaks of bubbling black. Below them, in a low, wide bowl of a valley, stood a vast spreading tree larger than any Neave had ever seen.

Terrible as it was, there was an undeniable majesty to the Red Tree. A thousand shades of crimson fluttered in its leaves, pulsing through bluish and bright red hues, as though the bare-stripped circulatory system of a living behemoth were threaded about its branches. Its upper boughs gleamed with ornaments of gold, crystal and painted bone: uncounted generations of gifts offered by its grateful human supplicants.

Even from afar, Neave could see that the nature of those gifts changed in the lower branches. They were asymmetrical lumps hung from cords of hair and sinew. One and all, they were the deep discoloured brown of organic matter caked with windblown dirt and shrivelled by the air.

Small figures ambled around the base of the Red Tree. Neave put out a hand, and wordlessly Shakana passed over her spyglass. Through it, Neave saw humans clad in garments woven of scarlet leaves. All were young, and many were injured. The majority of them were pale-skinned, with pink hair and red eyes, but there were others as well, with different complexions and foreign garb.

Side by side, they bent around the tree's enormous roots, busily digging channels in the soil. The same oily black contamination that Neave had seen in the forest was evident in the ground near the Red Tree, and it appeared that the humans were trying to scrape it away.

'What is that?' Neave asked, gesturing towards the black streaks.

'A legacy of an earlier attack,' Lorai answered. 'It is a magic of Chaos, but more than that I cannot say without closer study.'

'There's been a lot of that this mission.' Shakana took her spyglass back from Neave and examined the Red Tree and its surroundings herself. 'I'm all for Chaos battling Chaos, but it does trouble me that so many factions are after these scrolls.'

'Powerful weapons ignite powerful rivalries,' Hendrick said. 'Each wants to be the one to claim glory before their perverse masters.'

'It's not just that. Gerispryx was attacked by rival Chaos powers because her enemies wanted to steal the information she'd discovered,' Neave mused aloud. 'We saw their servants fighting in the Blind Queen's Maze, and we saw the outcomes. Pelokoa captured Gerispryx's sorcerer, her imprisoned scholar, and whoever that poor dismembered soul was in the salt barrel. The Red Tree had agents there too – that's how Lorai was able to trace it back and bring us here. If we could find it through its pawns, its remaining rivals might have been able to do the same. We know there's at least one faction unaccounted for.'

'What of it?' Shakana asked, lowering her spyglass.

Neave studied the faraway trench diggers, trying to determine how much of a threat they posed. They hadn't reacted to the Blacktalons' arrival, but perhaps their master felt it more urgent to remove the contamination from its roots than attack the Stormcast Eternals. 'This might be more than a rival entity trying to destroy the Red Tree before it could claim the scrolls. It could be that whoever poisoned the forest was also trying to seize whatever information the Red Tree had obtained about that artefact.'

'Meaning we should look for that information too,' Shakana said. She stowed the spyglass and drew her typhoon crossbow, sighting down its golden stock. 'Lorai, can you get us closer? Perhaps by summoning your mist again?'

'Yes. Though I must warn you that it may not work so well this time. You may be walking into a trap.' Lorai leant on her staff as she stood. Members of the Idoneth noble castes, the aelf had once told Neave, were taught from childhood that any display of emotion could prove fatal in their treacherous society, the crack through which Slaanesh could once again cast a shadow upon their minds. Lorai had internalised those lessons since she was old enough to swim, and they had not always been gently taught.

The Idoneth betrayed little feeling now, either. Only a slight tensing of her bluish fingers around the staff, and a glance at the Red Tree that lasted a fraction of an instant too long. Nothing else hinted at her fear. She stood, moving to the centre of the Black-talons' phalanx.

Mist rose around the bald aelf. It spread to surround the Black-talons, lifting Neave's hair in its cool wind and beading Hendrick's wolfskin cloak with moisture.

Ringed by Lorai's woven cloud, they went to confront the Red Tree.

Its thralls met them beneath the crimson leaves. These appeared to be living humans, unlike the headless husks that the Storm-casts had fought in the outer wood, but they were just as silent, and their movements were nearly as clumsy. Their faces and hands were painted with swirling designs of rose-pink pollen powdered over sticky sap. More pollen crusted their lips and the insides of their nostrils, so that they looked like they'd suffered gush-ing nosebleeds.

A woman with a pink puff of fungal hair swung at Neave with a feathered wooden staff. Lorai's mist trapped her blow, and once again the water drained from the thralls' bodies.

The effect was horrifying. It had been ugly enough on the husks, but on living people it was far worse. Within seconds, their eyes collapsed into sunken raisins, their healthy-looking faces withered into skeletal grins, and their bodies shrivelled into gaunt sacks distended with hard ridges where organs and fat happened to be sitting when they were dried.

Some of the Red Tree's minions, far enough back to avoid being caught and slain in the first wave, lifted their heads towards the sky like wolves baying at the stars. They stretched their lips wide and let out hacking coughs of reddish-pink dust, blowing it at the Blacktalons.

'We're being attacked by deranged pipers,' Rostus said in amazement.

'They're trying to poison us,' Neave said.

'They will not succeed,' Lorai replied serenely, lifting her robed arms. The mist rose with her, whirling faster. A film of trapped pollen gathered on its upper layer, twisting through the enchanted fog in a pointillist ribbon.

Shakana fired through the mist. Trailing twin tails of flame and steam, the quarrel streaked through Lorai's spell and unleashed a second inferno upon the Red Tree's thralls.

These fared no better than the first wave had. Their crackled skin and dust-dry hair went up as easily as the headless ones' leaves and wooden bones, and the heat of their conflagration reached Neave even through the protective haze of Lorai's mist. Steam bubbled across the fog where the dying humans beat at it, trying to force their way through with blazing arms.

As the first of them began to crumble into ash and embers, the pollen in their lungs crackled ferociously. The sparks were so bright that the organs burned incandescently, like twin skyflowers in the dark hollow of the victims' chests. The thralls coughed out pink-flecked smoke as they fell, and some of that smoke blew through Lorai's spell.

It wasn't much. The mist caught most of it. But the smoke particles were finer than pollen, and less prone to snagging on moisture, and they passed through where the pollen didn't.

At the first breath of it, Neave felt her throat swell and seize. The burned pollen had an unpleasant scent, but it vanished almost as soon as she registered it.

Her throat tightened further. She was being suffocated from within, betrayed by her own body and the pollen's poison. She felt that her head was very light, and her feet were very far away. But the Blacktalons were still pushing forwards, closing on the Red Tree, and the dizziness didn't keep her from fighting.

She spun through the fog, cleaving through burning bodies and whole ones, and her companions fought with her. All the Stormcasts dived in and out of the haze, striking when they could, retreating when they had to. Only Lorai stayed entirely within the mist, even as its outer bands grew dark with collected pollen.

Once more, the Red Tree's pawns stiffened and seemed to exchange some silent knowledge. Their bodies hunched, and the pink stains at their mouths and noses spilled out in messy bibs, as if they'd all been stricken by simultaneous haemorrhages.

The mist reached them, and drained the liquid from their bodies. Scant seconds later, the fire reached them too.

The thralls exploded into bursts of burning pollen. The smoke was cataclysmic. It engulfed Neave as she ventured out of the misty whirlwind to cut down a few more thralls; it swallowed Rostus and Hendrick. Perhaps it took Shakana and Lorai, too, despite the Idoneth's protective fog. Neave couldn't see.

All she could see, as the poisoned smoke filled her senses, was a sudden dimming of the light. And then darkness, and an endless fall of red leaves.

CHAPTER SIXTEEN

Sigmar, shield me. Sigmar, protect me. Sigmar, forgive my sins.

Voices in the darkness. Disembodied whispers. It took Neave a moment to realise the murmurs in this black and empty space weren't her own thoughts.

They might have been. She'd thought the same, so many times.

Sigmar, give me strength, for I am weak and afraid.

Sigmar, forgive my lusts, for my flesh harbours unworthy desires.

Sigmar, grant me peace, for jealousy torments my thoughts.

Save me, preserve me, make me wise, make me strong, make me good.

A small white light ignited in the darkness. It was a candle flame, strangely drained of colour, being cupped by an old woman in a hooded cloak.

Almost everything around the candle was lost to shadow. All Neave could see was the candle itself, the wrinkled hands holding it, and the carvings around the alcove in which the woman knelt. The stone was etched in a blocky design depicting hammers interlocked in a chain, and though Neave didn't recognise the specific sect it represented, she knew it marked one of Sigmar's holy places.

The old woman carried her candle to a votive stand where dozens of other pale candles flickered in the infinite night. Gently she set it in an empty holder, her lips moving in silent prayer. From the emptiness around her, a voiceless chorus whispered:

Sigmar, shield me. Sigmar, protect me. Sigmar, forgive my sins.

The woman knelt again in front of the fluttering votives. She touched a closed fist to her forehead, her mouth, and then her heart. That was an old ritual gesture, well established in the Cults Unberogen. Neave had seen it observed by hundreds of different groups.

The darkness is coming. The darkness is outside the door. It rises within. Sigmar, give me strength, forgive my lusts, grant me peace.

Without you I am weak. Without you I am unworthy.

I come to you in faith and need. I cannot hold without my god.

The woman opened a prayer book. Neave didn't see her get it. It was simply there, in her hands, which had been empty before. A twin-tailed comet surrounded by twelve stars glowed white on its plain black cover.

Again the woman's mouth moved in unheard words, but this time her chin was lifted towards the votives' light, and Neave recognised the shapes on her lips. *Through the aether and the heavens, our prayers are gathered. Through all the realms Sigmar hears us, every one. Though I walk among beasts, through iron and flame, I am not alone, and I fear naught.*

That was an old prayer. Ancient. No one had used that invocation since Archaon the Everchosen had seized and twisted the Allpoints into the maelstrom of nightmare it was today.

Yet the shape of the woman's words was modern, or so it seemed to Neave. She had no difficulty following the prayer, even though she knew that this invocation only survived as translations from archaic dialects.

The woman opened the comet-marked book as she chanted. Radiance from its pages shone up on her face, bathing her in beatific white light, and revealing that she knelt in a grand cathedral. She smiled, closing her eyes. Peace settled upon her.

Then the light changed. Threads of red appeared in it, staining the old woman's face with the patterns of leaf veins, or perhaps human veins.

Her smile faded. Worry creased her face. Eyes wide, she looked into the book of prayers, turning the pages with rising desperation as she searched for something to banish her fear. With each page turned, the red veins in the light grew wider, and the white glow thinned and dimmed.

Sigils rose upon the pages, which had been blank before. They were Chaos runes, so virulent even in this vision that Neave tried reflexively to look away, only to find her gaze pinned to the scene. The cover changed, too. The stars faded, and a glowing red crack split the comet's heart, warping it into the sign that Neave had seen on Pelokoa's stage and the Great Flayer's hides.

Bloody tears ran from the woman's eyes, staining the wrinkles that tracked down her cheeks. Her prayers twisted on her tongue, turning into vile imprecations, even as she sobbed in terror and tried to claw the words out of her own mouth.

The prayer book dissolved into twelve scrolls, each rolled into an uneven cylinder with one pointed end stained red. The scrolls were sealed with Sigmar's twin-tailed comet, but these emblems, too, bore the runic cracks in their hearts. Each scroll had an ember of cursed magic glowing at its core.

The votive candles' flames turned crimson. The candles went out, one by one, their flames snuffed into hissing darkness. In that gloom, Neave could see a vast but indistinct flock of hooded, faceless worshippers kneeling in the cathedral pews behind the weeping old woman.

The scrolls flew into the gathered faithful, striking them like arrows shot into an unwary army. Individual figures fell, and from each one that toppled, more cursed prayers rose, leaping onwards to new victims.

Sigmar failed me. Sigmar hurt me. Sigmar abandoned me in my faith.

The whispers turned bitter, wounded, bereft. Somewhere, a low voice purred, deadly as unseen rot spreading beneath a bandage. *I cannot hold without my god. You cannot hold.*

The cathedral's ceiling split with a deafening crack as the last of its worshippers fell. Plaster and stonework rained down. Through the gap shone the deep, luminous blue-violet of the aetheric void, and the shimmering bodies of the stars and moon against it.

The cathedral was in Azyr. Neave's vision froze momentarily in shock. No taint of Chaos could touch Sigmar's own realm. Azyr, and Azyr alone, had always been sacrosanct. It was said that Chaos had never reached it, not in a single soul.

But visions were imagined things. She had to remember that. None of this was real, or true. It was all a jumbled hallucination, like the woman reciting her ancient prayer in a modern tongue.

The fallen worshippers rose, stiffly and unsteadily. They turned to the sacred comet emblazoned above the altar, and they prostrated themselves before it.

As they did, a ripple of red light passed across the twin-tailed comet, echoing the rune that glowed within the scrolls. A single stroke of lightning sparked across the slash of sky visible through the crack in the roof. It was no natural lightning, but a flare of ugly smoke-stained red. Behind it came a clap of thunder that sounded like a daemon's laugh.

Then the rift vanished, and the cathedral appeared whole once more. The worshippers stood, and the terror was gone from them. Their hoods still hid their faces, but they appeared calm, and they moved with unhurried deliberation.

One by one, they passed by the votive stand, and each of them plucked a candle from its holder. A red spark burned at the tip of each wick, and the hooded figures cupped their hands to hide the poisoned flames.

The worshippers bore them away as they left the cathedral, and Neave *knew*, somehow, that they were going to other churches. Other congregations, other sanctuaries. Places where only the holy were welcome, and only true believers could pass.

Places where the seeds of destruction those believers carried might find fertile soil.

Neave coughed. Her throat burned and her lungs ached. She was too dizzy to know where she was or, for a disorienting beat, *who* she was.

Four cloudy figures crouched around her like vultures. She blinked, and their vaporous forms solidified into pale, red-eyed tree-thralls. Two were holding her arms, another was gripping her open jaw, and the fourth's cheeks were bulging as the man regurgitated a crimson-veined seed so large that it distended his throat and split the sides of his mouth as it passed through his lips.

Cupping the bloody-edged seed like a sacred chalice, the man brought it towards Neave's mouth. She could smell the contained corruption of it, like carrion buried in the airless depths of a swamp so long it had turned to corpse wax. Tiny white roots wriggled on its skin.

She wrenched her arms away from the thralls who were holding her and kicked the seed-bearer in the chest so hard his sternum cracked. The one who'd been holding her head let go and grabbed at her torso, trying to restrain the Stormcast. Neave kicked her too, although the angle was too clumsy for her to do more than knock the woman back into the crowd.

Lurching up to her knees, Neave threw an elbow into the thrall to her right, snapping the man's neck, and twisted to drive her other elbow into the one at her left.

She staggered back to her feet and took up her hurricane axes. Around her, the field had broken into knots of tree-thralls clustered around each of the Blacktalons. Hendrick and Rostus were isolated, seemingly stunned, and surrounded by mossy-haired tribespeople trying to force seeds into their mouths. Shakana and Lorai had wet cloths wrapped over their noses and mouths and stood within the shrinking ambit of the aelf's whirling mists, assailed by a horde of rapidly withering humans. Though the pollen still whirled around Neave, having so recently shaken off its effects, she seemed at least temporarily immune to the placid fugue it induced.

Neave ran towards Hendrick. Her axes blurred around her, cutting down seed-corrupted tribespeople with every step. With quick, sweeping slashes she slew the thralls surrounding her friend, then bent and jerked him back to his feet.

Hendrick swayed unsteadily. He stared at Neave without seeming to recognise her. Pollen and smoke smeared his face and stained his grey beard.

'Come on, Old Wolf. We don't have time for this.' The thralls were surging towards them again. Seeing nothing else she could do, Neave slapped Hendrick hard across the cheek.

A familiar fire lit in his eyes. He fumbled for his weapons, and Neave stepped back. 'Hendrick! It's me! Come on, wake up.'

'Neave?' Hendrick blinked and wiped the burned pollen from his face. 'Where–' He stopped, taking in the scene, and drew his sword. 'Never mind. Questions later.'

'Right.' Leaving Hendrick to fend for himself, Neave raced to Rostus' side.

The thralls had the big Stormcast pinned to the ground. Insensible and unresisting, he lay with his mouth open as they lowered another root-feathered seed towards his face.

As they neared their host's face, the roots sprang to life like the tentacles of a hungry octopus. They grabbed Rostus' lips and prised his jaw wide, aiming the seed's narrow end into his mouth. It slid in, pushing against his teeth with a wet grating noise.

Neave threw her axes. One smashed into the pink-haired thrall kneeling on Rostus' chest. The other sheared the seed in half, spraying the bald Stormcast's face with red-tinted sap. She ran to retrieve her weapons, kicking away a warrior who bent to seize one.

Rostus coughed and tried to spit the seed chunk out of his mouth. The sap-slimed roots clutched at his teeth and the insides of his lips, refusing to let go, even as they convulsed in their dying throes. Disgusted, Rostus grabbed the broken seed and pulled it away. 'What in Sigmar's–'

'Get up!' Neave yelled.

Rostus hurled the seed chunk into a thrall's face, shattering the woman's nose. Throwing the others off him with a heave of his slab-muscled arms, the massive Stormcast lumbered upright. He took a moment to look for his hammer, spotted it beneath three of the Red Tree's minions, and hoisted it out from under them, shaking them off like drowning rats from a driftwood spar.

Shakana and Lorai, the only members of their company who hadn't succumbed to the Red Tree's poisoned smoke, were still moving steadily towards the tree's massive trunk. Now that the Blacktalons were all back in the fight, Neave swerved to help them.

Lorai's whirling mists had shrunk to a narrow cyclone surrounding only herself and Shakana, but the Idoneth continued to drive her spell forwards, pushing a battering ram of fire before them. Leaves fell over them in a steady rain, drifting to the ground like dying butterflies. Some ignited as they passed through the inferno that blazed beneath the Red Tree's branches, but most just dropped, stained with a ribbon of black at their cores.

It took a moment for Neave to remember why that image struck her so strongly. *Venom flowing through the veins, corrupting the heart of...* what?

She couldn't remember. When she wiped the sweat and blood from her brow, her hand came away smeared with pink pollen and black ash. An astringent charred taste, like burned vith leaves, lingered at the back of her tongue, and her throat felt swollen and rough.

Coughing violently, Neave cut down another pink-haired tribeswoman. Fine white filaments knitted across the woman's wounds, trying to staunch the bleeding, but the damage was too grievous, and the Red Tree's magic too weak. The thrall fell.

The Blacktalons had nearly reached the tree. Through the smoke and the press of bodies, Neave saw that the Red Tree's immense trunk was fissured with rivers of weeping black. A rotten gap, clotted with globs of inky putrescence, had opened in its bole.

Deep within the hole, a fibrous red heart pulsed. Webs of exposed veins connected it to the tree's interior, and though these too had begun to sicken with creeping contamination, Neave had an instinctive suspicion that the true corruption of the Red Tree was far deeper and more ancient than the inky tracks that stained its skin.

This new disease, however, made it vulnerable. The Red Tree's bark had peeled away from its heart, and that left it open to the Blacktalons' strike.

'Rostus! Hendrick! Clear the path!' Neave shouted, charging forwards to cleave through the tree's remaining defenders. They just needed to give Shakana a clean shot at the heart.

Rostus nodded, understanding at once. Step by step, he smashed aside the Red Tree's followers in threes and fours with devastating swings of his hammer. The thralls banded together to stop him, but they hadn't the strength to hold him back, and their efforts only gave him a bigger target to crush.

Hendrick, moving with an old-fashioned courtly elegance that seemed wildly out of place in this fight, hewed down those who tried to attack Rostus from behind. With axe and sword, he carved a shifting half-moon of defensive space around the bigger Stormcast.

Between their blades and Lorai's life-draining spell, a gap opened. 'Shakana!' Neave cried. 'Shoot the heart! The heart!'

Shakana stepped through the wall of skirling mist and took aim. Only her eyes showed above the damp cloth she'd wrapped around her face.

Two thralls hurled themselves bodily in front of the sniper. Neave blocked them, cutting first one and then the other into pieces. The red spray stung her eyes, and another tribesman sprang out to grab Shakana's crossbow. His fingers sizzled against its golden stock, and Lorai's spell sucked the moisture from his veins, but the dying man hung on doggedly even as Sigmar's lightning crackled through his fingerbones. Blisters rose from his hands and were drained to sagging emptiness instantly.

Shakana lowered her crossbow with a jerk and squeezed off a quick shot, blasting the man away in a close-range burst of lightning. Even before his corpse hit the ground, she'd lifted and levelled her weapon at the Red Tree's wounded heart. In the same smooth movement, Shakana flared the weapon's arms to their widest setting.

Lightning gathered between the crossbow's golden spikes, coalescing into a ball of crackling white fury. Neave concentrated on holding off the attackers long enough for Shakana to finish gathering the energy she needed. From the corner of her eye, she could see the magic blazing brighter and brighter, until it looked like a star had fallen into the crossbow's core.

Shakana fired. A thunderbolt speared into the Red Tree's exposed heart. It hung for an instant, gold burning against angry red, and then it exploded.

A vast shudder passed through the tree. Acrid smoke gushed from the wound in its core and broke apart as it wreathed through the convulsing boughs. Red leaves poured down like stricken birds, hitting the Blacktalons with fleshy thuds.

From the rupture in the Red Tree's heart, the black taint poured like water from a burst dam, rushing out from the bole to the great tree's limbs. With stunning speed, its boughs rotted, sagged, and broke in a cacophony of splintering wood.

The thralls' pink eyes rolled upwards. As one, in silence, they collapsed.

In crimson drifts, the dead leaves of their master fell to cover them.

CHAPTER SEVENTEEN

'That damnable split comet again,' Shakana said moodily. 'You *all* saw it?'

'Yes.' Rostus rubbed his hairless temple, as if the memory brought a phantom pain with it. 'It was on the head of an eight-eyed serpent. The viper hid in the branches of a tree outside a house of healing, and when people came to pray over their sick and wounded, it spat poison into their ears. They carried it inside, and I couldn't see what happened there, but I could see the stained-glass windows sag and melt, and the holy images on them turn to blasphemies.'

'I saw it on a corrupted book of prayers,' Neave said. 'The pages tore themselves out, furled into sharp points, and flew into the hearts of the congregation. There they hid, and the faithful carried them out to the churches of Azyr.'

'Mine was on a crypt statue,' Hendrick said, reluctantly, unable to conceal his distaste at the remembered vision. He ran his fingers over his left gauntlet, where the twin-tailed comet had been embossed in gold. 'It depicted Sigmar in his glory, wielding

Ghal Maraz, but the comet under his feet was cracked, creating the same symbol you've described. The crack expanded, and eventually the statue crumbled into its void. Behind the marble and gold was a rotten hollow with a worm-eaten skeleton inside, as though that were the true face that the statue had been built to conceal. A black-armoured fist smashed the skull, and then there was… laughter. And a shadow with wings.'

'What does it mean?' Shakana shook her head, unconsciously imitating the motion that her star-eagle often exhibited when it, too, was frustrated. 'Is it meant to signify their purpose? A crack in the faith, a hidden taint weakening the Cults Unberogen? A vision of what they hope to achieve? Why do all our targets keep showing us this sign?'

'I'm not certain they are,' Neave said. Her gaze strayed back to the black stains that continued to seep from the Red Tree's heartwood and trickle down its dead bark. 'What I mean is, I think we're trespassing into visions they chose for themselves, or each other. Not us. Pelokoa's theatre was set for him, because he'd stolen information from Gerispryx and wanted to study it himself. That show was never meant for us to see.

'The Red Tree was fatally stricken, and its magic was already failing, before we came. It didn't have the strength to heal its thralls in combat even at the centre of its power, under its own canopy, where it should have been near a god. A creature that could hold off Nurgle for centuries should have been able to repair a few axe wounds easily, or stop Lorai from devastating its minions. But it couldn't. It was too near dead.'

'What of it?' Rostus grumbled, rubbing his mouth where the Red Tree's seed had grabbed at his lips with its prehensile roots. No marks remained, but clearly the experience had unnerved him. After the fighting was over, Rostus had rinsed his mouth repeatedly with various healing concoctions, and still he kept probing his teeth and cheeks with his tongue, looking for any hint of lingering contamination.

'There was another faction in the Blind Queen's Maze,' Neave recalled. 'The mercenaries. I didn't see how they could be related to the library of frozen books that Hendrick saw, but that doesn't mean they *weren't* connected. We encountered Pelokoa's revellers, the Red Tree's thralls, and the Champions of Vercaspior, all chasing Gerispryx's information. I think that final faction must have struck at the Red Tree.'

'Why?' Shakana asked. She looked more intent and less frustrated, like a hunting cat that had picked up the trail, and was both eager and relieved to be back on the chase. 'Simply to remove a rival from the hunt?'

'Maybe. But maybe...' Neave canted her head at Hendrick and Rostus. 'Could you tell which realm your vision showed? Or anything else specific about the location?'

Hendrick caught her meaning at once. 'Azyr. The crypt was built of Azyrite stone, in a very old style. There were inscriptions over the statue... I can't remember what they said, but I recall the script. It, too, was ancient Azyrite.'

'Mine was in Azyr too,' Rostus said. 'I didn't think it important at the time, but now that you mention it, the tree that serpent was hiding in was a blue sunveil. I don't believe I've ever seen one growing outside Azyr. And the images on the stained-glass windows weren't ones I recognised. I thought that was because they were the Red Tree's fabrications, but it might have been that they depicted scenes that were older than any stories I know.'

'Right.' Neave drew a deep breath, excited and apprehensive, as the pieces slotted into place. 'We know what these Chaos factions want, and why. They're vying for the scrolls that they believe will destroy our God-King. But I don't think they knew where to find them. Or, perhaps more accurately, I don't think the

Vercaspior faction knew. But perhaps the Red Tree did. Ancient as it was, with roots that delved deep into the buried history of the realms… it might have dug into secrets that none of the others possessed.'

'And that's why the Red Tree's visions were all in Azyr? Because this other faction forced it to show them clues about where that secret weapon could be?' Rostus' brow smoothed, then furrowed again. 'But if it's in Azyr, they can't get it anyway. Chaos cannot reach our realm.'

'Chaos hasn't been able to reach Azyr *in the past*,' Neave corrected him. 'We can't take the future for granted. Sigmar would not have given us this assignment if the risk weren't real.'

'Let me seek Sigmar's wisdom. Perhaps he can guide us to the truth.' Dusting his hands on his thighs, Hendrick gazed up through the Red Tree's falling leaves.

Decay had continued to spread, with the inky stain sweeping through the dead tree's limbs. Its branches collapsed unpredictably, higher boughs often taking down lower ones with their weight as they crashed to the ground.

Unstable as it was, however, the Red Tree was unquestionably the highest point in sight. Hendrick spent another moment charting his course, then sprang up into the lower branches and began climbing. Though some broke off under his feet and snapped away in his hands, the Old Wolf managed to catch himself on a lower limb or swing to an adjacent one every time.

Shakana shaded her eyes, watching him go. After a moment, she went up on her toes, squinting at something Neave couldn't make out. 'I think I see something.' She clambered up the Red Tree's limbs, slipping a few times as stricken branches cracked under her weight.

Despite the treacherous footing, Shakana moved nimbly. She vaulted up to the higher reaches, where she plucked some of the ornaments hanging from the Red Tree's boughs. Hurriedly she slipped back down. 'We should go. That tree's going to come crashing down as soon as Sigmar's lightning hits it.'

Neave nodded, and the Blacktalons retreated to await Hendrick's return from a safe remove.

On a low hill, well away from the Red Tree's corpse, Shakana showed them what she'd brought down. She held a dented steel prayer amulet, its sacred hammer scratched and blasted; part of a heavy cloak reinforced with a layer of chain sewn between its panels of leather and fur; a fragment of crystal, mazed with white lines; and one of the parchments from the Blind Queen's Maze, which held a map depicting a mountain range.

All were marked with the split comet, and each time the symbol had been created by sheer happenstance. The twisting scars of stains and scorch marks, gouges and crusted bits of gore, combined on each of the trinkets to form the same disturbing emblem, again and again.

After examining each one, Neave passed them to Lorai. The Idoneth had taken out her cyfar compass again, and was sitting cross-legged in front of its pearlescent bowl. Wordlessly, Lorai swept Shakana's trinkets over the water's surface in ritualised spirals and then set them aside, staring at reflections that only she could see.

'There were more,' Shakana said, 'but I couldn't reach them all. It was odd. Higher up, where Hendrick went, I didn't see anything with this symbol. There wasn't anything lower, either. But where I stopped, there must have been over a dozen of these things, all hanging side by side.'

'As if the Red Tree had told its servants to find them, and all the symbols occurred together, in a burst,' Neave mused. She picked up the bit of cloak Lorai had discarded, and looked at it again. Its construction was familiar. She played the blood-stiffened fur and thick leather between her fingers, and then she had it. 'This was the style of cloak that the puppets on Pelokoa's stage wore.'

Shakana pursed her lips. She glanced at the distant tree, as if second-guessing her decision to leave some of its ornaments behind. 'So you were right. They *were* all scavenging the same clues from the Blind Queen's Maze.'

'Perhaps. We should know more soon.' Neave glanced meaningfully up at the sky. Storm clouds were gathering in a grey vortex over the top of the Red Tree.

Only a few seconds after she spoke, a blue-white bolt of lightning stabbed down from the heavens, striking the dead tree in a blinding flash. An earth-shaking thunderclap sounded, followed by the lower, longer groan of the tree splitting apart as it burned.

The Blacktalons turned to watch, and together they fell into an awed silence. Terrible as the Red Tree had been, the sheer size and majesty of its burning form demanded their reverence. Night had begun to fall, and in the lowering darkness, the blaze stood out like a divine beacon across Ghyran.

Hendrick came limping towards them with the fire at his back. His face, cast in shadow, was haggard over his soot-stained beard.

'The storm continues,' he told them, sitting heavily. The wind turned, carrying a drift of smoke from the Red Tree's bonfire. It smelled not of wood, but of burning bone, like the funeral pyres of tribes on the Great Parch, who let their dead dry in the baking heat and then burned them with no more than a handful of grass for tinder. 'We have slain four of our five targets, as the God-King charged us to do, and only one remains. But the black vortex at the centre of this affair has only grown stronger, closer, and deadlier, even as it hangs by a single thin tether to this world.'

'Who's the last target?' Neave asked. The wind turned away again, and she was relieved. Though the smoke carried only the faintest whiff of poisoned pollen, it still reminded her of the Red

Tree's hallucinations, and she didn't care to relive those. 'Where do we find it?'

Hendrick shrugged in weary apology. 'The vision did not tell me. Several times it… tried to, I believe, but a grey gloom fell over my sight, and all I could perceive was a faceless, winged shadow. I could not even tell whether the shadow was that of mortal, daemon, or beast.

'I believe something interfered with the God-King's sending, and after three tries, the vision shifted. I saw a monastery on a high mountainside, covered in such thick ice that it seemed to be carved not in stone, but into the heart of winter itself. Bloody footsteps stood at its door, though I could not tell whether they led in or out. In either case, I believe we will find the trail there.'

The library of frozen books. 'If we can find the monastery,' Neave said.

'That part, fortunately, is easy.' Hendrick didn't sound especially relieved by that. Just tired, and perhaps a bit worried. 'I've been there before. It is known as the Sanctuary of the Winter Sun, in Aqshy. Over the ages, it has had other names, but it has always been a brave and faithful stronghold of the Cults Unberogen. Many staunch Stormcast Eternals have been called from the warrior priests trained there. For it to appear in this context is troubling.'

'Lorai?' Neave asked. 'Can you tell us anything more?'

The Idoneth lifted her inscrutable gaze from the cyfar compass. In the firelit night, her bowl cast shimmering waves of blue and lavender across her face. 'I have searched for the next soul to track, and I have found nothing.'

Neave nodded, disappointed but unsurprised. If Sigmar's communion hadn't been able to give them a clear mark, she could hardly expect that the Soulscryer's spell would fare better. 'Have you found anything else?'

'Yes.' Lorai spread her thin fingers wide and swept them over the surface of her bowl. As the water began to darken and swirl, she beckoned the Blacktalons near. 'Your earlier guess did not err. The Red Tree sent its roots deep and far into the soil, burrowing through centuries of history buried in stone and clay. It drew out the memories of creatures long dead, siphoning fragments of their knowledge through the loam of their bodies. This it did before it was corrupted, and did more avidly once Chaos had consumed its soul.

'That is how it found the Great Flayer, and Gerispryx, and the other threads in the tapestry we follow. The ornaments Shakana found were the mementoes that the Red Tree ordered its faithful to procure. It used the resonances of remembered pain in those objects to guide its roots as they plunged deeper, seeking insights from forgotten ages.

'I cannot tell you what it found. The traces are too faint, too tangled, and too contaminated by malevolence for me to unravel. But I can tell you that another hunter found the Red Tree before we did, and forced it to reveal what it had uncovered.'

'Varstrom,' Lorai intoned. Hearing the name again sent a shiver of apprehension down Neave's spine. 'That is the name that the Red Tree dug up from the depths of decayed history. That is the great secret that the black poison pulled from its heart. Varstrom.'

'Varstrom is the key to the storm,' Neave murmured. 'That's what Pelokoa's servants kept saying when they were questioning the scholar they seized. Now we know, for certain, that's what they're all after. But where is it? *What* is it?'

No one had an answer for her. A great groan rolled across the land, breaking the hush. Slowly at first, then accelerating towards the earth ever faster, the Red Tree toppled in an immense cascade of sparks, heaving up the ground as it fell. Overturned dirt and torn roots smothered the fire, casting the night into near-total black.

In the darkness, Neave said: 'Let us pray. Let us pray, together, and then let us hunt.'

CHAPTER EIGHTEEN

The nearest usable realmgate was the Aerdrych Ihaldreth, in the hands of the Velsachi Ordrann grove of the Sylvaneth. Sometimes called the Greyleaf Grove, the Velsachi Ordrann were a reclusive but storied branch of the tree folk, who had kept Alarielle's faith steadfastly even when their green goddess retreated from her realm.

They had been rewarded for their fealty with the honour of guarding the Aerdrych Ihaldreth, and they did not take that duty lightly. Neave and her companions were greeted courteously at the silver-leafed borders of their territory, and then immediately assigned an honour guard, who watched them with impassive dignity.

The Blacktalons did not object, for the Velsachi Ordrann were valuable friends and dangerous foes, and there was nothing to be gained by offending them. Although diplomacy was hardly among the Blacktalons' primary duties, they understood the delicacy and importance of Sigmar's alliances, and could play the role of gracious guests when required. Besides, the Sylvaneth had proven themselves in battle many times, and their bravery was worthy of respect.

The leader of their escort, Telvurai Splinter-Spear, was a tall, slender Sylvaneth with an antlered brow and a silvery cast to her wood-like skin. Luminous seedpods, like droplets of solidified moonlight, glimmered about her brow in muted shades of green and twilight blue. A pronounced spiral grain rippled along her limbs, which had a softly polished sheen. For her to be assigned to the Blacktalons' honour guard was a sign of considerable respect, for Telvurai was among the Greyleaf Grove's most distinguished champions, and was seldom sent away from their borders.

'You slew the Red Tree,' she said, after she had exchanged politenesses with the Blacktalons. The Sylvaneth's deep, blank eyes and tiny mouth revealed nothing of her thoughts, and her voice was a low, reverberating ripple, melodic and emotionless as a river's flow.

'Yes,' Neave said. She was surprised the Sylvaneth knew about it already, but saw no point denying the truth.

'She might have been one of us,' Telvurai observed, as she led the Blacktalons through the whispering trees towards the Aerdrych Ihaldreth. Tiny glowing spirits flitted about them on gossamer wings, like luminous wildflowers floating on the breeze. 'Long ago, before the touch of ruin took hold. She might have been a great instrument in the spirit-song.'

They passed through a colonnade of stately, symmetrical trees whose limbs intertwined to create a great green tunnel high over their heads. Neave couldn't see the Sylvaneth guardians in the greenery, but she had no doubt they were there, poised and vigilant against any threat.

'I'm sorry,' she told Telvurai, unsure how to read the Sylvaneth's tone.

The antlered Sylvaneth turned her head at an impossible angle, owl-like, without shifting her shoulders. Still no feeling revealed itself in her liquid gaze. 'No. If she was once among us, it is better that she was destroyed. Once blight reaches the heartwood, there is naught to be done but to burn it, root and branch, before the disease spreads. Otherwise all the grove will fall.'

'Still, it is a loss. Perhaps not the Red Tree's death, but its corruption,' Neave said.

Telvurai didn't answer. The Sylvaneth turned back again, and with long, fluid strides led them to the realmgate.

The Aerdrych Ihaldreth was a leafless tree, winter white and starkly beautiful. It was not wood, but stone: a petrified tree that had turned to pearl or alabaster rather than striped grey rock.

In the centre of the tree, suspended like an immense jewel in its trunk, was the realmgate. It was an opalescent disc of pale, swirling colour, like a mosaic of emerald, lapis lazuli and dark amethyst filtered through a thin pane of mother-of-pearl. Tendrils of translucent magic emanated from its edges, hissing softly in the hush of the grove.

'Go,' Telvurai said, as the other Sylvaneth in the honour guard arrayed themselves to either side of the realmgate. 'May the Everqueen smile upon your work.'

Neave lifted a fist in salute to the Sylvaneth and stepped into the tree.

A surge of vitality swept over the Stormcast as she walked through the realmgate. Every particle of her skin tingled. Each breath carried a rush of energy and clarity that coursed through her body from fingertips to toes, banishing her fatigue and filling her with the crystalline, adrenaline-spiked alertness that she normally felt only on the brink of battle.

She had heard that the life energies of the Aerdrych Ihaldreth affected non-living creatures in unpredictable ways. Nagash's servants had been physically or psychically obliterated by the onrush of vitality into their undead forms. It was said that Nurgle's plague knights exploded as their diseases, spurred to new heights of fecundity, consumed their hosts. There were legends, too, of Khorne's frenzied berserkers receiving such lopsided torrents of strength that their muscles ripped through their skin and shattered their bones.

Whether these stories were true, Neave didn't know. She couldn't recall any battle in which the armies of Chaos had been able to pass through the sacred realmgate. But the Aerdrych Ihaldreth was ancient, and Ghyran had lain in Nurgle's power for centuries, so perhaps it had once been otherwise.

If so, no trace of the Ruinous Powers' taint remained. Still alight with the euphoria of the realmgate's life energy, Neave stepped through to the baking heat of a courtyard in the fortified town of Melynhael. Under the shade of billowing white sunsails, Freeguild soldiers armoured in fiery chelskin capes and spiked bronze caps kept a watchful eye on the new arrivals.

Neave saluted them and stepped aside as the rest of the Blacktalons came out behind her. They were all well familiar with Melynhael, a trade hub that supplied food and lumber to the great city of Hallowheart, and transported gems, arcane minerals and realmstone back to Ghyran. They'd used it as a base for missions in Aqshy before, and Neave rather liked the town. It had a courageous, practical spirit that appealed to her.

This time, however, the Blacktalons didn't have the luxury of spending days on rest and resupply. They were racing against prophecy, and none of them knew how long they had until the storm broke.

Even before the soldiers of Melynhael had finished returning Neave's salute, the Blacktalons were gone.

East and south they ran, skirting the Ruins of Ahramentia, then south into the Sorrow Peaks. In the blistering windless valleys, brittle ashes crunched under the Blacktalons' boots, and the air shimmered like the mouth of a baker's oven on a winter morning. Smouldering fissures snaked through the smoking earth, drawing flocks of long-tailed puffwings that fed on their superheated exhalations.

Neave led the Blacktalons away from those burning valleys, up steep mountain trails cut into razor-edged obsidian. Pillars and arches of wavery black glass rose around them, and in their depths, fiery daemonic eyes sometimes burned.

They passed rivers of false water that shimmered with sweet promises of quenched thirst, but delivered only tongue-shrivelling, volatile mineral oils. Geysers of blue flame punctuated the twilights, while dawns broke over the soot-crusted remnants of gargantuan war engines and arcanomechanic fortifications, built in another age and now reduced to fitfully echoing shells inhabited by superstitious tribes.

The Blacktalons climbed higher. At altitude, cold began to overcome the relentless heat of Aqshy, though even under a mantle of cinders and snow, the Sorrow Peaks maintained their fiery nature. Intertwined rivers of obsidian and ice, one frozen hard as the other, ran down the mountainsides in beautiful, treacherous cascades. The Sorrow Peaks' white cloak tore open regularly in fountains of hot air and spitting magma, and their howling winds bore sharp fangs of rainbow-streaked volcanic glass.

It was here, in the uppermost reaches of the Sorrow Peaks, that the Sanctuary of the Winter Sun stood.

Neave had heard of the monastery before, although she had never personally visited. It was a semi-legendary stronghold of the Cults Unberogen, with a historic significance out of all proportion to its small population and remote location. For centuries, the dedicants of the Winter Sun had maintained a collection of tribal relics, sacred artefacts, ancient war machines and other esoterica significant to their faith. The nature of the order had changed from a monastery of ascetic contemplation to a fighting order and back several times, but always their primary duty had been the maintenance and protection of their archives. The Sanctuary's collection was narrow but exceedingly deep, and reached back through an extraordinary span of time.

Over the years, several Stormcast delegations had come to examine the Sanctuary's archives. They had written favourably of the mortal worshippers' diligence, but some of their accounts also expressed concern that such valuable treasures were left to the care of a small contingent of humans in such an isolated fastness. At least twice, the Stormcast Eternals had removed materials from the Sanctuary and taken them to better-defended sites.

The remainder of the Sanctuary's collection, however, had been left in place. Its dedicants might be few in number, but their training and discipline were of the highest order, and the stronghold's inhospitable location was deemed a significant deterrent on its own.

As the Blacktalons neared the Sanctuary of the Winter Sun, Neave saw what the chroniclers meant.

Reaching the monastery required a long climb up bitterly cold and wind-hammered trails. The mountain's natural defences were augmented by squat, thick-walled towers that tapped magma veins for warmth. Those towers also diverted the molten rock into immense, brass-mouthed spouts that jutted from their heights, threatening to bury the paths beneath deadly crossfires of lava at the touch of a lever. While the towers' dedicants were plainly awed by the Blacktalons' arrival and the honour being done them by the Stormcasts' visit, Neave was pleased to note that they still insisted on formally asking her name and purpose. She gave it gravely, knowing that she was as close as these worshippers were likely to come to the presence of Sigmar himself, and conscious of her dignity as his representative.

Past the final set of towers, the Blacktalons came to the Sanctuary proper. It was a surreal sight, for the monastery was so deeply buried in ice that it resembled a shipwreck in a frozen sea. Its contours were dimly visible through the layers of compacted snow and ice, but what was visible was as much shadow and suggestion as actual stone.

A dark hole burrowed through the ice to the monastery's gates, and though it was at least fifteen feet in diameter, it was so profoundly dwarfed by the bulk of the frozen fastness behind it that Neave felt a moment's doubt about whether she and her companions would fit through.

She knew from the tales how it had been built. To protect the monastery from scouring mountain winds and their endless barrage of volcanic shrapnel, its faithful had pumped entire lakes' worth of water out over the mountain's face, where it froze into thick, armouring layers. As the ice eroded and began to strain under the weight of embedded shrapnel, the monastery's inhabitants poured more water out to reinforce and replace what had been lost.

Over centuries, the Sanctuary of the Winter Sun had developed into a frozen labyrinth. Its older levels were inaccessible and permanently entombed in ice, having been filled in by decades of pumped water and slowly pushed down the mountainside by the weight of newer layers.

Only the permanent structures carved into the stone, and the upper layers tunnelled out of the ice, were actively maintained. The older, abandoned sections had been compacted into a mass of ice and debris that served as a foundation for the rest. Yet even these were valued by the Cults Unberogen, for they meant that the Sanctuary of the Winter Sun was one of the rare places in Aqshy where history was not regularly consigned to the flames.

The monastery's entire history was preserved in ice. And though

Sigmar's mortal followers could no longer access the farthest reaches of that history, the Children of the Winter Sun believed with absolute certainty that, should he ever wish to do so, the God-King could crack open their icy archives with a single blow of his hammer and retrieve all the wisdom stored within.

With any luck, the key to their quest was somewhere in the upper Sanctuary, and Neave wouldn't need Sigmar's hammer to get it.

The library of frozen books. She wondered if the Sanctuary was the place that Hendrick had seen in his vision. It seemed likely, but they had no proof yet.

A short path, framed by chipped and battered obsidian statues, led to the ice tunnel. The path was inlaid with twelve golden discs, each bearing the likeness of Ghal Maraz. A chime rang out as the Blacktalons moved across each disc, and the hammer etched on its golden face filled with magical light. When they came to the last, the same emblem appeared on the monastery gates, a sliver of gilt and charwood dwarfed by the slabbed rough walls of ice, ash, and embedded obsidian on either side. The light echoed off the ridged walls of the ice tunnel and glowed within its depths, illumining the entire face of the mountain.

The Sanctuary's gates opened. Four heavily cloaked figures stepped out. Three wore smoke masks and shaggy ursal pelts over padded armour.

The fourth was the only one with her face uncovered. She was a woman in her late middle years, with light brown skin and a calm, authoritative intensity that reminded Neave of generals she'd known.

Perhaps she was one. Sigmar's wars were fought on many fields, both spiritual and corporeal, and this woman was plainly accustomed to at least one of those. Her greying hair was tucked beneath a crisp white wimple clasped in place with gold chains, and she wore the holy hammer of Sigmar proudly embroidered at either end of her ceremonial stole.

'Be welcome to the Sanctuary of the Winter Sun, honoured Stormcasts,' she said. Subtle magic amplified her voice, allowing her words to carry through the bitter wind. 'I am Aliquaille, keeper of Sigmar's sacred flame in this humble house.'

'Thank you,' Neave called back, squinting against the debris-riddled wind. Bits of cinder and glass pinged off her sigmarite armour. 'I am Neave Blacktalon. I'm afraid we have little time for pleasantries. My companions and I are hunting an enemy of the faith, and the trail has led us here.'

'Then you must come in.' The woman stepped aside, beckoning them through the gates.

Neave followed their human escorts into a cavernous ice-walled chamber. Heatless, sorcerous lights cast a blue glow across the frozen walls and debris-flecked floor. Empty sockets in the ceiling showed where larger chunks of hardened lava had been prised out before they could melt loose and fall on the monastery's inhabitants. Apart from a few bare stone benches and a hammer-and-flame mosaic on the floor, there was nothing in the room.

'In hardship we learn strength,' Aliquaille said, seeing Neave take the measure of their surroundings. 'This is the way of the Winter Sun. We offer shelter, but not comfort, for we would not insult our fellows in faith by presuming them to be so weak.'

'A strict faith,' Neave said, careful to keep her tone neutral. It was often so with sects of the Cults Unberogen that took root in inhospitable areas. Hardened by difficult environments, their people took pride in their toughness, and eventually came to hold it as a holy virtue.

'We would follow no other.' Aliquaille shrugged with a small self-deprecating smile. 'But you did not come to hear us preach to you of Sigmar's faith. You *are* his faith, made flesh. Tell us how we may serve.'

'A danger has come here, or is coming,' Hendrick said. 'We do not know which. It may already have arrived, or it may be imminent. Have you had any strange visitors recently, or observed any unsettling phenomena?'

'No,' Aliquaille said. 'The only travellers we've received in a fortnight, apart from yourselves, are the traders who bring our supplies, and a small band of Sigmarite scholars who wished to research some manuscripts in our deep archives.'

Neave drew an audible breath. *It is the library.*

Hearing her reaction, Hendrick leant forwards intently. 'What manuscripts?'

'Nothing of great importance, or they would not be consigned to the deep archives. Treatises arguing the major positions on the Fourth Schism of Prismatikos, I believe. Mildly heretical. But surely nothing that should warrant the attention of the Stormcast Eternals?'

'I can't yet say,' Hendrick told her. 'Are they still here, these scholars?'

Aliquaille paused. A flicker of puzzled trepidation shadowed her smooth brow as she registered the Blacktalons' interest in this news, but she maintained a dignified calm. 'Yes. They have been studying in the deep archives since they arrived. They went down again just this morning. I expect they will join us for the evening meal, if you wish to speak to them then.'

The Blacktalons exchanged a look. Hendrick said: 'Let's not wait that long. Will you show us to the deep archives? I'd like to see what they're researching.'

'Of course.' Aliquaille took one of the cold blue lights from the walls, holding it aloft. 'Please, honoured Stormcasts, follow me.'

CHAPTER NINETEEN

'What can you tell us about these scholars?' Hendrick asked. 'Where did they come from, and who was their leader? Did you notice anything unusual about their habits or manner?'

'They called themselves the Vorgemi, and claimed to hail from the Opal Isle,' Aliquaille told them, as she led the Blacktalons through the upper reaches of the Sanctuary of the Winter Sun. Already she seemed sceptical of this information, and she glanced back frequently at the Stormcasts. Although too disciplined to ask openly, she was clearly searching for some explanation of what they wanted with the scholars. 'Their leader was a woman named Ithyrac. Their dress and habits were foreign, but this is not unusual. Nearly all our visitors have customs and mannerisms that seem strange to us. These Vorgemi were not extraordinary in that regard.'

'What mannerisms of theirs struck you as strange?' Neave asked.

'They wore black lenses over their eyes,' Aliquaille replied, 'and hid their faces under leather hoods, which they explained were necessary in their homeland due to the continual brilliance of the fires in the region, and the many gems which refracted that fire. These articles had developed considerable cultural significance, and so the Vorgemi did not wish to remove them even here, in our sanctuary, where there is no necessity for such things. They seemed to be able to see well enough to navigate the ice halls safely, so I did not insist.'

Behind her back, the Blacktalons exchanged another look. *The Champions of Vercaspior*, Neave thought, and did not say. There was no need. It was foremost in all their minds.

Ahead, a pair of heavily cloaked guards stood beside an archway built of black stone blocks. Each block was inscribed with protective runes and prayer sigils. At the centre of the arch, a luminous blue stone pulsed with gold sparks, filling the chamber with glittering reflections. Even from ten paces away, Neave felt the strength of the holy magic warding the arch.

Aliquaille bowed her head and traced a ritual symbol across her chest.

'Summer Saint.' The guards returned her greeting deferentially, and stepped aside to let the Stormcasts through.

'Summer Saint?' Neave looked curiously at the woman. She wasn't familiar with that title.

Aliquaille then touched the hammer embroidered on one end of her stole. She glanced at the symbol reverently, and let the garment fall back into place. 'The Sanctuary's elders have honoured me with that position. The Summer Saint is the keeper of the Sanctuary's spiritual legacies. I teach my fellows about Sigmar's gentler, kinder aspects. His patience, his forgiveness, his love for all who strive to follow his ideals, however flawed our efforts. That is what summer means in this part of the world, you see – the brief, welcome season of kind sun and blooming life.

'The Winter Saint is my counterpart. She is the master of battle, and represents Sigmar's martial nature. The Children of the Winter Sun dedicate themselves to both aspects. We harden ourselves in winter to protect the memory of summer. But,' Aliquaille added with a self-deprecating shrug, 'winter lasts much longer in these mountains than summer.'

On the other side was darkness, and an icy stairwell that plunged down in tight spirals. Stone saints watched them from the monastery's alcoves, their robes and armour spiked with ice. Some bore carved hammers, while others brandished spell scrolls or held stone lanterns inscribed with comets and sacred runes. Their garb and weaponry were archaic even to Neave's eyes, giving the graven figures an air of undimmed determination.

Ours is a legacy held for millennia, they seemed to say. *You guard it now, and you must not fail.*

Lifting her blue light high, Aliquaille started down.

'Is it unusual for scholars to come all this way to seek out the deep archives?' Hendrick asked casually, betraying no more than polite interest. Coarse cinders and pulverised debris had been scattered over the icy steps to improve traction, but they remained distractingly difficult, particularly since they'd been cut to human scale, and were too small to be comfortable for the Stormcasts. 'The Sorrow Peaks can be quite harsh, especially this high. It seems a great deal of trouble for some minor point of historical interest.'

'Faith drives people to extraordinary deeds,' Aliquaille said. Her footsteps were light and measured, hidden by the thunderous echoes of the Blacktalons' boots in the icy hall. 'Particularly the God-King's faith. What might seem hardships to outsiders are only tests of dedication for true believers. Many of them choose the challenge simply because it is there, and worthy.

'But it is also true that the Sanctuary of the Winter Sun is held in reverence because so much of the history of Aqshy is written in smoke. The people of this realm burn bright and die young.

251

Living memory is swiftly lost, and often it is the only history a tribe has. What is paper, in the Realm of Fire, but kindling? The tribes sworn to Khorne scorn bookish ways, and even those who might choose to learn the art of binding thought to ink seldom have that luxury.

'Consequently, it is rare, terribly rare, for anyone to have what we have – detailed records of the life of Sigmar's faiths in this land. Ways of dress, communal prayers, songs of glory and mourning, herbs burned in sacrifice. Much of it is of little interest, except to those now dead and their descendants. But we keep it all, to honour them and remember that they held the torch before us, and kept its flame alive. We will not discard their memory.

'And sometimes people come to read their words, and remember who they were, or try to. I would think that you, Stormcast Eternals, might understand the value of that exercise more than most.' Aliquaille paused and looked back at them again, inviting their thoughts. Or, perhaps, merely offering a moment of understanding.

Neave felt the woman's words strike an unexpected chord. It was true that Stormcasts could go to great lengths to protect their vulnerable memories, or to retrieve even the faintest glimmer of one that had been lost to Reforging. Why should mortals not feel the same?

Besides, Hendrick had said that many Stormcasts had been forged from the souls of those trained and tested in the Sanctuary of the Winter Sun. No doubt some of them returned in the hope of remembering their own lost, mortal selves.

What would she have written, if she'd been trying to memorialise the spirit of her own living tribe for the future? What would she have written if she were trying to preserve something of her own human soul for *herself*?

She didn't know. That version of herself was too far gone. Despite numberless centuries of hurling herself after one lead or another, pursuing misty shadow-selves who beckoned her from across the chasms of time and death, she still didn't know who she had been in life, or why she'd been chosen to serve as a Stormcast.

But she could guess that if she were writing for a reader in the unknown future, with the assumption that this reader would be a fellow Sigmarite but one who remembered nothing about Neave or her tribe, then she'd be tempted to record all she could about what made her, and her people, unique among their fellow believers. She might dispense with the veils of indirect language, assuming that her reader would respect the priorities of their faith, or might simply be too far removed from her own current day to need such safeguards.

What use would it be to maintain the secrets of a fortress' inner workings in an age long after that fortress had crumbled? Why not record the details as precisely as possible, so that someone in that distant future could recall the full glory of what once had been?

Now, as a Stormcast, Neave knew the answer to that question all too well. But as a human, and especially a human in Aqshy, she might have answered it very differently.

And if thousands of others had made similar decisions, all embedded in the deep ice beneath the Sanctuary...

'The trove of secrets here must be immense,' she said aloud.

'Yes,' Aliquaille agreed. 'It became too much for our archivists to maintain after only a few centuries. The Sanctuary has only a small complement of believers, and across the years, many of its leaders have viewed their primary duty as preparing Sigmar's armies for war in the present day, not safeguarding old secrets for their descendants. The ice archives have not always been a priority. Even when they were, the cataloguing was... inexact. But we do try to keep everything. Perhaps someday it can all be unfrozen and properly sorted.'

'Someday,' Neave murmured. Who could say? Perhaps it would

be so, at least for these people, in this corner of the world. For the Blacktalons, the war never ended, but that was because they hunted Sigmar's enemies across all the Mortal Realms. If one lived in a single place, for the span of a single life, peace could feel like a real and lasting thing.

As they walked, descending ring after ring into the monastery's lower levels, the hall grew narrower. Rostus had to pick his way down sideways, and his shoulders scraped against the walls. The statues in the alcoves looked even older, and some of them receded into the ice.

The steps, initially steep and small but well defined, began to bowl in the middle from the pressure of untold feet, and then eroded into slippery lumps. The carpet of cinders sank into the ice, which had melted and refrozen so many times that the debris first created a crunching layer of frizzled hole-pocked ice, and then vanished beneath slick greyish white.

Aliquaille's blue light bounced off strange shapes embedded in the looming walls. They'd reached the deep archives, and the halls here were carved from, and into, rooms that had been flooded and frozen. Fragments of Aqshian weave-paper, impermeable to water, floated off submerged shelves, recalling the parchments suspended in black nothingness in the Blind Queen's Maze. Books of acid-scribed metal plates, pierced and linked by rings, glimmered in the depths. Bits of woven-grass furniture and broken glass drifted among them, the latter almost invisible in the ice. Statues lay slantwise like drowned corpses caught in the chambers of sunken ships, and the bottom third of every room was a jumbled carpet of heavy objects: obsidian urns, tarnished antique armour, stone sarcophagi, arms and barrels from dismantled siege machines.

Occasionally, something sparked in the black depths, as if responding to the light that Aliquaille carried. It was quick and elusive, making Neave think of the glowing fish that darted through the deep seas of Ghyran and Ghur.

'Stormsparks,' Aliquaille said, catching one of Neave's glances at the frozen lights. 'Old magical devices, imbued with the God-King's power, that preserve his sanctuaries. They strengthen the integrity of these rooms against their own weight, and help keep the monastery from collapsing down the mountainside. They also guard against enemies of the faith, although that was more of a concern in centuries past than it is for us today.'

'May it ever be so,' Neave said politely, hiding her doubts.

The path continued, abruptly broadening into fresh-cut, crisply edged steps between cleanly shorn walls of ice. Rostus sighed in relief at the wider dimensions, although he still had to duck his head to keep from crashing into the ceiling.

'This part is newer?' Hendrick asked.

Aliquaille nodded. 'Newer, and also older. The halls below this point had become too hazardous for regular use, so they were fully frozen some years ago. When we need to cut our way back into the sealed parts of the Sanctuary, dedicants use ice cutters to carve out fresh paths. We cut these recently, at the request of the Vorgemi, who wished to delve into records too ancient to be otherwise accessible.'

'What else would have been in that area? Were there other materials stored alongside the treatises they said they wanted?' Neave asked. She had a fair guess at the answer already, having seen the disorganised contents of the other frozen archives, but she wanted to know for sure.

'I don't know what else would have been there. Something, certainly. We don't have the luxury of space to arrange things otherwise. What it might have been, however, I cannot tell you. The records are inexact, at best, and if the nets break, pieces occasionally drift from room to room when they are flooded.

Even so, nothing is lost here. Our records are engraved on metal or etched into weave-paper, so they may withstand both flood and flame. Our knowledge may be buried, but it is never lost,' Aliquaille said. She paused at the next landing, raising her light to look over the dark, cramped hallways that stretched away on this level. Needles of freshly cut ice lay scattered about the floor. 'This is where we brought the scholars. They should be...'

She broke off, eyes widening. The woman didn't say anything, only drew in a sharp breath, but that was all the alarm the Black-talons needed.

Drawing her axes, Neave shouldered to the fore, Hendrick close on her heels. Behind them, Aliquaille flattened herself against the frigid wall, her distress unspoken but palpable.

At the edge of Aliquaille's blue light lay a heap of corpses in the simple grey robes and heavy fur cloaks of Sanctuary dedicants. They appeared to have been killed quickly and quietly, for the bodies bore no defensive wounds and Neave could see no signs of struggle.

'Ystia,' Aliquaille whispered, distraught. 'Orendis. Why?'

Because the Vorgemi are the last faction seeking the scrolls, Neave thought, as suspicion crystallised into certainty. These were the agents of Chaos who had struck the Blind Queen's Maze and the Red Tree's heart, stealing the clues that had led them to this place. Now they'd stolen the Sanctuary's secrets with equal mercilessness.

Each victim had been struck down by a single blow to the heart or the back of the head, delivered with such inhuman force that it pierced cleanly through their skulls and sternums. They'd been shoved to the side of the room in a careless tangle, where they lay welded together by a cold river of blood.

With a chime from Lorai's staff, light flowed along the icy ceiling, rippling outwards in green-blue waves that illumined the icy archive where the dedicants had died. It flowed over a room that was, essentially, a single enormous block of ice wormed with narrow passages through which humans could walk, and Stormcasts could crawl. Stormsparks hovered in the depths, but unlike those they'd encountered earlier, these were burned out.

Loose nets of woven brown grass floated within the ice, and after a moment, Neave was able to use these to decipher the seeming chaos of the ice blocks. The entire library, including its shelves, had been carved out of ice. At some point, the shelves had been filled with sealed scroll cases, artworks and pottery book-urns. Those shelves had been strung with grass nets to keep the lighter artefacts from floating away, and then they'd been flooded. What Neave had initially taken for a solid block hadn't always been one; it was only when this portion of the monastery had been sealed off that it had become so.

Someone had hacked rough gaps out of the ice shelves, then pulverised the chunks for whatever lay within them. Shattered pottery cases and handfuls of discarded pages, torn out and cast aside because they'd been frozen together and refused to separate, suggested that whoever had ransacked the room had been looking for a book, or some other writing.

'Do you recognise any of these pieces?' Neave asked. 'Can you tell what the Vorgemi were looking for here?'

It took a moment for Aliquaille to respond. Eventually, however, she tore her eyes from the dead and shook off her shock. 'No. Nothing that was any more important than the contents of any other room. I don't understand why the Vorgemi would have done this.'

Neave shrugged. She bent to pick up a clump of frozen pages, waiting for Lorai to melt the ice so that she could pull them apart. 'They didn't want your people to know what they were taking. Whatever it was, it must have been obvious enough that taking it openly risked ruining their pretence of being true Sigmarites.'

A thread of magic stretched across the frozen pages, thawing them. Gently, Neave separated the soaked papers, managing to keep them mostly intact and legible. She scanned the archaic writing quickly, then paused and read over it again, with greater concern.

Holding the text out to the other Blacktalons, Neave showed them the index in the back, then a part of the spine frilled with the stubs of ripped pages. 'Varstrom. This atlas spoke of Varstrom. Look. It's here, in the index, though the Vorgemi tore away the referenced pages. Varstrom is a place, not a person. This book held a map of it. *That's* why they seized it and fled.'

'How would these Vorgemi escape the Sanctuary? Are there other exits?' Hendrick asked.

Aliquaille shook her head. 'From the upper levels, yes, but down here? Everything is frozen. The only way out would be–'

'To cut a new path,' Lorai finished for her. The Idoneth gestured into the frozen deeps, and the light shifted obediently, illuminating a small opening tunnelled into the ice at a steep slope, almost straight up. Handholds pocked one side.

The tunnel had been cut without concern for the shelves or their contents. Books and urns had been sliced in two by the superheated ice cutters, and their pieces lay on the floor next to chunks of cracked ice. Dull grey stormsparks dotted the walls, their magic exhausted by futile efforts to guard against these enemies of the faith.

Neave glanced at the deceased dedicants. They'd been stripped of their ice cutters, and the tunnel made by the Vorgemi was too small for the Stormcasts to use. 'Lorai?'

'Ice is water, and water flows,' the Idoneth said. Already, the tunnel was softening like clay in unseen hands. Bass groans and low creaks, profound as the cracking of the earth's bones, reverberated through the chamber as the tunnel reshaped itself to admit the Blacktalons.

'I can see them,' Lorai murmured, her eyes filmed over with a sheen of pale blue. 'They are waiting for us with weapons drawn in the hallowed halls.'

'The Vorgemi?' Neave asked.

'No. The Children of the Winter Sun.' Lorai blinked, and the film cleared from her gaze. 'They have let the Vorgemi pass already. They are waiting for us.'

CHAPTER TWENTY

'That's impossible. The Sanctuary of the Winter Sun is faithful to Sigmar,' Aliquaille blurted out, as the Blacktalons turned on her. There was no overt threat – there was no need – but the tension was sudden, and very sharp. 'We have always been loyal servants of the God-King.'

'For their sake, I hope that's true,' Shakana muttered. She was already reconfiguring her crossbow to its rapid-fire setting. Stowing the weapon in its sling, the sniper fell in behind Neave as they climbed up the ice tunnel, back towards the monastery's inhabited levels.

The tunnel cut cleanly through the upper archives, bypassing the staircase that the Blacktalons had descended. It came up through the floor of each archive room and ascended through the ceiling, using walls or shelves as ladders between. Cool water slicked the handholds, so freshly carved that they hadn't yet frozen over.

The Vorgemi hadn't spared any of the Sanctuary's treasures as they'd slashed their way up. Bisected funeral masks and the cleaved shields of nameless heroes, their shorn edges gleaming with raw, bright metal, jutted from the tunnel's rippled walls. Meltwater trickled down the broken masks like tears, and though she knew the destruction of these things was only a minor sin compared to all else the Vorgemi had done, Neave was nevertheless outraged by the casual indifference with which they'd vandalised these relics of faith.

The Children had dedicated generations of their lives to preserving the memories of the fallen, and the fact that these funerary icons were such obscure and minor things – consigned to the deep archives, forgotten in tombs of black ice – only made Neave angrier. *This was all that remained of them.*

Grunts and the rasp of chainmail against ice echoed from the tunnel over Neave's head. The Vorgemi climbed quickly, but not as quickly as Stormcast Eternals. With Lorai's aid, the Blacktalons were gaining.

Twice they passed the cooling corpses of lone scholars who'd been surprised amid the shelves. They encountered no one living, however, until they came to the final archway, demarcated by stark black blocks and a glowing blue keystone, that marked the boundary between the Sanctuary's warm heart and the cold archives it kept for the dead.

Thirty armed and armoured warriors awaited the Blacktalons there. They stood in formation in a practice hall ringed by the shields and arms of venerated heroes. The warriors wore the heavy cloaks of sanctuary dedicants, scarred by years of wind-lashed cinders and volcanic glass shards. Spiked helms of leather and bronze covered their faces, and the holy hammer of Sigmar shone on their chests and pauldrons.

Their leader was a tall woman armoured in bronze and gold, her heavy plate styled to evoke the sigmarite of the Stormcast Eternals without insulting them by overt imitation. She wore a stole similar to Aliquaille's, but shorter and pinned at shoulder and breastplate so that it would not come loose when she fought.

'Iriveya?' Aliquaille asked in confusion as she came to the archway and looked over the warriors in their unsmiling ranks. 'What is this?'

'Please stand aside, Summer Saint,' the gold-armoured woman replied in stiff, formal tones. 'This test is not yours. We will accept Sigmar's blessing, if you wish to give it, but we understand if you do not. Against the God-King's champions, our courage must be measured on its own.'

'I don't understand,' Aliquaille said. It was half protest, half plea. 'Why are you holding arms against the Stormcast Eternals? These are Sigmar's chosen. The Vorgemi are our enemies, Winter Saint. They pretended to be of the faith, but that was a lie. They've murdered the Children of the Winter Sun, and–'

'You must stand aside, Summer Saint,' the gold-armoured woman said again, and this time there was an edge of nervous impatience to her words. 'Please. I will not ask again. Do not dishonour our order by standing in the way of our greatest trial. The God-King himself has recognised our courage and discipline by sending his Stormcasts to test us, and we will not be found wanting.'

The Winter Saint's words, and the ready postures of the warriors behind her, filled Neave with sudden dread. 'We aren't here to fight you.'

The gold-armoured woman nodded, grimly satisfied. 'As it was foretold. Ithyrac informed us that you would say this. We respect your willingness to protect our dignity. But we do not need you to save our face. We will not decline Sigmar's challenge. The Children of the Winter Sun have always met the God-King's tests, and we will not fail now.' She raised her sword in formal salute. 'We welcome this chance to prove ourselves worthy. I pray we'll earn our place in your ranks.'

She raised her short stabbing sword. Behind her, the Children of the Winter Sun did the same, brandishing their blades in a single swift movement. 'Children! Our test is upon us. Do not flinch! Do not falter! Show Sigmar the strength of your faith!'

'This is madness,' Rostus breathed. He unlimbered his great hammer, but held it across his body in two hands, unwilling to commit to the fight yet. Slush dripped from his shaggy cloak, pattering onto the polished floor. 'Do they think this is how they'll become Stormcasts?'

'There is no test,' Neave cried to the dedicants, even as she took a step back. She did not draw her axes, but she fell into a defensive position, and she sensed the other Blacktalons arraying themselves at her back. 'We did not come to the Sanctuary for you. Our task lies elsewhere. Please, just *get out of our way.*' They'd been so close to the Vorgemi, and their enemies were gaining distance with every second.

But the Children of the Winter Sun weren't listening. They formed a steel-fanged blockade between the Blacktalons and the exit through which the Vorgemi had fled. Neave's confusion turned to anger, and then despair. *They leave us no choice. We* must *catch our quarry.*

Shakana had reached the same conclusion. The sniper's crossbow sparked with deadly energy. She dropped into a crouch, taking aim at the warriors.

'No!' Aliquaille shouted, rushing to put herself between the lines.

But it was too late. The gold-armoured Winter Saint led the charge. 'Children of the Winter Sun! Let us prove ourselves to the God-King! *Attack!*'

Neave sprinted across the cavernous hall and grabbed Aliquaille, jerking the woman away from a sword thrust that would have gutted her. As the woman stumbled, Shakana's crossbow stitched lines of lightning over her head, across the soldiers' ranks. The first row fell, drilled cleanly through helms and gorgets, but those behind them charged past the corpses.

Rostus broke their wave. His hammer swept the soldiers pitilessly aside. One crashed into a wall alcove, toppling an age-weathered stone saint from its plinth. The statue hit the floor and broke with a thunderous crack. Its head rolled over the chipped floor and stared blindly at the empty space where it had stood, and for a wild instant Neave imagined the nameless saint was trying to turn his eyes from the carnage.

She wished she could do the same.

It wasn't merely that the Children of the Winter Sun were attacking the Blacktalons. It was that they did so with fanatic determination, and with no sign of fear – either for their lives, or for their souls. *Do they really believe this is Sigmar's will?*

Terribly, tragically, it seemed so. The warriors' eyes were alight with awe behind their open-faced helms, and they cried to Sigmar even as they attacked his god-forged champions. Fixed in their own fanatic conviction concerning the God-King's wishes, they were deaf to the Blacktalons' calls to stop.

'Please, no,' Aliquaille sobbed, but no one heard her except Neave.

Hendrick tried disarming a warrior by shearing off the head of the man's spear, but the soldier cast the stump aside and drew his ice cutter instead. Gouging the red-hot tool into an icy wall, the soldier created a blinding veil of steam. Hendrick was forced to squint against the hissing rush, and another warrior seized the advantage. He swung his own ice cutter in hard, searing a sooty streak across the Stormcast's plated thigh.

Hendrick snarled and swept his sword around again. The warrior raised his ice cutter to block the blow, but Hendrick's blade snapped effortlessly through its rune-scribed metal and buried itself in the man's chest. The warrior crumpled, spraying blood in a wide arc that steamed against the cold stone walls and bubbled black where it struck the ice cutter.

'The Vorgemi are escaping,' Lorai said, low and urgent. 'They have reached the outer slope. A conveyance awaits them there.'

Neave bit back a curse. The time for mercy, if they'd ever had any to spare on that luxury, was running out fast. 'Yield!' she shouted at the remaining Children. 'You will not win this fight! Your deaths do nothing to honour Sigmar. *Stand down!*'

Their only answer was a redoubling of their attack. Three came at her with short obsidian-tipped spears and shields of volcanic glass reinforced by holy sigils. They fought well together, two always pressing the attack or raising their shields for cover while the third sought out weaknesses and blind spots.

Neave killed them all in seconds. Her hurricane axes split their spears and shattered their shields, then took their heads. The trio died as they'd fought, in unison, and she could spare scarcely a second to mourn them before the next warrior came rushing at her with sword readied.

'*Stop this madness!*' Neave shouted in frustration, and again her cry met only a wave of renewed ferocity.

A soldier pushed another statue out of its alcove towards her, trying to knock her off balance. Neave sidestepped it easily, and the statue shattered into chunks of stone and age-brittled armour, drawing another anguished moan from Aliquaille.

Neave leapt over the statue. She killed the soldier with a backhand swing as she passed, then dropped another who'd been crouching beside the alcove, hoping for an opening. Their bodies fell, side by side, over the statue they'd destroyed.

There has to be a better way. Sigmar would have been able to stop the Children without killing them. The God-King would have had the wisdom to break through their delusion, or the charismatic force to make them stand down even if they clung to it.

He would have known how to subdue them without resorting to lethal measures.

But Neave could think of only one option, and it was uncertain. 'Lorai! Can you bind them with water, or freeze them in place?'

'Only if you wish me to lose sight of the Vorgemi.' Alone among their number, the Idoneth had taken no part in the fight. Her eyes were filmed over with sparkling lenses of ice, and she turned with a distracted stiffness that had her looking at where Neave had been standing five seconds ago, not where she was now. 'They have taken a conveyance. It is difficult to see through the snow, but I believe it has wings. It moves quickly. I cannot track them through the blizzard and stop these warriors simultaneously. You must choose one, Blacktalon.'

'The Vorgemi.' Neave gave the order without hesitation, but not without grief. A hard lump tightened her throat.

She didn't bother asking the warriors to yield again. They'd refused reason; they had chosen the blade. The best she could do was make it fast.

The holy tapestries dripped with blood, and the remaining statues were defaced by the scorching swipes of ice cutters and the gore of their sworn defenders. Crimson washed over the floor and froze, and the survivors tripped over the bodies of their comrades, yet none of the Sanctuary's soldiers surrendered. Not one.

Their courage was as extraordinary as it was dispiriting, for they had no chance of prevailing, and still they fought on to the last breath. Crippled and dying, they clawed for their spears.

Finally, after an eternity of excruciation that lasted less than five minutes, it was over. All of the Children of the Winter Sun were down.

The last of them, a muscular young woman with sweat-matted red hair already freezing to the floor, looked up at Neave through dimming eyes. She tried to smile, but only coughed. 'Honoured Stormcast. Did we pass your test?'

'There never was a test,' Neave said heavily, too demoralised for anything but the bitter truth. She glanced over at Lorai, partly to see whether they could yet pursue the Vorgemi, but also so she wouldn't have to look at the woman she'd slaughtered.

The Idoneth had her head cocked at the ceiling, calculating the most efficient angle for an ice tunnel. After a moment, she raised her hands, and bored a smooth circular hole between the ceiling's ribs, like an ice-edged whirlpool grinding through the stone. But digging through stone blocks was slower going than tunnelling through ice had been, and it would be several moments before the Blacktalons could pursue. Neave had no choice but to look back at the dying soldier.

It wasn't clear whether the woman had heard what she'd said. The warrior's eyes were cloudy with coming death. Her lips tried to form a question, but she hadn't the strength to speak. She sucked in a shaky breath and tried again. 'I know it is unworthy to ask such a thing, and Ithyrac warned us it was meant to be a secret. But I... I still wish to ask. Did we prove ourselves? Will we be chosen to join you?'

'I cannot say,' Neave told her, both because it was true and because it was the only solace she could offer the dying woman. An acid hatred for this Ithyrac, who had fatally deceived so many faithful warriors, burned in her chest. So, too, did her guilt for being the Vorgemi's unwitting weapon. 'That is for the God-King to decide, not me.'

'Of course. Yes.' The woman exhaled, and for a moment Neave thought she'd died. But then her eyelids fluttered, and she whispered: 'I thank you, honoured Stormcast. Thank you for letting us prove our faith. For testing us as no one else could. For–'

'Neave, the tunnel's up,' Hendrick said. He'd heard enough of the conversation to be gentle, but the mission was the mission.

Neave nodded. She closed her eyes, squeezing away the bitter tears that welled in them, and pushed herself to her feet. Her armour felt heavier, or maybe she herself felt weaker. *They were worthy of you, Sigmar. Deceived, but worthy. I was not.*

But she could not dwell on that, and there was nothing to be gained by staying longer. The redheaded warrior had died. Neave climbed onto a broken statue, preparing to leap up to the tunnel. Shakana and Rostus had already gone, and Hendrick was in the midst of pulling himself through the ceiling. With a final heave and a shower of ice flakes, his boots disappeared.

Aliquaille lifted a hand. The woman's eyes were puffy and reddened, her cheeks wet with tears, but she straightened with an undeniable resolve. 'Let me come with you.' Seeing Neave's refusal beginning to form, she hurried to add: 'The Vorgemi came here. Ithyrac came here. They must have done so for a reason. I know the Sanctuary and its secrets better than anyone alive. Perhaps Sigmar put me in this place to help you.'

And her cathedral has become a charnel house. By my hand. By ours.

That shouldn't have mattered. Neave knew better than to let sentiment sway her.

But in the bloodied, freezing ruins of what had once been a holy sanctuary, surrounded by the bodies of loyal Sigmarites she herself had slain…

She was human enough to find it difficult to refuse. *If Sigmar did not want us so, he would have taken these feelings away.* But the God-King had not chosen to make his Stormcasts emotion-less killers. He'd chosen to leave them with memories, impulses, desires, dreams. He'd chosen to leave them *human*, as much as they could be, and Neave trusted his wisdom when she didn't trust her own.

If Sigmar meant for her to feel regret and shame at the thought of abandoning Aliquaille amid the carnage they'd caused, there was a reason for it. Perhaps that was even why he had allowed the Children of the Winter Sun to sacrifice themselves so pointlessly.

Neave didn't really believe the God-King would spend the lives of his faithful so callously… but it was true that she would never have considered letting Aliquaille accompany the Blacktalons if not for the Children's deaths.

So perhaps there had been some purpose to the tragedy, after all. This entire mission had been guided by prophecies and premonitions, and Neave still had little concrete information on the Blacktalons' final target. Perhaps there really *was* something a scholar from the Sanctuary of the Winter Sun could tell them.

Perhaps this was Sigmar's hand, drawing her a sign.

Neave offered her own hand. 'You'll have to keep up.'

Aliquaille took it. Eagerly. 'With Sigmar's strength, I shall.'

The tunnel took them up, and up again, through ice and stone and ruptured pipes that had once channelled warmth from the volcanic taps, and now vented their precious heat uselessly into Lorai's chill bore. It came at last to a semi-natural cave overlooking the mountainside into which the Sanctuary had been built. Despite the shrieking winds that battered the cave's stone-and-grass doors, a strong odour of sulphur and lizard droppings met the Blacktalons as they emerged into the biting cold.

Stone stalls, heavily grimed with rippled cakes of soot, took up a little more than half the cave's space. They looked like they'd been built to hold something thrice the size of a horse. Harnesses, bits and grooming tack hung in neat rows on a pegboard beside the stalls. Shovels and rakes leant against the wall nearby.

Otherwise the cave was empty.

Aliquaille frowned at the vacant stalls. Heaps of frozen droppings littered them, but the beasts that had left them were gone. 'Where are the vulcanaurs?'

'I believe they've been slaughtered.' Rostus walked to the cave's mouth. A thick shield of ice had been poured over the doors' outer faces, reinforced by more of the glowing stone beads they'd seen in the depths, but the bar holding them together was gone, and the wind bashed them violently to and fro. The big Stormcast caught one of the doors and held it halfway open, though his muscles strained with the effort of keeping it steady.

Through the gap, Neave could see the bodies of several black-and-red scaled beasts slumped on the ledge outside. They had long necks, serpentine tails and fan-like wings, and even in death they held a handsome dignity. Icy snow was accumulating in grainy drifts against the bodies, and shards of wind-hurled glass spiked their glossy scales.

Raising a padded sleeve over her face in a feeble shield against the debris-laden winds, Aliquaille moved forwards to look over the ledge beside Rostus. She came back with blood streaming down her brow from a shallow but ugly gash, and a face grimmer than that small wound warranted.

'They killed three of the vulcanaurs, but the rest are missing,' Aliquaille told them, wiping the blood away from her eyes. 'Over a dozen lived in this eyrie. These beasts are fiercely loyal to their kin. If the Vorgemi stole them, that's bad enough, but if they slaughtered a few and left the bodies to enrage the survivors…'

'It doesn't look like that's an "if",' Rostus rumbled. He squared himself in front of the ice-clad doors, readying his hammer. 'Brace yourselves.'

CHAPTER TWENTY-ONE

'Don't kill them,' Aliquaille said. She was already retreating back into the monastery, using the stable door instead of Lorai's ice tunnel. 'I can speak to them. Please. Only give me the chance.'

'Do we believe her?' Shakana asked, crouching behind a stall and shifting her crossbow to its middle setting. She reached into the case behind her shoulder to draw a handful of crystal-tipped bolts that Lorai had scribed with runes of power, and fitted one into place.

'Yes,' Neave said, although that was more hope than conviction. 'I believe Sigmar sent her to us for a reason.'

'I hope you're right. This is going to require some tricky shooting, if we want to keep these things alive.' Shakana glanced over her shoulder. 'Lorai?'

The Idoneth drew back her sleeves and shifted her staff to the crook of an elbow, freeing her hands and arms. 'I am ready.'

'Rostus?'

'Ready. I'll block the–'

The rest of his words went up in flame. An enormous blast of fire slammed into the outer doors, curling smoky tongues through the gaps above and below them. The doors' thick plates of ice vaporised, filling the cave with a rush of sulphurous steam.

Rostus grunted, bracing himself against the doors' stone ribs to hold them together. Steam and meltwater poured over him, obscuring his face and form so that he appeared to be a boulder of pure brute strength. Woven grass, stripped of its icy shell and abruptly dried by the obliterating heat, crackled and burned around his hands.

He stood his ground. Blistered, straining, head lowered and heels set against the fury of the flames, Rostus gave up not an inch. The doors, bolstered by his determination, held.

The firestorm crested, broke, and pulled back. Rostus heaved for breath, his head hanging. His sweat had evaporated in the first rush, but now it poured forth, dripping from his chin.

'Now!' Shakana cried.

Rostus gathered his strength, pushed past the pain, and threw the scorched doors open.

Two winged, serpentine creatures hovered outside the cave. They were much larger than the bodies Neave had glimpsed on the ledge earlier. Now that she could see them side by side, she realised with sickening certainty that these must be adults, and the ones that the Vorgemi had slain had been juveniles. Their offspring, most likely.

The adults, unsurprisingly, appeared furious. They were also beautiful: sleek, muscular beasts with four large wings fanned out in pairs along their backs, whip-like tails, and draconic heads. Their hides were the glossy black of fine obsidian, fissured with glowing red heat-lines between each scale. Those radiating lines of heat widened and converged around the creatures' abdomens, which glowed like the forges of the gods.

Neave realised that the firestorms had been created not, as she'd assumed, by some equivalent to dragon's breath, but by the creatures furiously beating their wings to fan the heat of their internal furnaces. Now, it seemed, their fiery energies had been temporarily depleted, but their rage had not.

Shakana shot them, one after the other. She hit one in the sternum, just above the incandescent red fissure of its belly, and the other in the base of a forewing. Both quarrels shattered on impact. Their enchanted tips caused no real damage, but released a gush of magically contained water instead.

Lorai seized control of that water, animating it into liquid ropes, thick as her wrist and stronger than iron, that bound both creatures in mid-air. As they began to fall, she sent smaller tendrils into the mountainside and froze the vulcanaurs in an icy likeness of a spitting spider's web. The beasts shrieked and battered their tails against the stone, but neither could escape.

'I cannot hold them for long,' the Idoneth warned. 'They will melt free with the heat of their bodies, once they regather their strength. The effort required to sustain ice against their power would leave me useless for days.'

'Where is that woman?' Shakana demanded, looking about for Aliquaille.

As if in answer to her question, the monastery's inner door opened. Aliquaille rushed out, holding a golden horn set with red gems and inscribed with holy sigils encircled by the winged forms of vulcanaurs. She put it to her lips and, after a pause to catch a gasped breath, blew.

Neave expected a thunderous song, but the golden horn made no sound. Instead, it blew a cloud of incandescent sparks, which shimmered through intricate patterns like a shoal of tiny glittering fish, darting and weaving through the air.

From that sparkling fire cloud emanated a scent of burning

incense, heavy and yet ethereal, smelling of sacred woods and cold smoke caught in hushed cathedral halls.

The pinned vulcanaurs lifted their heads towards the fire cloud, and though Neave's view was limited by the angle and the stable doors, she had the sense that they saw and understood something in the sparks. Their heads lifted towards the cloud, and the curve of their necks suggested alert, wary comprehension.

'I cannot hold them much longer,' Lorai warned, 'and more are coming.'

'Let them go,' Neave said. Her hands tightened on her axes, though she kept her stance neutral. 'Let's see if Aliquaille calmed them.'

Lorai murmured a sibilant word, and the ice holding the serpentine creatures against the mountain wall dissipated into water, then steam. Both vulcanaurs plummeted fifty feet or so, then caught themselves and rose up with swift beats of their wings.

In flight, the vulcanaurs were astonishing, and Neave was briefly mesmerised by their balletic beauty even as she appreciated their danger. They caught the Sorrow Peaks' capricious gusts in their wings as easily as gulls coasting on trade winds, and rode them with pirouetting playfulness. Within moments they'd risen back to the stables, cutting almost straight vertical courses through the air, and hovered beside the ledge.

Heat shimmered over the vulcanaurs' glowing red midsections, and they fanned it with one pair of wings each as they drew curlicues in the air. This time, instead of launching a conflagration, the vulcanaurs created their own answering cloud of sparks. It, too, scintillated through a complex display of colours, shifting from white to gold to red, with wavering accents in fast-fading blue and violet.

Aliquaille walked closer to the vulcanaurs and inhaled deeply through the horn. A few sparks were sucked in through the wide mouth, but it hardly seemed to change the overall pattern. Still, after a moment, the woman nodded, and blew out again, creating a second fire cloud that mingled with the animals'.

'What does it mean?' Rostus asked, eyeing the overlapping clouds warily. The big Stormcast watched the vulcanaurs with undisguised curiosity, but also a deeply held tension. Fire often brought back bad memories for him, Neave knew; it had taken his family, and even now Rostus sometimes had difficulty looking straight into flames.

'She'll give us answers when she has them,' Shakana said, flatly enough that it sounded as much threat as reassurance. 'Neave, do you really want to trust this woman?'

'"Want" isn't quite the word,' Neave replied. 'I have a sense that it's what we're meant to do. Call it an instinct.'

Nodding noncommittally, Shakana slid the rest of her water bolts back into their case and shifted her crossbow back to its widest setting: heavy, lethal blasts of lightning. She laid it unobtrusively on the ground beside her, mostly hidden by her thigh, where she could reach it in an instant if the vulcanaurs turned against them.

A few moments later, Aliquaille turned from the ledge and came back to them. Her eyes were reddened and her cheeks flushed from heat and wind. 'The Vorgemi captured three adults with black chain harnesses, then slaughtered their young to provoke the remaining vulcanaurs into a rage. It nearly worked. Had they not recognised the sparkhorn, they would have killed you, believing you to be in league with the interlopers who murdered their nestlings and the dedicants who tended the stables. All their human friends are dead, they say.'

Rostus scowled and flexed his fists. 'Second time today these Vorgemi have tried to use Sigmar's own faithful against us. I'm beginning to dislike the bastards.'

'Where did they go?' Neave pressed.

'South. Towards the Earthscar.' Aliquaille touched a band of red gems near the mouthpiece of the horn, and gestured towards the vulcanaurs on the ledge. Each of them wore a jewelled band of similar make about its left foreleg. 'We can track them with the horn, and they can sense each other as well. Storms are so common in the Sorrow Peaks that the Sanctuary banded our vulcanaurs long ago, so that we would not lose one another if gales blew us apart.'

Shakana raised an eyebrow. Neave could see that the sniper was slightly mollified by this new information, but the change in her demeanour was subtle enough that it was likely lost on Aliquaille. 'They'll sense us as well?'

'Yes. If we pursue on the vulcanaurs, their beasts will be able to sense their wing-mates approaching. But they are willing to carry you, if I go along as well. They are… upset with the Vorgemi for capturing their kin. Being forced to bear unwanted riders is a particular abomination to them. They are strong-willed creatures, and proud, and to be so easily broken by Chaos… It has enraged them. They want revenge.'

'We'll be more than glad to help them,' Rostus assured her. 'So. The Earthscar. What can you tell us about that?'

'That is what the vulcanaurs call the Pershenal Gap.' Aliquaille touched one of the snapped chains that dangled from her wimple, tracing the holy symbols with a fingertip. 'Legend holds that it was created by an ancient and vengeful god, long forgotten and likely dead, who hurled his spear into the earth. He had become incensed by the world's sins, and sought to kill the realm itself. When lava floods and plagues of smokeblights failed to satisfy his thirst for destruction, he assailed Aqshy with his own weapons, and he wounded it grievously.

'Whether or not the Pershenal Gap is a god's wound in the world, it is indisputably a poisoned place. The gap cleaves into the mountains' heart, belching gases and vapours that kill even the smoke-breathing beasts of Aqshy. Magma burbles up continually from the rift, and those who have seen it say that it seems consciously malevolent, striking at living creatures and sabotaging explorers' equipment as though guided by some cruel sentience.

'They say, too, that the Pershenal Gap is haunted by the spirits of the restless dead,' Aliquaille added, with a note of hesitancy. 'Gheists who could not find their way to Shyish, and who are cursed to haunt this world until they're freed.'

Shakana had finished stowing her weapons while Aliquaille spoke. She glanced up from checking their fastenings. 'What would draw the Vorgemi there?'

'I don't know,' Aliquaille answered. 'The Pershenal Gap holds nothing but death.'

'No,' Neave said. 'The Pershenal Gap holds the secret to Varstrom.'

The flight through the Sorrow Peaks was extraordinary. For a few rare, glorious hours, the mountain gales quieted their fury, allowing the vulcanaurs to fill their wings with wind and soar over the glowing, black-webbed peaks. Snow shivered on the high mountains, often collapsing abruptly as lava or volcanic gas vented beneath the deep drifts. There was seldom much warning: an imperceptible quivering across the snowpack, followed by a thunderous avalanche or a geyser of displaced snow that shot hundreds of feet into the air, vaporising into steam midway.

From afar, the sights were beautiful rather than terrifying. The fountains of snow and steam created ghostly rainbows over the peaks, and the rivers of lava glowed brilliantly against the broad, rippled black-and-white fields of cinder and snow. The Sorrow Peaks were imbued with a primeval, elemental grandeur, and Neave had never seen it laid out before her in this aerial view. It felt like a glimpse of a world new-forged, not yet seen by any but the gods.

The vulcanaurs carried them across the sky with determined

speed. Aliquaille had helped the Blacktalons adjust the saddles and harnesses to accommodate their stature, although trying to make the human-sized gear fit Rostus was a hopeless task. Nevertheless, the vulcanaurs bore his weight without complaint, and if anything, seemed even more eager to wield him as a living weapon against their foes.

Their anger, though not directed at the Stormcasts, coursed through them as intensely as their heat. Neave could feel it pulse against her like a second heartbeat.

It was an anger she shared.

The other targets on this mission had been abominations, but of a sort she'd faced and fought many times before. Gerispryx and the Red Tree, Pelokoa and the Great Flayer: all had prised at the Blacktalons' weaknesses, undermining the Stormcasts where they could, but they had done so directly, enemy to enemy. Their hatred held a certain honesty.

Ithyrac and the Vorgemi hadn't done that. They'd lied to the dedicants of the Sanctuary of the Winter Sun, deceiving them into a suicidal attack on Sigmar's own Stormcasts, and had tried to trick the vulcanaurs in similar fashion. The Vorgemi had slaughtered the creatures' young in the hope that the bereaved adults would retaliate against the Blacktalons, and it would have worked if not for Aliquaille's intervention.

Using innocents was abhorrent enough, but manipulating fellow Sigmarites into being slaughtered by Stormcast Eternals was vile. Neave hadn't been able to shake her disgust, or her guilt, since it happened.

They were supposed to be better than this. They were supposed to be champions of the faith. All the Blacktalons were, but Neave especially.

She was their leader. It was by her command that they killed, or didn't.

And what she had chosen…

It wasn't a choice.

Ithyrac had forced her hand. Rationally, coldly, Neave knew that was true.

Emotionally, she couldn't shake her conviction that if she'd been wiser, quicker, more insightful, she could have – *would* have – found a better solution than killing the Sanctuary's dedicants. A worthier Sigmarite would have found a way. Somehow.

But Neave hadn't. It hurt, and although she knew it was unworthy to admit to such base emotions, that hurt left her wanting revenge.

Ahead, a wall of black smoke rose from the mountains to the sky, visible only as a starless blot against the night. The vulcanaurs had flown through the descending dusk into darkness, and now they dived into the mountains' shadows, plunging the Blacktalons into a vastly deeper blackness.

Fine grit filled the air. An odour like coal smoke, but bitterer and laced with unpleasant, throat-burning metallic notes, enveloped the vulcanaurs and their riders. Neave had donned her gilded mask against the cold already, and was glad she'd done so, as coarse volcanic dust grated against the metal. She lost sight of her companions, and could barely see the fissured red glow of her own vulcanaur's neck beneath her gauntlets.

'How much further?' Neave asked Aliquaille, who was saddled just in front of her. The vulcanaurs were accustomed to carrying two riders apiece, but only Neave and Aliquaille, and Shakana and Lorai, were light enough to travel in pairs. Hendrick and Rostus had to ride alone, and the largest of the vulcanaurs – a grizzled female that Aliquaille said was known as Blue-Eye for her scarred and milky left eye – was hard-pressed to carry his weight and keep speed.

'Not far. The Vorgemi descended only a mile ahead,' Aliquaille called back. She had pressed the golden horn directly against the vulcanaur's skin, and seemed to be able to communicate by breathing through the instrument that way.

Neave relayed this information to the other Blacktalons using Lorai's enchanted water-drops. It was the only method they had of communication through the rushing winds of their flight, especially since they now couldn't see one another through the smoke-filled night.

The air grew hotter as the vulcanaurs began to descend. Wind-blown grit scoured Neave's skin through every tiny gap in her plate. She could still feel dust on her tongue, but she couldn't smell or taste it any more. A few minutes ago, the metallic stench of the smoke had made her light-headed, and the dust that sifted through her mask had tasted of sulphur and caustic ash, but all of that was gone.

Instead a thick, muzzy warmth began to wrap around her temples. It tightened steadily, constricting her head until her vision blurred and an insect-like buzzing filled her ears. Phantasmal shapes loomed in the darkness, reaching for her with clawed hands that dissolved into grainy smoke just as they were about to close around her face.

The vulcanaur was diving much faster, plummeting at such velocity that Neave wondered whether they weren't just falling. She tried to ask Aliquaille what was happening, but nothing came out of her mouth except more buzzing.

Neave shook her head, but the noise only grew louder. She was so dizzy that she might have fallen out of the saddle if she hadn't been strapped in. Or perhaps she *had* fallen, and was too disoriented to realise that she was tumbling head over feet, through poisoned clouds, into the molten void of the Pershenal Gap.

The faces in the smoke crowded around her. They were enormous and crude, like figures moulded from mud by someone only dimly familiar with human shapes. Their eyes were no more than shallow suggestions, but their great sagging jaws stretched wide enough to swallow Neave whole. *Faces painted on a tent,* she thought, but she couldn't remember from where.

The clouds' vast mouths moved in cataclysmic words, but there was no sense to them, only a rhythmic, pounding intensification of the buzzing that hammered at Neave's skull. It pressed and pulsed, threatening to shatter her bones from the inside out. The air in her lungs swelled until she was forced to cough it out in puffs of hot sulphur, and couldn't begin to breathe anything back in.

Suddenly cold sluiced over her. Pinprick flashes shot across her vision. The smoky faces dissolved, and a chill silver radiance spread across the sky, which *was* the sky, clear and unmistakable, spangled with icy stars overhead.

Neave lay flat on her back, breathing hard, staring up at the alien sky. Cold stone pressed against her from below and rose up around her in desolate unlit structures, simultaneously foreign and familiar.

An aching emptiness filled her core. It was such a profound absence that at first she couldn't conceive of what was missing – as if, without notice, her face had been erased into a smooth blank, or the axes had vanished from her side. The loss cut that deeply into Neave's identity. It stripped to the marrow of who she was.

After an impossible, eternal moment, she realised what was gone.

Sigmar. She'd lost her god. The comfort of his presence within her, the strength she took from his faith in her, and hers in him... It was gone. She felt nothing when she reached for him. Only a void, empty as a cave without echoes.

Neave was distantly surprised that she could still breathe, see, and think. Could a Stormcast *exist* without her god?

Evidently so, even if it felt unutterably strange.

Her companions were scattered nearby, all similarly dazed,

along with the stunned and twitching vulcanaurs. They seemed to have been thrown onto the ruins of a market square in an abandoned city. Dead black weeds, bent and withered, rattled in gaps between the flagstones. Vacant windows looked down on them indifferently from high towers encircling the square. The buildings echoed the architecture of Azyr, all sunburst spires and grand orreries, but something about their shapes seemed… off, somehow.

The colours were wrong, as well. Everything around them was monochrome, and even the Blacktalons themselves seemed washed in grey. *Where* are *we?*

Neave sat up just in time to catch a flicker of movement from one of the nearby towers.

Movement, and metal. Instinctively she rolled to the side, taking cover behind the toppled bowl of a broken fountain.

Barbed crossbow bolts pinged off the overturned basin, leaving black-inked gouges in the stone. Looking up, Neave caught a glimpse of the shooter's conical, goggled helm pulling away from the window.

They'd found the Vorgemi.

CHAPTER TWENTY-TWO

The screech of the crossbow bolts snapped the Blacktalons out of their stupor. They scattered, Shakana and Hendrick crowding alongside Neave behind the overturned fountain's bowl, Aliquaille huddling behind the crumbling statue that had once poured water into the basin, and Rostus taking cover behind the corner of a building to the others' right. There was something peculiar about the lines and material of that building, Neave noted in a small part of her mind, but the immediate threat gave her no time to dwell on it.

The vulcanaurs shook their heads and flapped their wings, but they were slower to shake off their daze. Crossbow bolts hammered the beasts as they clawed back to their feet. Some skidded off their sleek black scales, and one burst into flame as it struck a vulcanaur's bright-hot abdomen, but others slammed home.

The draconic creatures screamed in pain, a high vibrating shriek like serrated blades grinding against one another. The red-banded leathery fans on either side of their faces flared out in rage, and they leapt into the air, circling up through the cold silver-flashed sky to the windows of the tower where their assailants lurked.

Swiftly the vulcanaurs positioned themselves in front of the tower, as they'd done outside the stables at the Sanctuary of the Winter Sun, and beat their wings rapidly as their abdomens began glowing with heat. Hotter and hotter they burned, glowing red, orange and incandescent gold from their chins to the base of their tails. The heat from their blazes reached Neave on the ground, three hundred feet away, and she had to turn her helmed face away from the glare.

The vulcanaurs loosed their inferno. Four firestorms converged on the tower's upper half. Stone blocks cracked apart in the heat. The air shuddered and shimmered as it boiled.

Then, without warning, something exploded inside the tower. If the vulcanaurs' collective blast had been a conflagration, this was the death of a small sun. The concussion lifted Neave off the ground and threw her hard onto her back.

Cracked stones burst apart, shredding the skies. All four vulcanaurs were hurled out of the air. One, mortally wounded, hit the flagstones with a bone-cracking thud and did not move again.

Four other vulcanaurs launched themselves from nearby roof-tops, closing in on either side. In a coordinated attack, they assailed their former wing-mates with claw and fang.

The new vulcanaurs' fury was startling, unnatural. They thrashed their heads in wild screams, but only hoarse strangled croaks escaped their throats, and they lashed their tails against the roofs with such careless violence that they tore their own flesh apart on the stone, leaving spatters of flesh streaked with scales. Neave saw rune-scribed collars glowing darkly about their throats, and understood immediately that those cruel implements of Chaos had driven them into a frenzy.

The Blacktalons' vulcanaurs, still reeling, offered no resistance.

They flapped and scratched at the market square's stones, unable to stand, let alone fight back. Doubtlessly they would all have been killed, had Shakana not risen up onto a knee and started firing at the attackers.

Lines of golden lightning stuttered across the smoking flagstones and punched black-edged holes into the corrupted vulcanaurs. One of Shakana's shots drilled through a vulcanaur's eye, dropping the creature instantly. The others reared back, making their raspy half-voiced cries.

If Sigmar had been taken from the Blacktalons, his gifts hadn't. Neave took heart from that, and hurled her axes after Shakana's shots. She hit the closest vulcanaur in the chest and throat, gouging bloody holes in its hide.

Slow, too slow. The damage Neave could do like this didn't compare with the carnage she could inflict up close. It took a full second for her axes to fly through the air, and she was exposed when she stepped out of cover to retrieve them. She snarled in frustration. *This won't work.* Rostus and Hendrick were even more handicapped; they were close-quarters specialists, ill-suited to ranged combat.

Another volley of crossbow bolts came from the towers overlooking the market square. These came from the damaged towers to either side of the one that had been rigged to explode.

'Shadow jumpers,' Shakana muttered as she ducked back behind the fountain basin. A quarrel hit the stone and deflected past her head.

Neave nodded, having had the same thought. The ambushers had originally fired from the centre tower, now demolished, and they'd moved to the towers on either side without crossing any of the empty space between. Therefore they had some magic that enabled them to leap from one place to the next. She'd seen servants of Chaos use blood, crystals and mirrors as short-range gates, but in this place, shadows did seem most likely.

'Light?' she suggested.

Shakana was already pulling a pair of bolts from another of her special cases. She thumbed her crossbow to the middle setting and fitted a bronze-tipped quarrel into its slot. 'On it.'

Neave motioned to Hendrick and Rostus, then to the towers. Both nodded in response. They, too, had seen the quarrels' flight, and no more needed to be said.

Lorai's voice echoed through the ear-phials. 'I will stay to protect the beasts. If our situation is as I believe, we will need them to leave. They must survive, or we cannot.'

'All right,' Neave murmured. She glanced at Shakana. 'Go.'

Shakana fired her bronze-tipped bolts into the towers' vacant windows, one after the other. They shattered on impact, flooding the towers with golden light and shaking more stones loose with a twinned, deafening boom. If the light was not quite as brilliant as Neave had expected, it was nevertheless more than sufficient to turn both towers into lighthouses in the night.

Even before the bolts struck, the Blacktalons were moving. Neave charged into one of the towers; Hendrick took the other. She heard Rostus' heavy tread behind them, and trusted that he would follow whoever seemed to need him more.

The tower was eerily silent when Neave rushed in. Its ash-black stone had a translucency reminiscent of the darkest smoky quartz, though with a violet tinge that suggested amethyst instead. The sparse furnishings were made of the same material, dotted with cushions and hangings in faded violet.

Everything looked faintly moth-eaten, or eroded, as if it had been carved from sand and lapped by gentle waves. Edges were blunted, smooth surfaces subtly pitted, embellishments and decorations worn to lumps and dimples. None of the busts on the bookshelves had faces, and the few books sitting beside them hardly even seemed to be books. They were just the shapes of books, devoid of lettering on their spines or titles on their covers, and Neave had the distinct sense that if she tried to open one, she'd find it a uniform mass, without any pages to turn.

The monochrome strangeness of it made Neave feel as if she were walking into yet another hallucinatory vision, like the one the Red Tree had inflicted on her. The feeling intensified as she realised that the walls were hung with small painted icons of Sigmar, though the images were all oddly indistinct, with the god's face blurred to a featureless smudge. They were old-fashioned, too, depicting Sigmar in archaic armour and with his beard braided in a fashion Neave had only glimpsed in the oldest cathedrals of Azyr.

Whoever had lived in this place had been a Sigmarite. That much seemed clear. Little else was, but neither was it relevant to the task at hand.

Neave rushed up the stairs. A black-helmed Vorgemi met her on the steps, brandishing a barbed spear. She threw an axe into his chest, expecting an easy kill, but the weapon passed through his body without resistance and clattered on the wall behind him.

Illusion. Neave hissed in comprehension just as the false image vanished and the real Vorgemi blinked into view, two steps to the side of where she'd thought he was. He stabbed at her. She swung a forearm down, knocking the weapon aside, but it was close. The Vorgemi was faster than she'd expected, and Neave herself was slower.

Sigmar, grant me strength. But the simple comfort of the prayer eluded her. Neave had repeated those words innumerable times, and Sigmar had never failed to fill her soul with reassurance when she'd asked.

This time, there was no answer. Only silence greeted her prayer. She was alone.

It cracked her confidence. She dispatched the Vorgemi clumsily with her remaining blade, taking three strokes to finish what one should have done, and stumbled heedlessly past the corpse. So disoriented was she that Neave almost forgot to retrieve her fallen axe as she passed by.

Two more Vorgemi blurred out of the shadows on the next landing. They might have been scorched by Shakana's blast; it was hard to tell, with their black armour in the gloom. No weakness showed in their fighting. They attacked ferociously and with disciplined skill, one moving swiftly to exploit any gaps the other opened in the Blacktalon's defences. Worse, they slipped through the shadows, vanishing just as her blades were about to bite and reappearing behind her swings.

Neave was faster and stronger, but she was alone, and still shaken by the God-King's failure to answer her call. She swung at the closer Vorgemi, who melted into darkness to elude her. The other stabbed down with a barbed spear, hooking the edge of Neave's breastplate. He wrenched at the haft, trying to throw her off balance.

She kept her footing, but had to drop her guard. The first Vorgemi saw an opening. He stepped back into solidity, and his spear came darting in.

Neave grabbed it. She didn't have a choice. The spear hooked into her armour meant the Vorgemi could throw her off the stairs if she shifted her weight too far. Instead she seized the weapon and, praying that its poisoned teeth couldn't bite past her gauntlet's blessed sigmarite, jerked it forwards.

The Vorgemi fell. Sidestepping and releasing the spear as he tumbled past her on the stairs, Neave cracked an axe into the back of the man's helm. Her blade bit through metal and bone, and spat out pulped, bloody brain.

His companion didn't flee into the shadows. He dropped into a defensive stance, spear drawn back and poised to strike. From above, Neave heard heavy, hurried footsteps, and understood that the Vorgemi was buying time for his superiors to finish whatever task had brought them here.

Neave threw her axes at him. One after the other, lightning and steel blurred into a deadly wheel. The Vorgemi dodged the first and deflected the second, his reflexes nearly fast enough to match Neave's own.

Nearly. She lunged and snagged his ankle with a gauntleted hand, and then closed her fist as hard as she could. Steel plates crunched in her grip, and wet warmth spurted out. The Vorgemi snarled – he didn't scream; he wasn't human enough for that – and then he made no sound at all, because Neave dragged him down and fired her boltstorm pistol point-blank into his helm.

She grabbed her axes and ran past the black-clad corpse, moving faster with each flight. The beating of leathery wings reached her from outside, accompanied by a rapidly rising heat. Neave felt as if she were running towards a bonfire, but her only worry was that she might not reach it in time.

At last she came to the top. The tower's uppermost floor, which contained only a single large chamber, had been blown apart by the explosion of its neighbour. A great ragged hole tore through the ceiling and two walls, laying the chamber open to the violet-streaked sky. A mosaic of the night-clad heavens had adorned the domed ceiling, and pearly fragments of stars and moons rained down from its ruins as Neave mounted the final stairs.

Five Vorgemi met her at the threshold, spears levelled. Daemonic runes gleamed wetly on the heads of their spears, pulsing as though they'd been cut into living flesh rather than black steel. Behind them was a taller figure, lithely muscled and unmistakably female even with her obscuring black armour and goggled helm. She tucked something small and luminous into the front of her breastplate, then vaulted out of the blasted tower into the night.

Neave started to pursue, but the Vorgemi held her off. The liquid that dripped from their spears rose into the air as smoke, tangling into a briar of spiked, shadowy vines. Insubstantial as they looked, the shadow brambles were solid enough to draw blood, and they reached for Neave with a hundred grasping creepers.

She chopped them away ferociously, but the shadow brambles grew back as quickly as she could hew them down. Neave snarled in frustration as she watched her target begin to sprint away across the square.

Deliverance came in Shakana's thunderbolt. Another blast rocked the night, and the Vorgemi went flying in lightning-wracked spasms. Neave slashed through the remaining vines and raced past the black-armoured bodies. With a single bounding leap, she flew off the tower after their leader.

The corrupted vulcanaurs overtook her. Neave heard the leathery snap of their wings and felt the radiant heat wash over her back. The air seemed to pull away from her in a massive inhalation, like the sea withdrawing before a tsunami.

She knew what was coming. Neave lowered her head and ran faster, reaching for the utmost extent of her Sigmar-granted gifts. She took hold of the winds aetheric, and with the God-King's blessing, rode them.

Time seemed to hold still about her. Buildings blurred to either side. The sky stretched into a dull black smear. Neave's quarry snapped into focus before her, a lone point of movement in a paralysed world.

Neave readied her axes.

The goggled woman turned. She raised a gloved hand towards Neave, slowly, as if she were moving underwater. In it was a twisted piece of metal painted with a Chaos sigil, and as she lifted the unholy mark, she mouthed a blasphemous word.

A wave of hideous force punched into Neave, lifting her off her feet and slamming her to the ground. Her armour clanged on the cobblestones, but the noise was oddly muted, and she barely felt the pain. Vile sorcery washed over her in an invisible verminous tide as she struggled, and it left a coating of squirming filth over her body even after it released its grip.

Neave pushed herself up with both hands, hacking for breath. Foulness filled her mouth and clogged her nostrils. Every muscle in her body ached to the bone, as if she'd been running for days without rest. The sensation of phantom worms sliding over and under her skin gradually faded, but still she felt defiled.

Worse, the goggled woman had put four hundred yards between them, and the Chaos vulcanaurs were closing in.

Something was coming up behind them, though. Darker shapes, three of them, blotted out the faint silver stars. Two were more or less steady. The third rose and fell, straining desperately with each beat of its wings. Neave could just make out the dim red fissures running across each creature's underbelly.

The Blacktalons were coming, mounted on their own vulcanaurs. The bobbing creature had a great black lump between its wings, and from its size alone Neave knew that had to be Rostus. She felt a surge of gratitude, both to her companions and to the valiant vulcanaurs, whose determination was fierce enough to stay on the chase while bearing such burdens.

The Chaos vulcanaurs wheeled to meet their pursuers. Gold and orange flared in the sky, leaving burning trails in the dark as both groups of vulcanaurs began fanning up their firestorms. Shakana's crossbow spat lines of brighter light across their smouldering glow, and a rising haze of steam around the winged forms suggested Lorai was at work as well.

Neave redoubled her efforts to catch the goggled woman. Her Sigmar-granted speed had been drained, and she could only run with ordinary swiftness, but she wouldn't give up the pursuit.

By now they were far from the market square. They'd run through residential neighbourhoods, arcades of workshops and artisans' stalls, tiled bathhouses, and palaces of learning and commerce. Churches and shrines stood on nearly every block.

Once this had been a wealthy city, splendid and pious, but all that remained of it were vacant silhouettes. Neave never saw another living thing, nor even any movement save that of her own chase. Not a breath of wind stirred the pennons on the market stalls. Every building Neave passed was dark and indistinct, creating a surreal impression of a shadow city that, despite being real enough to run through, had never been any more alive than a theatre's painted backdrop.

Now she and her target were racing through a silent park of circuitous paths that wound through wild-looking rock formations veined in amethyst. Worn obelisks dotted the gardens, as shapeless as the sculptures in the Vorgemi's tower. Black shrubs and ebon grasses grew around the paths, and though Neave had neither time nor inclination to study them, something about their shadowy forms tickled at her memory.

The artifice of their surroundings hadn't changed. If anything, it had only become more pronounced during Neave's pursuit. Not everything cast shadows in the pallid starlight – only some of the buildings had shadows, and neither Neave herself nor the woman she chased did. Cobblestones and weeds crunched into the same grainy black dust under Neave's feet, sending up puffs of smoke with every step. She had a disorienting sense that the landscape was crumbling into unreality all around her, as though she ran through the dream of someone slowly awakening.

The goggled woman cut smoothly through the tangled paths, seeming well familiar with their ways. Through the obsidian-leaved trees ahead, Neave saw a tall, spired cathedral gleaming darkly in the endless night. A single main tower dominated its silhouette, stretching higher than anything else she'd seen in the city. The sight of it rang a distant bell of recognition, though Neave was sure she'd never seen this particular cathedral before. Pale lights haloed its base and flickered unsteadily in the lancet windows.

Her quarry veered towards the holy place. Neave followed. She could see, now, the mighty hammers carved into the gallery pillars and the twin-tailed comets that arced above the doors.

Those comets were cracked down the centres, their hearts split in an ugly pattern she'd seen too many times before. Shadows filled the crevices, weeping down the broken comets like cold blood.

The woman slipped into one of the cathedral's side doors and was gone. Neave moved to follow, but a deeper patch of night swept over her head before she could close the gap. Fire streaked the earth beside her, missing her by just a few feet. A four-winged form roared past on a rush of superheated air.

Sparks popped on Neave's armour and sizzled in her hair as the Chaos vulcanaur blew by, wings churning. Air pulled in around it, lifting the cinders from the Stormcast's shoulders. The next pass would be too close to miss.

She risked a glance up. The vulcanaur was barely thirty feet overhead. One eye was missing, its rear wings were raked with bloody tatters, and claw marks ran across its scaly hide, but it seemed oblivious to these wounds. The core of its body glowed with heat, increasing rapidly.

Neave strained to outpace the beast, knowing it was hopeless. She couldn't outrun the blast that was coming.

Within the cathedral, a pinpoint of smoky red light began to move, visible through the filigreed windows. The sight of it in this holy place, even one gone cold and desolate, filled Neave with rage and grief. She took her axes in her hands and turned towards the Chaos vulcanaur, determined to go down fighting, and simultaneously despairing that it was *this* fight that would end her quest.

Hopelessness threatened to overwhelm her. Yet even as a shadow of despair fell over her, a literal one loomed in the sky.

Another vulcanaur, larger, also wounded, and weighed down by a massive shape slumped between its straining wings. *Rostus.*

How the battle-scarred female vulcanaur found the strength to climb higher in the night, Neave would never know. But it did. Injured, overloaded, wearied by age and strain, Rostus' vulcanaur clawed its way above its Chaos counterpart. Its belly held no more fire of its own, and merely reflected the brilliance of the fire blast that the Chaos vulcanaur was gathering to obliterate Neave.

Rostus crawled forwards to his mount's neck. His face appeared over its shoulder, and the creature listed to the right under his weight. 'Neave! I hope you're not taking all the glory for yourself!'

His call wasn't purely for her benefit. The Chaos vulcanaur lifted its head, momentarily distracted, rather than obliterating Neave at once.

That opening was all he needed. Arms outstretched, Rostus stood, teetered precariously, and jumped from his vulcanaur's back to the one below. The big Stormcast's sheer mass was deadly enough; with thirty feet of freefalling velocity behind it, he hit the Chaos vulcanaur like a living cannonball. Beast and Blacktalon careened together towards the ground, Rostus wrenching at the thing's wings as they spun in a pinwheel of uncontrolled flame.

They hit the cathedral courtyard together in a convulsion of stone and fire. Windows shattered above them, raining glass into the inferno of the vulcanaur's demise.

Neave raced forwards, but the intensity of the blaze held her back. As she shielded her face from the heat, the flames suddenly dipped with a hiss of steam.

Another vulcanaur descended, with Lorai and Aliquaille on its back. Crossbow quarrels jutted from its flanks, and the insides of its nostrils were crusted with blood and soot. Nevertheless it bore them down carefully, spreading its clawed toes wide on the paving stones and lowering itself to the ground as it lifted its wings to ease their dismount.

Mist wreathed the Idoneth's hands and rose from her high-collared robe in gentle wisps. It pushed back the fire that had engulfed Rostus and the Chaos vulcanaur, revealing two bodies in the centre of a blackened crater. Charred and smashed together, lit from behind by the half-ring of flames Lorai hadn't extinguished, they looked like a single monstrous corpse in the dark.

'Will he live?' Neave asked. Rostus hadn't discorporated into lightning, so she assumed he wasn't dead, but, she realised, that might not be true. If they were cut off from Sigmar in this place…

'I will do what I can,' Lorai said softly. She walked towards the courtyard in a billowing cloud of fog, leaving the vulcanaur and Aliquaille behind. 'You can do nothing to help. Finish the mission.'

Neave nodded, looking up at the cathedral. With the bonfire of the vulcanaur's death blazing across the windows that remained intact, she'd lost sight of the red spark. It was in there somewhere, though, as the servant of Chaos worked her way through the sanctuary like a gut worm bringing death to its host.

Readying her axes, Neave stalked towards the open doors.

'Let me go with you.' Aliquaille's face, washed by firelight, was a golden mask of resolve. She looked, for a moment, oddly like a Stormcast herself. 'Please. Let me walk beside you in this place.'

'Where *are* we?' Neave asked. She had guessed that they were somewhere in Shyish, given the violet tinge to the darkness and the vast silences of the dead city. The Realm of Death held innumerable underworlds, as many as there were visions of the hereafter that mortals could imagine. One could spend lifetimes studying them without scratching the surface.

But this place was different from the other parts of Shyish she'd known. The uneven shadows, the faceless tapestries, the grass and earth that crumbled to ash underfoot... and the absolute emptiness.

If this was an afterlife, why did it hold no souls?

'I am not certain,' Aliquaille admitted, 'but I believe it is drawn from the memories of Azyr. *Old* Azyr.' She pointed to the solemn statues that stood beside the cathedral doors, the graven emblems on the galleries, and the cracked windows with their stained-glass saints. 'That statue depicts Saint Bertralm, who called down a holy comet to destroy the heretics of Iselfyrd, sacrificing his own life as the price of invoking Sigmar's wrath. The next one is Saint Anselore, who starved to death in purity rather than partake of her captors' debauched feasts. The constellations carved in marble you must surely know. You have seen them with your own eyes, whereas I have only seen sketches in books. But I, too, recognise the Seven Archers, and Dracothion's Wing.

'And that ring of stars,' she added, pointing to an arc of glimmering amethyst in the sky, half hidden by pearl-grey clouds, 'is the Crown of the Broken King, who was slain by Sigmar in the Age of Myth, and whose constellation has been extinguished in the true world for ages unknown.'

Neave looked up at the cathedral again. A chill of delayed recognition shivered through her. The shadow-plants in the garden, the pattern of the windows' panes, and yes, the stars overhead... she *did* know them. They were different, but not so different that she couldn't see the truth of what Aliquaille said.

'What does it mean that this sky holds dead stars?' she asked.

'I cannot say,' Aliquaille admitted. The woman clasped her arms close about herself, holding the golden chains of her office for whatever comfort the metal could offer. Awe trembled in her voice, and fear. 'But I suspect the answer is in that cathedral. May I go with you to find it?'

'Yes,' Neave said.

CHAPTER TWENTY-THREE

A reverent hush settled around Neave as she stepped into the cathedral. The moment that she and Aliquaille crossed the threshold, they were enveloped in grave serenity. Soft purple light slanted through the stained-glass windows, illuminating the stern stone faces of the statues that overlooked the altar and marched in armed rows down the sides of the grey tombs in the aisles flanking the nave. Cold incense and faded smoke, the ghosts of long-snuffed candles, drifted through the still, heavy air.

'The windows have healed,' Aliquaille murmured in astonishment.

It was so. The windows that had shattered with the vulcanaur's fiery crash were intact, shining in the curious night as if they'd never been touched.

'Were they broken when we came in?' Neave wondered aloud. She couldn't remember. Now that she reached back for the memory, she found that many of her recollections were alarmingly vague. What had been certain a moment ago seemed to have become suddenly, maddeningly elusive.

She couldn't remember the sigil on her own armour, or whether Hendrick's was exactly the same. The colour of Shakana's cloak escaped her. Did Rostus crinkle his eyes just so when he was about to tell a joke he was convinced was funny, and was equally certain that no one else would like?

Had the cathedral windows been broken?

'Yes,' Aliquaille said. 'The sceptre of Saint Essevel was shattered, and the two beside it, which I do not know. All have healed.'

'Good,' Neave responded vaguely, unsure why she was saying it. She ventured deeper into the cathedral, hunting for the red spark she'd glimpsed from outside. So many of the Vorgemi had readily given their lives to allow her time to escape, Neave knew it could only be one person. *Ithyrac.*

Beyond the echoing coolness of the nave rose a great tower, where the light of hundreds of windows overlapped into a layered, ever-shifting pool of radiance. The shields and helms of honoured warriors ringed the tower in ornamental racks stacked higher than the eye could follow, and between them flickered circle after circle of tall, thin candles burning with violet flames.

As she crossed the threshold into the tower, Neave felt the cathedral's aura of solemnity deepen towards sorrow. Betrayal, grief and determination cut through the sea of sadness like leviathans through the seas of Ghur, and like those great behemoths, they trailed powerful, disorienting crosscurrents in their wake. The profundity of the cathedral's emotions struck Neave mute, and left her feeling like a ghost in her own skin.

Whose sorrow was she feeling? She didn't know. Not her own. These were someone else's memories, someone else's hurts. But they struck a chord that resonated within Neave's core, as if she were experiencing the lost sensations of her own past lives, all of them, at once.

'Do you feel the sorrow here?' she asked Aliquaille. She kept her voice down, not wanting to disturb the cathedral's silence. It seemed important, for some reason, to respect that.

The woman gave her a sidelong look. Perhaps there was something confused in it, or perhaps Neave only imagined that. 'Sorrow?'

'Yes. I feel a… sadness here. Do you?'

'I don't think so. It's hard to say.' Aliquaille tried a smile, and then gave it up, shivering. The purple candlelight tinted her wimple and shadowed the sacred symbols on her stole. Tiny flames reflected in her irises. 'I thought myself pious, and close to the divine, but in a place such as this… I feel the God-King all around me, in a way that I had only briefly touched during the deepest meditations. Now he is near, so very near, and I am… shaken, Stormcast. This must be how you always feel, with the lightning in your soul.'

'Perhaps.' Neave didn't remember. She had lost almost all sense of her own mortal life, and despite her long search for the truth, was no closer now than she had ever been. One thing struck her sharply, though. 'You feel Sigmar here?'

'Yes.' Aliquaille's stare was uncomfortably penetrating. 'Don't you? He's everywhere, all around us.'

Neave reached out, silently imploring Sigmar for reassurance, but felt nothing in return. The God-King's absence was, if anything, even starker in the cathedral. With so much pain and loss suffusing this holy house, she couldn't understand why she didn't sense him. *What is this place?*

And if she, a Stormcast Eternal, felt only sorrow answered by emptiness, why did Aliquaille feel the presence of their god?

Neave pushed away her doubts and fears, and tried to focus amidst the tides of emotion that swelled through the cathedral. She drew slow breaths, scenting the air, and listened for any trace of Ithyrac's movements.

Below us. There. The creak of a door moving on stiff hinges, and the faintest scrape of soft leather boots on stone.

Neave looked about for a staircase, but saw none.

Perhaps Aliquaille had noticed one while Neave had been distracted by the cathedral's unearthly atmosphere. 'Have you seen any stairs descending from this level?' Neave asked. 'Ithyrac's gone below us. What would be down there?'

Aliquaille took a moment to consider her answer. 'This cathedral is built in the Azyrite fashion, and a very old form at that. I'm not familiar with all the nuances of its sculpture or configuration. But in most realms, and particularly in Azyr, the archives would be kept below ground, shielded from destruction by storm winds.' The woman looked up at the tower, and the centuries of honour and courage memorialised in its trophies of war, and turned away reluctantly. Plainly she longed to study the legends and holy histories captured in those shields, even in the face of their mission's urgency. 'The stairs will most likely be in the transepts.'

'Show me.'

Aliquaille bowed her head and led Neave through the candle-lit tower towards the transepts. These opened from either side of the tower, through archways encircled with the signs of long-forgotten tribes and noble houses. A stairway descended from each of the transepts, lit up by candles that burned brighter than those in the tower.

Neave listened for a moment at each archway, then took the one on the right. 'She went this way.'

'*Sigmar, grant me strength,*' Aliquaille whispered, overcome by awe. She touched the carved stone with a wondering hand as she passed through. 'During countless cold nights in the Sorrow Peaks I prayed for guidance. More than once, Sigmar answered me with the gift of visions. In my dreams I have seen this archway. This very one, Stormcast.'

Neave didn't answer. She still felt nothing but Sigmar's absence. Rather than dwell on that despair, she focused on pursuing Ithyrac.

Running would have drowned out any noise that her quarry made, so Neave moved slower, stalking her prey rather than chasing her outright.

The stairs led down through black stone walls illumined by a soft violet haze from the depths. Each block was subtly translucent, more akin to smoky quartz than basalt, and as Neave descended, they began to shift around her.

A dusky purple light, barely noticeable at first, emanated from the blocks in the lower level. With each turn of the staircase, the stones appeared more ethereal and their glow intensified. By the time the two women reached the archive landing, they were bathed in twilit radiance.

It wasn't only light that leaked from the spectral stones. Grief poured from them, so intense that a knot choked in Neave's throat and a cold pain lodged in her chest. *Sigmar, my king, Sigmar, my god, do not forsake us. Do not condemn us. We are not sinners, O God-King. We are your true and faithful servants.*

The words weren't hers, the pain wasn't hers, but Neave could not shake either. In the ghostly glowing stones she began to see faces, and to hear prayers whispered by long-dead lips. *Hear the names of the innocent. See the faces of the righteous. Know that we are yours, Sigmar. We are* yours, *O God-King. Do not cast us aside!*

Imploring hands rose up in the stones. Weeping eyes turned hopefully towards her. The faces in the blocks were only indistinct phantasms, impossible to identify by age or gender, and stripped of all but the merest suggestions of hairstyle and adornment. Neave thought most of them were human, but she wasn't even certain of that.

They were true Sigmarites, though. The force of their faith radiated through the stones as strongly as the light that shone from them, brightening in Neave's presence as if it sensed, and responded to, Sigmar's divine power in her Stormcast form.

It dizzied her, and she put a hand out against the stones to steady herself. At once the light surged brighter, and the prayers of the dead battered at her soul.

Protect us. Hear us. Grant us mercy, O God-King.

'He didn't, you know.' Ithyrac stepped casually from the shadows, which unfolded around her in the shape of black spectral wings. The ghosts fled from the goggled woman's presence, leaving the stones dark at her back. 'Sigmar. He granted them nothing but destruction. His own faithful. It's good to see you, Blacktalon. I was wondering when you'd come. It took longer than I'd anticipated. I thought you were faster.'

Neave blinked. She'd been so distracted by the cathedral's apparitions that she had failed to notice Ithyrac's presence. Even if the Vorgemi had been hidden by illusion, she should have caught some trace, if she'd been sufficiently alert.

She realised, abruptly, that she didn't see Aliquaille either. The Summer Saint was gone. The room held nothing but amethyst-glowing stones behind Neave's back, and dark ones behind Ithyrac's. Past the goggled woman was a shadowed entryway, the only possible exit if Aliquaille hadn't gone back up the stairs.

'Are you looking for your little human pet? Don't worry. She's well out of the way.' Ithyrac laughed. Her helm distorted it into a vibrating, insectoid trill. 'I'd tell you she's safe, but that would be a lie. I sent her to discover the truth, and that makes her dangerous indeed.'

'What do you know of the truth?' Neave snarled, drawing her axes. She was angry, and glad of it. Anger burned away the fog of voices and confusion, and restored the clarity of purpose she hadn't felt since she'd come to this strange void of an afterlife and been severed from Sigmar. 'Was it the truth you fed the Children of the Winter Sun? The truth you used to harness and break their vulcanaurs? You are a creature of lies, as are all servants of Chaos. Nothing else.'

'No doubt it comforts you to think that.' Ithyrac slid her knives out in answer. Her blades were long and slightly curved, and finished in matt black except for a greenish tint along the edges. Rather than spring to the attack, however, she continued to lounge lazily against the wall. 'But no. As the Dark Master knows, nothing is so deadly as the truth. Particularly not to you, or your vainglorious hypocrite of a god.'

Neave gave her rejoinder in steel. She took three swift steps to close the distance, and swung with both axes, one aimed at the woman's face and the other at her throat.

It hardly seemed that Ithyrac moved, yet she wasn't there when the hurricane axes cleaved the air. Amethyst flashed across the wall's black stones as the goggled woman slid away and Neave's hands swept harmlessly past. The distorted faces of the blocks' spirits rose up like drowned corpses bobbing to the surface of a sea, mouthing their soundless prayers.

Ithyrac's laughter snapped Neave's attention back to her. The woman was ten feet away, leaning against another wall, apparently unbothered. She reached up, slowly so that Neave could see what she was doing, and unbuckled her goggled helm.

Lifting it off her head, Ithyrac revealed a plain, practical face with a strong square jaw and impish eyes. Her black hair was cut short and her brown skin was creased in the windburnt fashion of most Aqshian tribespeople. Long green talons capped her fingers, but nothing else about her revealed her allegiance to the Dark Gods.

'Did I strike a nerve?' she taunted. Then crimson sparked in her eyes, and the bones of her face rearranged themselves under her skin, stretching wide at the jaw and spiking out at the temples. When her smile faded, so did the daemonic aspect, but she no longer looked convincingly human to Neave. 'I suppose I did. But then, you're an easy target. All it takes is a gibe aimed at your god to court a Stormcast's ire.'

'You are unworthy to speak of him,' Neave growled, and charged at the woman again. This time she deliberately aimed her axes wide, swinging one high and the other low and to Ithyrac's left, to test the extent of the Vorgemi's illusions.

The second axe bit into something solid, though Neave's first blade rang uselessly against the stone. Ithyrac grunted, and her image stuttered and flickered, as if she'd momentarily lost control of whatever enchantment displaced her true position. Her smile vanished as she jerked away from Neave's attack, her black armour badly scored. Blood trickled from between the plates.

'I am entirely worthy,' Ithyrac spat back. Tiny fangs emerged from her gums, warping her words with a sibilant hiss. She circled away from Neave, shadows blurring around her to obscure her form and movements. 'I was one of you once.'

'More lies.' Neave didn't want to waste breath talking to this creature, but the words were out of her mouth before she realised it. The idea that the Vorgemi would claim to share any form of kinship with a Stormcast Eternal filled her with too much disgust to contain.

'No lie. I was a faithful Sigmarite. A champion of the faith. Not a Stormcast, thankfully. Unlike you, I managed to avoid the eternal enslavement of my soul.' Ithyrac punctuated her words with swift arcs of her blades. Hidden by the swirling shadows around her, they were difficult to see and near impossible to block. Steel screeched against sigmarite and then came back again, hitting the same weak points a second time as Ithyrac tried to puncture Neave's defences.

Neave didn't answer. She focused on the fight, listening more than looking. The Vorgemi's sorcery deceived the eye, but only muffled the ear. *There.* She caught the tell-tale tension of Ithyrac readying another feint, and swung an axe in to meet the oncoming lunge.

The blow landed with satisfying solidity. It hit the Vorgemi's breastplate hard enough to crush the metal inwards. She staggered back, hurt too badly for the illusions to hide.

The cloak of shadows rose higher, enveloping Ithyrac protectively as she snarled in pain. She lashed out in a flurry of rapid stabs, leaving constellations of bright metal punched in the enamel of Neave's plate. Several of her blows pierced through the chain-mailed gaps between plates, and others hit hard enough to dent Neave's armour in turn. 'I was one of you. Why do you think I came here? Why do you think I *cared*? Because I devoted too much of my life to a god of lies, and he deserves to be unmasked.'

'Was it for truth and justice that you murdered so many souls?' Neave scoffed, straining to cover her laboured breathing and the rapid weakening of her injured left arm. Her ribs throbbed under her heavy armour. The pain flared hot when she twisted or lunged, an unmistakable warning that she didn't have long left to fight.

'For the truth, yes. A truth that will bring justice.' Ithyrac swept her blades out at Neave again, but she wasn't trying to strike the Blacktalon. Her knives flung darkness out in overlapping arcs, writing a complex design in the air. The Vorgemi uttered a guttural incantation, and the shadows spread into a web that choked Neave's sight and wrapped around her arms, binding them to her sides. Another spasm of pain wracked her ribs under the pressure.

Ithyrac's voice moved away, and relaxed into cruel mirth once more. 'The truth might even enlighten you. Where do you think we are, Blacktalon?'

Follow her steps. The Vorgemi still hadn't realised her oversight. She'd blinded Neave, and she seemed to be throwing her voice to disguise her position, but she wasn't hiding the sound of her footsteps.

Neave had to keep her distracted. She let some of her pain seep into her voice, knowing it would gratify the woman, while she quietly tested the strength of the shadows gripping her arms. Agony seared her injured side and shoulders at the movement. She allowed some of that to show, too. 'Shyish. We're in the Realm of Death.'

'No.' Ithyrac laughed, but her merriment was twinned and distorted by her shadows, and it gave Neave nothing to pursue. 'If Varstrom were there, we'd have found it long before. My master searched that realm from core to edge. But the people of Varstrom were never allowed to rest among the dead. They might have revealed Sigmar's sin, you see. Had their souls gone to Nagash, the Great Necromancer would have learnt what they knew. Sigmar couldn't allow that. He buried them here, in Ulgu, creating a false underworld where the souls of his betrayed believers could be hidden until they rotted away. Forever, if need be. As long as it took for Sigmar's secret to be finally, fully erased.'

'A secret you intend to use as your weapon,' Neave said, listening for any clue that might betray the Vorgemi's position. She blinked, showing Ithyrac that the shadow-web still blinded her, and struggled against her bonds just hard enough to be convincing. *Let her think me helpless.*

Inwardly, the Blacktalon burned with rage. It wasn't only the blasphemies that the Vorgemi kept spewing. It was her smugness, her insistence that *she* was somehow in the right, that all the monstrous things she'd done were justified because they could be used to tear down one of the few bright beacons of hope still left in these blighted realms.

I will kill her. Neave clung to the thought, pulling strength from it.

The Vorgemi was talking again. 'Naturally. What do you think the Varstrom scrolls *are*? A spell? A rite of destruction? Perhaps they are, but their power is not mere magic. It is the *truth*. A truth Sigmar has done all in his power to destroy.' The daemonic woman struck out with both daggers.

Her footsteps scuffed the ground. The air whistled between her blades. Neave heard her chance, and took it.

She threw her full strength against the shadowy bonds. They ripped apart, and Neave leapt at Ithyrac even as the Vorgemi lunged.

The daggers punched in. One was turned aside by the sigmarite plate. The other wasn't. Flashes of violet and black streaked behind Neave's eyes, interrupting the grey murk of Ithyrac's spell, and she heard herself gasp as the blade sank into her body.

But she didn't falter. She seized Ithyrac and pulled her close, dispensing with her axes entirely. A blind hit wasn't likely to kill the Vorgemi, and then Neave would have to find her all over again. But if she grabbed Ithyrac, and never let go…

The woman writhed and stabbed furiously at Neave's arms and shoulders. The angle was awkward, though, and she didn't have much leverage. Her daggers scraped against the sigmarite without biting through.

Sightlessly, Neave fumbled one hand towards Ithyrac's throat while holding her pinned with the other. No shadows deceived her now. She found the Vorgemi's gorgeted neck, wrapped both hands around it, and began to squeeze.

'It doesn't matter,' Ithyrac said, hoarsely, as Neave's fingers tightened around her throat. Leather and metal groaned in the Blacktalon's grip. Still, somehow, the Vorgemi tried to laugh. 'Perhaps it's even better this way. Your human saint,' – she coughed, struggling for air – 'wanted the truth of your god. I showed it to her, and she leapt.

'Now she knows, Blacktalon. She's seen the truth behind her golden idol's mask, and it will destroy her. It will destroy *him*.

'But what of you Stormcasts?' she asked, and her laughter was a blade Neave couldn't dodge. 'Even knowing the lie, you'll be bound to him. What will that do to you? Will you go mad? Tell yourselves the mortals deserved it, because they were only mortals, and flawed in their faith, unlike you? I hope so. That would be delightful. If Sigmar's special hounds, forged to protect the weak, convince themselves that mortals don't deserve protection *because* they're weak… Why, then you really would be cast in the mould of your god.'

Neave didn't answer. She only squeezed harder. Her breaths grew raspy with pain and effort, while Ithyrac's grew weaker as her gorget gradually gave way to Neave's throttling. For a long, terrible moment, they sounded almost identical, panting together in the dark.

Then the gorget cracked, and Neave closed her hands completely around Ithyrac's throat.

Breathless, she held her grip long after Ithyrac had stopped struggling. Then, she let the body fall. The shadows cleared from Neave's vision, but her body still ached, and her thoughts were unfocused. Her heart remained desolate. She dropped her trembling hands to her sides. In the sudden silence, her anger began to cool, abruptly overwhelmed by a sense of unmoored dread. She had hoped, somehow, that Sigmar would return with the Vorgemi's death, but she was as alone as ever in this place.

As she stood, her legs almost gave way beneath her. Where were the other Blacktalons? Where was Aliquaille?

Exhausted beyond thought, Neave stepped over the corpse to the archive doorway. The room had brightened considerably with Ithyrac's death. Only the body and the floor beneath her were dark. Elsewhere, the shades in the walls were no longer cowed by the woman's presence, and glowed with the full force of their spectral light.

Again their hands lifted in silent plea, and their cheeks hollowed around mute prayers, but the ghosts were trapped in their shining prisons, and Neave moved past them without pause. She could do nothing for the dead. Her concern was for the living.

Darkness surrounded her in the cathedral's archive. The walls were made of the same strange haunted stone, but the spirits beyond this doorway seemed distant and disinterested. Violet glimmers flickered in the stones' shadowy hearts, but they did not rise towards Neave as the others had.

The aura of grief that had suffused the cathedral tower was even stronger here. It washed over Neave in crushing waves, burying her beneath the impossible, scouring weight of someone else's mourning. She could scarcely breathe in the grip of that devastating sorrow, and wondered how Aliquaille could withstand it.

Bare stone shelves filled the circular chamber in a series of concentric rings. The spectral shapes of scrolls and books lined those curved shelves, but the only substance that remained to them were skeletons traced in dust. A puff of breath and they'd collapse, leaving only their glowing ghosts behind.

Holy sigils and sacred hammers marked the books' spines and scrolls' seals. Twin-tailed comets blazed from the covers, their lines incandescent in the gloom. Neave wasn't surprised to see that the ghosts of this place kept their library alive in memory, even after the actual documents had crumbled into oblivion.

This, not the tombs or altars or even the shields arrayed in their honoured displays in the tower, was the cathedral's true heart. This was where the core of its afterlife burned.

She found Aliquaille sitting in a stone chair at the centre of the library's circular labyrinth. Votives flanked her in wrought-iron candle trees, their flames pale violet and their holders worked into the sharp curls of twin-tailed comets encircling mighty champions. At their feet, and the candle trees' bases, were the piled corpses of Sigmar's enemies: orruks, Chaos-warped monstrosities, and the primeval beasts of a world long gone.

Other shapes, crafted not of iron but of memories caught in amethyst light, lay at their feet too: women, children and men wearing the same holy symbols as those who stood over them. Illusory smoke rose up from their bodies, and scorch marks marred their wet, dark clothes.

Aliquaille lifted her head as Neave approached. Streaked tears glistened on her cheeks. She lifted the long, curling scroll that spilled over her lap and rolled on to the floor, and then let it drop hopelessly again. More scrolls, scribed on the same paper by the same hand, overflowed from large boxes stacked in front of her chair.

The scrolls, unlike everything else Neave had seen in the dead cathedral, appeared whole and intact. Purple light flowed through them, but it pulsed within the paper, not the ink, as though preserving the writings rather than replacing them.

'What are they?' Neave asked, gesturing towards the scrolls with one hand. She became aware for the first time that Ithyrac's blood, drawn by the crushed edges of the woman's gorget, dripped from her gauntlets. Glancing back, she could see the dark trail spattered in her wake.

'Proof,' Aliquaille said. Her voice was very small, and sad, and lost. She looked up at Neave with the same wounded, imploring need as the faces in the walls. The scroll trembled against her shaking hands. 'Proof of Sigmar's treachery, and his cruelty towards his own faithful. Proof that he is a murderer, and that his murders were driven by cowardice. Proof that he is a *monster*, Stormcast.

'Our god, a monster.'

CHAPTER TWENTY-FOUR

'So our enemies have long claimed,' Neave said carefully, moving closer to Aliquaille. She kept her stance relaxed and her hands in plain view, trying to appear non-threatening, as the chamber's shadows engulfed her. Violet phantoms rose and fell in the stones of the catacomb's walls, but Neave kept her gaze fixed on the living woman.

She sensed no taint in the room, though the arcane energy that swirled through the air was so intense that it left ghostly images at the periphery of her vision. The taste of silver tingled on her tongue.

Still, it was not hostility that Neave sensed from the power coiled within the cathedral. What she felt was a deep, aching sorrow, leavened with piety and… hope?

Yes. It was hope that emanated from the walls around her, palpable as the chill damp that breathed from an ordinary castle's dungeons. Hope that had been disappointed, perhaps many times, but had not yet been destroyed.

She felt hope, and she felt faith. Bruised and battered, but still clinging to the fundamental certainty that a true god, a just god, would hear the prayers of his worshippers and be moved.

But moved to *what*?

'These were their prayers.' Aliquaille gestured to the scroll spilling over her lap. Her fingers trembled over its lettering, weak as the wings of a dying bird. 'They prayed to Sigmar to show them mercy, and he… He shunned them. He didn't even *listen*, Stormcast. He did not…'

'Who prayed?' Neave still didn't see any immediate threat, and relaxed slightly. For the first time, she studied the chamber's gheists with care.

Around Aliquaille's feet, spectral figures in amethyst light, none larger than the woman's hand, prayed and prostrated themselves in tearful supplication. Each one seemed to have only a few gestures, which they repeated again and again, trapped in brief but endless loops of memory.

More figures moved in the surrounding walls. Each was trapped in its own stone block, like a prisoner confined to a solitary cell. They seemed unaware of the other spirits around them, and of Neave and Aliquaille in their midst. Like the tiny gheists that ringed Aliquaille's chair, they were caught in loops of remembered anguish, continually acting and re-enacting the same scenes from their long-past lives.

'The people of Varstrom,' Aliquaille whispered. She let a hand fall to the unseeing figures by her chair, and to Neave's surprise, the spectres moved slightly around the woman's fingers. They didn't pause in their repeated mournings, but they stepped to the side, as if avoiding a wall that had presented itself in their path. 'I didn't know what that name meant, when we came here, but now I do. It was a city. A city, and its people. They lived so long in peace, protected by Sigmar's strength in holiest Azyr, that they…

they forgot the cruelties of Chaos. In forgetting, they became vulnerable.'

The aura of grief that choked the room softened minutely as Aliquaille spoke. The spirits in the walls seemed to shift in response to her attention, and different images bloomed and unfurled in the nearer blocks. Aliquaille tilted her head to watch them, and Neave followed her gaze.

In one, a bespectacled scholar pored over texts from other realms, each marked by the metallic scales on its cover or the radiant light that shone from its words. Each of the arcane tomes she studied seemed innocuous enough on its own, but as the captured memory went on, the scholar began to notice redactions and lacunae in her texts. The mystery of the missing information seemed to intrigue her more than the original subject of her studies, and she sought out increasingly esoteric sources to piece together what she'd deduced must have been hidden.

In another, a fierce warrior who, lacking real battlefields to test his prowess, found his prize-fights less and less satisfying. He took on impossible matches and inflicted terrible brutalities on his competitors, and yet with each bout, his hunger for true combat only grew.

Another block showed citizens who'd grown bored with the ease of their lives, and others who sought escape from crushing pressures and a vague, indefinable dissatisfaction that they didn't know how to resolve. Together, they brewed strange intoxicants and knotted themselves into one another in ever-stranger configurations, trying to find solace, or at least oblivion, by overwhelming the senses of the flesh.

'Their pursuits did not – yet – open the way for Chaos to reach Azyr,' Aliquaille said softly, as the shadows in the stone blocks continued their ghostly dance. 'But their indulgences came ever closer to crossing that line, and Sigmar grew afraid that the excesses of

Varstrom might allow his most grievous enemies to touch his sacred realm.

'He sent them warnings of his displeasure. But mortals interpret portents as they will, and those who had already begun to stray refused to see their danger. They were in Azyr, Sigmar's own home, and believed themselves beyond the reach of harm.'

In the stone blocks, the scholar found her books blackening to illegibility as she turned the pages, yet she seemed to think this was some wizard's obfuscation ward rather than Sigmar's own hand at work. She attempted at first an incantation, and when that failed, she redoubled her efforts to decipher what had been lost.

The warrior found his weapons rusting in his grasp. His axe's blade dulled and flaked despite careful sharpening; his sword's steel pitted and the hilt cracked apart in mid-swing. These disasters only fuelled his bloodlust, and he bludgeoned his next opponent to the ground with his bare hands, howling in victory as his victim lay insensible at his feet.

As for the hedonists...

Neave looked away. 'If that was what Varstrom's people became, Sigmar was right to smite them.'

'Was he? None of them actually fell, Stormcast.' Aliquaille regarded her with quiet reproval. 'The God-King feared they would become susceptible to Chaos' influences, and perhaps they might have, in time... But when he struck them down, they were only people. Flawed, weak in faith, subject to temptation... but people. Not monsters. And they were not alone in the city.'

The woman gestured to the nearest wall. The images that Neave had seen earlier receded, and their stone blocks went dark. Others, previously shadowed, lit up. Amethyst phosphorescence swirled within them, taking on the shapes of new spectres.

They showed ordinary people, going about ordinary lives, in a city that shone as a bright mirror of the gloomy ruins Neave had walked through. People bought bread and laughed over tea in marbled squares ringed by starry-windowed towers, while the shining moons of Azyr spun in the skies above. Children danced in a masked parade for Saint Tisarel's Day, and bells tolled the holy hours.

A faint echo of the cathedrals' song reverberated from the memories trapped in the walls, and though Neave could barely make out the sound, she shivered with recognition. Sigmar's holy houses still sang those same melodies.

'These were the citizens of Varstrom,' Aliquaille said. 'Their only offence was that they didn't repudiate their fellows, even knowing that so many had begun to slip. But how could they purge those who had not, truly, fallen to Chaos? Sinners they might be, but these were their friends and family, bound by ties of kinship and tradition. And they lived in Azyr, under Sigmar's eternal light. They never believed that the shadows spoken of in whispers might reach them there. They trusted in the all-knowing power of our god, and by that trust sealed their doom.

'Yet there were others who sensed the danger. Sigmar's priests felt his displeasure, and as they realised the enormity of the threat, and the deadly complacency of the citizenry who refused to believe it, they worked desperately to stave off disaster. These scrolls were their last, best attempt to turn aside Sigmar's wrath.' Aliquaille touched the shimmering letters again, and the spirits at her feet, and in the walls, shivered as if a cold wind had blown over them.

'What are they?' Neave asked, wondering what could hold such power over the shades.

'Names,' Aliquaille answered. 'The names of all the innocents who would die if Sigmar wiped Varstrom from Azyr. For that was the punishment the God-King threatened – if the people did not heed his warnings, and repent for their failings, then he would smite them and the entire city. His priests, true in faith, believed that Sigmar would not be so cruel if he understood how many blameless lives would be lost – and all over the fear, only the *fear*, that Chaos might gain a foothold in Azyr.

'So, they wrote them down. Hundreds, thousands. And they gathered those names here, in the heart of the city's greatest cathedral, and built a throne in which Sigmar was meant to sit and read them. It was a grand chair, worthy of a God-King, but it sat among the mortals, so that he could see things as they did.' Aliquaille paused, and her gaze sought Neave's. 'As you do, Stormcast. I cannot help thinking, knowing what I now do, that perhaps he meant for you to walk among us, and see our lives at our level, to avoid repeating his mistake.'

'The mistake of destroying Varstrom?' Neave said. She felt numb.

Aliquaille bowed her head. When she looked up, her eyes were fierce, though her mouth trembled with emotion. 'Wasn't it? These souls still believe that Sigmar will come to them. They keep their faith alive, embedded in his cathedral, hoping he will reward them for their long belief.

'How many centuries has it been? Yet the shades of Varstrom cling to their faith, even as their number dwindles and their underworld crumbles. Where is this place? Shyish? Ulgu? *Azyr*? Wherever it is, it has been closed off from all the other Mortal Realms. The dead have been exiled to wait until their souls erode and their memories are lost beyond retrieval. But still they believe. Still they hold faith, and their light flickers in these walls. Waiting, hoping, for the God-King to hear them, and honour their names.'

'He will never do that,' Neave murmured. She'd meant the thought only for herself, but Aliquaille took it as a challenge. The woman sat straighter on her throne, and the letters on the scrolls flared as she held them up.

'Their names must be known,' Aliquaille said, lifting her chin so that the golden chains dangling from her battle-stained white wimple glittered in the gloom. The sacred emblems engraved on their ornaments and embroidered on the Summer Saint's stole seemed to catch what little light there was; Neave couldn't tell whether it was only her imagination, or the shades casting their faltering strength towards those holy symbols. 'Their sacrifice must be honoured. The Cults Unberogen is strong enough to withstand the revelation that Sigmar himself has erred, and repented. What more profound lesson could there be? Even a God-King can misjudge. His faithful will understand, and will take greater compassion on themselves, and each other, after studying his example.'

No. The thought hit Neave suddenly, and yet it was something she'd always known, somewhere deep below the surface, where the unspoken truths of her existence swam.

Mortals could be fallible. A god could not.

A god could be forgiving. Mortals could not.

That was, Neave now understood, why Sigmar needed his Stormcasts, perhaps partly why he had created them. They were his intermediaries, walking amongst mortals and seeing the world as they did – precisely as Varstrom's priests had hoped the God-King would, and as Sigmar had understood he no longer could. A Stormcast's decisions, if correct, could be taken as their god's. But a Stormcast's errors were their own. Mortal believers seldom credited the flaws in a Stormcast's judgement to Sigmar. Their God-King remained remote and infallible in the high fastnesses of Azyr, and his worshippers could take solace in the belief that he, himself, would not have made the mistakes that his lesser agents did.

Varstrom, however, had been crushed by Sigmar's own hand. The God-King had rendered his own judgement on his followers, and it had been devastating.

And wrong.

That was the crux of it. Neave felt it deep within her core. Sigmar

319

had ignored the pleas of his own clergy. The danger he'd feared had been real, but in her heart of hearts, Neave couldn't contest what Aliquaille had said. Destroying a city out of fear and haste that some of its people *might* succumb to temptation was, in her estimation, cowardice.

If his faithful ever learnt of it, surely it would destroy them.

For that, Neave believed, was another law of human nature. In every society, there were always some who leapt to condemn others' moral trespasses, and who relied on divine scripture to justify their harshness. She'd encountered them many times in her journeys with the Blacktalons, and on a few rare occasions, she'd even been tasked with removing the most extreme offenders to preserve the integrity of the faith.

But if it became known that Sigmar himself had purged an entire city in sacred Azyr to eliminate the corruption of its mortal sinners, then there'd be no holding back the extremists. They'd have the God-King's imprimatur for all their harshest deeds.

A bitter heaviness sank into Neave's chest. Only one course lay before her.

'You are not wrong,' she told Aliquaille, as she walked through the whispering ghosts to approach the woman on her throne. Stone and glass crunched beneath her boots, where windows and gheist-blocks had crumbled under the weight of the cathedral's age.

It truly was a beautiful chair. Varstrom's finest artisans had poured their hearts into its crafting. Even in this shadow version, dulled and faded as the spirits who sustained it slowly evanesced, Neave marvelled at the intricacy of its detail and the brilliance of its polish. Dark jewels traced the twin-tailed comet on its back and marched in rows along the arms. The likeness of Ghal Maraz, worked in burnished metal on the headpiece, shone through the cathedral's gloom.

Neave looked at the throne, and its holy images, so she wouldn't have to see the woman seated upon it.

Her expression betrayed nothing. Her hands remained empty.

Yet Aliquaille knew. She gathered the fallen scrolls into her lap, and she looked up at Neave with a profound, resigned disappointment. 'You do not share my faith.'

'No,' Neave said, then stooped to take a shard of glass from the floor and drove it up through the woman's jaw into her skull.

It was swiftly done. There was, Neave hoped, no pain. Aliquaille collapsed on the throne, and though her blood spilled hot over the Blacktalon's gauntlets and darkened her armour, it flowed through the spectral throne without leaving a mark.

Neave took up the tangled scrolls. The paper was ancient, fragile, and soaked with the spreading red stains of Aliquaille's death, but still it held together in her hands. Amethyst light pulsed through its crumbling curls, preserving the aged paper and translating its archaic script to letters that Neave could read.

Gesparis, baker, 34.

Hedania, scribe, 58.

Letia, new-married, 19.

Caudos, child, 5.

Isphera, child, 7.

Neave exhaled, slow and controlled. She waited for her heartbeat to steady.

Then she took a pen from Aliquaille's writing case, and dipped the nib in the saint's blood.

Bracing the paper across one of her gauntlets, she wrote with the other hand:

Aliquaille, saint.

She didn't know the woman's age. She doubted that it mattered. No one would ever read these names, least of all Sigmar God-King.

He had turned his back on these people, and had locked away

their souls to perish of silent neglect, so that not even the dead would be able to tell of his betrayal. Far from listening to his worshippers' pleas, he'd muted them forever.

Neave understood why. If the secret escaped, it would destroy the Cults Unberogen. All the good that the God-King had wrought in all the centuries since, all the mortal souls he'd protected and given meaning – all of it would be imperilled by this revelation. That was the vision of the cracked comet that all their enemies had done so much to bring about. The Varstrom scrolls didn't hold a spell, after all, but something far more explosive than any sorcerer's ritual: the truth.

Neave tucked the dead saint's pen back into its case. She piled the scrolls high over Aliquaille's body, heaping them onto the throne until she couldn't put any more on the pile. Ghal Maraz vanished beneath curls of purple-laced paper, as did the twin-tailed comet, and the body of the murdered woman sitting in the God-King's chair.

There were more scrolls piled up around the throne. Neave couldn't unearth them all, let alone move them. *How many died here?*

Too many. Too many for her to read, too many for a God-King to face.

Sigmar, my lord. Neave's throat was a knot. She felt tears drip from her chin, though she didn't know when she'd started weeping.

She was a Blacktalon. Her duty was to kill those who threatened the faith. That was Sigmar's sacred charge, and she'd never faltered in all these years.

Never had it come so near to breaking her.

With shaking hands, Neave took a firelighter from one of the pouches at her side. She seldom used it, but the alchemical device obediently summoned a flame when she clicked its engraved brass switch. Its vivid orange seemed impossibly vibrant in the cold, shadowed solemnity of the gheists' cathedral.

'Why?' she asked no one. The ghosts, trapped in their fading memories, didn't answer. The dead saint, buried in scrolls, didn't answer.

Sigmar did not answer.

Aliquaille had sensed the God-King in this cathedral, but Neave never had. *Because he isn't here,* she thought, and knew it for the truth.

What the Summer Saint had sensed was the communion of believers: all the souls that had joined in prayer and gathered to worship their god together. That could, for the mortal cults, come very close to the essence of faith. She'd mistaken their fellowship for the presence of the divine.

But a Stormcast Eternal felt Sigmar directly, as the source of their strength and the driving force of their existence. The faith of mortals, however strong, was no substitute.

Sigmar was not here. He never had been, and never would be. It was, perhaps, the one place in all the Mortal Realms that he could least bear to look.

And Neave, loyal killer that she was, had smothered his fear with her own.

'*WHY?*' she screamed into the dark.

The cathedral swallowed her agony. It didn't give back so much as an echo. If it hadn't been for the raw, ragged pain in her throat, Neave wouldn't even have known she'd cried out.

She dashed away her tears. It was useless. Too many more came.

Always she'd told herself, when the Blacktalons had to resort to the blade, that Sigmar would have had a better answer. Would have been wiser, more perceptive, more resourceful. Would have been a *god*, worthy of the name.

That belief was shattered. Instead, where she reached for her faith, Neave felt only a scoured, hollow misery. She didn't even have the consolation of the other Blacktalons to lean upon. They were elsewhere in the shadows of Varstrom, ignorant and thus innocent. And while Neave had no wish to take that from them, it left her to face the shock alone.

There was no idol of flawless wisdom enthroned in Sigmaron. There was only a father with fallible judgement, and imperfections, and fear.

Is that enough?

Neave stared at the fire in her hand. She'd nearly forgotten she held the flame. It was so small. It offered no warmth, and little light, as far as she could feel through her numbness. But its orange tongue was real, and vibrantly alive, as nothing else was in this place.

She put it to the scrolls.

The flame caught. Neave released a breath. She hadn't been certain that the paper would burn – she'd thought perhaps the magic that preserved its names would also shield it from destruction by fire. But the flame took hold, and soon it spread through the names of the dead.

Each name flared as it burned. Shadowy magic warred against hungry flame, and for a second it held the line, keeping the letters alight in the air as the paper crumbled to ash around it. Then, inevitably, it surrendered, as its material anchor to the world was lost.

As the names of the dead disappeared, the spirits in the walls began to vanish as well. One by one, the glowing blocks went dark. The aura of pain and betrayal that filled the chamber began to loosen, not with forgiveness, but with the simple black silence of forgetting.

Again and again the pattern played out. Fire and magic inscribed the names of Varstrom's lost innocents in the air, writing an incandescent memorial that sparked, shimmered, and was gone.

Neave stood in the midst of it, welcoming the sting of the smoke and the bite of the cinders as part of her penance. She stared at the names as they rose over the ashes, not trying to read them, only to bear witness to their burning litany.

Sigmar never would. His servant would have to suffice.

She couldn't tell whether Aliquaille's name lighted like the rest. By the time the pile had reached its blood-soaked base, the tangle of names was too thick to tell any one from the others. They churned through a haze of smoke flecked with burning paper, brightening and dimming in entwined spirals. If the Summer Saint's was among them, Neave didn't see it.

Her body was there, though, and it burned with the scrolls. Garlands of violet and gold tumbled around it, and then consumed it.

Neave stayed until the last embers died. The cathedral fell into complete darkness around her. No spirits lingered in its walls; no sorrow wreathed its altar. The throne that Varstrom's people had so lovingly crafted for their god was gone, banished along with the spirits whose hope had sustained it.

If she were truly fortunate, Neave thought, she might perish too, and lose this memory to Reforging. Wouldn't Sigmar welcome the opportunity to erase the last memory of his deed?

She hoped so. She prayed for it. As fervently as she'd ever prayed to the God-King for anything, Neave prayed that she might be given the gift of death to forget this.

But she did not pray aloud, for there was no one to hear her in the ashes.

Brushing the grey remnants of the scrolls from her armour, and feeling nothing at all, Neave left.

Outside, the world was crumbling.

As Varstrom's souls faded into whatever nebulous fate – or final death – awaited them beyond their purgatorial prison, the false underworld that had contained them faded as well. Even before she'd set foot in the cathedral, Neave had noted how eroded and shapeless many of Varstrom's peripheral buildings and details were. As she emerged from Aliquaille's pyre and her own grief, however, she saw the entire city collapsing into dust.

The cathedral's stained-glass windows had gone blind grey, and the lines of solder between the panes trickled down like rainwater. The spired towers resembled cones of burnt incense, soft and pitted and waiting for the merest hint of wind to blow them away. In the courtyard, the statues were slumped piles of dust on crumbling plinths, and the garden plants had lost their leaves, standing only as brittle skeletons that were ready to collapse at a touch.

As Neave walked away from the cathedral, the desolation intensified. Most of the larger buildings still stood, but decay crept along their foundations and support beams, stretching up to claim walls and roofs as swiftly as fire consumed paper.

Within minutes, Varstrom would be no more. Its secret could be fully and finally forgotten… except by her.

The other Blacktalons were gathered just beyond the cathedral courtyard, and their reaction to seeing her was immediate.

'Neave!' Shakana cried, rushing forwards. She clapped Neave in a rough embrace, then took a step back, looking her over for wounds. 'Thank Sigmar you're alive. We'd worried you'd perished in this place.'

Neave stared at her, too soul-weary to speak. Shakana's relief turned to confusion, then worry. 'Are you all right?'

When Neave didn't answer, Hendrick cleared his throat. 'It's done?'

'It's done.' Neave didn't try to hide her listlessness. She couldn't have if she'd wanted to.

'Aliquaille?' the Old Wolf asked.

Neave shook her head. 'But it was quick. No pain.' *Not of the body.* The soul was another story, and one she had no wish to tell.

Instead she surveyed the Blacktalons, noting the missing face among them. 'Rostus?'

'Fallen.' Hendrick grimaced, and glanced to the dulling sky. Its stars had guttered out, and the suggestion of infinitude created by its layered clouds and streaked lights was gone as well. A flat, artificial grey remained, and a hint of red near the horizon, where they'd come through. 'Lorai got him back through the realmgate before he succumbed, at least. Sigmar willing, we'll see him again soon.'

'Sigmar willing,' Neave echoed. The words had never felt so empty.

Hendrick's bushy grey eyebrows rose. Concern filled his eyes. '*Are* you all right?'

Neave shrugged off his question, as she'd shrugged off Shakana's. 'Our task is done. The target is slain. Nothing else matters.'

'Other things do matter,' Hendrick said gravely. He clasped Neave's forearm in a brusque warrior's greeting, holding it a second longer than he usually did. 'I don't know what happened, but I do know that we are here for you, Neave. You do not fight alone. You have us. The Blacktalons, your friends. You have Sigmar.'

'I know,' Neave said. She looked at Hendrick, really *looked* at him, and then at Shakana and Lorai. The Blacktalons. Her friends.

She thought for a moment. Perhaps she did have Sigmar, too, as flawed as she'd learnt he was. *A god who was once a man cannot be held to perfection.* Humans had human frailties. As the Stormcasts sometimes did, and as Sigmar evidently had.

Is that enough? Neave asked herself again. Could she follow her god so fervently, knowing how grievously he'd failed?

She hadn't had an answer before. She didn't have one now. Later, when the wounds weren't so raw, she could think about that again. Until then, it was enough that she had her comrades. It would have to be enough.

There is still beauty in the Mortal Realms. There is still hope.

There was still purpose. There had to be.

'We should leave,' Shakana said, pointing skywards. The faraway red glow of the realmgate had begun to dull, as if the collapse of this small, strange shadow-life had reached the gate as well. 'No time to waste if we want to see Rostus again, or much of anything else.'

'Yes.' Lorai approached them with the vulcanaurs. Although they still bore the half-healed marks of their recent wounds, the beasts seemed much restored, and their glossy scales shone with sacred ointments. Neave noticed, belatedly, that Hendrick's case of healing unguents sat lighter on his hip, and Shakana's silver lamp had gone out.

Doubtlessly the decision had been purely practical. The vulcanaurs needed all their strength if they were to bear the Blacktalons up through those hostile skies to Aqshy. Nevertheless, it struck Neave as fitting that the Blacktalons should make some small atonement for all that the Sanctuary of the Winter Sun had suffered in the name of faith. *Let us heal what we can.*

Neave climbed onto her vulcanaur's back. Aliquaille's saddle should have sat before her, but it was gone. Someone had taken it off, most likely to tend the vulcanaur's wounds, and had learnt there was no reason to put it back.

She looked away, lifting her face towards the sky.

Ahead, the lifeless grey of Varstrom's heavens gave way to turmoil. The clouds were ominously dark around the realmgate's red pulse. Thunder spiked between them, and angry winds roiled them like a cauldron's steam. It promised to be a brutal flight.

Neave welcomed it. She needed a new fight. Something purer, cleaner.

Something that could purge her of this one.

'Come,' she said. 'Let us hunt.'

EPILOGUE

In Hammerhal Aqsha, Neave prayed.

She prayed in the sanctum fortress of the Blacktalons, and in the gilded halls of mortal cathedrals, and among the rough basalt shrines of the myriad Aqshian cults, whose burning pendants flung comet trails of sparks in the hot red wind.

Did I do the right thing? Was it necessary? Sigmar, my god. Why?

She heard no answer. Neave didn't know whether this was because there was none to give, whether Sigmar felt one had already been made apparent, or whether he wished to test her with this scruple.

But slowly, like dawn emerging over low hills, she felt the warmth of the God-King return to her soul. She saw his glory reflected in the faces of his worshippers as they gathered to pray, and heard it swell from the choristers as they joined their voices in song. It was embedded in the stones that mortals cleaved from the lava-licked hills, smoothed, and raised into bulwarks of civilisation.

Sigmar's strength was here, and the promise of his protection, and in watching the daily activity of life in Hammerhal Aqsha, Neave understood and accepted the full weight of what she had done beneath the shadowy cathedral of her dreams.

This was what the God-King's faith made possible. This was what she had protected. And if there was a bloody secret buried amid the bedrocks of its foundation, perhaps that was a fair price to pay to keep the edifice standing.

Too many people lived in it for Neave to countenance its collapse.

The realisation did not, exactly, remove the weight of doubt that she felt. But it lightened it somewhat into something she could carry. Neave still hoped to lose the memory on the Anvil of Apotheosis someday, so that her faith might be restored to the pure and uncomplicated strength it had been before.

She did not yet know how to master the alternative.

Time blurred.

Memories swam together, tangled in the murk, and sank to the depths or glided past in unrecognisable forms. Again, Neave walked through the Blacktalons' sanctum, the arched halls of mortal cathedrals, and the smoke-trailed shrines of native cults, and felt both embraced and lost.

She couldn't remember why it felt important to do these things, or witness these rituals. The mortal worshippers were always honoured by her presence and eager to welcome her, and Neave felt Sigmar's radiance fill her as she took up a verse in song. But afterwards, there was confusion.

What had compelled her to seek out these moments? She couldn't recall.

Had she been hurt? Lost? Distraught in her faith?

If so, the wound had healed. Neave searched her memories and found only a faint, nebulous sense of sadness, which might merely have been wistfulness at being unable to recall the original memory. Something skirted the edges of her mind, something deeper, but it was elusive. A phantom of her dreams, and no more.

She was returning from one such foray when Hendrick, perspiring still from a round in the sanctum's fighting rings, saw her and raised his hand. 'Neave!'

Neave smiled, glad to break away from her own ruminations. 'There you are, Old Wolf.'

'Where have you been? I expected to see you in the practice halls. We have visitors, brothers from the Perspicarium. They've made no secret of their eagerness to test themselves against you.'

'I was praying.'

Hendrick's expression shifted slightly. He rubbed his bearded chin, looking to the copper-tipped cathedrals in the distance, and then back to Neave. 'You've been doing a great deal of that lately. Prayer is important, of course, but… is something troubling you?'

Neave shook her head. 'No,' she said, relieved and slightly surprised to find that it was true. 'I thought there was, but it's gone.'

This only seemed to concern Hendrick. He took a step nearer, clasping her upper arm to offer steady reassurance. 'What is it, Neave? What do you remember?'

'Nothing.' Neave returned Hendrick's steady, searching look, then stepped back, breaking his grip with an apologetic shrug. 'I didn't mean to worry you. Perhaps there *was* something that troubled me, but it's faded. For some reason, I just wanted to see Sigmar the way his mortal worshippers do. So, I prayed with them.'

'Ah. Forgive me for worrying.' Hendrick's weathered face creased in relief, and a hint of amusement. 'What did you learn from them?'

'I don't think I *learnt* anything,' Neave said. 'It was more about what I felt.'

'And what was that?'

'Strength,' Neave murmured, and a warm glow filled her at

the thought. She closed her eyes, remembering. 'Pure and holy strength, Hendrick. Safety. And, an unquestionable peace.'

In an empty place, cold and lonely, the shadows stirred.

A shape rose from the darkness, outlined in shifting gloom. There was no one to see it, and little of it to be seen despite its enormous size. Shadows clung to it like a dancer's veils, revealing only glimpses of what lay beneath. A glossy scale, the curve of a horn, an expanse of tenebrous wing. No more.

It glided over piles of dust that had once been market halls, tiered fountains, the marble-columned homes of a contented people. A grand and glittering cathedral, built to house the hopes and prayers of its faithful.

All ashes, now. The walker in the darkness let out a soft, derisive snort as it flicked a foot through the heaped dust, scattering it in a silent puff. 'Your shining city came to this, false one. How many generations of loyal belief? How many songs, in how many holy halls? Repaid by betrayal, reduced to ash, extinguished down to their very souls… and still your foolish servants believe. Still, they are blinded.'

The charred remains of a serpentine creature lay in a shallow crater of dust. It hadn't rotted, for there was no life in this place to make it rot. Instead, it had dried to sticky arcs of sinew and muscle stretched between cracked bones and stiffened scales: a fossil in flesh and skin.

Beside the corpse was a blackened arc of splintered stone, left by the impact of a second body hurtling from the sky. The scar earned a shadowed sneer as the walker passed. 'Even now, you dare not fight yourself, with muscle and raging heart. All this fear and loathing, and yet you hide and hide, and send your puppets out to bleed and die in your stead.'

The shadowy walker stepped down into a hollow in the dust-cloaked earth. The eroded remnants of spiralling stairs were barely perceptible as depressions in the ash. Flakes of burnt paper seeded the drifts of dust, and a goggled black helm lay half-full of ashes nearby.

Not far from the helm, another partially dried corpse lay face down in the ash. The walker approached it, turned it over with a foot, and slipped its hand into the dead woman's pockets and pouches with unsentimental efficiency until it came up with a shard of smoke-stained crystal.

Tiny faces reflected from the crystal's facets: a broad, bald figure in gold; a slender bluish aelf, whose face was half hidden behind a diaphanous veil; a grey-bearded warrior whose dignified mien drew a curl of the lip from the walker; a dark-skinned woman with an intent expression and a regal star-eagle perched on her shoulder; and, finally, larger than the others and in the centre, a fierce-looking woman in the last days of her youth, with hair shorn short on the sides and gathered into a tail at the back, and Sigmar's regalia shining bright upon her armour.

'The false god's most precious creation,' the walker whispered, as the crystal's other facets went blank and the image expanded to fill the entire prism. 'Neave Blacktalon.'

A pale orange shimmer danced across the crystal's face as the image cleared and shifted into the same woman, face twisted in fury, throttling the life out of the crystal's bearer. The sheer savagery of her attack was breathtaking.

'What do you remember, Neave Blacktalon? When the truth of who you are finally returns,' the walker whispered, fascinated, as it tilted the crystal to and fro, studying the Stormcast's rage, 'what will you remember? And, what will you *do?*'

ABOUT THE AUTHOR

Liane Merciel lives in Philadelphia with her husband, two big unruly mutts and her preschooler, the unruliest of them all. Her work for Age of Sigmar includes *Blacktalon* and the novella *Red Claw and Ruin* that featured in the portmanteau novel *Covens of Blood*.

THE HOLLOW KING
by John French

Cado Ezechiar, a cursed Soulblight vampire, seeks salvation for those he failed at the fall of his kingdom. His quest for vengeance leads him to Aventhis, a city caught in a tangled web of war and deceit that Cado must successfully navigate, or lose everything.